ALLIANCE OF EQUALS

ALLIANCE OF EQUALS

A New Liaden Universe® Novel

SHARON LEE &
STEVE MILLER

ALLIANCE OF EQUALS

Copyright ©2016 by Sharon Lee & Steve Miller

Liaden Universe® is a registered trademark.

A Baen Books Original

Baen Publishing Enterprises
P.O. Box 1403
Riverdale, NY 10471
www.baen.com

ISBN: 978-1-4767-8148-8

Cover art by David Mattingly

First Baen printing, July 2016

Distributed by Simon & Schuster
1230 Avenue of the Americas
New York, NY 10020

Library of Congress Cataloging-in-Publication Data

Names: Lee, Sharon, 1952– author. | Miller, Steve, 1950 July 31– author.
Title: Alliance of equals / Sharon Lee, Steve Miller.
Description: Riverdale, NY : Baen Books, [2016] | Series: Liaden Universe ; 19
Identifiers: LCCN 2016010526 | ISBN 9781476781488 (hardcover)
Subjects: LCSH: Liaden Universe (Imaginary place)—Fiction. | Life on other
    planets—Fiction. | Space colonies—Fiction. | BISAC: FICTION / Science
    Fiction / Space Opera. | FICTION / Science Fiction / Adventure. | FICTION
    / Science Fiction / General. | GSAFD: Science fiction.
Classification: LCC PS3562.E3629 A79 2016 | DDC 813/.54—dc23 LC record
available at https://lccn.loc.gov/2016010526

10 9 8 7 6 5 4 3 2 1

Pages by Joy Freeman (www.pagesbyjoy.com)
Printed in the United States of America

THANKS TO . . .

Patrick Shawn Bagley, for the gift of his expertise—
for being a good sport
and
an exemplary human being

TO . . .

Paul Myron Anthony Linebarger, for Nostrilia

AND TO . . .

Alan Baker, Alice Bentley, Sally Erikson, Robert Haines,
Terry Hazen, Melita Kennedy, Gail Wineland Martin,
Hanneke Nieuwenhuijzen, Maurita Plouff, Mike Proctor,
Marni Rachimel, Trude Rice, Kate Reynolds,
Frances Silversmith, Sarah Stapleton, Stan Thornton,
Bridget A. Wheeler-Gehrling, Stanley Whitaker, Anne Young

for their participation in the Great *Alliance of Equals* Typo Hunt.

All uncorrected typos are, of course, the fault and the
responsibility of the authors.

CONTENTS

· · · · · · · · · · · · · · · · · · · ·

ALLIANCE OF EQUALS

CHAPTER ONE

. . . .

Dutiful Passage

HE RUSHED HER, A TALL TERRAN MALE, OVERTOPPING AND OUT-massing her. Padi dropped back one step, flat-footed and cen-tered, knees flexed—and he was on her, keeping himself tight, seeking to overturn her with his speed, and flatten her under his weight. She ducked inside his reach, snatching at belt and elbow, twisting her upper body, letting him lift himself over her shoulder. Momentum, it was all his own momentum, and, in the last instant before she let him go, she straightened, adding her motion to his, *throwing him* with every ounce of strength she possessed before she released him—and continued the spin, completing the move and dissipating unused energy.

Her late opponent hit the floor some number of his own body lengths down the room. Hit, rolled, and leapt to his feet; turned...

...and bowed, as vanquished to victor.

"Your follow, having thrown your attacker far away?" he inquired in Terran.

Padi's bow was from student to teacher.

"I would have run, sir, and been many blocks distant before he regained his feet."

"And if he had a partner at the top of the street?"

"I would have shot her," she said coolly, "and run on."

"I see."

1

Arms Master Schneider looked around the practice room, as if he were seeing something other than the padded walls and floor.

Padi folded her hands and waited. Arms Master Schneider took time with his words, and there was no speeding the man up, no matter how much one might wish it. Padi supposed it another sort of practice, and did her best to recruit herself to patience.

"I wonder," he said eventually, walking toward her, his posture soft, and his hands unthreatening. Padi remained at center, and allowed her hands to unfold into neutral positions at her sides.

Her instructor did not seem to notice; he continued to walk gently forward, his eyes on her face.

"It's very natural," he said, resuming speech without giving voice to what it was he had wondered, "to want to throw an enemy as far from yourself as possible, gaining the opportunity to run. But it seems to me, Padi, that your solution to a rush is invariably to throw." He smiled, and added, "Even if you are able to throw impressively far."

He paused, well inside Padi's defense space, and settled deliberately, hooking his thumbs in his belt.

"We're fortunate to have such ample practice space, but I wonder what you would do, if you were on port, and had to counter an attack in, let's say, a small space. An alley, a vestibule, even a 'fresher? What, for instance, if the person standing peaceably next to you suddenly—lunged?"

He did so, far too close for mercy. There was only one imperative, here: survive to protect her pilot, and her passengers—a little boy with two infants in his charge.

She knew the answer; she had drilled the answer until it was reflex.

Ducking, she stepped into his lunge, raised a hand and snapped into a short, savage jump. The extended palm should have caught him under the chin, but Arms Master Schneider was far too canny for that. He arched into a backflip, using the space he had only just been scolding her for utilizing. Padi landed lightly in place, shaking her arms to release the energy she had withheld. Delivered with full force, the strike to the chin would have snapped her attacker's head back and broken his neck.

It was of course very bad form to kill one's instructor; besides, she liked Arms Master Schneider—and it *was* practice. Even if the blow had landed, he would have been in no danger, though he might have had a headache, after.

"Your reasoning?" he asked, from two body lengths away.

Padi bowed.

"You had posited cramped quarters and an assailant well within my space. The only sure answer in such a case is a kill. I cannot risk a deflection; I might find myself snatched and immobilized, unable even to call a warning. I cannot risk a prolonged engagement, if indeed, as you had also offered, the first attacker was one of a team. I am alone, and I must prevail quickly, if I am to survive."

There was a long silence while Arms Master Schneider mulled over his store of words.

"Let's try another scenario, in that same small space, in a confusion of wind and darkness, let's say. A person is grabbing for you, and crying out. What's your answer?"

Padi frowned, and paused to consider the question twice, suspecting a trick, but a second examination revealed nothing that might change her answer.

"It is the same," she said calmly. "I must take definitive action."

"And if it's later found that the person who reached for you was asking for your assistance—or warning you of danger? Your answer would kill an innocent—even an ally—no differently than a villain."

But this is play-acting! Padi thought irritably.

"The only intent I can be certain of is my own," she said, which was straight from the training tapes they had Learned on the Rock. "Others depend upon me. I cannot risk myself."

"What do you risk, by dancing an avoid before the kill?"

"Time," she said promptly. "Tempo. Opportunity."

Arms Master Schneider pressed his lips together, which he did when he was considering something especially difficult.

"We have a few minutes left," he said eventually. "Let's practice some of the common avoids. Particularly, we should pay attention to how much time is lost to the move, and if tempo can be preserved—or even created. You will take the part of the attacker."

He bowed, and she did. Both centered themselves.

"At will," he said, and Padi launched into action.

· · · ❋ · · ·

There was no new correspondence in his mail queue.

There was, for instance, no letter from the Terran Trade Commission confirming the committee's decision to upgrade Surebleak Port from Local to Regional. Such confirmation had been promised to him by the committee chair no later than the end of the *relumma*, which was fast approaching.

Additionally, there was no letter from Lomar Fasholt, which he had been expecting daily, if not hourly, since Theo had reported that his former trade partner had broken with her Temple, and subsequently disappeared from her homeworld.

Nor, for that matter, was there a message from Theo, acknowledging receipt of his pinbeam, and reporting that she, her ship, and her crew were en route to Surebleak and the safety of Korval's clanhouse.

Shan glared at the empty inbox. It hardly seemed fair or fitting that a circumstance which ought to have afforded real, if fleeting, pleasure should instead generate strong feelings of frustration.

He felt his fingers moving in a soothing, familiar rhythm, glanced down and saw a chipped red gaming counter, its edges showing naked wood, moving across the knuckles of his left hand. The token crossed the last knuckle, his hand turned, palm up, to catch the thing before once again setting it on its journey.

He sighed.

He had acquired the gaming token, and the fingering exercise, elsewhere, and some little while ago. In fact, he had lately considered himself quit of both, having gone so many days undisturbed by either, only to find them manifesting again, and with the *Passage* barely out of the home port. Simple sleight-of-hand, that was all. Completely unremarkable, save for the manner of its...acquisition.

Three times, while he watched, the token walked across his knuckles. At the end of the fourth journey across the back of his hand, it did not fall into his waiting palm, but seemed instead to vanish into plain air. That would, perhaps, have been comforting, if he did not know with a certainty that had nothing to do with logic, or even understanding how the trick was done, that the token was, now, in his right front trouser pocket.

Blast the thing.

He took a deep breath to cool his irritation, and looked back to the screen.

Certainly he had other work to fill his idle hours, even if he had no mail.

The touch of a key banished his unsatisfying inbox and brought the sketch of the new trade route onto the screen.

It was, truth told, a malformed and unbalanced thing, hardly worthy of a novice trader, much less a master. He knew how to build routes, of course, but the sad truth was that most of his work as Korval's master trader had been the maintenance and modification of long-established routes built by the master traders who had gone before him.

He hadn't built a major new route since...well...since the Bestwell-Kessel-La'Quontis Route, the year that Padi was born.

"Admit it, Shan," he said aloud, "you've gotten soft."

There being no argument forthcoming from himself, he reached for his wineglass and sipped, eyes on the inelegant shambles adorning his screen.

He might, he thought, putting the glass aside, be somewhat kinder to himself. The route as described revealed not so much a master trader whose skills had atrophied, as a master trader who was required to feel his way, combining discovery with design.

The first part of the route—*that* had been well enough, with six stops of light trade, all at ports known to Korval ships, if not to *Dutiful Passage* herself. At each of those six ports, in addition to the trade, he and Priscilla had met with allies and business partners, to strengthen old ties, and to build new ones, where necessary, the two of them empowered by the delm to speak with Their Voice.

They were now embarking upon the second phase, wherein they would be on the search for new trade partners, allies, and business associates. They would also, in this phase as in the former, be demonstrating to the universe that Clan Korval, doing business as Tree-and-Dragon Family, *was* doing business; that it was not afraid of its enemies, nor ashamed of its past actions. Miri had dubbed the plan *playing chicken with the universe*, but she had agreed with him, Priscilla, and with Val Con, that the demonstration was required.

Though the actions that had seen Korval banished from Liad had been justified, not to say necessary, they had—people, rumor, and politics being what they were—their character to redeem, and the sooner they began *that* work, the sooner they would succeed.

Also, they labored under another piquant truth: the clan's purse was...less than plump. Oh, they were by no means destitute, and Ms. dea'Gauss was hard at work establishing new income streams and researching new investments.

Still, there had been a cost in removing themselves, and their finances, from Liaden society, and Liaden economy. In the long term, Liad would pay the larger portion of that invoice, which, while satisfying to contemplate, did nothing to mitigate the necessity of Korval's holding household while establishing a firm base of operations on a rather backward planet, and seeking to expand their resources.

Historically, the clan had expanded resources through trade. And it was his duty, as Korval's master trader, to build new routes—strong, viable, profitable routes—and build them quickly.

Which he had best be about.

So. Their first new stop on the route they were simultaneously discovering and building was Andiree in the Kinsa Sector. According to the *Guild Quick Guide*, Andiree was a solid port, rated Safe, for whatever comfort that might lend to the naive, or those who made it their business to be *un*safe. It declared itself Terran, yet had included in its colonizing population a small number of Liaden artisan clans.

That was of interest, being something like the situation in which Korval now discovered itself. The Liaden artists of Andiree, rather than forming an enclave from which the greater planetary society was excluded, as Liadens had done on other worlds where they were the minority population...the artists had embraced the local culture, first on the level of craft, as they joined with those who shared their passions for pottery, sculpture, painting, paper-making, carving, and weaving, and from that base spreading out, into, and finally joining with the planetary society.

According to the anthropologists who had studied the place, what had occurred over time was *not* the assimilation of one population, with its customs, into the other, but a melding that had produced a separate-but-equal third society with entirely new customs. The primary unit of personal allegiance, for instance, was neither clan nor family, but guild. Contract marriage existed, but between guildmasters only, as a political tool, rather than for progeny. Balance existed, administered formally through the guilds, while Balance between individuals was socially unacceptable.

Shan sighed. Andiree was perhaps a glimpse of Korval's future, though it was difficult to imagine Surebleak's blunt and rugged culture allowing itself to accept anything of Liaden sensibilities—or even Korval House custom.

It was...profoundly disturbing, to think that they—that *who they were*, and had been since the Great Migration itself—would be lost within a generation or two...

The door to his office hissed slightly as it opened and he spun from his screen, coming to his feet as his lifemate entered.

She paused, brows knit, as the door closed quietly behind her. "Shan? What's wrong?"

In addition to her *melant'is* as lifemate to the thodelm of yos'Galan, and captain of the *Dutiful Passage*, Priscilla Delacroix y Mendoza was also a Witch—or, according to Liadens, a *dramliza*. She would have read his emotions even as he now read hers, thereby learning that she was tired, and slightly irritable. A meeting with the third mate, then, he thought, moving around the desk.

"Nothing so much as *wrong*," he said, opening his arms. "I was only reflecting on Korval's future, and how we will soon become strangers to ourselves."

Priscilla stepped willingly into the offered hug, her arms going 'round his waist. She sighed, deeply, and dropped her head to his shoulder. He lay his cheek against her soft curls, and breathed in her fragrance.

"He's a bit stiff in the honor, the third mate," he murmured.

Priscilla hiccuped a small laugh.

"He is, isn't he?"

She sighed again, and he tasted the particular tang of a relaxation exercise, even as her body softened against his.

"I ordered a tray brought to us here," she said, straightening slowly out of the embrace. "I hope you'll join me."

"Breakfast or supper?" he asked lightly.

"Both—or neither. Or perhaps a midnight snack, before I seek my bed." She smiled at him, and added, "My *lonely* bed."

He laughed.

"Underhanded play, Priscilla!"

"Nothing more than the truth." She tipped her head. "The change in Korval's estate worries you."

"Not our estate so much as our future," he said, moving toward the cabinet. "May I pour you a glass of wine?"

"Please."

Priscilla preferred white wine. He poured generously.

"Val Con was pleased to leave Liad, though not," she added thoughtfully, "necessarily with the manner of it."

"Val Con is yos'Phelium, *and* a Scout. He's obliged to find the—*former* homeworld tiresome." He sighed, and shook his head. "It may be that I refine too much. After all, if we're to become something else, it was Father who began it, with his Terran lifemate. Only see what came of that!"

"Even more Terran lifemates?" Priscilla asked, taking the glass from his hand with a smile.

"Three, so far, in the following generation," he agreed, turning toward the desk to retrieve his own glass. "The gods alone know what—or whom—Nova may embrace."

"If anyone," Priscilla said, and glanced toward the desk an instant before the incoming message chime sounded from the comm.

Shan stepped 'round the desk and tapped a key.

The letter in-queue was from James Abrofinda.

Shan smiled. He was fond of James Abrofinda, and met him too seldom. He'd been a Tree-and-Dragon contractor for at least twenty Standards, and—

Notice of Buyout.

Shan blinked, and sat down, carefully, in his chair.

Immediately after Korval's action against the Department of the Interior base beneath Liad's surface, which had, regrettably, left a crater in Solcintra City—he had received quite a number of buyout notices, most from Liadens, as would be expected. He had by this time rather thought he was done with buyout notices. To receive one now, and from such a source—a Terran smalltrader running a long, stable route; open to trying new, or slightly outrageous, cargoes; quick to communicate what worked and what didn't...

But, wait, there was a letter, too. Shan tapped a key, and felt a light hand settle on his shoulder.

"I thought we'd seen the last buyout," Priscilla said.

"As I did, but here—James has done us the kindness of explaining himself..."

A quick scan put him in possession of the facts. James had come in to Capenport, where he was not only well known, but expected. Before the hull was cool, the port had slapped him with a fine equal to half his cargo—

"Because he's our contractor?" Priscilla said, reading along with him.

"And because Capenport decided that Korval committed crimes against a planet and is therefore outlawed," Shan read the next bit aloud.

> I'd been hearing some muttering here and there about Tree-and-Dragon turning bad, but I put it down to the usual. This, though—I'm a small shipper; I can't afford another fine like this one.
>
> Outcome is that I dumped the cargo, next port up, and cleared the logos and call signs off the hull and out of my landing packet. I never thought I'd do this, but there's no other way; I'm buying the contract out. The deposit's been made to my usual account. I'm sorry for it, there's no acrimony in it, except for the pinheads at Capenport. You and me, and the Dragon, we're in Balance, but we can't do business.
>
> Here's my advice: change the trade name, if you want to keep on with the family business. I don't like to think about what might have happened if Pale Wing or the Passage had come onto Capenport, considering what they felt was just punishment for a contractor.
>
> Be careful, Shan.

He sighed, and leaned his head back into Priscilla's hip.

"A rational man, James. Of course, change our name is just what we *can't* do, the delm being adamant in their opinion that we have comported ourselves with impeccable *melant'i* and are in no way ashamed of our actions."

"Korval revealed and weakened a hidden enemy of Liad and its people," Priscilla said, her fingers quietly kneading his shoulders. "Not only have we done nothing wrong, Korval is a hero."

"Not to hear the Council of Clans tell it. And various news sources. But I agree—Korval's honor is unscathed, and our *melant'i* in the matter of the Department of the Interior is pure." He sighed.

"Poor James. A two-cantra buyout on top of that fine? And he'll have dumped the cargo at salvage rates," Shan said.

"Send the money back. Tell him it's compensation for his loss; that Tree-and-Dragon doesn't expect its contractors to bear the expense of false accusations."

Shan laughed. "Priscilla, that's reasoned like a Liaden."

"No," she said seriously. "It's reasoned like an honorable person, who wants to do well by those who have done well for him."

A chill froze him for a moment before he shook his head.

"Yes, I *am* going to have to become accustomed, aren't I?"

"It'll come," Priscilla said, and he felt the brush of her emotions—amusement and concern, with concern the greater part of the mixture.

"I suppose it will," he said. "Padi's generation will be the last, I think, to consider themselves Liaden. Those who follow will be *Bleakers*." He sighed. "Who names a planet *Surebleak*?"

Priscilla laughed. "It was descriptive, surely?"

"Oh, surely . . . and still is. Until Mr. Brunner gets those weather satellites up and tuned, and even then, I fear we'll only have graduated to Halfbleak."

"Our house will be there," she murmured, which was perhaps an attempt to give his thoughts a more cheerful direction, in which she was partly successful.

"Our house will be there if ever Architect vin'Zeller will finish with the plans and send them to us! I'd hoped to break ground during the current year's summer. If we need to wait through another winter—"

A chime sounded, sweet and high: the door annunciator.

"Your midnight snack arrives," Shan said to Priscilla, and raised his voice slightly. "Come!"

The door whisked aside, and Arms Master Schneider brought his tall and muscled self into the office. He paused and inclined slightly from the waist, his compromise between a bow and a Terran nod.

"I hope I'm not inconvenient," he said.

"Not in the least," Shan assured him, considering the swirl of the man's emotions. "What may I be honored to do for you?"

Jon came another step into the office, and gave them each a solemn glance, in turn.

"Well, sir, ma'am—I'd like to talk to you about Padi's defense training."

CHAPTER TWO

. . . .

Dutiful Passage

PADI YOS'GALAN BOUNCED OUT OF THE LIFT AND TROTTED DOWN the long hall toward Hydroponics. She was smiling.

Dance lessons always left her warm, and... happy. It wasn't just the exercise, though *that* was certainly welcome, it was also the knowledge that she was good at *menfri'at*—which was the name of the defensive art most commonly taught to pilots and other spacers. Of course, she had begun her lessons long before the remove to Runig's Rock, and had enjoyed them from the first. It was a particular pleasure to feel one's muscles working cleanly together in quick, sure movements.

She had, she thought, slipping into Hydroponics, comported herself well during the test session she had just completed with Arms Master Schneider. It was her expectation that she would find a reassignment to a more advanced class on her duty screen tomorrow.

That pleased her, too. One *liked* to do well; to excel at whatever one did. Grandfather Luken said that the drive to excel was at Korval's heart, and Padi believed that he was correct. After all, was it not said that *There are fifty High Houses—and then, there is Korval?*

Padi caught her breath, warmth fading a little, as she opened her locker and retrieved her belt-kit.

For that was a thing said on *Liad*—which was no longer *home*, because Korval's name had been struck from the Book of Clans.

Now, on Liad, they would say, *There are fifty High Houses.*

Now, on Liad, they would say, *A Dragon does not change its nature.*

Which was perfectly correct, and nothing to do with the clan if, if *lesser persons* failed to take the time to understand the Dragon's nature...

A chime sounded, discreetly, and there came the soft fizzing from the room beyond that meant the misters had come on.

Padi caught her breath. She was going to be late!

She threw her belt over her shoulder, slammed the locker door and half-ran to the assignment station. Her hand broke the beam, and she was logged in precisely on time. Sighing, she accessed the duty roster, belting the kit 'round her waist while she scanned the screen, looking for her name; finding it near the bottom, with the notation *Tank Gr2, thinning.*

She touched the screen, acknowledging receipt of her assignment, and again ran her eye down the list, to find who else might be working this shift.

Head Technician Varoth was in her office; the red triangle that meant *do not disturb* next to her name. Good. Padi had no desire to disturb the head tech.

Faw Chen was listed as on-shift in Hr6, repair. Padi grinned.

Hr6 shared an aisle with Gr2. She would have company— agreeable company—this shift.

Still grinning, Padi jogged down the aisle toward her assignment. Faw Chen had only come aboard at Billingston, filling the hole left in the roster by Din Ref dea'Ken's resignation. She was a few Standards older than Padi, willing to answer questions and to ask them. Not that either of them would shirk their work, of course, but they might exchange some conversation, and working with Faw Chen was *much* preferable to sharing a shift, and proximity, with Inleen, Padi's fellow 'prentice, or with Head Tech Varoth. Jeri, the other garden tech, was agreeable enough, but not much given to talk.

She turned the corner and there was a thin woman in green overalls, bent diligently above Tank Hr6, a toolbox open on the shelf beside her.

"Faw Chen!" she said. "I'm glad to see you!"

The gardener looked up, a ready smile on her face.

"I'm glad to see you, too! And on time!"

That was a joke. It might even be a joke with a point turned toward Inleen, who, in Padi's experience, had never in his life been on time.

"Only imagine the ringing scold I would earn from the head tech if I were late," Padi said, pulling the log for Gr2. Jeri had marked out the sections that wanted thinning, and, in Gr3, two sections that needed to be deadheaded. Padi nodded to herself and moved to the first marked section.

Gr2 was peas, and the first section was, in fact, fearfully over-grown. Padi dutifully performed the required measurements, testing the medium for moisture and acidity, logged the readings, and finally leaned in to run her fingers lightly over the fragile green seedlings.

Thinning was soothing work in its way, though her attention, and her care, as well as her hands, had to be *in the garden*, as Tech Varoth had it.

One needed, first, to observe the segment to be thinned, iden-tifying the robust plants and those that were less so. On the first pass, those plants that were clearly failing would be removed, and sacrificed to the composting frames. The second pass would take those seedlings that were somewhat more robust, but still unthrifty, and so on, until only the healthiest and strongest seedlings remained.

She hummed as she worked, a wordless little tune she had learned from Grandfather Luken, when they had sheltered in the Rock together. The leaves were cool against her fingertips, and her attention was wholly engaged.

"Do you think she would?" Faw Chen asked quietly.

Padi blinked, her fingers fumbling among the seedlings. She raised her head, but Faw Chen was bent over her section, a diagnostic stick in her hand.

Padi frowned, trying to recall her last—ah, yes. Tech Varoth's likely reaction to Padi being tardy.

Despite her determination to do well, Padi had felt from the beginning that Head Tech Varoth had taken her in dislike. She had not been able to discover why this was so. At first, she had wondered if there might be some deficiency in her work, but, if that were the case, surely the tech would merely have corrected her, instead of barely acknowledging her presence, on the increasingly rare occasions when their schedules put them on the same shift?

"Why wouldn't she scold me?" she asked Faw Chen, turning back to the seedlings. "She certainly scolds Inleen when he's late."

"True. But Inleen's mother is not the captain of this ship."

Padi blinked, her fingers gone still among the seedlings, wondering what Inleen's lineage had to do with—

"As your mother is, the captain of this ship," Faw Chen continued, her voice gentle.

Padi looked down at her fingers, and moved them among the cool leaves, working deliberately now, as she tried to think how best to explain, for it was an error of culture that Faw Chen posited—and a very disturbing conclusion drawn from it...

"My *mother*," she said, her voice as careful as her fingers. "*My mother* is Vestin yos'Thomaz Clan Ebrim." She raised her head slightly and saw Faw Chen pause, her head cocked to one side. She said nothing.

Good, Padi thought, she wants to understand. To learn.

"Now," she continued, still careful. "Now, it is true that Priscilla Mendoza and my father are lifemates, but that doesn't... among Liadens, what that means is that she has come into Clan Korval—our clan—but she's not *my mother*. She's an elder-in-clan..." Because lifemates were understood to have one *melant'i*, and Father was *certainly* Padi's elder-in-clan, as well as Thodelm yos'Galan, which meant that Priscilla, too, held a thodelm's duty—and none of that, Padi realized, would answer the question that Tech Varoth and Faw Chen, too, needed to have answered—and might even confuse the issue.

She paused, sorting through necessary and extraneous details. One could not, after all, teach a whole culture in one day! However, if one separated the involved *melant'is*, one might simplify *enough*, without simplifying *too much*.

"What must be understood is that the *melant'i* of an elder-in-clan resides *within* the *clan*. The ship has its own order of *melant'i*—of command and discipline. On ship, the captain is captain for all the crew, and administers discipline with an even hand. The captain of the *Dutiful Passage does not* permit crew—*any* crew—to be slovenly in their work."

Somewhat breathless, she paused. Faw Chen had turned away from her work and was watching Padi closely.

"Do I explain that well?" she asked tentatively.

"You explained it very well," Faw Chen said, and turned back to the tank.

Padi sighed. She had hoped that she wouldn't have to ask, but she must know!

"Did you mean me to understand that Tech Varoth would...
not...instruct me as she might Inleen, because of this...
misunderstanding of my relationship with the captain?"

There followed a long silence, during which Faw Chen had
several instruments out of the toolbox. There came a definitive *pop*
from inside the tank, and a soft exclamation from the gardener.

Padi bit her lip and bent back to her own task, trying to
recapture the rhythm of the work.

"I am, I think, a step over a line," Faw Chen said at last.
"Let me try to reassure you while not moving any further in
the wrong direction."

There came another pause. Faw Chen was replacing items
into her toolbox, a frown on her round face.

Padi looked down, and frowned herself. She had pulled a perfectly healthy seedling, rather than the less-healthy plant beside
it. So much for keeping her mind *in the garden*.

She placed the culled seedlings into the composting tray, then
straightened, not willing to risk another life to her inattention.
Across the aisle, Faw Chen also straightened, and turned to face
Padi.

She bowed, gently, in some mode particular to her own people.
In depth it was close enough to the Liaden bow between equals,
which was...not quite exact, Faw Chen being Padi's senior in years
and in training. Still, it would do as a demonstration of goodwill.

Padi bowed in return.

Faw Chen smiled.

"Yes. I think I may say that Head Tech Varoth and I were
discussing the operations here in the garden. The tech is pleased
with your work, and your comportment. The mention of your
relationship to Captain Mendoza came as a comparison favorable
to yourself while being unfavorable to another of the staff here."
She tipped her head. "Have I explained that well?"

So she had compared well to a co-worker. Almost, she could
hear Tech Varoth's voice, "Gods thanked, at least *he's* not the
captain's daughter; and *she* doesn't stint her work!"

"You have explained well," Padi told Faw Chen. She thought
for a moment.

"Are you in a position to carry my explanation to Tech Varoth?"

"I am, and I will," Faw Chen said firmly. "Also, for my own,
better, understanding, I will speak with the cultural officer."

The cultural officer was the librarian, Lina Faaldom, who had access to Scout tapes, and, if necessary, to Scouts.

"May I," Faw Chen asked softly, "ask another question in the same direction?"

Padi felt her stomach twist a little, foreseeing the question, but it was perfectly reasonable that it be asked. It was, in fact, necessary.

"Yes," she said, and managed a smile. "But quickly, or I will not finish my shift-work."

Faw Chen smiled.

"Quickly, then: you *are* the child of the master trader?"

"Yes, I am." She licked her lips. "Again, *melant'i* comes into the matter. *On this ship*, I am the master trader's *apprentice*, and anyone who thinks that Master Trader yos'Galan will permit error or sloth from his heir, his apprentice, or anyone who is under his hand, must... must not know him very well!"

Faw Chen laughed.

"Well said! And now, having done with my work, I will leave you to yours. I will note in the log that I diverted you to my own purposes, which will placate the head tech, should you not finish."

"Thank you," Padi said. "But I would, really, rather finish."

Faw Chen smiled.

"Of course you would," she said.

· · · ※ · · ·

Vivulonj Prosperu stopped at Gilady to take on supplies. Leaving those details with Dulsey, the Uncle went below to check on their guests.

"How fare the pilots?" she asked when he returned to the galley.

Uncle tipped his head, frowning slightly.

"Progress is satisfactory. He rushes headlong toward waking while she prefers a more deliberate pace. I have amended his speed somewhat, though more for the comfort of the ship than because I fear he will do himself harm. With such an abundance of pure material, there is very little chance, now, that he will fail. Still, I would not have him precede her by too many days. Enough so that he might guide her, but yet not so much that he... becomes bored, shall I say?"

Dulsey laughed.

"A pilot at leisure is a fearsome creature, to be sure!"

"Just so," said Uncle, with a slight smile. "And a bored Dragon twelve times more so!"

"There is that," Dulsey acknowledged, and used her chin to point at the entertainments screen.

"There is a news packet," she said. "It might make for an amusing hour."

They had, of course, received a news packet, as part of the station's service. It would be old news, space being wide, and Gilady not well positioned within it. Still, there was sometimes something of interest in such packets, and they were, as Dulsey said, often amusing.

"It might, at that," Uncle said. "I will brew tea."

"Ynsolt'i," Dulsey murmured, scanning the items list.

"One is hard put to suppose that anything of interest could have happened at Ynsolt'i," Uncle said, pouring tea.

"That is precisely why we must view it," she said. "Imagination clearly fails us."

"I agree."

Dulsey cued the proper episode, and the two of them gave the screen their attention.

The nightmare of congestion that was Ynsolt'i's normal traffic state unfolded before them, as seen from the angles of perhaps a half-dozen ship-eyes. It was a moment before it became apparent that it was not merely the crush of ships, but one ship in particular that was being followed.

"*Bechimo*," said the Uncle, who had reason to know those lines well, and leaned forward slightly in his chair, watching as the ship was maneuvered into a tight approach, with scarcely room for even a mathematical variation.

"If the pilot sneezes, *Bechimo* will bounce off of that rig," Dulsey said, apparently forgetting that whatever had happened there had been finished long ago.

Behind the tightly boxed ship, another phased in—a corsair with the lines of a predator. Breath caught, they watched as more hunters appeared. Orders were issued; *Bechimo* was to yield to escort, and prepare to surrender to authority.

The answer to that was remarkably clear, as if the pilot had spoken directly into the comm of every ship about Ynsolt'i.

"Orsec Twelve, First Class Pilot Theo Waitley, on *Bechimo*, flying for Laughing Cat, Limited, here. Be advised that we're targeted by three unannounced ships and that we are targeting in return. I am directing my Exec and my ship to take immediate defensive and responsive action as required. We will not comply with your request while, outside, hunter ships approach."

Evasive action, indeed! The Uncle realized that he had been holding his breath and took in air, his whole attention pinned to the screen.

There was too much noise; pilots objecting; pilots demanding—the tumult went unheeded as *Bechimo* ran, and returned fire until the hunters, one by one, were lost in traffic.

Except for one.

That one...leapt forward, firing what the energy grid at the bottom of the screen classified as neutrinos.

Bechimo returned fire; the attacking ship was hit—The vid flickered, and when it steadied again, *Bechimo* was gone.

There came more noise: pilots demanding to know what had happened, some few clever souls proclaiming that *Bechimo* had Jumped, others claiming that a Jump in such traffic was impossible, the other ship must have been killed in the same blast that had taken the hunter...

When at last it was over, Uncle took a deep and not entirely steady breath, and leaned back in his chair, hands folded over his belt buckle, a slight frown on his face.

"You're not amused?" Dulsey asked, her voice quieter than usual.

"On one level," he said slowly. "One must allow Pilot Waitley and *Bechimo* to be formidable. And one might almost feel, a little, sorry for the poor agents of the Department. How could they have considered it possible that *Bechimo*'s crew would give themselves up? What were they thinking, to provoke and attack, with so many witnessing their actions?"

He flung a hand up and toward the screen, fingers sketching disdain.

"*This* is the enemy Korval cannot defeat."

"Nor can we," Dulsey observed drily.

He sniffed. "Nor *have* we. Yet."

"Fair enough. But at this pace, there will be nothing left for us; Pilot Waitley and her ship will have eaten them all."

"Perhaps not, though certainly they are within their rights to take as many as they deem fit." He shifted somewhat in his chair.

"It is unfortunate that the actions of idiots pressed *Bechimo* into an indiscretion—again, with so many eyes upon them."

"I mislike that neutrino bath," Dulsey confessed. "It seemed *Bechimo*'s shields were thinning... badly."

"I thought so, too. And while we may sit here, comfortable in the knowledge that they long ago outmaneuvered brigands, within the moment it must have seemed as if there was nothing else to do, save Jump. The situation is regrettable—but survivable, most especially given Seignur Veeoni's work, eh?"

Dulsey smiled.

"In fact. When will she publish more widely?"

"An excellent question. I think it must be soon. Very soon."

· · · ❉ · · ·

"Andiree will be the first new stop on the route," Father said, as Padi brought him his wine. Before he had asked her to refresh his glass, they had been talking about her cartography coursework, but she knew him too well to be found on the wrong foot by so minor a change of topic as that.

"So it will," she agreed, placing the glass on the flat disk of green-and-blue mottled stone that served as a coaster. Padi remembered the stern-faced person who had given it to him—Ambassador Valeking of Granda—as a gift of good faith. Ambassador Valeking hadn't liked Father; her dislike so plain that Padi, who had been present at the meeting in her *melant'i* of cabin boy, had tasted sour grapes for hours afterward.

Father had been amused by the Ambassador, though Padi hadn't been able to fathom precisely why. And in the end, neither dislike nor amusement had mattered, so far as she could see; Korval and Granda together reread the standing treaty, no changes were made, and both parties signed, accepting the terms for the next twelve years.

Oh, and Father had gotten a pretty stone coaster.

"How do you plan to mark this momentous event?" Father asked as she settled into the chair across the desk from him.

She considered him blandly, her best trading face in place.

"I plan to mark the occasion by taking on cargo that I will sell for profit at Chessel's World," she told him, seriously.

Father's eyebrows rose. He picked up his glass and settled back. "But how piquant! Tell me more."

The urge to sit up straighter and stiffer in answer to his comfortable slouch was almost irresistible. Nonetheless, Padi resisted it, sitting respectfully at attention, as befit a 'prentice in the presence of a master, but with muscles relaxed and face bland.

"My studies have shown me that Chessel's World is the largest importer of *milaster* in its quadrant. Demand long ago outgrew the planet's ability to produce it. The homegrown sort is triple-A grade, and is reserved to the Redcap caste and above. The rest is imported, which means that the lower castes pay too much for a product that is often inferior."

"Shocking," Father murmured, his silver eyes half-closed. "But tell me how you will turn this sad situation to your hand."

"Easily enough," Padi answered. "Andiree produces *milaster*— enough for its needs, which are modest, and a surplus, which is sold for export."

She leaned forward, her elbows on her knees and her eyes on Father's face.

"Andiree *milaster* does eventually find its way to Chessel's World," she continued, "but it is transported slowly, via serial transfers between looper ships. By the time it arrives at its market, it is not in the best shape, nutritionally, and the transport costs have raised its price considerably, though the trader's margin is small."

"This is dreadful; neither side of the trade is satisfied!"

"No," she dared to correct him. "Both sides are, grudgingly, satisfied, but neither is *happy*."

"However, you have a scheme that will repair this situation."

"I have a scheme that will deliver a superior product to market, and which will provide a profit. For us. *Dutiful Passage*."

He raised his glass and gestured with it, an invitation to continue.

"The *Passage* is not a loop ship; we propose to Jump from Andiree to Chessel's World. We will therefore have only our own transport expense in the equation, with whatever the cargo itself costs. At Chessel's World, we can undersell our competitors, very slightly, while earning a significantly larger profit, for a superior product."

"My recollection of the lists suggests that *milaster*, despite its popularity at Chessel's World, is a low-end item."

"Yes," she acknowledged. "That makes it fitting spec cargo

for a 'prentice, who is neither plump in pocket, nor likely to be sought out in the marketplace for her name alone."

"How much do you intend to commit?"

She named a figure: fully half of her original spec fund for this trip, reserving those small profits she had gained at their previous ports.

"Depending on supply, of course," she added.

"That is quite a lot of money," he commented.

She allowed herself a smile. "I wish to become *considerably* plumper in pocket."

"As who does not? Well, you appear to have thought the matter out. Please, keep me informed of your progress."

"Yes, Master Trader."

"Excellent. Now, I fear, I must come the parent for a moment, and allow you to know that Arms Master Schneider has been to see me, expressing some concern regarding your defense training."

Padi blinked. "Concern?"

"Indeed. He praises your abilities in *menfri'at* lavishly, and is quite convinced that you will eventually excel at a higher level. His concern, however, has to do with your—let us say your *willingness to embrace* the ultimate answer to all questions. He expressed it thus: 'If she was in a street scrape, there wouldn't be anybody but her left standing.' As arms master, he finds that you are too willing to adopt a single-solution stance to multiple—oft-times complex—problems. Such inflexibility weakens your defenses. He also confided his concern that this dependence upon one solution springs, not from control, but from a lack of confidence in your own abilities. He has therefore recommended that you be placed into the *daibri'at* class taught by Lina Faaldom. This will necessitate a very slight change in your schedule, which I trust will not discommode you in the least. You will begin with Master Faaldom your next on-shift."

Padi took a breath, and another, struggling slightly. She had expected to be moved from her dance class, yes—but to a higher level within *menfri'at*!

If Arms Master Schneider had been *concerned* about control, why could he not have spoken *to her*, his student? Surely *he* did not share Tech Varoth's absurd notion that her kin-ties meant that she could not be corrected!

She took a hard breath, aware that Father had stopped speaking and was looking at her with curiosity.

"Surely, if my moves lacked control," she said keeping her voice even, though she wanted to shout. "Surely, if I were *inept*, Arms Master Schneider had only to correct me."

"It is not, as I understand it, your moves which lack control," Father said, his eyes on hers, "but your motivation."

"I . . . don't understand," she said, trying not to feel as if she had . . . failed. *Daibri'at*—that was for babies! Well, no, of course it wasn't. Hadn't Syl Vor practiced *menfri'at* with them at the Rock? Very focused he had been, too, and his kills the cleanest of any of them, though she and Quin had been dancing for years. But *daibri'at* hadn't a *use*; it was all about describing graceful movements, and breathing into the moment. It was, it was more akin to flower arranging than *real* dance.

"Padi."

Father's voice was soft, warm. She blinked up into his face.

"Sir?"

"I wonder, child, if you've been experiencing any discomfort? If perhaps your head might pain you at odd times, or you are suddenly disoriented, or . . . frightened, for what seems to be no reason?"

In fact, she thought irritably, he was wondering if she was *cha'dramliza*—a Healer—which she assuredly was not, nor would she ever be. Of that, she was determined.

Oh, it was reasonable to expect that she might be—Father himself was a Healer, and so was Aunt Anthora, though Aunt Anthora . . . well. In any case, Korval was strong in the *dramliz* talents; talents that typically manifested when one became halfling.

However, just because many of Korval became Healer or *dramliza*, did not mean that *all* of Korval did so. One need look no further than Quin and Cousin Pat Rin to find kin who were not Healers.

As *she* was not a Healer, nor ever would be.

She shook her head, and smiled for Father's care, which was proper, and really, she was quite fond of Father and did not wish for him to worry.

"No, sir; nothing like that. I'm only running to keep up, so if sometimes I seem odd . . ."

"No odder than usual, I think," Father said, and gave her

one more considering look before leaning back in his chair and reaching again for his glass.

"Well, now, I have heard your plans for Andiree and Chessel's World! Would you care to hear mine? I fear you'll find them considerably less bold than yours, and so I warn you!"

"Only if you will explain what you mean to accomplish by meekness," she said.

He smiled.

"Did I say *meek*?"

CHAPTER THREE

· ·

Dutiful Passage

IN ADDITION TO HER DUTIES AS LIBRARIAN AND CULTURAL OFFI-
cer, Lina Faaldom served the ship as a Healer. Padi had been
in the habit of considering her a sensible woman; the information that she was master of a dance as trivial, as *purposeless*, as
daibri'at...had come as a shock. But, there. Quin was...mostly...
quite sensible, wasn't he? And didn't he, regardless, spend time
better used for reading, or for exercising, threading beads along
wires and chains? Some of his creations were quite pretty, and
could at least be given as gifts, and worn. And some cachet
accrued to the creator when others willingly wore his handmade
trifles, even if the stones were semiprecious, at best.

By contrast, this...*daibri'at* left no residual that might benefit one or one's acquaintanceship. Of course, when one danced
menfri'at, there was no *immediate* benefit, saving that gained
through exercise. The real benefits became apparent when one
was set upon by brigands and obliged to defend oneself or one's
comrades.

The aim of *daibri'at*, as far as Padi could divine, was...to
look pretty.

In short, she thought, moving briskly down the hall toward
her class with Master Faaldom, *daibri'at* was a waste of her time.

She did, however, have her orders and her schedule, which was
why she was on her way to one of the smaller practice rooms. It

had occurred to her, while she showered, that the case of Lina Faaldom being a Healer might not be...an accident. Father might well have asked a colleague for an evaluation of his daughter's proclivities and talents.

After all, Father clearly *expected* her to come Healer—perhaps he even *wished* for his heir to share his talent. One didn't like to disappoint Father, of course, but—no. She was *not* a Healer. It was simply not possible.

However, the more she considered the notion that Lina Faaldom had been asked to provide a second opinion, the more she believed that she would find herself a class of one for *daibri'at*—which had the effect of lifting her spirits somewhat as she came nearer the practice room. After all, if *daibri'at* practice was a mere subterfuge, then she would be back dancing *menfri'at* at her *proper level* within a shift or two.

That thought cheered her so much that she was nearly dancing in fact when she reached her destination, and put her hand against the plate.

The door whisked open—and her mood crashed, from bright cheerfulness to dark despair.

For she was not Lina Faaldom's only student in the dance of *daibri'at*. There were five others in the room ahead of her.

And one of them was Arms Master Schneider.

· · · ✳ · · ·

Shan tapped the keypad, and reached for his glass.

His first glance at the messages in-queue failed to discover the words, "Terran Trade Commission." It was beginning to be worrisome, this lack of communication from the Terran Trade Commission.

He had initially considered it a positive sign that the honored members of the Rating Committee hadn't laughed in his face, or issued a flat *no* on the spot, but had rather promised to take the matter of upgrading Surebleak Port's rating under advisement, review the files he had provided, and contact him with their ruling in three Standard months.

As that date came ever more near, he was beginning to suspect that their unusual agreeableness had been nothing more than a stall.

Well. He closed his eyes and indulged himself with a few

deep, calming breaths before opening his eyes to consider his message queue again.

Carresens-Denobli...

He blinked, touched the access key, and eased back into his chair's embrace, his eyes still on the screen, and a communication he had never thought to see during his career as a master trader.

In short, he was looking at a working memo from the Carresens Syndicate, under the signature of one Janifer Carresens-Denobli, Trader-at-Large. Trader Carresens-Denobli styled the memo a "first exchange of thoughts." He confessed that he had only just begun thinking of Surebleak as a port of potential interest to the Syndicate, and thus his first thoughts were necessarily incomplete.

> *Other matters will doubtless occur to each as we discuss this in more depth, trader-and-trader. I offer here, as my first thoughts, a loop that accommodates Surebleak and also Ashlan, which is an anchor port for three Carresens long-loopers and many others, of the small-loop ships. I am thinking, too, of Nomi-Oxin-Rood, which is something much on the lines of Surebleak—there is potential, but nothing that would tie it into existing routes. If there were to be a new loop, perhaps a hybrid loop, though I have not thought deeply on this, it may be that the potentials of Surebleak and Nomi-Oxin-Rood may be realized, to the mutual benefit of traders.*
>
> *I append a list of such cargoes as might be of interest to Ashlan and Nomi-Oxin-Rood, for which I have some information. Also, I append a list of those cargoes which are standard on Carresens ships, in our loops which now exist.*
>
> *Of very great interest to me is information regarding those items which might find favor with the traders of Surebleak, and also perhaps an indication of specialty items, which might show well in the Festevalya, and so open up the mind of the wider universe to Surebleak.*
>
> *I await in lively anticipation your first thoughts regarding this enterprise, which may be directed to me at the beam code below.*
>
> *Sealed by the hand and will of*
> *Janifer Carresens-Denobli*

Carefully, Shan set his glass aside.

Of the several names he had given to Theo as possible contacts along the exploratory loop he had launched her upon . . . of those several contacts, he had supposed from the beginning that the Carresens would roundly ignore Korval's overture and their ambassador.

The Carresens, after all, had no need of outside trade arrangements; they were complete in their trade family and their vast, intersecting network of loops, and felt no need to expand their range, or change their methods.

Until, apparently, now.

He tapped up a new screen and filed a query for Janifer Carresens-Denobli, then flipped back to reread the good trader's "first thoughts," and open the appended lists.

They were remarkably complete lists, for mere "first thoughts." One might almost wonder if the Carresens—or if *this particular* Carresens—had been expecting contact from Korval.

The list of the trade goods commonly carried by Carresens ships made for fascinating reading, revealing, as it did, quite a bit regarding the nature of the Carresens loop and long-time trade worlds.

Shan drew a careful breath.

What in the name of the gods had Theo said to the man?

The console chimed then and he flipped back to the research screen, learning in very short order that Janifer Carresens-Denobli not only stood as one of the Carresens three Ranking Traders, but was also a senior trade commissioner.

"The question changes," Shan murmured, picking up his glass, and draining what was left. This was no ordinary Carresens trader. How had Theo *gotten an interview* with this person?

But that was obvious, wasn't it?

Her ship.

Putting aside the fact of its sentience, the ship . . . was an old ship, with, let it be said, *interesting* lines. A ship that had been specifically built, a very long time ago, to be a long-looper.

Carresens and Denobli would not yet have merged families and routes, Shan thought, when *Bechimo* had been built. And if the present-day family members hadn't quite seen anything like those lines, rest assured that they had records. Almost definitely, they would have been in contact with the Uncle, trade being one of his many . . . hobbies.

In fact, it wasn't at all unlikely that the Carresens or the Denoblis—either or both—had invested in the building of *Bechimo*, many, many Standard years ago.

So, then, Theo wins an interview with a high-ranking Carresens trader because of her ship. The Carresens might even be excused for thinking that the ship was a message.

And so one of the three Carresens elders set himself to explore just what, precisely, that message might be, and if it was to the benefit of the Carresens.

Well, well; how novel. How *exciting*. He would have to consider carefully, and offer Trader Carresens and his Syndicate as fully realized "first thoughts" as he had been offered.

Surely, there was profit to be made, for all.

They only needed to work out the details.

· · · ❄ · · ·

"And here arrives a new practitioner of our art," Lina Faaldom said, as Padi stepped into the room, the door falling closed behind her. "Join us, please."

Padi slipped her boots off and moved six steps across the soft floor, bowed to the master's honor and straightened to meet a straight, honey-brown gaze.

Lina Faaldom was very slight, and somewhat shorter than Padi, who, after all, came from a clan known for the height of its members. She seemed to project—perhaps, being a Healer, she *did* project!—a cool serenity that put Padi immediately on her mettle. She was here to take a *lesson*, not a *nap*!

The master was seen, perhaps, to smile before she inclined her sleek head.

"Please, allow us to know your name," she said, and raised a hand slightly, as if to restrain Padi's enthusiasm. "Here, we are all students. Therefore, we share call-names only."

"Yes," Padi murmured, and bowed to the five who stood patiently in a semicircle before the master. "I am Padi."

The student closest to her, who she thought worked in the cafeteria, bowed. "Riean."

Next in line was Arms Master Schneider, who bowed and murmured, "Jon"; then a woman whose face bore the marks of many years, "Keslis."

Then was Caz Tar, with an outworld accent; Padi thought him

about Quin's age. And she had certainly seen the next student, Brisalia, among the maintenance crew.

"Lina," said Master Faaldom, in her cool voice. "Please, Padi, take your place beside Riean. You will want to have an arm's width or more between you; we stretch wide here!"

This was apparently a joke, greeted by several chuckles. Riean grinned, and obligingly stretched his arms out at shoulder height, giving Padi her range. She nodded her thanks and took up a position beside, apart, and slightly behind him.

"Good," Master . . . Lina said. "As I have said, we are all students here. Some of us have been studying longer, but *daibri'at* is a discipline which may be studied for a lifetime, the diligent student finding always some new facet to explore. The art has been described as a many-petaled flower; also as a multifaceted gem. And we come together, as students, to *practice*, each at our own level. As the eldest student of the art present, I often lead our practice. However, this is not always the case. Any one of us may lead a practice. And each of us will be asked to do so."

She looked at them each, one by one, then said, "Since we have a new student among us today, who will explain our art?"

"I will," said Brisalia. "*Daibri'at* focuses the student's attention on movement. It's . . . inward-turning. We pay attention to the movement, and our mind's connection to our muscles, instead of focusing on the results of our movement."

"As we do in *menfri'at*," Arms Master—Jon—added.

"That is a useful contrast," Lina said. "*Menfri'at* is an outward-looking art. It *acts upon* others. *Daibri'at* is inward-looking. From it, we learn the intent of our movements."

The *intent* of her movements? Padi thought. Surely, when she kicked at a target, or an assailant, she *intended* to connect; to disable the threat? What other *intent*—

"So, having described what is essentially indescribable, let us begin our practice. Please find your center—feet under hips, weight evenly distributed. We will bring our arms up until our palms touch over our heads, and we will take four complete breaths before lowering our arms to our sides."

Padi was already centered—one thing *menfri'at* had taught her was to *always* be centered; you never knew, after all, when an attack might come—and raised her arms until her palms touched.

...only then seeing that...Lina and the rest were still in the process of raising *their* arms, slowly and deliberately. She slid a surreptitious glance at Riean, and saw his eyes half-closed and his face rapt in concentration, as if the process of centering himself and beginning this simple movement had triggered some deeper process.

She looked to Lina again, seeing that her palms were now touching over her head, and watched as those four "complete" breaths were executed, as slow and as measured as a pilot might take them, in preparation for board rest.

Then, the arms came down, as slowly, if not more slowly, than they had risen. Padi lowered hers, as well, struggling to match the agonizingly slow pace, and found she was trembling and slightly sweaty by the time her fingers were pointing toward the floor again.

Lina opened her eyes and smiled.

"Next, we will raise our arms, as we just did, and, when we have completed four breaths, we will bend at the hips and bring our hands to the mat."

Once again, the agonizingly slow rise of both arms. Padi grimly kept pace, pilot instincts, honed for precise, rapid action, abraded almost past bearing. At the top of the form, she breathed four complete breaths, hinged at the hip and bent until her fingertips touched the mat.

A drop of sweat plashed against the mat between her feet and her fingers. Padi breathed in, feeling her muscles shake with the need to *move*, breathed out, four times, and came up again to her full height.

"Excellent," said Lina. "Now, place your right foot ahead of your left on the mat, bring your hands up as if you are holding a large ball, immediately before your heart."

Padi followed the form demonstrated, bearing down until her muscles ached, refusing to allow herself to snap into a series of kicks, or to simply collapse cross-legged to the mat and have done.

"Very good," Lina said, and smiled directly into Padi's eyes. "Now, breathe in, and pivot from center, keeping your ball directly before your heart..."

CHAPTER FOUR

· ·

Tarigan
In Jump

THEY WERE IN JUMP, EN ROUTE TO BIERADINE, AND THE PILOT
had given copilot Tolly Jones leave to grab a snack, and stretch
his legs. There was 'mite in the galley, so he added hot water and
stirred up a mugful. Unlike some spacers, it wasn't his drink and/
or food of preference, but it had its uses as a quick pick-me-up,
which it happened he needed. The pilot was pushing them, just
a little, nothing bone and blood couldn't put up with, stipulating
that bone and blood was what you'd call *in form*.

Which he wasn't, quite.

He swallowed the 'mite as fast as he could, put the mug in
the washer and exited the galley, turning left, to take a little
walking tour of *Tarigan*.

She was a tidy ship, augmented in interesting ways, which
Pilot Tocohl had already drilled him on. The pilot wouldn't suffer one bit of damage if he did something stupid that breached
the hull, but he'd be a dead man, and it was courteous of her
to notice his disability in that regard and take steps first off to
be sure he was safe on the ship.

His tour ended, as it had on his three other walkabouts, at
the alcove that held the autodoc. He paused at the side of the
single unit, palm flat against the opaque hood, and frowned at
the status board.

Haz—his former partner, in Port Security, Hazenthull nor'Phelium—had taken a couple hits for him, which normally would've made as much difference to her as getting slugged with a marshmallow. She was that big, and that tough. Too bad for her that the particular sort of marshmallows she'd caught had come out of the gun of one of his late...directors, and they'd been poisoned. It was a particularly nasty poison the directors employed, which he knew from personal experience, but him and the pilot'd gotten Haz into the 'doc plenty quick. He'd expected her to be up and around by now.

The good news was that the 'doc had consistently reported that she was on the mend. In fact, the end-of-treatment display was finally lit up this time. He leaned close to have a look.

Fourteen hours 'til the hood came up. He patted the top of the 'doc softly, as if Haz might feel his hand and take some comfort from knowing he had her back.

Just like old times.

He patted the 'doc once more and left the alcove, heading for the bridge.

"How fares the Explorer?" the pilot asked from her station.

She was a sight for tired eyes, was Pilot Tocohl. Smooth and personable and specifically nonthreatening, the curve of her gleaming white chassis suggesting something feminine; the smallness of it hinting at vulnerability. She moved herself about the ship by floating a few inches above the deck plates—nothing so crass, or noisy, as wheels or skis. He hadn't worked out if her motivating force was antigrav, magnetics, or a tightly focused and utterly silent air pad. It seemed rude to ask.

It was Tolly's opinion, as an expert in the field, that there wasn't the least need for Pilot Tocohl to sit station. Pilot Tocohl had direct access to all ship's systems right there inside her pretty little head, or he was a three-nosed Andulsin frog.

"She's got a healed-by date," he said in answer to his pilot's question. "Fourteen hours from now this bridge is gonna be full up with big, stubborn woman, who'll be wanting to talk to her captain, stat."

"I shall be very glad to see her, and in such condition," Pilot Tocohl said composedly. "In the meantime, I wonder, Pilot, if you will answer some questions for me."

"Do my best," he said, like his stomach hadn't kind of cramped up, hearing that. "Understand that I don't know the answers to all the questions."

"Oh, yes, I do understand that," she said. "Before we begin, let me request that you not lie to me. If you do not wish to answer a question, simply refrain from doing so."

"All right, Pilot," he said, and slipped into his chair. "I'm curious myself, though. The—my contact, who approached me about this project...he has my credentials."

"Indeed, your credentials are...impressive," she said. "And you are undeniably resourceful. Our mutual contact was quite clear that you are a mentor of great talent. The most talented in your field, he said."

"To be fair, the field isn't that big, the Complex Logic Laws bein' what they are."

That the pilot was herself a violation of the Complex Logic Laws went without saying. His being hired as copilot was to cover for her. She was a prototype, so the script went, some kind of a cybermech pilot, sophisticated, but stopping short of illegal. Which was why she sat station. He was along for the ride, to observe, to make notes, and to abort her if something went wrong.

However, his contract had two sections to it, and the second part engaged his services in evaluating and, if possible, socializing, a newly realized AI, who had come to awareness under unspecified, but difficult, circumstances, unmentored.

He didn't have anything against sitting copilot, but he might not have taken the contract just to give Pilot Tocohl cover, seeing that his own blanket had lately developed a considerable number of holes. The second part of the contract, though...that had grabbed his attention and it hadn't let go.

Never mind that the Complex Logic Laws made Pilot Tocohl and all her kind out to be rogue devices, bent on destroying human life. If encountered, according to the CLL, an AI was to be confined, deactivated, or destroyed; nobody was to take it into their heads to *build* one for any reason whatsoever, under pain of death.

It hadn't always been that way. Truth said, it wasn't that way, even now. AIs got born...not as a frequent thing, but often enough that mentors were needed. They worked the underside, but not one mentor Tolly'd ever met or heard of had minded that.

Pilot Tocohl turned toward him, the flat screen at the apex of her slender core column showing the shadow of a face, smiling a shadow smile.

"The field may be small, but that does not negate the fact of your mastery, Tolly. Our contact praised you in the highest terms. I have no questions there."

Tolly took a breath.

"Where do you have questions, then?" he asked her, but he already knew.

There was a small pause, as if Pilot Tocohl needed a moment to gather her thoughts. Tolly sighed gently.

"A sigh, Pilot Tolly?"

"I was thinking I'd like to meet the mentor who had the teaching of you. I could learn a thing or two." He paused, and added, just to be clear, "No disrespect, Pilot."

"Certainly not. If you think such a meeting would be of use, I will ask my mentor if he will see you, when this mission is done."

"I'd like that, thanks."

"You are very welcome. And now, I fear, my questions.

"What are you, Tollance Berik-Jones?"

That was asked well enough that he was persuaded she already knew. No point in lying, then, or in remaining silent. "I'm a manufactured human, Pilot. The *human*'s so I don't offend the Complex Logic Laws."

"There are also laws against manufacturing humans, I believe."

"A lot harder to prove 'manufactured.'"

"I see."

There came another pause, as if the pilot were considering his answer.

"Are you the Uncle's?"

He blinked. Hadn't seen that one coming.

"No, Pilot," he said, not surprised that she knew the Uncle— and that she expected the same of him. People on the underside knew their neighbors, that was all.

"This vulnerability of yours, which you have been working to ... limit. How much danger does it bring to our ship, and our mission?"

Well, that *was* the question, wasn't it?

"Pilot—I don't know. The pool of available directors is pretty small." He allowed himself a moment of grim humor. "Smaller, now, thanks to Haz. Even if they mean to have me, no matter what, it's going to take time for word to get back to the school; time to send another team out; and then they have to find us. I'm not saying it's impossible that they will..."

"I understand," she said, after his words ran out. If she'd been human, Tolly had the notion she'd've sighed right then.

"This vulnerability—what is its nature? An implant? A construction? Something biologic?"

He shook his head. "Pilot, I don't know." He hesitated, then decided it wouldn't do any harm to tell her. "I figured to steal the specs, back when I was young and really stupid. I can tell you that the directors keep them locked up tight. And that they're stinting of praise when one of the students shows initiative and has a go at the locks."

"I see. Describe to me, please, the effects of control."

"My will is overridden; my...self is submerged. I am compelled to do such things as the operator deems necessary. When I have completed a mission, I am allowed to return to...what I believe to be myself." His felt his lips quirk. "This may be a flaw in the system."

"Perhaps so. One would assume that there was a reason for it, however."

"Yes'm. Could I ask you a favor, copilot to pilot?"

"Yes."

"If it seems to you that I've fallen...victim to my vulnerability, will you please kill me?"

Her face came fully visible for an instant, before the pilot angled the screen downward and tipped slightly forward in a bow.

"Yes," she said. "I will."

It soothed him to hear her say it, which was maybe stupid. Still, he figured her good for the promise; whoever'd designed Pilot Tocohl had been uncommon clever; *she* wouldn't be caught in any whistling glamor.

It came to him then that he had two solid allies, standing at his back, given what Haz had already done for him and that thing the pilot promised. Two allies; people he could depend on, without question.

He couldn't remember, in all his life, having so much as one ally, and he hoped, his eyes prickling a little as he looked to his screens—he very much hoped that he would stand just as firm, for them.

"One question more, Pilot Tolly."

He drew a breath, and turned back to face her.

"Yes'm?"

"I wonder if you have heard a...rumor, let us say. Presently, I hold it no higher than that—a rumor of a very old AI recently wakened. The Uncle may be in it—there's that rumor, also—but surely he would be, so it's no surprise, there."

An ancient AI waking—*reawaking*, it would be. And if it were reawakening, then it had likely fallen asleep due to lack of needed repairs...

The Uncle was well placed to repair such a thing...

Tolly laughed, and shook his head, looking up at the pilot with an apologetic grin.

"I haven't heard any such rumor, myself, but I've been out of the loops, this last while." He felt his grin widen.

"Sure would be interesting, if true," he said, and saw an answering grin in the shadows of the pilot's face.

"It would be," she said. "Wouldn't it?"

· · · ·❄· · · ·

A chime sounded.

Shan raised his head, blinking out of an abstraction of First Thoughts. It occurred to him, somewhat distantly, that this was not the first time the chime had sounded.

Or the third.

A quick series of taps saved his document, and cleared the screen. He spun his chair about, and reached for his glass—which was empty.

"Come!"

The door opened and Lina Faaldom stepped through, tiny and definite, brown hair just slightly disheveled, as if she had only now come back inside from a turn in the garden.

He considered her; most especially, he considered the flavor of her emotions: determination wedded to a certain wariness. Determination—certainly, he knew Lina to be a determined woman, a Healer of rare skill; devoted to helping those who were perhaps less determined to achieve and maintain Balance.

Wariness, though...that was not at all like Lina. Oh, she was hardly a fool, and certainly he had seen her frightened a time or two in their long friendship. Caution, he might expect, but wariness...?

"I have disturbed your work," she said, pausing a mere three paces into the room. "Forgive me, old friend. Tell me when I will be convenient, and I will return at that hour."

"In fact, your arrival is a happy circumstance, and not only because I'm always pleased to see you," he said. "I fear that I may have been overthinking something. It will do me good to step away from it and entertain another problem for a time."

He tipped his head and gave her a half-smile.

"You *do have* a problem for me, don't you, Lina?"

He expected a laugh; she produced a slightly harried smile.

"I fear so," she said, drifting forward again, and slipping into the chair.

No, this was not much like Lina. Shan considered her again as she settled herself: determination, wariness, puzzlement.

Well.

"Would you care for wine?" he asked. "I am about to pour for myself, as my stupid glass has come empty. I can't think how it might have happened."

That earned a slightly less harried smile, and a small inclination of the head.

"Wine would be pleasant, thank you."

Lina drank red. He rose and filled two glasses, placing hers on the desk near her hand before he once again took his own chair.

He raised his glass. She raised hers. They drank.

The wine was pleasant, though spiced with increased dismay. He thought he understood that she was unsure of the best way to broach her topic.

"Best to leap in with both feet," he murmured.

Lina moved her shoulders, neither a shrug nor a shiver. "It seems I must, since I have no facts to lay before you, merely feeling."

"We are Healers; emotion is the primary tool of our trade."

Lina sighed, and sipped her wine again. Shan allowed a breath of calm to waft between them, which took only the tiniest of liberties with their long friendship. Unless Lina chose to see it differently, of course.

She smiled slightly.

"Thank you," she murmured.

She put her glass aside with a tiny click, and raised her eyes to his.

"As we had arranged, Padi came to class and danced *daibri'at* today. I will say immediately that I have had students who were more eager to embrace the art."

"Was she disrespectful?"

Lina shook her head.

"Disrespectful—no. Perhaps a little disdainful, at first—but that is not unusual for one coming to the Small Dance after having partaken of *menfri'at*. I had the impression, when she entered the room, that she had not expected to find so many co-students. Definitely, she was...displeased to find Jon among us. She kept her temper, however, and after an initial misunderstanding regarding the timing of our dance, she comported herself well."

She reached for her glass and sipped again, frowning.

"I noted that it was very difficult for her to move in proper rhythm. She wanted speed; *her body* wanted speed. To move so slowly was, not merely a novelty, but physically stressful."

Shan swirled the wine in his glass; looked up to meet her eyes.

"She is a pilot, with a pilot's reactions; newly come from an...intense course of specialized training."

Lina nodded. "From which spring Jon's concerns: that the specialized training had been too intense, and had unbalanced her judgment. His hope is that the Small Dance will assist her in reasserting her balance, as he and I have seen it do for other dancers."

She paused, and Shan considered her carefully.

"You have reason to believe that this therapy will not be of benefit to Padi?"

Here was the crux; he felt the heat of her frustration even as she blew out her breath.

"Padi...is—oh, bah! I will say it, and it will sound like idiocy, but perhaps we two may then parse it into sense. Padi, old friend, *does not relax.*"

Shan laughed.

"Korval as a clan is driven to succeed. Surely that hasn't escaped your attention? Padi is very much a child of Korval. Worse, she is one of Korval who has been forcibly diverted from her life-path and her plans. She is running hard to catch herself back up."

He stopped here because Lina was shaking her head.

"It is...something more than that. Something *other* than

that. You have studied the Small Dance; what is its purpose, aside from focusing intent?"

He *had* studied *daibri'at*, when he had been Trader yos'Galan and scarcely older than Padi was now. Its principles and purposes had long ago entered his general repertory of skills. Trying to isolate its purpose, rather than seeing it as a part of the tapestry...

"Options," he said. "*Daibri'at* defuses reflexive action, and opens the mind to possibility."

"Yes. It is, at its heart, a tool to relax and to expand the awareness." Lina drew a hard breath. "Padi does not relax. She is *always* on high energy. Even at the end of our practice, when we sit together and breathe...I saw her"—a sharp headshake, as if Lina was out of patience with her inability to find the perfectly correct words—"I saw her divert the energy, rather than accepting its benefits."

Shan frowned.

"Divert it...where?"

She gave him a wry look.

"That, I did *not* see. However, I may make a guess. As she rose to leave, I noticed the suggestion of stone in her aura, as of walls within."

Shan blinked.

"You think Padi is hiding something, and is diverting energy from everything she does in order to keep a...secret...behind walls?"

"Yes! I knew you would shape it sensibly!"

Well, he might have done so, but the feat gave him no joy; not when the next question was, naturally, *Hiding what?* closely followed by *Why hadn't he noticed?*

But, no; he *had* noticed. The children—*all* of the children, save perhaps the infant twins—had returned from Runig's Rock... changed. The nature of the training—the very *reason* for their presence at the Rock—who would not be changed by such things? And he had noticed, not walls, but a reserve, certainly. Priscilla had also noticed...and Anthora. Between them, they had made the decision to give the children time to heal themselves—if Healing was indeed required—while their elders kept watch. It was a conservative course; self-healing was in almost all cases to be preferred.

"I had noticed a certain...reserve," he said carefully, not wishing to lie to Lina, and equally unwilling to burden her with Korval secrets. "I would not have said a *wall*."

Lina nodded. "It is well hidden. I think I would have not seen it, but that I had just danced, and was thus open to all input. Which leads me, old friend, to the last of the problems I have to place before you today."

He raised an eyebrow and inclined his head.

She smiled.

"It comes to me that Padi is a halfling."

He raised his hand.

"You will say that she is ripe to come into her powers. I ask her, as often as I might without becoming entirely tedious, you understand—and she denies the classic symptoms of onset. I also scan, of course, but I've found nothing to indicate a budding Healer."

"I venture to predict that Padi will come *dramliza*," Lina said.

"Based on this glimpse of stone?"

"And the fact that it is so very well hidden, yes." She seemed about to say more, but at the last moment changed her mind.

Shan, however, knew what she might say—that a *dramliza* coming into her power was a far different—a far *more dangerous* thing—than a Healer coming into hers. Such a coming of age might even endanger the *Passage*.

"I will speak with Priscilla. Will you be available to assist, should we decide it best to force the issue?"

"Certainly. One dislikes such methods, as I know you do, but the ship..."

Indeed, the ship.

Lina rose and bowed as between equals, which put a fine point on the discussion they had just completed: Healers discussing the proper concerns of Healers.

He rose and returned the bow, then walked her to the door.

CHAPTER FIVE

. . . .

Dutiful Passage

THEY WOULD BREAK OUT INTO REGULAR SPACE WITHIN THE NEXT ship half-day, and begin Andiree approach, the *Passage* sending information packets and news ahead.

She would be on the trade bridge with Father, trading catalogs, questions, offers, invitations, news packets. The catalogs would be her priority; Father would answer queries, and review the catalog entries that she marked for his interest, if any.

Depending on the planet, and the number of traders on-planet seeking an early and advantageous connection, the double shift on the trade bridge might be either exhausting or boring. It would, in any case, *be* a double shift, and she ought, really, to be sleeping now rather than studying.

Padi sighed and rubbed her eyes. She'd been diverting two hours of her sleep shift to study since the *Passage* had departed Surebleak, having long ago found that she didn't need much sleep—not really.

Not when there was so much work to do . . .

Not when there was so much *catching up* to do.

Father had said she would be running double time, in effect, taking two lines of training simultaneously: cabin boy and 'prentice trader. He'd told her, quite seriously, that even with the double-track training, she would very probably not meet her goal of achieving her trader's license on her eighteenth Name Day. He had been quite kind, and laid the fault where it belonged, on the attentions of the *stupid* Department of the Interior, which had taken Korval so very much in dislike, and had therefore interrupted *everyone's* proper life-course, and not on any deficiency she had displayed. He had said, too, that it was no shame to stand a full trader on one's nineteenth Name Day, which goal he was confident she could meet.

She had chosen to, well... not *discount* his words, no. She had merely chosen to see them as a *challenge*. After all, it wasn't as if she had come to the *Passage* with no training at all. She had served two trips as cabin boy on *Pale Wing*, one of Korval's first-tier tradeships, and would have transferred to the *Passage* herself for the next long circuit, save that Plan B had been brought into effect at the most inconvenient moment conceivable, sending her, Quin, Syl Vor, the twins, Grandfather Luken, and Cousin Kareen scurrying to hide in Runig's Rock.

There they had taken lessons of a very different order, in addition to their usual school fare, and accelerated piloting study—disappointingly, on the sims—while they had waited for word that Korval's enemy had been vanquished.

In truth, their sojourn in the Rock had not been so ill as it might have been, given close daily proximity to Cousin Kareen, who was a stickler of the *first* water. Quin had minded it, of course, in addition to being all a-twitter over Cousin Pat Rin, when, if he had only taken a moment to consider—but there. Quin was made of nerves. *She* had known there was no reason to worry, though she did allow that she might have felt differently, had it been *her* father who had failed to report in, not once or twice, but *at all*...

In any case, eventually, they were called home. Or, not precisely *home*, but to Surebleak, a planet of which *no one* had ever heard, nor was that circumstance anything to wonder at, once one actually saw the place.

It had all been rather bewildering—indeed, it was still... unsettling... to recall that *Surebleak* was now the home port of *Dutiful Passage*, and the seat of Clan Korval.

Father and the delm—including Uncle Val Con, who had been away for so very long with the Scouts, now joyously returned to the clan, and bringing to Korval a completely unexpected lifemate, who was forthwith revealed to be a Tiazan of Erob, so *that* was all right...

Father and Priscilla, the delms, and Cousin Pat Rin—all of them had been there, around Liad, when it had happened. *All* of them had taken a hand in the event.

And they had explained, very carefully and very thoroughly, exactly what *had* happened; why, and what the stakes had been, not only for Korval, but for all of Liad; and why they dared not fail nor take half measures.

Padi understood the situation perfectly, though the Council of Clans had not, which had led to Korval's removal to Surebleak in the Daiellen Sector.

Father had explained, privately, to her and to Syl Vor, why Trealla Fantrol—yos'Galan's own house—had to be razed, which had made her *angry*. Then she found that Jeeves had brought all of her things and had arranged her new suite, in Jelaza Kazone—Korval's first, and most ancient, house—exactly as it had been in her own, lost rooms, and perhaps she had, just a little, cried...

Well. One could have accommodated even *so much* change, in the service of destroying this Department of the Interior, so that it would do no more harm, to Korval, or to anyone else.

But, as it transpired, the Department had *not* been destroyed, it had merely been wounded, though badly.

Indeed, the Department had been so grievously wounded that anyone might have thought they would withdraw from the field. Father told her that this had been expected.

Only... the Department had not withdrawn. They had, unexpectedly, and perhaps unwisely, after the most modest of pauses to rest and recruit themselves, *increased* hostilities.

And *that* was why they—herself and the other youngers, and Grandfather and Cousin Kareen—had been removed from the clan's safe place at Runig's Rock.

Not because their enemy had been utterly vanquished, and their name ground into the dust, but because there was no certainty that the Rock would not come under attack in the mad increase of hostility.

One might have supposed from this that the delm intended them to sit quietly under guard at Surebleak, but no, *that* had not been the plan, at all. Korval needed to establish itself upon its new homeworld: there were trade routes—trade routes advantageous to ships based upon Surebleak—to be built, alliances to be redeemed and lives to be lived.

"Korval," had said Uncle Val Con, in his *melant'i* as delm...
"Korval is ill-suited to the role of mouse. We began as dragons,
and as dragons we shall go on." Here, he had sent a stern look
to *Father* and added, *quite* unfairly, "*careful* dragons."

Careful dragons meant that the *Passage* herself would not
take port at any of the worlds they called upon, but would rather
remain in orbit, while crew was given leave, or went about the
ship's portside business in groups of no less than three.

Which was a circumstance, Padi thought, stifling a yawn, not
entirely convenient for one who would learn to trade, and for whom
a solitary ramble around port might reveal treasures untold—or, at
least, unanticipated wares which might be turned to profit.

Behold, for instance, Andiree. She was already scheduled to
go down in Father's group, and while she was not fool enough
to think that a 'prentice had nothing to learn from a master
trader, her own attempts at trade could not but be influenced
by his presence. He might hold himself back, but folk would see
the big amethyst ring of a master trader, and they would *bargain*
with him, no matter they *spoke to* the 'prentice.

It was a vexing situation, and one that she had been considering since the schedule had arrived in her duty queue. She
could hardly refuse the assignment—she *didn't want* to refuse the
assignment! It was far more than an honor to watch Father at
work! And he was going to be concentrating on artworks! Merely
she wished to be certain it was *her skill* that carried *her trade*,
rather than Father's ring. She had great hope for the *milaster*
scheme—perhaps too much hope. The transaction had somehow
acquired a weight in her mind, as if turning the *milaster* around
at a handy profit would define her fitness for trade.

Ridiculous.

Well.

She sighed again.

Father was a Healer, after all. Perhaps he could simply suggest to the breeze that he was a sack of potatoes, and thus be
safely ignored.

Her screen beeped, reminding her that she had been staring
at the same page of text for twelve minutes—and without, she
thought irritably, having read a word of it. She might as well
have gone to bed, if she was going to waste her study time in
dreams and regrets.

Irritably, she closed the text, promising herself that she would catch up her deficiency by studying tomorrow over breakfast... well, no. She needed to review the tolerance tables over breakfast, so she would be ready for her shift with Cargo Master ira'Barti. Over lunch—but no. She would be on the trade bridge by then; Father had promised a cold tray at the console, and a *large* bottle of tea...

Oh, she would *find* time! Perhaps she would be less distracted next-shift, and be able to borrow another, *productive* hour from her sleep schedule.

For now, though, she'd best go to bed.

· · · ※ · · ·

"Hey, Haz?"

The voice was familiar, even welcome, but entirely out of place. Even so near a comrade as Tolly had become, he had no place by her berth. Indeed, should the Elder find him...

"C'mon, Haz, rise and shine!"

Blades and blood! If he kept up in such a manner, he would see himself dead before this day was out, and by her hand, before she obeyed the order to turn the weapon upon herself.

She extended an arm, meaning to snatch and stifle him—

"Ouf!"

Her elbow smacked into a barrier; her hand smacked her nose hard enough to bring tears.

"Yeah, sorry 'bout that. We had to fold you up some to get you into the 'doc. Gonna take some unkinking to get you out." There was a pause.

"Be a lot easier if you'd open your eyes and get with the program. The pilot's gonna be needing me back at the board for breakout. An' you don't wanna be stuck in there, now you're awake. You're awake, aren't you, Haz? 'Cause, if not, maybe I should wait to thank you for saving my life."

Recent memory came boiling back then. Tolly, the whistle, the woman striking him with the butt of her gun, opening a gash on his face. The kick of her weapon against her palm as she neutralized the threat to her partner.

She opened her eyes.

Tolly's face was above hers: tan skin, freckles, even features that she had come to understand soothed Terrans and Liadens alike. His hair was an undistinguished yellow, and his eyes were blue, neither particularly dark, nor noticeably pale. At the moment, they were squinted slightly, as if he were looking into a bright light, or straining to see something clearly at a distance.

"You are yourself again?" she demanded. "You were not late for your ship?"

But he had said something just now, had he not, about break-out and the pilot wanting him at his board?

"I'm myself again *and* I made my ship, all because of you," he said, giving her a grin. "C'mon, now, let's get you up on your feet."

Some while later, unkinked, on her feet, and in the galley, second handwich half-eaten, Haz considered what Tolly had told her.

Wounded and in danger of her life, she had been brought aboard the ship that had contracted his services, and placed in the autodoc. The pilot's mission was of some urgency; Tocohl was reluctant to put her lift back, and also reluctant, so Tolly had it, to endanger one in the service of Clan Korval. Pilot Tocohl had, therefore, contacted Captain Robertson herself, and obtained her permission for Hazenthull's attachment to the mission.

"How is it that the captain gave her permission so easily?" Hazenthull asked.

Tolly was leaning against the counter, a mug in one hand, from which he occasionally sipped tea. "Pilot Tocohl's known to Korval," Tolly said. "One of the first things the pilot said to me, once we got you situated, was that this ship doesn't count Korval as trouble."

Hazenthull thought about that, around another bite of handwich.

"I will make myself known to Pilot Tocohl," she said eventually. "She is not among the lists of allies which I was given to learn. Also, I should report in. Commander Lizardi—"

But, given Tolly's recital of events, Commander Lizardi had likely struck Hazenthull nor'Phelium from the lists of Port Security several Surebleak days ago.

"Captain Robertson being aware of your situation—and ours—it wouldn't surprise me if she right away called Commander Liz and explained your leaving so sudden."

The captain, of course, understood chain of command, Hazenthull thought, finishing the handwich and reaching for the mug of plain water. It had surely been done as Tolly said, and already someone else walking her beat...beside a partner who was not Tolly Jones.

She finished the water, stood, and placed the mug into the washer, waiting a moment while Tolly dealt similarly with his mug.

"I will," she said again, "make myself known to Pilot Tocohl."

"Sure thing," Tolly said. "You stay right here; I'll send her in."

· · · ✳ · · ·

"It might be," Priscilla said, sipping her wine, "that Padi's being prudent. Runig's Rock generated a great many secrets. She might well have locked them behind walls."

They were in their private quarters, and at their ease, having ruthlessly rearranged schedules to gain two shifts together—saving an emergency call upon the captain, naturally. There was also the possibility of an emergency call upon the master trader, but that was not nearly so likely. At least, not until they came out of Jump.

"I spoke to Lina," Priscilla continued. She was reclining on the lounge, her long, slim shape draped in a starry blue robe that bared her breasts—a fashion from her homeworld, where Priscilla had been the initiate of a goddess. In comparison, Shan's robe of deep red 'broidered with yellow flowers, and belted at his waist, was the merest commonplace. He sat on the rug beside the lounge, looking up into her face, and her eyes, like black diamonds beneath arching black brows.

"Lina hasn't had another glimpse of this wall, though she's still aware of Padi shifting the energy raised in the dance... somewhere." She smiled slightly. "She asked me to tell you that her least-willing student has become over these last few sessions... somewhat more willing."

Shan lifted his glass high. "Behold me, relieved! One naturally wishes one's heir to accumulate accolades, but 'least-willing student of *daibri'at* in the history of the dance' is not quite in the line of one's fondest hopes."

Priscilla laughed.

"She already has '*avid student of menfri'at*,'" she pointed out.

"There is that. Am I to understand that Lina remains willing to wait, to watch with the rest of us, and to hope that the child wakens to her fullness with—shall we say—as little trauma as possible?"

"She'd rather not force Padi into her power," Priscilla said, her eyes serious. "Neither would I."

"Nor I. The Healers are in accord."

He raised his glass again, in salute. Priscilla raised hers. There was a small, sharp clink as the rims kissed, and they drank.

A moment only to savor the vintage before Priscilla raised her glass once more. Shan lifted his in echo.

"To the bright life who would share our lives and our love. We invite you to this time and this place, where we will welcome you and treasure you." She drank with a flourish, and set the empty glass aside.

Shan did the same, though with perhaps more puzzlement than flourish.

Priscilla extended a hand.

Her skin was cool and smooth, her fingers pale as cream against his brown palm. The familiar sweep of her aura simultaneously soothed and thrilled him.

"Priscilla?" he ventured.

"Yes, my love?"

"Are we going to have a child?"

She smiled, and he did, giddy with her joy.

"If the Goddess is willing—and you are."

He bent his head to kiss her hand.

"Willing, though laggard. Why now, I wonder?"

A dark thread rippled through her joy, gone before he could read it.

"If I say that the Goddess came to me in a dream and told me that now is the time, the soul which will come to us as our child is ready . . . will that make you less willing?"

He considered that seriously. His respect for Priscilla's faith did not particularly extend to her goddess, whom he regarded as unnecessarily meddlesome. On the other hand, the delms had made it clear that full nurseries were a priority of the House. Not that the delms were anything less than meddlesome themselves.

However, the thought of holding their child, with Priscilla's black eyes and softly curling hair, fair melted him where he sat.

He shook his head, and smiled wryly.

"Let us leave it there—I am willing. No! I am eager."

"Not too eager, I hope," Priscilla said.

She swung her legs over the side of the lounge, drawing him to her as she sat up.

He rose to his knees, and kissed an upstanding nipple, the shiver of her delighted lust warming him.

"Not too eager," she repeated, running her fingers through his hair. She slipped a hand beneath his chin and raised his face. "We have hours," she whispered, and kissed him.

· · · ☀ · · ·

Padi was at Runig's Rock, and she was afraid.

So much depended on her—on all of them—but *she* was the only one who was afraid. Quin was grim, and Syl Vor serious, but they weren't *afraid*. They didn't huddle in their beds after lights-out, shivering with nothing more than *fear*.

Grandfather Luken and Cousin Kareen were quite matter-of-fact, even when discussing those plans of evacuation the success of which depended upon them staying behind to hold the enemy, to buy pilots and passengers time to board the ship, time to tumble out into space, and be well away. Time bought with Kareen and Luken's *lives*, which they very well knew, and yet—*they* were not afraid.

Padi yos'Galan, whose duty was to stand copilot, to protect the pilot, and the ship, and the passengers—*Padi yos'Galan was afraid*.

Syl Vor, whose duty was the most terrible of all—to protect the babies. To keep them quiet, and warm; fed and calm.

And, under no circumstances, in no conceivable situation, was he to allow them to fall into the hands of their enemies. Syl Vor carried a pistol, and Grandfather had very carefully explained who those pellets were for, and that Syl Vor must be very quick, and very certain, and that he must not miss when it came to the last shot.

Syl Vor was solemn; he was earnest. Syl Vor did not want to hurt the babies, his cousins. Certainly, he did not want to hurt himself.

But Syl Vor was not *afraid*. He absorbed his duty, learned what he must do and the manner of it. He drilled; he danced; and sometimes, in the evening, when drills and dance and lessons were done, he would sit and draw pictures of home: certain of the cats, Jeeves, the east flower garden, the stream, and the stepping stones...

Of them all, each holding duties far more terrible than her own...only *Padi yos'Galan* was afraid. Sometimes, in the night, she was so overcome with fear that she *cried* under the blankets;

her fist stuffed in her mouth, lest she wake Quin, who had sharp ears, even in sleep. Not that Quin would mock her, but he was her pilot. He would question her ability to do her duty—rightly so. He might properly bring his concern to Grandfather, who would—what? There was no one else to take Padi's duty. Grandfather held a third-class license; Cousin Kareen was no pilot at all. *She* was Quin's copilot; that duty was hers, and hers alone, and she could not let fear cripple her.

"Ah!"

The cry woke her, and she sat up, chest heaving with sobs, her face wet with tears. Lights came up, illuminating her familiar quarters on the *Passage*—where her screen, stylus, and boots were all floating significantly above the surfaces where they had been resting when she sought her bunk.

No! Not here, not now!

She covered her face with her hands, and swallowed, taking a deep breath against the sobs, just as she had done, the night she had decided, on the Rock, what she must do with her fear.

That night, she had completed a pilot's breathing exercise, and when the sobs had subsided, she had lain down and run the Rainbow, telling herself at the end of the sequence not to sleep, but to arise, with sharpened senses, and go to the practice room.

She had done that, without waking anyone, and there, she had danced. In her mind's eye, she had danced inside her room at the end of the Rainbow, and her dancing had built a closet, made of stone. She had stepped into the closet and screamed out all her fear and all her tears. When she was empty, she exited, and locked the closet behind her.

Aboard the *Passage*, with less than two hours until the end of her sleep shift, she could not go to any of the practice rooms. The ship would note her deviation from schedule, and alert Father, or the captain, or the officer on duty. She would have to explain herself, and it was the last thing she wanted to tell anyone—least of all Father—that she was a coward—and that she had lied to him.

So, then.

Shivering, but no longer crying, Padi slipped out of her bunk. She glared at her boots, which were floating at about the level of her nose, breathed in, and snapped, *"Behave!"*

They hit the floor with a solid thump. Behind her she heard

the stylus strike the desktop and roll, and her screen settle with a bump.

Padi looked about her quarters. Far too cramped *here* for *menfri'at*.

But it was not, she thought suddenly, too cramped to dance *daibri'at*. For focus, was it? And to make her aware of her intent? Yes, certainly.

The closet had weakened since its creation. She would reinforce it; make it so strong that the fear would never break free again.

She took a breath, brought her imaginary ball in front of her heart, and called upon her intentions.

CHAPTER SIX

· ·

Dutiful Passage
Andiree Approach

THEY HAD MADE GOOD USE OF THEIR HOURS TOGETHER, SHAN thought with a certain satisfaction, as he settled in behind his desk. No doubt, it was very wrong of him to wish that they had hours—even days!—more ahead of them.

"Which, of course, you do," he told himself, as he opened his mail queue. "Or so one trusts. Viewed correctly, in fact, this small interlude of labor provides an opportunity for you to recruit your strength."

Priscilla was on the bridge, as a captain ought to be, during breakout. Soon enough, he would himself be on the trade bridge, eager 'prentice in attendance, and the entire Port of Andiree clamoring to do business with them.

Or not. Ports were fickle things, and had become more fickle still in these new circumstances in which Korval found itself.

But, there! One would strive to think happy thoughts. Anthora swore that a positive attitude had the ability to change worlds.

. . . which was a fairly unsettling thought, considering the source.

The breakout bell sounded; the *Passage* shifted into normal space with scarcely a quiver. Shan smiled, and turned to his screen as it flashed and cleared, gong announcing an incoming emergency report.

✳   ✳   ✳

It was a preliminary report, very brief, with a promise of details to follow:

Pale Wing, one of Korval's first-line ships—in fact, the ship on which Padi had served as cabin boy—had been fired upon on approach to a port where she was well known and, previously, welcomed.

Shan drew a hard breath, his stomach clenching, reaching for the comm even as it buzzed. He touched a key.

"Yes, Priscilla, I have it," he said.

"The detailed report just hit," she said. "Forwarded to all pilots and reserve pilots. Meeting at fifteen hundred hours in the second-level conference room."

"I'll be there," he said, turning back to his screen and the detailed report.

· · · ✳ · · ·

Hazenthull leaned against the counter where Tolly had been, and closed her eyes, the better to think.

It was true that she was the least of the small-Troop which had come under the command of Hero Captain Miri Robertson, who had vanquished the Fourteenth Conquest Corps. Though she had received several so-called "therapy sessions" from Lady Anthora yos'Galan, who had the ability to reach inside heart and mind and make such adjustments as were deemed necessary...

Despite this, she, an Explorer, had not progressed nearly so well as even Diglon Rifle. Diglon had embraced their new circumstances with enthusiasm, and set himself to learn...everything, while she... found comfort only in her work cycle at the port, in the simple duties of a guard, as if she were nothing more than a Rifle herself.

Comfort in routine, and then, when Commander Lizardi had paired her in duty with Tolly Jones, something more than comfort. Something that she had not felt since before the Elder had fallen.

Comradeship.

Tolly Jones had deserted his post, and she—she had followed after him, to ensure that he came safe to his next destination. She had chosen—*chosen*—her partner over the Troop.

She had chosen her partner over her service to the captain, if it came to that, though she had not expected to find herself—

The door to the galley whisked open. Hazenthull straightened, hand rising in a salute to the pilot's honor...

... and hesitated a damning instant before completing the strike to her shoulder.

The pilot was small, seemingly fragile, perfectly clean and white. Perhaps she glowed somewhat. Or, thought Hazenthull, perhaps it was merely that she was so *very* white, that she *seemed* to glow in the galley's low lighting. Certainly, she *floated*, a little distance above the decking, wafting forward under some noiseless compulsion.

"Good waking to you, Hazenthull Explorer." The voice was mellow, and female. She spoke Terran with a light, lilting accent. "I am Tocohl Lorlin, pilot. Allow me to welcome you aboard *Tarigan*, and to thank you for your care of my copilot."

"You are welcome," Hazenthull said, which was an important civilian phrase.

There was a pause. The screen at the apex of the pilot's body tilted slightly upward, and Hazenthull saw the shadow of a woman's face.

"Perhaps I distress you, Hazenthull Explorer. Speak frankly, please."

Hazenthull drew a breath.

"Pilot, not... distress. Surprise. Is it permitted to inquire into your nature?"

"Certainly. I am an autonomous intelligence; a full individual person."

Hazenthull nodded. Such persons lived, as she had learned, a perilous existence, pursued by mercenary hunters, should they reveal themselves, whereupon they would be stripped of their personhood and either enslaved or killed. Jeeves, the head of Security in the House of Korval, was one such, and she subordinate to him in rank.

It would not, of course, be wise to mention Jeeves to Pilot Tocohl. She might, however, say something of the truth.

"I have met your like, Pilot, and I am no friend of the laws which oppress you."

The shadow face might have smiled.

"That is well said, thank you. I will tell you that I am well acquainted with Jeeves, and it was he whom I called when you fell into my care. He queried Captain Robertson regarding her orders, given the urgency of our mission, and naturally recorded her response. I will make that recording available to you.

"Regarding the status of this ship and pilots—our mission is *most* urgent. We are bound into a situation that is not…necessarily stable. It may, in fact, be quite dangerous. Your presence on our team would mean that Tolly and I would be able to more fully concentrate on our primary mission, knowing that you will ensure our safety while we do so."

"What is this mission?" Hazenthull asked.

Pilot Tocohl bowed slightly.

"The mission is very complex and quite…secret. You will appreciate that, for the safety of the pilots and of the mission, I cannot divulge more until I have your agreement to be a part of our team."

"The captain has given me to you," Hazenthull pointed out.

Pilot Tocohl tipped her screen to one side.

"And yet, if you do not like the assignment, or feel that you cannot support us, it would be best for all concerned if you were to leave at the first opportunity. We will be coming out of Jump at Bieradine. You may leave us there, if you so decide. I will transfer funds sufficient to a safe and comfortable layover, until a Korval ship arrives to take you home."

Staying safely by herself held…less appeal than it might. Hazenthull drew a deep breath.

"I would hear the tape and review the file on Bieradine," she said, adding courteously, "if the pilot pleases. Also, it may assist the pilot in her own deliberations to know that I, too, am a pilot."

"I have your résumé from Jeeves," Pilot Tocohl said. "Based on it, and on what Pilot Tolly has told me of your partnership, I believe that we could do no better than to have you with us on our mission. My only hesitation lies with you. If you cannot give your full support, then it is best for all that we part."

"I understand," Hazenthull said, and then, though her mind was already made up, "My decision will be clearer, once I have heard my captain's instructions."

"Of course. There is a study room beyond the galley. You may be private there. I will give you full access to everything save the particulars of the mission."

"Thank you," Hazenthull said, "Pilot."

"Thank you," the pilot said. "For your patience in the face of this…irregular circumstance. Please, follow the orange line on the floor. It will lead you to the study room."

Hazenthull glanced down, espying the thin, bright line running along the decking.

She bowed slightly from the waist, and turned to follow the path to the study room.

· · · ❋ · · ·

Shan touched a key and scrolled down through the report.

The details were horrifyingly similar to the attack upon *Bechimo* at Ynsolt'i, and let it be known that *Pale Wing* was nothing like an independent sentient ship with the gods only knew what Old Tech capabilities built into his systems. A tradeship, built—*well built*—in Korval's own yards, she was a fine vessel, was *Pale Wing*, with a fine crew aboard her. But, as one must phrase it, in the case, *only* a tradeship, and no more able to maneuver sprightly in tight traffic than an average rock.

There it was, on his screen—*Pale Wing* on the approach to Liltander, an extremely busy trade hub, very much like Ynsolt'i. The ship was well known to Traffic; indeed, *Pale Wing*'s pilot and Liltander's Traffic Guide greeted each other as old friends might, and fell easily into a routine well known to both. Everything proceeded in a seemly and normal manner until, with *Pale Wing* deep inside the pattern, constrained by other traffic, two light-craft, armed, and with perhaps the appearance of police cruisers or hunter ships, arrived and attempted to divert them from their designated path and final docking.

An appeal was made to the Guide, who said, angrily—so it seemed to Shan, listening at his desk—that the matter had passed out of her hands.

The light-craft again demanded that *Pale Wing* alter course, on threat of specific violence—and the pilot complied with the order.

To a point.

Ama ven'Tyrlit sat as captain of *Pale Wing*, a woman of great personal fortitude, and a master pilot besides. The next maneuver had her mark on it—bold to the near edge of insanity and impeccably executed.

Pale Wing inched through traffic, not quite on the coordinates given, but near enough that it could be seen that a good faith attempt was being made to comply. Only when she was clear of the tightest congestion was it revealed what that small deviation had gained her.

A freighter loomed between *Pale Wing* and the hunters; a relatively clear avenue before her, and it was a mad dash then, at velocities that made him catch his breath, with the hunters scrambling to be away from the freighter.

By the time they were in the clear, it was too late, at least, for the easy fulfillment of that specific promise of violence.

Pale Wing had aligned herself with Traffic Control, where she commenced to keep station, while sending out a broadband call for a guild mediator.

And there the matter stood. The hunters might yet have fired, but the risk to the station, or their own visibility, stayed their hand. The call for a guild mediator ought to have frozen all pieces in place, of course, but Shan had no illusions about that, had there been fewer witnesses.

He leaned back in his chair, staring at the last scene from *Pale Wing's* video log—the two hunters, looking very much like those that had threatened *Bechimo*, waiting just outside the shadow of the station. And *Pale Wing*, just *inside* that shadow, holding an entire station hostage to the good behavior of savages, while a world, and more, watched.

A call went out for a guild mediator. Liltander being a hub, there was bound to be a guild mediator—or three dozen—lying about, waiting for something to do to pass an afternoon or evening.

Shan swallowed, his stomach sour. Self-preservation aside, a ship endangering a station was not something that any mediator worth his certification would overlook. There would at least be a fine, if not an interdiction, and while the hunters would very likely reap more, and worse, that was very cold comfort indeed.

The screen beeped, indicating that the log had skipped ahead four-point-six Standard hours, to the arrival of the mediator, and his judgment.

Shan reached for his wineglass.

The guild mediator had leveled a fine—not as large a fine as it might have been, but more than negating any profits *Pale Wing* might have expected to wring from the traders of Liltanderport, had she been permitted to resume docking.

Which she was not.

The guild mediator suggested that *Pale Wing* take up whatever goods were waiting for her, send down any directed cargo by tug—and quit Liltander space.

What befell the hunters was even less satisfying, as they had been able to produce documents linking them to the local security net, as contractors. The guild mediator could do little but remand them to the discipline of their chief, which he did in the strongest possible language.

The log entry ended. Shan closed his eyes, ran through a quick focusing exercise, and opened his eyes to the message waiting light.

A letter of apology was in-queue from Captain ven'Tyrlit, who offered her resignation, if he wished it; and a letter from *Pale Wing*'s trader, the redoubtable tel'Brakin, begging his instruction.

· · · ☼ · · ·

Some hours later, she was back in the galley, a mug of tea cooling in her hand while she stared at a particularly uninteresting piece of decking. She had finished her review of the files Pilot Tocohl had released to her, and—

"What's the problem, Haz?"

Tolly hitched up onto the edge of the galley's long counter and sat there, arms braced on either side, booted feet swinging above the decking.

Hazenthull stirred, and sighed. Tolly was a skilled reader of people, and while they had not been partners for a very long time, they had been an effective team. Tolly himself said that they *clicked*, as if they were two modules that operated well enough on their own, but which, joined, became a single, deadly efficient device. It was nothing to wonder about, that he saw her at brown study and correctly deduced that she was ill at ease.

She raised the mug, tasted cold tea, and grimaced.

Shifting out of her lean, she turned toward the pot.

"Would you like tea?"

"Sure, tea'd be fine," he answered, and waited while she poured, taking the cup she gave him between his palms, and lowering his face into the steam.

Hazenthull resumed her lean against the counter, holding her mug carefully in one hand.

"You decide to leave us at Bieradine?" Tolly asked, raising his head, and giving her a straight look from guileless blue eyes.

Though he was considerably smaller than she was, being Terran to her Yxtrang, Tolly was not a child, nor was he a simpleton; Hazenthull had known that since the first patrol they had made together. She had lately, however, begun to think that he was... even more complex than she had supposed.

"I read the file on Bieradine," Tolly continued, after he had taken a sip of his tea. "Looks like a nice place for a vacation. Lots to do—climb mountains and swim lakes until you get tired, then go on down to the city, and take it easy, tour the museums..."

"I am not leaving the ship," Hazenthull said heavily. She knew from experience that he was capable of continuing to spout such nonsense, for—well, until someone or something diverted his attention.

"Well, I'm glad to hear that," Tolly said. "I'd miss you."

That was...not quite nonsense, though it partook of certain Terran cultural cues of which she was not entirely certain. That he would miss her—they had been partners, after all; they had each trusted the other to guard their back. That was not something that faded...quickly. If it faded at all.

Did she not miss the Elder, still? And that despite her sessions with Lady Anthora. She had been his junior for...very nearly her entire career as an Explorer. He had been a constant of her life, until she had...

"Haz? If you're not leaving us, then what's the problem?"

She sighed.

"The problem is that...the captain gave me to the mission—"

Tolly sat up a little straighter.

"Haz, this is your decision. If you don't want anything to do with the mission, say it; we'll put you off with a nice draw account and the pilot'll square it with—"

"No," she interrupted. "Hear me. I do not know what the mission is, but you do. Pilot Tocohl does. The captain must also know what the mission is, and has judged that I will be of benefit to the team. Even if the pilot had permitted me to learn the mission before making my decision, I could not...reverse the captain's orders in this. Because she *is* the captain."

"And she's got both pieces. Yeah, I see that."

Tolly sipped his tea. After a moment, Hazenthull sipped hers.

"Being who and what she is," Tolly said slowly, "Pilot Tocohl has...feelings, let's say, about people being denied the right to make their own decisions."

Hazenthull blinked.

"I had not considered that," she said. "But, to make a decision, one must have..."

"...sufficient data. Yeah." He sipped once more, and lowered the cup. "She didn't exactly think that through." He looked up into her face and gave her a grin. "If I was called on to give a professional opinion, I'd say Pilot Tocohl hasn't had a lot of practice at this yet."

She frowned.

"Surely the pilot can hear what we say."

"Sure she can, but we haven't been disrespectful, and I can express my professional opinion." He sighed.

"Tell you what, Haz, since you've made your decision to stay, based on the data available to you, just like the sensible woman I know you are, let's ask the pilot to release the mission files so you can get up-to-date. In the meantime, what I can tell you, since you've decided to stick with us, understand, is—we're bound for Jemiatha's Jumble Stop, which is located at the far end of nowhere, near enough. They got a little bit of a problem with an AI born too fast and without proper training."

"This is why the pilot goes. This is one of her...people she seeks to aid."

"That's it," Tolly said. "It's also why I'm going. I told you once—remember?—that I was a specialist. Training AIs, that's my specialty. 'Mentor'—that's the job title."

He put the cup on the counter at his side, and slid to his feet.

"Since you're staying aboard, we can Jump-in/Jump-out at Bieradine, which'll please her—and me, too, come to say it."

"I will tell the pilot my decision now," Hazenthull said, shifting out of her lean to put her mug aside.

"Good," he said, turning away, and turning back to her when she said his name. "Yeah?"

"The woman on the port," she began...

The woman she had killed for him—the woman who had addressed him as *Thirteen-Sixty-Two*, and struck him in the face with a gun when he did not answer quickly enough...

She shook her head—the Terran gesture signifying frustration at her own inability to choose between the multitude of questions she wanted to ask him.

"Who was she?" Tolly murmured. "She was tel'Vaster's backup."

"Tel'Vaster was the man who tried to shoot you in the back?"

"That was him. Her name was Glinz Pirl-Dorn. She . . . both of 'em . . . were directors—sorta the direct opposite of Pilot Tocohl, when it comes to matters of free choice."

"She spoke as though she . . . owned you."

"Well, by her way of thinking, she did own me—or at least considered me hers to use. It happens that I think otherwise—and there hangs an interesting story, maybe, but I'm going to have to tell it to you sometime else. Tea break's over and I gotta get back to my chair."

Hazenthull took a breath, and brought her index finger to her forehead in the gesture that meant, among the Troop, that a promise was offered.

"Let us make a pledge," she said, "to trade the tales of ourselves."

Tolly blinked, then returned her salute.

"Let's do that," he said solemnly. "Soon."

· · · ✴ · · ·

They had attacked *Pale Wing*, the stupid, *stupid* Department of the Interior, because it was *of course* the Department of the Interior, the mode of attack was *exactly* the same that they had used to contain—to *try to* contain—Cousin Theo, whose very refusal to be captured, or to stand by to be boarded, ought (one would think!) to have taught them *something*.

But, no, they were *idiots*, the entire Department of them, however many there were, and surely not one over the age of six!

Pale Wing! She had served on *Pale Wing*! She knew Trader tel'Brakin well, and Captain ven'Tyrlit, too! She had friends among the crew! Why, she might have been on board herself—but no, that route went nowhere. What was at issue was the stupidity of the *entire* Department of the Interior. They were so completely incapable of learning *anything* that they would very likely continue to assault Korval ships! Why, they were so *stupid* they might even try to capture the *Passage* in this witless manner, despite Cousin Theo having actually killed *at least* one of their ships, and *Pale Wing*—

Padi drew a breath.

What Captain ven'Tyrlit had done...had been very wrong. To endanger the station, and the lives of all who lived and worked there? No, that was not the choice of an honorable pilot. The safety of the ship could not trump the lives of those who were not of the ship.

And, yet, one did perfectly understand *why* the captain had made that particular choice. She may even have thought it a safe enough bluff, perhaps failing to understand the depths of stupidity from which the enemy operated. Captain ven'Tyrlit would not have known, perhaps, that those pursuing might well have fired upon *Pale Wing*, despite her position, simply because they were *too stupid* to comprehend that sometimes missiles go wide of their mark.

Or, Padi thought, they might not have *cared* if they holed the station, so long as they had also taken their prize.

She had been at the debriefing session, of course, with the rest of the ship's pilots. Priscilla—the captain, rather—had taken the few questions which had been raised, including one regarding perhaps modifying *Bechimo*'s "specialized equipment" so that it could be installed in other Korval ships. The captain had said solemnly that she would consult with Captain Waitley, and then recalled the *Passage*'s own capabilities to the minds of those assembled.

"The *Passage* does have smart shielding and patterned defense shields," the captain said. "We welcome ideas for upgrading, or improving our existing systems—anything that may increase our ability to defend ourselves in the case of such a close-in attack. It would seem that our enemy has a bias. Ways in which we can exploit that bias to our advantage would also be helpful. Any suggestions or ideas should be presented to Third Mate Tiazan."

She had then asked for more questions, of which there were none, and dismissed everyone to stations.

And that was where Padi was headed now—to the trade bridge, the master trader having left the meeting during the question period.

It would, Padi thought, hardly be wise to arrive at her station in a state of active anger. She needed to concentrate her mind on the incoming catalogs and offers.

Therefore, she punched the call button for the elevator, then danced a few steps of *daibri'at* right there in the hallway, confining her anger to the stone keep that already held her fear.

CHAPTER SEVEN

· ·

Andireeport

MASTER TRADER YOS'GALAN HAD PURCHASED HANDMADE PAPERS and pens turned from local woods. Padi watched as he was now examining pottery bowls with a crystalline glaze that the attending artisan swore made them virtually unbreakable.

"What an interesting idea," he said to the square-faced woman. "Is this a house glaze, or your own innovation?"

"My own," she said with a slight bow. "I have always been a great reader. Some years back, I found a monograph regarding crystal knives produced by a certain tribe of beings known in the broader universe as Clutch Turtles. Their knives were proven to be virtually indestructible, and—well. Pottery is a fragile thing, and we suffer in the far trade for it. So, I set myself the task."

She picked a bowl up from the display shelf, a winsome work in swirling deep blues, the fluted lip all cream and white. It reminded Padi of a wave racing toward shore; she yearned to hold it, and find how the shape fit her hand.

The artisan threw the bowl at the tiled floor.

Padi cried out in protest, and felt her face heat, even as the bowl struck the tiles with a bell-like clang, and settled, entirely unshattered.

"I am impressed," the master trader said.

The artisan bowed, and continued the motion, plucking the

bowl up, and straightening. She looked to Padi, a smile on her face, and glanced at the master trader.

"It is permitted to give a gift to one who would not see beauty destroyed?"

"It is a handsome gift, for an apprentice," he said, his voice perfectly neutral.

Padi felt her cheeks warm again. She had displeased him. Well, of course she had! What trader squeaked aloud during the trade?

"We were all apprentices once," the artisan said, the bowl balanced delicately on the tips of her fingers. "I still have the bowl my own master gave me to place by my bed, so that every morning when I opened my eyes, I would see it, and recall that I strove to bring beauty and balance into the world."

"A wise master. I hope that I may be as wise." He bowed slightly. "I am honored, that my apprentice should receive so apt a gift."

The artisan smiled even more fully. Padi bowed to her honor, more deeply than Father had done.

"It is a wonderful bowl," she said. "I will strive to be worthy of it. Thank you."

"You are very welcome," the artisan said. "The bowl pleases me, as well. And it will please me to think of it voyaging in space, supporting an eager apprentice along her path to master."

Her bow suggested master to apprentice, though there was something in the hand motion—perhaps, Padi thought, master-to-an-apprentice-not-her-own.

"Allow me, please, to wrap this, and place it in a sack, so that you may carry it more easily on port."

The sack had long handles. Padi hitched them over one shoulder and nestled the bowl against her side. The master trader had spent another few minutes with the artisan, arranging for the *Passage* to take samples of her work, and had left a beam code and an infokey for the guild master's pleasure.

They paused now in the common corridor: the master trader, herself, and Vanner Higgs, who made their third. Mr. Higgs's official title was Technician First Class; he was also part of the *Passage*'s security detail. Before coming to them, he had been a technical sergeant with a mercenary unit. His primary responsibilities there, too, had to do with technologies and connectivities, though he had of course had battle training, as well. He had told her, when a previous schedule had placed them on port together, that it was much more peaceful being a tech on the *Passage*, because no one was trying to kill him while he was setting up the equipment.

He stood now, patiently, a little apart from her and the master trader, his eyes alert; not a technician at this moment, but a security person, on duty.

"Well, Apprentice? What do you think of the potter's wares?"

"They're very beautiful," Padi said, recalling the bowls, cups, and art objects on display. Everything in the shop had been pottery—down to the glazed tile floor. "But they're handmade; she cannot possibly produce enough to make it profitable for her to trade off-planet."

"Now, there's an interesting question. Did you see the discreet sign above the wrapping desk, *Contact the Guildmaster for Bulk Orders*?"

Padi frowned. She *hadn't* seen the sign; she had been too interested in the wares. Another failure; a trader sees *every*thing, just as much as a security guard.

"No, sir; I didn't," she confessed.

"It was, as I say, discreet. I have asked that the guildmaster be in touch, should our information interest her. I confess that I am agog to hear how they manage bulk orders—and what 'bulk' may mean to them."

"I am interested in those topics, as well," she said.

"I will be certain to keep you informed," he said affably, and looked over her head to give Mr. Higgs a nod.

"Vanner. We're about to forsake the halls of civilization for the noise and confusion of the Fruit and Flower Market. Are you afraid?"

"Not so much, sir," Mr. Higgs said genially. "I been on Gaston Prime during the Feast of the Founder. That spoilt me, kinda, for fruit markets."

"I understand. I will, therefore, content myself with a warning concerning the flowers."

"Always look twice at the flowers, sir."

"An excellent policy." Master Trader yos'Galan turned to Padi. "You are now lead trader. I will recuse myself, insofar as I may. Does this satisfy?"

"Yes, Master Trader."

"Splendid. Allow me to carry your parcel. A trader should have her hands and her wits about her when she goes in to negotiate."

"Yes," she said slipping the bag off her shoulder and handing it to him. She felt a slight pang as he slipped the handles over his own shoulder, which was ridiculous, of course. Father would certainly take very good care of such a bowl.

"Thank you," she said, and nodded to Mr. Higgs before setting a brisk pace down the cool hallway, through the door, and out into the day port.

Padi had done her research, so she knew where the nearest east-west jitney station was, where to debark and which slideway would convey them directly to the fruit section of the Fruit and Flower Market. She told over this information to Father and to Mr. Higgs, in case they should become separated, which was wise, for she and Mr. Higgs did lose Father on the slideway, which was very crowded.

They stepped off at the Fruit Market landing, just the two of them. Padi turned just as Father exited the slideway. He gave her a nod.

"What a terrible crush, to be sure! How fortunate that they all seem to be going someplace else!"

"Fortunate, indeed," she said, drawing a deep breath to calm the flutters in her middle. She felt like she had when she had taken the test to find if she was, indeed, a pilot of Korval.

Well, one knew how to cope with sky-nerves, after all. She closed her eyes briefly, accessing a quick calming exercise. Her stomach settled into its usual place, and her hands immediately felt steadier.

Opening her eyes, she nodded to Father and to Mr. Higgs, and pointed toward the platform stairs.

Technically, *milaster* was not a fruit, but a nut—the kernel of the *laster* fruit, very little of which escaped the appetites of the population of Andiree. The kernel, however, was not so well-regarded, though it was perfectly edible, and, indeed the population of Chessel's World regarded it with a passion to rival that of Andiree for the fruit.

In terms of trade, the matter could not have fallen out more satisfactorily. The kernel, which was durable and easy to ship, was desired off-world, while the delicate fruits were desired on-world.

Padi paused to take her bearings by the corner markers. Her destination was at the intersection of Blue-Flower and Green-Fruit, which was—*there*, to her left. She had turned right one row too soon at the top of the grid.

"There's our corner," she said, turning to Mr. Higgs, who smiled and nodded. She glanced beyond him, to where Father . . .

Father was gone.

No, that was absurd; there was no crush of slideway travelers here in the hall, merely a few dozens of shoppers, some merchants standing at the entrance to their booths, and a few 'bot cleaners. Padi spun slowly on her heel, as if seeking the corners one more time, for verification.

Father was nowhere to be seen.

She blinked, feeling a little unsettled in her stomach. It was true that he had said he would recuse himself. But, surely, he would not have left the group without a word at least to Mr. Higgs. And *certainly* he would not have violated the order that all crew on port travel in threes, *or* in the company of a member of the ship's security team.

One more breath; one more glance around—the last, lest she attract the attention of a floor monitor, and that *would be* embarrassing, to be delivered to her destination by a monitor, as if she were too green to have studied the map beforetime.

Her glance crossed that of Vanner Higgs. He tipped his head, very slightly, to the left. Padi looked beyond his shoulder, her eyes snagging at once on the merest shadow; a faint suggestion of silver hair, strong nose, and shoulders outlined by a dark blue shirt sketched upon the warm, market air.

It would appear that Father had, indeed, suggested to those surrounding that he simply . . . was not present.

While it disturbed her that such a subterfuge—even born of Healer talent, as it must be—had very nearly fooled her, at the same time she was grateful that Father had found a way to clear the trade for her.

Padi sighed, quietly, and raised her hand to point again at their corner before moving off in that direction.

· · · ✦ · · ·

Well, *that* had been unexpected!

Shan looked down at his own hand, relieved to see that broad, brown member, with the carved amethyst of a master of trade sparkling cheerfully—one might say, *smugly*—there.

It had given him a bad turn, just a moment ago, to look down and *see* nothing, though he could *feel* the hand perfectly well, and each finger when he wriggled them and the weight of the ring.

Granted, he didn't often suggest that he wasn't present, but on those occasions when he had, the effect had been more as if those around him had simply forgotten that he was there. If one was determined enough, one could see beyond the suggestion, as he had found one evening to his sorrow, when he had been trying to avoid an overzealous suitor.

In no case had *he* ever forgotten he was present—nor had he ever vanished before his very eyes.

Happily, he had been able to bring himself back from total absence to what seemed to be a shadow of himself by concentrating on what he should be seeing. It was as if he had applied too much force to the original suggestion, and gone one step deeper, into *actual* invisibility.

Which was nonsense.

At least, he *thought* it was nonsense.

He felt his fingers moving and glanced down at his hand, watching the shadowy red counter walk across foggy knuckles.

Drat the thing, he thought irritably. The counter hesitated in its journey, as if it had heard the thought. *That* was interesting.

He focused his attention on the counter.

Go away! he thought at it, as sternly as he was able.

Between one knuckle and the next, it vanished.

Shan blinked, and reached into the usual pocket.

No counter.

He checked the other pocket.

No counter.

Well, good. He was delighted to be rid of the blasted thing. Only...

Where had it gone?

He took a breath. A problem for later, if problem it was. He'd speak to Priscilla about it. In the meantime, he followed Padi down a narrow, sparsely populated aisle to a booth sporting a red-and-blue checked awning; a rosy-cheeked man wearing a white apron over a bright red shirt stood behind a red counter supporting four large glass jars, each containing a brightly colored foodstuff.

Padi pulled her Andireeport trade card from her pocket, and approached the counter. Vanner stopped just short of entering the shop, standing at ease, his eyes roving up and down the aisle, surveying the meager crowd.

Shan stepped into the shop itself, though not so close as the counter. He wanted to be able to watch, and to hear. Padi had seemed rather nervous earlier, though this was not by any means her first time as a buyer.

Well, and sometimes the work itself steadied the nerves. Certainly, she seemed cool enough now, as she bowed to the gentleman, and extended the card.

· · · ❄ · · ·

"Trader yos'Galan, welcome!" the red-cheeked man bellowed, his smile showing an amazing number of very white teeth. "I am Gustav rel'Ana, proprietor of the Laster Garden. How may I serve you? We have, fresh and amenable to stasis, candied *trovyul*, salted ginger, and dehydrated *spinginach*. For your special customers, we have also a small amount of *laster* chutney. Such a treasure does not often come to our port location, but last year saw a *laster* harvest as none before, and we are able to offer a few—a very few!—cases of this Andiree delicacy to discerning buyers."

Merchant rel'Ana's voice was loud, as if he were shouting at her from across the aisle, rather than the width of the counter. Padi kept her face smooth and did not back away from the assault upon her ears. She did, however, answer in a soft and mannerly voice that would have astonished Cousin Kareen.

"The chutney," she said, diverted briefly from her agenda, "can it be put into stasis?"

The man's smile became . . . less broad, and his cheeks became redder. Padi wondered if she had been maladroit.

"The chutney, Trader, no. You do not put *laster* chutney into stasis. You tuck it tenderly into the best stateroom, as if it were your own child."

She *had* been maladroit; she scolded herself, she should have known better. Hadn't her research told her how fragile the *laster* fruit was? Surely that would be the case for anything made from it.

"I am desolate to have no such tender accommodations available to the chutney," she said. "I have only heard tales of this rare foodstuff, and for a moment, I allowed my hope to interfere with my good sense."

The smile widened again. She had redeemed herself.

"But, if not the chutney, what brings you to me?"

"I am in search of *milaster*," she said. "Quite a bit of *milaster*. I am informed that you sell in bulk."

"I do, yes! However, Trader, I must warn you that the kernels, they will lose . . . taste, texture, nutritional values after only a very short time in stasis. They remain edible, but they do not remain *excellent!*"

"I understand," Padi assured him. "I plan to deliver within the toleration period."

"Hm." That was said quite softly; the smile entirely vanished now, as he studied her from brown eyes squinted into slits.

"How much bulk *milaster* will you buy, Trader?"

Now they were approaching the correct course. Padi looked directly into those calculating brown eyes.

"That will depend upon how much you have to sell, and at what price and condition," she answered.

Gustav rel'Ana's eyebrows rose.

"Well, then," he said. "If you please, Trader, step over to the side counter, just there. I will call for assistance here, and then—we will talk."

· · · ❊ · · ·

There was a tiny ripple in the air by her ear, as if a flutterbee had passed quite near.

Priscilla looked up from her work screen, frowning slightly. Flutterbees were not expectable in the office of a captain hard at work inside of a starship in orbit . . .

There.

A glow of dusty red drew her eye, on the desk between her coffee mug and the keyboard. She took a careful breath, and extended her attention, remembering how this very same game counter had been waiting for her—for Moonhawk—when she had come to Weapons Hall, to gather those things that she would need, as the captain of a warship around an embattled planet. Then, the counter had been sparkling with Shan's presence, when he had been separated from the ship, his fate unknown. It had comforted her to know without doubt that he was alive.

When matters were settled, and they were rejoined, the counter had left her and...returned, to Shan.

"Stupid object," he'd told it, "I'm not Lute."

Only he *was* Lute, in the same way that she *was* Moonhawk, old souls both. She had been taught at Temple that she was "Moonhawk's vessel," and that her strength as a Witch came from that special relationship with one of the oldest priestesses of their order.

Lute had, according to history and myth, been Moonhawk's companion...across many lifetimes. He was not himself a priest—there were no priests at the temples on Sintia—but he had, often, been acknowledged as a Man of Power, though some histories referred to him as a mere cunningman.

While she would never suggest to Shan that his gift came from his special relationship with Lute, it was clear to her that there was...an interest.

She touched the red counter with the tip of one finger, read the tale of its recent adventures, and smiled.

Shan had sent it away in a fit of pique, and it had come to her, apparently being unwilling yet to return to Lute, or to Weapons Hall.

Priscilla focused on the battered item, imprinting *I love you* into its wooden soul, and then murmured, "Return."

She lifted her finger.

There was a flash of red, brighter than the counter itself, followed by that small disturbance in the quiet air of her office.

The tiny uncluttered triangle of desk space between her coffee mug and the keyboard was empty.

Still smiling, Priscilla returned to work.

· · · ※ · · ·

Padi's knees were shaking, and her hair was damp with sweat, but she had managed the deal, and gotten what she wanted, at a price that was...very nearly...what she had intended to pay.

Gustav rel'Ana had produced a sample of what was in his storerooms, along with certifications from the growers and harvesters. She had scanned them with the reader provided by the port, and found them authentic—which was to say, the port transmitted to her the Laster Cooperative's confirmation that the information she had been given was true and correct.

The samples tasted good to her—the nutmeat was firm and a little sweet, very pleasant in the mouth—but she was certainly not an expert on freshness. The certifications from the growers co-op included a list of nutrients, and a graph showing the rate at which each degraded, in stasis and on the shelf.

Gustav rel'Ana wanted more per unit than Padi's limit, but again, her research stood her well. She didn't quite have to walk away from the counter before her view prevailed, though it had been a near thing.

And in the end, he had gotten a little of his own back: because of the method by which the nuts were packed and sold, she was required to overbuy, for he would not break a sealed unit.

She signed the sales chit; gave him the code for the tug which would be bringing the *Passage*'s pod into orbit, and the deal was done.

"It has been a pleasure, Trader yos'Galan!" the vendor told her, shouting again. "Come to me whenever you have need of *milaster*. I will be very glad to do business with you again!"

That made her a little uneasy, but the papers had been signed; the delivery scheduled, and the money, she was certain, already transferred out of the port account with her name on it. Master Trader yos'Galan would surely critique her performance on the shuttle lift to the *Passage*, and she would learn then if she had been foolish beyond measure.

She exchanged bows with the vendor and found her way out of the booth, Mr. Higgs falling in beside her, Father—still rather indistinct—beside him. Gods, she wanted a cup of tea and a quiet place to sit and gather her composure.

That... was not her usual reaction to a completed trade. Most usually, she felt exhilarated, and curious to see what else the market might offer. Today, she only wanted to leave. However, she was not alone. Indeed, she was in the company of a master trader, who had not necessarily shared all of his requirements with her.

"Is there business yet to do?" she asked.

There was a slight pause, as if Mr. Higgs waited for the master trader to speak. When there was no contribution from that quarter, he said that he had no other business, and that they were coming up on time for the shuttle, anyway.

Padi nodded and led the way toward the slideway, her stride somewhat less energetic than it had been on the way in. She wondered if Gustav rel'Ana had a *nerligig* or another, less legal, mood regulator concealed inside his booth.

The slideway platform was just ahead. She forced herself to walk more quickly.

· · · ✳ · · ·

Shan felt something settle in the depths of his pocket, and sighed.

It was nice while it lasted, he thought, watching Padi, ahead of them. The child looked exhausted, which was likely those short sleep shifts catching up with her at the far end of an unexpectedly vigorous session of trade.

He had been wary of broaching the topic of sleep shifts. As a mere father, his concern would surely be set aside for her own necessities, and he was loath to bring the master trader into the matter.

Well, they would have a conference on the lift to the *Passage*; he would mention it then, in the context of the effectiveness of the trader on the floor. *That* might set her to thinking.

He put his hand into his pocket and pulled out the red counter; it was glowing somewhat, and he felt, as plain as a kiss on his cheek, Priscilla's love, warm and steady.

Closing his fingers around the token, he smiled to himself. At least now he knew where it had gone. Best if it had returned to Weapons Hall and the improbable edition of himself he had met there, Lute the magician. Failing that, it was ... good that it took itself off to Priscilla, who had the skill to deal with it, rather than landing in the pocket of some random trader, or dealer in antiquities.

Ahead, Padi was angling toward the ramp that led to the slideway platform. Several people were clustered near a booth there, and one of those turned his head, spotted Padi and detached himself, his course set to intercept.

Shan took a deep breath, thrusting the counter back into his pocket, and deliberately thought himself very visible, indeed.

· · · ✳ · · ·

Padi saw him out of the corner of her eye, a male in local clothing, perhaps a little older than she was, his height and his features combined to convince her that he was Liaden. He was coming toward her, deliberately, as if he knew her.

She had never seen him before; she was certain of it.

Liadens were no longer safe, and the agents of the Department of the Interior were demonstrably stupid enough to walk up to them openly and demand that she, and Father, and Mr. Higgs come with them.

If he didn't try anything *stupider*.

Still, she thought, recalling to mind her lessons in *daibri'at* and Arms Master Schneider's advice . . . Still, it might be something else. He might be on another trajectory altogether, and not on course for them.

She altered her course somewhat; the boy altered his course, still aiming to cut her off.

Padi took a breath, taking in the surroundings with a quick glance. Open enough, some people, but not a crowd, and he seemed to be by himself.

She stopped, centered, and faced him.

He smiled, wide and delighted—*not* Liaden—and came forward more rapidly.

She flexed her knees. Though he wouldn't be much to throw, she was briefly grateful that she had given Father her bowl.

"Well, what's this, an acquaintance late met?"

Father's voice was loud in her ear, and there he was, completely solid, and abruptly between her and the approaching target, her bowl in its sack over his shoulder.

"Padi, do you know this young person?"

The boy stopped, confusion on his face. Perhaps, Padi thought, he was wondering where Father had come from.

"No, sir," she said, in answer to his question. "We have not met."

"Ah. But perhaps it was myself you wished to speak with?" Father asked.

The boy shook his head.

"Your pardon, sir, it was . . . the lady. I thought I did know her, the resemblance—but I see that I'm wrong! Pardon, sirs! Lady!"

He bowed, a shapeless thing, neither Liaden *nor* Terran, and without waiting for an acknowledgment, turned back the way he had come.

Padi let out a long, shaking breath.

"Well, now," Father said, looking down at her from his height. His voice was mocking, but his eyes . . . were not.

"Wasn't that easier than killing the poor lad?"

She hadn't been going to *kill* him, Padi thought. Unless he had proven a threat, of course.

"I didn't know him," she said, her voice sounding angry in her own ears. "If he was a threat, I wanted to be prepared."

"Exactly correct," Father said. "And now that he has been properly chastised, I suggest we board the slideway and go home."

CHAPTER EIGHT

. . . .

Chessel's World

PADI SETTLED INTO A HARD PLASTIC CHAIR IN THE SELLER'S SEC-
tion of the Chesselport Grand Auction Hall. There was no real
reason for her to be in the hall; all of the important transactions—
saving the sale, of course—had been handled at the auctioneer's
docket, in the antechamber. There, she had registered her cargo,
provided a unit sample, her receipt, and the certifications and
verifications from Andireeport and the Laster Cooperative. The
cargo had previously been moved to the bidding bin assigned to
the *Passage*, along with the goods Master Trader yos'Galan had
on offer—tame stuff, there, the Number Three Mix; none of the
goods he had taken on at Andiree, nothing at all *interesting*,
really. Number Three Mix was the blandest of the six standard
trade mixes the master trader had to hand.

In Padi's opinion.

Of course, she thought, looking up at the upcoming auctions
board, he probably wanted to learn something from his offering:
how many bid and at what price; who had bid; if they accepted
or rejected the trade catalog offered free to all who asked; how
many actually made contact with him after accepting the catalog;
and if they had anything potentially *interesting*, or only useful,
to offer the habitants of an upcoming port.

He, of course, wasn't here to watch the auction—master traders had far more lucrative matters to tend. The auction was...

an introduction, that was all. A way—one way—to get his name out on the port and into the mouths of the street vendors. He, himself, had been invited to a reception at the portmaster's office later in the local day, and was currently contacting prominent names on port, to arrange for meetings before and after.

Padi sighed where she sat, her eyes on the board. One vendor had bid on her offering, at the usual market rate. She twisted her fingers together and reminded herself that this was only one bid—and likely an automatic, as it had come so quickly. The bidder hadn't had a chance to read the documentation, really, and to understand why what she had on offer had value.

She sighed. The reception. Ordinarily, she would have been at the reception, too, as the master trader's 'prentice, but the invitation had specified "Master Trader yos'Galan" and "no guests." It seemed an odd thing, and she had said so. Father had merely said that he had seen odder and told her that she would, therefore, need to see to the auction of her cargo without his help.

Which was a joke, naturally enough, and the reason why Padi came to be able to indulge herself at the public auction, with only Third Mate and Pilot Dil Nem Tiazan, and Comm Tech Sally Triloff at her side. The third mate was kin, of course—Korval and Erob allowed such relationships, so often had the lines been crossed—though very much her elder. He had, in fact, come out of retirement to oblige the captain when she sought to fill those posts left vacant by the...events on Liad. Despite his age, his hair was *quite* red; he was stern, and had little to say for himself. He had voiced no objection to Padi's scheme of sitting for a while to watch the bidding; merely, he had settled into a chair near, though not next to, her, pulled a reader out of his pocket and was immediately immersed in a book, or a report, or...

Sally was another matter. Padi felt that Sally would rather have liked to walk about the port, instead of sitting in an auditorium watching the apprentice trader stare at the bid boards and bite her fingernails. She really *ought* to suggest that they wander to Sally's whim; after all, the auctioneer had her comm code and would transmit the details when—if—the lot sold. The auctioneer also had her account information on file; her portion of the sale, less the auctioneer's percentage and such taxes as the port levied, would be automatically forwarded to it.

There really was no reason to sit here and monitor the board herself, as if her attention might influence the outcome.

She leaned toward Sally, her eyes still on the board—and abruptly straightened, breath-caught.

Another bid had come in, appreciably higher than the first; a bid more in line with the worth of the product described in the documentation she had provided the auctioneer. Padi forced herself to breathe, swallowed—and a third bid came in, this one even more substantial than the second.

Padi's chest hurt. She was...it was going according to plan! *Her milaster* would be known as a superior product and she would be paid...her research had suggested that she would net... between two and three percent more than the degraded *milaster* that came to Chessel's World via the loop ships. The profit was good, of course, but the *real* prize would be if she could parlay today's sale into a *standing order*. If she could turn *that* trump, why, she would have had a hand in shaping the route itself, and would win for Chessel's World the honor of a scheduled stop.

She stared up at the board, her hands clenched on her lap, blinking as a fourth bid came in, slightly higher than the bid before, which might mean that momentum was slowing, but it couldn't have topped out already...

"Padi?" A light hand pressed her sleeve. "You okay?"

Padi felt a jolt of guilt. Sally. She had been going to offer Sally the lead, which was only balanced and fair.

She turned, and smiled deliberately into the tech's dark eyes.

"It is my first large offer at auction," she said, and saw a tiny expression of disappointment cross the woman's face.

"But," Padi continued, "I can follow the bidding on my comm." She pulled the unit from her belt. "I will make certain of my channel, and then let us go out onto the port—if you will lead us?"

Sally smiled widely, pleased. Good.

"I'd really like that," she said—and her smile faded slightly. She turned to look at Dil Nem.

"Sir, do you wish to lead, on port?"

It was a courtesy for his rank, Padi knew, and it spoke well of Sally that she offered it, when she plainly wished the position herself.

The third mate looked up from his reader, and lifted a shoulder.

"I have no need to lead," he said, in strongly accented, but perfectly intelligible Terran. "Please, find for us the hidden delights of the port."

Sally took that as a challenge; Padi saw it in the flash of her eyes.

"I'll be happy to do so, sir," she said, and looked to Padi. "Have you found your channel?"

"I have," she said. "I may be heard to ping every now and then, as new bids come in."

"Fair warning," Sally said. She stood, a grin on her face, and nodded toward the closest exit. "There's our way out."

Chesselport was open to the weather, which was agreeable. Her research had revealed that Chessel's World at this latitude and longitude enjoyed clement weather, with no great variation in temperatures and no extended rainy season. Other geographies on-world did labor under these inconveniences, but they did not intrude upon the port. Following Sally down broad streets lined with shops, Padi was reminded of the days when she had accompanied Father up and down Solcintra Port as he pursued his duties there.

The comm on her belt pinged as they walked, but she resisted the temptation to look at the screen every time. Every other time, that was well enough; it was a good compromise between a trader's care for the trade, and a proper enthusiasm for a crew mate's skills.

For Sally was a skilled leader. Unlike some other crew mates, whom Padi charitably did not name, even to herself, Sally had a sure instinct for interesting streets and a good eye for a shop likely to hold unusual wares.

Padi was particularly impressed by a shop hosting a live demonstration of what she gathered was a traditional dyeing technique. It would seem that Dil Nem and Sally were similarly struck, for neither protested Padi's suggestion that they stay to watch a second demonstration.

The dyer noticed their interest and rewarded it by draping a finished scarf in graduating shades of green around Dil Nem's neck with a smile.

"It becomes 'ee," he said. "Wear it in health."

For a moment, it seemed to Padi as if Dil Nem might refuse the gift—then he bowed smoothly.

"I thank you," he said, and Padi, just behind him, added, "Have you a card? If anyone asks my kinsman where he came by such a handsome scarf, we want to give good directions."

The man grinned. He produced a card from the pocket of his apron with a flourish, and handed it to Padi.

"There's a smart kitlet," he said. "For that, your own scarf, and your friend, too!"

He was as good as his word: Sally's scarf was a deep crimson with pale pink borders, and Padi's sported a swirling pattern of misty violet and deep purple.

After leaving the dye shop, Padi's comm pinged three times, on a rising tone. She snatched it off her belt and thumbed on the screen.

She stopped, staring.

"Bad news?" Sally asked, from beside her.

"No..." she said slowly. "I don't think so. My lot sold at"—three-and-a-half percent over average!—"a good price. But I am wanted by the auctioneer, to sign an...affidavit."

· · · ❖ · · ·

The traders of Chesselport were a standoffish lot, Shan thought, leaning back in his chair with a frown. Working with the port directory and trade bios, he had created a list of traders to contact, from most desirable to least, and had spent the last hour and a half calling them, in order. He had not expected to complete the list before it was time to depart for the portmaster's reception, but he had expected that he would have at least six appointments to keep afterward.

As it happened, he was disappointed in both of his expectations, for he had called every name on the list, and still lacked three-quarters of an hour to his departure time, and...he had not one appointment to show for his labors.

True, he had only managed to speak to a handful of traders personally, but every one of them had been busy, or had nothing to offer at this time. To the latter, he had said that it was an introductory visit only, whereupon they, too, were busy.

It was...unprecedented. Staring up at the ceiling, arms folded behind his head, Shan tried to recall if he had ever in his life found a port where *no one* cared to speak to him. Even on Dayan, so long as he remained in the port proper, and in the company of a woman, he found traders willing to talk with him. Not necessarily *to trade* with him, he having made the genetic error of being male, but to show wares, in case he happened to know of a ship properly captained by a woman, where the trader was also a woman of a clan whose delm was a woman.

Really, it was quite lowering. He was beginning to enter into Theo's feelings of rejection.

Perhaps he had erred in the matter of the auction. He had wished to feel out the market, as, one had assumed, the market had wished to feel out a new trader come to port. Lot Number Three, commonplace as it was, generally produced good results in that regard. The simplicity of the offerings very often served to soothe those who might be wary of that new trader on port, thinking that he might be too dear, or one of those fellows who dandled in exotic wares and would scarcely admit that there might ever be the possibility of a market for hairbrushes.

He sighed at the ceiling, and closed his eyes.

Had he come up against local custom? Was he, in fact, precipitate? Ought he to have waited until the portmaster's reception? The Chesselport World Book had not mentioned an introduction protocol, but the books were sometimes blind in . . . interesting ways. If it was so ingrained—that one must be introduced to a stranger by a person of suitable status before one might interact with said stranger—it might very well go without saying, for what civilized person would behave differently?

He snorted lightly.

"Assume that you've sinned against custom, Shan," he said aloud. "Go to the portmaster's gather, become introduced, and hope that the traders you contacted out of order are of a uniformly forgiving—"

A gong sounded loudly.

Shan spun the chair, his hand flashing out to the keyboard— *alert incoming*, that ugly noise meant.

Something bad had happened.

· · · ❄ · · ·

"No, I will not sign that."

Padi looked directly into the auctioneer's eyes.

"I did not enter stolen goods into the auction, and I do not agree to forfeit my profit. I showed you the receipts and the certifications. You accepted them and placed them in the bid packet with the rest of the information." She paused, and deliberately lifted an eyebrow. "Did you not?"

That was, perhaps, a bit too much, from a 'prentice trader to an auctioneer, but she was angry, and she was *certainly not* going to sign this... this *affidavit* admitting a crime she did not commit, nor was she going to allow them to keep the proceeds of her sale—the *considerable proceeds* of her sale.

"The receipts and certifications are legitimate," the auctioneer said. "I regret that we accepted them before we were informed that the lot is part of an ongoing criminal enterprise. I advise you that signing the affidavit and forfeiting the funds is your best option."

"I will do no such thing! I am connected with a registered and well-respected tradeship, the *Dutiful Passage* herself! Show me this ongoing criminal enterprise."

"The burden of proof is not on me," the auctioneer said.

"Relinquish my profits," Padi said, proud of how stern and steady her voice was. "I will not sign the affidavit; you may take it away."

"Trader, I cannot. The law is clear. Profits from a criminal enterprise are forfeit to the port. Those who do not sign the affidavit reveal themselves as criminals in fact and are taken up by Security."

She felt a presence by her left shoulder; heard low-voiced Liaden in her ear.

"Trader, perhaps it is best to sign."

"No!" she said sharply, to Dil Nem and the auctioneer alike. "I shall *not* sign. What I *will do*, however, is file a report with TerraTrade. This is theft."

"Very good, Trader," Dil Nem said, in loud Terran. "Let us return to the ship."

He took her arm. She thought about resisting him, but what more could she do here? The auctioneer was adamant; there seemed little hope of recovering what was hers, short of holding him at gunpoint—and perhaps not even then.

The pressure on her arm increased. She relaxed, deliberately, and allowed Dil Nem to turn—a simple pivot, very smoothly done—and the three of them exited the hall.

No one stepped forward to prevent it.

"The shuttle," Dil Nem said, once they were outside, "quickly. Comm Tech, please call ahead, inform the pilot that we will require immediate entry."

"Yes, Third Mate," Sally said, and in a moment Padi heard her on the comm, crisply relaying the third mate's orders.

Padi's knees were shaking, and she could scarcely think, for the anger burning in her breast. Her plan had merit! She had sold her cargo at a fine profit—which the auctioneer refused to pay out—and it wasn't fair! It *was* theft, and she would not—

"Best to bring it before the master trader," Dil Nem murmured, and more loudly, "Comm Tech, please ask the pilot to contact Captain Mendoza and Master Trader yos'Galan. Say that the trader has lost her profit to . . . port legalities. Say, *ongoing criminal enterprise.*"

"Yes, Third Mate," Sally said again, and once more there was the sound of quiet consultation behind Padi's back.

"You may," Padi said, "release me, Third Mate."

He cast a measuring look at her. She met his eyes firmly, and after a moment, he released her arm.

At the same time, however, he increased his pace—not running, *never* running. A person running on port only inspired others to run after her. He was, however, walking very briskly, and therefore several steps ahead of their small group when they came 'round the corner and onto the street that lead to the shipyard.

"Halt!"

Three large persons dressed in the livery of Chesselport Security stood before them, two with weapons leveled.

Dil Nem halted, and threw out an arm to stop Padi. She, in turn, looked over her shoulder for Sally, who was looking over *her* shoulder . . .

. . . at three more uniformed persons behind them, each also holding a weapon.

· · · ✳ · · ·

"Master Trader, a message from Comm Tech Sally Triloff, on port with Third Mate Tiazan and Trader yos'Galan, forwarded by the shuttle pilot on-world."

A chilly breeze blew across the back of Shan's neck. He took a deep, quiet breath.

"Please proceed, Comm Tech."

"Yes, sir. Message follows: Trader yos'Galan has lost her profit to... port legalities. The auctioneer wanted her to sign an affidavit, which she refused to do. Reason given for confiscation: involvement in an *ongoing criminal enterprise.*"

Roner Jerethine, that was the tech's name. An unflappable individual, in Shan's experience, this moment sounding just a bit breathless.

"Continues," the tech said. "The three have been placed under arrest by armed Chesselport Security, and are being escorted to the magistrate's office, where they will be incarcerated, fined, or both. The pilot heard, through the open comm, a man's voice state in Trade that those found to be complicit in *crimes against a planet* have in the past been executed."

There was a small pause, as if Comm Tech Jerethine was swallowing his horror as Shan was swallowing his, then, "At this juncture, the pilot says the comm was taken away from Tech Triloff; he heard her protesting, and demanding that it be returned. There was a very loud noise and the unit went dead."

But this was ridiculous, Shan thought. *Crimes against a planet* meant piracy and aggression, and while some worlds did, indeed, hang convicted pirates, the charge itself was ludicrous. *Dutiful Passage* was an honorable and well-known tradeship. She...

He closed his eyes.

Dutiful Passage had stood above Liad, weapons live, backing an action that had seen Terran mercenaries on the ground at the spaceport, that left a gaping hole in its largest city; an action that had *killed people*, innocent people, who had simply been going about their lives...

Crimes against a planet, indeed.

"Same message relayed to Captain Mendoza, sir," Tech Jerethine said. "She's talking to Chesselport Magistrate Office now."

"Thank you, Roner," he said, as calmly as if Padi was on board and at *daibri'at*, beyond all possible threats against her life. "Please ask the captain to call me, when she's done with the magistrate."

"Will do." Shan thought he heard a note of sympathy in the man's voice. "Anything else for me, sir?"

"Not at the moment, I thank you."

"Right then." A deep breath. "Jerethine out."

CHAPTER NINE

··

Vivulonj Prosperu

SOMETHING HAD WOKEN HIM: THE MOVEMENT OF AIR AGAINST his cheek, the whisper of fabric against skin, a...chime?

Perhaps a chime, he thought, though he did not find it in recent memory.

The dream of a chime?

That was very possible. He had all his life been attended by chimes, buzzes, clicks, and bells. The comfortable chiming of the study clock, counting the hours. The warning bell as a ship broke from Jump into real space. The click of a comm switch being depressed. The sharp buzz denoting the end of a class period.

Perhaps he was late abed, and his dream-mind had produced a chime to rouse him.

He took a breath, tasting mint; felt a cool breeze kiss his cheek.

Well, best he rise, then, if he were slugabed, and see to the order of the day.

He opened his eyes to a dim and featureless chamber. The walls were smooth, the floor was smooth, both dark; reflective enough that they seemed to glow somewhat in the meager light.

There appeared to be no door in the wall, nor hatch in the floor, nor aught else in the chamber, save himself and the piloting couch upon which he lay.

A careful breath before he rolled lightly to his feet. Again, he tasted mint, and . . . something else, familiar, but borne away in the chill rush of memory.

Doors.

There had been doors. He remembered the old wooden door, the main door into Jelaza Kazone, the Tree-and-Dragon worn smooth by the palms of countless homecoming Korval pilots.

But that door had been . . . locked? No. Korval's door had been . . . beyond him. He remembered lying prone on the chilly plain, dry grasses scratching his face. Stripped of everything but thought, he accepted that he would never again put his palm against that door, or feel the latch work under his hand.

He remembered, next, her voice, rousing him, questioning him, prodding him to attend her; to pay attention; to *live.*

I have found us a different door, van'chela. *You must trust me.*

Of course he trusted her; how else? She was his pilot, his lifemate, his love.

It was only after she had bullied him to his feet, and taken his hand firmly in hers . . . it was only when he had seen it—them—those *different doors* she had found, that he began to fear that she had bargained poorly for their lives.

They were not *doors*, the portals she had found for them, but tunnels; as dire a pair as ever he'd seen, each filled with a horrifying blare of light. He had tried to stop their advance, to turn, to avert . . . but he had been weak with dying, and the wind that had sprung up to harry him—to harry *them*—had overpowered him, even in his horror.

The wind pushed harder. Her hand gripped his, strong and sure, and her voice came to him over the roar, steady and clear.

You will not lose me! Daav, I swear it!

The last thing he remembered, as the light burned out his vision, and the wind filled up his ears, was her hand slipping out of his grasp.

And now, this place, and him awake, perhaps not dying, not now; or alone in some solitary afterlife.

She had sworn that he would not lose her. He remembered that and chose to believe, in this moment, at least, that she had the power to guarantee such a thing.

He drew a breath. The air was drier, he thought. Warmer.

"Aelliana?" he called.

His voice vanished into the dimness, swallowed by smooth walls.

There was no answer.

Well.

She was not always immediately present, after all. Sharing one body as they had, these last twenty Standards and more, yet still she had the ability to go...elsewhere, beyond his conscious touch. If he insisted, she would answer; irritable, perhaps, or a little sharp—which he surmised meant that he had interrupted her at work.

But, she answered, had always answered, after he had learnt that, despite the evidence of his eyes, she was not dead, but... transferred, somehow—the *her* of her—into, but apart from, his own personality and thought processes.

The how of that transfer, and her survival—well, it had been the Tree, of course, meddling, as it did, and in the case, to good cause.

"Aelliana?"

His voice was sharper this time; it cut some little way into the silence around him.

The air was growing decidedly warm, and worrisomely thin. He accessed a pilot's mental exercise to calm himself and walked forward, striking boot heels deliberately against the floor.

...and heard nothing. He might as well have walked Scout-silent, for all the sound his steps gave up.

He reached the far wall and leaned forward, placing his hands flat against the dull surface. For an instant, his palms were warmed by ungiving metal. He was panting now; the air was *hot*, and she did not answer him.

He knew, then, that she would not answer; that she was gone, not merely absent. At the last, she had not been able to keep her word, which meant he was...

...alone.

He sagged against the wall, which vanished under his hands, sending him tumbling headlong into some other place that was bright, and cool, though his lungs still labored, and she was gone...gone...away from him and he would die, now, of being alone...

"Look at me!" a voice snapped. "Daav yos'Phelium Clan Korval!"

The voice belonged to someone who was not Aelliana, but—the voice knew his name. An ally, perhaps a friend.

He made the effort to open his eyes, shuddering, gasping,

though there was air here, only his muscles had locked, and he remembered...remembered the terrible time immediately after... after he had seen her fall, shattered by the fragging pellet, blood like crimson rain, and he screaming for both of them...after...

...after, his brain had struggled to accommodate the violence done to it, had he only known it at the time. He had seizures that had taken his breath, leaving him unable even to sob. Pain would slice through his head like so many lightning bolts, until there came an excruciating black explosion, and he would lose knowledge of...everything...

Gasping, he looked up into a man's face, twisted with anger, or fear.

"What ails you?" the stranger demanded.

He tried to get air, enough air to speak, but all he could manage was the single word—the word that told his doom.

"...gone..."

A shudder wracked him. He couldn't *breathe*. A hard hand fell onto his shoulder, pressing him flat, even as he caught the scent familiar to him since childhood.

"Here, Pilot," the other said. "Take this."

He saw it before another shudder forced him to close his eyes.

Somewhere, close at hand, a bell screamed a warning.

"Daav, eat the pod."

Eat the pod?

If he had breath to spare, he might have laughed. As it was, he turned his head away, and forced the words out, for the other was not clan; he did not know that the aid he offered was...

"...not ripe..." he choked.

And knew nothing else.

· · · ※ · · ·

They had been brought to the magistrate's office, which was long and thin. Four rows of three chairs each faced a desk upon a dais. Behind the desk was a wall with a plain door in it. The door was shut.

Padi and Dil Nem Tiazan and Sally Triloff...they were sitting in the first row of three chairs. Three guards stood between them and the raised desk.

Three guards, Padi thought, was respectful, but not very efficient. In addition to carrying a large weapon, each wore an armored vest and hard boots. Two guards outfitted in such a manner would have been a more efficient use of personnel. Had they wished to bind the prisoners, one would have been more than enough.

However, they had not been bound, though the chairs they had been forced to occupy were so ill-formed that Padi could scarcely conceive of *any*one being comfortable in them. They were Terran-sized, of course, which meant that her feet, and Dil Nem's, swung above the floor. Sally's feet did meet the floor, but the armrests were at a bad height for her, and the seat was too deep; she'd tried to sit on the edge, but her guard had leaned closer, forcing her to sit awkwardly back, her legs bent in the most uncomfortable-looking way imaginable.

Padi's guard didn't care that she sat on the edge of the chair; he loomed over her so closely that she could smell his perfume. He had laughed loudly when the leader of the team had asked, back on the street, which of them was Trader yos'Galan. Far from reprimanding him for discourtesy, the leader had given Padi into his particular care. Perhaps he had a specialty in guarding traders.

Now, while the other two guards maintained a seemly silence, her guard talked, loudly. His topic of choice was the proper disposition of pirates, especially those who preyed upon—his choice of phrase—the innocent population of an unprotected world.

Which was simply absurd. Most civilized worlds had protections in place. Liad, more advanced than some, had the planetary defense net... which hadn't actually protected the planet, now she recalled, because Jeeves, utilizing the Captain's access, had shut it down. But the concept...

"You ever see anybody hang?" her guard asked now, shouting as if she were on the shuttle, lifting for the *Passage*, where she very much wanted to be.

"Hey!" he said when she didn't answer, his voice even louder. "You ever seen anybody hang?"

"No," she answered shortly.

He leaned closer, so that she had to tilt her head far back to meet his eyes, and smiled, showing his teeth.

"*I* have," he said.

"Oh, you have not!" Dil Nem's guard exclaimed. "There's not been any hangings here for fifty years! More, maybe!"

"Did! Saw a tape they made of the last one—*thirty* years ago, not fifty." He looked from his mate back to Padi.

"What they do, see, is they tie a cord around the neck of the pirate they're gonna hang, and they tie the other end to a steel grid. The pirate stands on a platform, right in the middle of a trap door. When the knots've been tested, the trap door springs open, the pirate falls, and—*snap!*—the rope catches, the neck breaks, and she's swinging there, by the rope around her neck, her feet kicking a little bit until they get the message that she's dead." He nodded and looked over to his mate, whose pale face seemed paler than it had been a moment before. Not that Padi blamed her; her own stomach felt decidedly unsettled, and she couldn't rid her mind of the picture of a woman, head lolling, the rope biting cruelly into the delicate skin of her throat, swinging gently . . .

"That's what's done with pirates and murderers," her guard finished, and suddenly leaned very close, staring down into her face.

"That's what they're gonna do *to you*, probably. You're one of 'em, yos'Galan; that's *your* name, isn't it?"

The picture of the woman swinging by her neck changed. Padi saw pale brown hair, disordered in the fall and its abrupt ending, tangled over her own face; her own feet in the very boots she wore today kicking feebly against death . . .

"Scared?" he asked then.

"Well, sure she's scared!" That was the other guard, grabbing Padi's guard by the shoulder and hauling him back. "Comes to that, *I'm* scared—and *you're* scaring me! I'm putting you on notice, right now: I'm talking to Cap about you *and* Riley. Judging's for the magistrate to do. Our job is to make sure they stay here for it, not to scare 'em, or intimidate 'em either."

"Bruller likes to scare little girls," commented the third guard. "Makes him feel big."

"Hey!"

He spun toward this new attack, the movement leaving his side completely open.

Padi took a breath, put her hands flat on the arms of the stupid chair. She'd have to lift and leap, because her feet were so far above the floor, but that was fine; she had energy and trajectory; she could launch herself upward, break his neck with one blow, and—

Dil Nem's hand clamped hard around her wrist; a shadow slipped between her and her target—the second guard. She was shaking her head, looking pointedly at Padi's hands.

"Just stay peaceful, Trader," she said softly. "Magistrate's on her way. Bruller don't have anything to do with her judging."

Dil Nem's fingers were going to leave a bruise, Padi thought with a faraway feeling of calm. She met the guard's eyes and nodded. She could feel the adrenaline singing in her blood, mixing badly with her upset stomach. Deliberately, she focused, and brought up a pilot's breathing sequence. Calm, calm at the board...

· · · ✳ · · ·

The man called Uncle stood with his hand on the hood of the birthing unit, staring up at the status board, reading the battle of wills described in the lights and gauges there.

For the moment, *his* will, expressed through the equipment, was the stronger; *he* could keep Daav yos'Phelium alive—insist that the other man not die, despite his obvious wishes. That circumstance would maintain for precisely so long as the Uncle kept his patient imprisoned in the birthing unit.

"*...gone...*"

Uncle frowned after that ghostly word, uttered as if it explained all.

And perhaps, he thought, it did explain...much.

If the man had noticed the absence of his lifemate, utilizing whatever sense he had developed over the years of sharing his essence with her, he may have assumed her dead. Whether, then, he had of his own will turned his face from life in order to follow her, or his body had simply obeyed some Tree-made, cell-level imperative, mattered not at all.

Then, there was the thrice-damned pod. *Still* not ripe?

The Uncle was inclined to think badly of Korval's Tree.

Then, he was inclined to think again.

In order to live, Daav yos'Phelium required the presence of his lifemate. The pilot had himself intimated as much; supporting evidence was provided by the stubbornly unripe pod.

It was therefore necessary to place Aelliana Caylon into a slightly accelerated birthing cycle. She must be present the next time Daav was brought to consciousness. If he died then, within the circle of his lifemate's arms, then the Uncle could consider that he had done all that he might, as one who operated in ignorance of the Tree's intent.

There was some risk in accelerating Aelliana Caylon's rebirth, but not, the Uncle thought, again considering what the status lights told him—perhaps not as much risk as holding Daav yos'Phelium long to life against his will.

The Uncle nodded once before turning from the birthing unit to replace the pod in its container, putting it back into the locker that also held all of the man's clothes and those possessions that he had on him when he had been savagely attacked by his enemies.

Closing the locker, the Uncle quit the cubicle, bound for the place where Aelliana Caylon labored toward birth.

· · · ✳ · · ·

The door behind the desk opened.

"All stand for Magistrate Tinerest!" called the third guard.

All three guards fell back then, giving them room to stand. Padi slid off the chair to her feet, Dil Nem's hand still tight 'round her wrist, as he came off of his chair.

"Step forward now," the second guard said. "Stop on the red line."

The three of them stood side by side on the red line, and looked up at the magistrate sitting behind a dark metal desk on a slightly raised dais. She was an old woman, her face lined with experience and cunning. Her eyes were pale blue, and very sharp. She looked the three of them over slowly, as if she were committing their faces to memory, then glanced down at the screen on her desk.

"Trader Padi yos'Galan, Third Mate Dil Nem Tiazan, Communications Technician Sally Triloff," she read, and looked at them again. "Which of you is Trader yos'Galan?"

Padi straightened and met the sharp gaze.

"I am, Magistrate."

"I see." She sighed, and again glanced down at her screen.

"I apologize for keeping you waiting; I was on comm with Captain Mendoza of *Dutiful Passage*. She provided documentation pertinent to the case, which I reviewed in preparation for our discussion here."

The magistrate raised her head and met Padi's eyes.

"Trader yos'Galan," she said briskly, "the profits from your trade are forfeit. This is a matter of both law and pragmatics. Specifically, the law as it is now in force was properly applied; it is the policy of the magistrates to reward the proper application of the law, in order to promote an environment where the law is more often followed than circumvented."

Padi bit the inside of her cheek to remind herself to keep silent.

The magistrate nodded.

"You would like to say that pragmatism favors the port—and so it does. However, pragmatism also favors your ship. If I were to order that your funds be released, in opposition to the law which is now in force, you and your ship would become *objects of interest*. I place before you the notion that your ship is already of interest to far too many people, no few of them, as I learn from Captain Mendoza, unsavory in the extreme.

"Now. As the information provided by Captain Mendoza casts reasonable doubt upon the contention that *Dutiful Passage* is an ongoing criminal enterprise, I will absolve you of one small, but very important, detail of law. You will *not* be required to sign the affidavit which implicates your ship in criminal activity. Do you understand everything I have said?"

"Ma'am." Padi took a breath, and met the magistrate's eyes straightly. "I don't understand why *Dutiful Passage* still bears the burden of *possible dishonor*. In light of the information provided by the captain."

The magistrate nodded again.

"That's a reasonable question. The answer is that I am not the only magistrate on Chesselport, but one of a court of seven. I must convene a full meeting of my sisters so that we may review this new information together and come to a consensus. Obviously, we have not had time to meet, and I do not wish to inconvenience you further by insisting that you wait upon our deliberations, which might easily consume several days. What I am able to do, within my own court, is let the record show that, in light of evidence produced and verified as genuine, I—in this instance only—have set the matter of an ongoing criminal enterprise aside as irrelevant to the case.

"Having done this, I find that there is no case. There is no reason to fine you, or to incarcerate you. Therefore, you are free to go *directly* to your shuttle and lift to your ship, as the port allows. In order to ensure that you will, indeed, go by the most direct route possible, my own car will take you to the yard."

She looked down to her screen, and said, "Dismissed."

CHAPTER TEN

. . . .

Dutiful Passage

SHAN LOOKED AGAIN AT THE INCOMING MESSAGE QUEUE AT THE bottom of his screen, which was simply absurd; the comm would chime if a message came in. Gods knew, he had work to do, but he couldn't seem to . . . settle his mind.

In fact, the only useful thing he'd done in the last two hours was to send his regrets to the Chessel's World portmaster, citing press of business. One ought, at least, to keep up appearances, even if one now suspected one's prospective host of duplicity.

Or, perhaps, especially.

Deliberately, he flipped open the file on Langlast, their next likely port o'call, and began to read the precis.

Five minutes later, when he realized that he had read the same page four times without recalling a single word, he admitted that he might benefit from a quick session of self-healing, to reestablish focus and deliberation.

He stood and moved into the center of the room, setting his feet firmly, and deliberately relaxing his shoulder muscles.

Focus, he thought. Yes. Focus and cool deliberation.

He closed his eyes and took six deep breaths, relaxing more deeply with each, until he sensed the change of place, and opened his eyes to the soft fogs of Healspace.

He breathed in the fog. It had a mouthfeel like spun sugar, and tasted of citrus. Well, focus had been called for, after all.

Best that the Healer and the one to be healed both had their wits about them.

Again, he filled his mouth with fog—this time, the taste was sharp and pungent—and relaxed into an aspect of calm objectivity as he waited for the one who had called him here.

The fogs before him parted, and a man stood forth: tall and lean; his hair the silky white of a young child's that had never darkened into gold; with silver eyes under thin, slanted white brows; a face that was long and sharp and brown. He wore a wine-colored shirt, and a purple ring flashed on his hand.

Shan the Healer extended a hand; Shan the Trader met it. Emotions flowed between them: worry, fear, and anger. Quite a lot of anger, which was... not usual. He was an even-tempered man, until he was not.

Still, it was a straightforward thing: merely a Sorting, a Soothing, and a Sharpening. The personality matrix was firm, informed by love, commitment, and clarity of purpose. There was no indication that the unusual levels of anger had eroded either his heart or his ethics.

Excellent.

Shan the Healer reached forth and commenced the work: Sorting the tangled, hot and cold emotions; Soothing the troubled soul; Sharpening the beleaguered intellect.

It went well, the work, and nothing out of the ordinary, nothing unexpected, until, abruptly, a weight fell upon his senses, and the edges of his Sight darkened.

He withdrew slightly from the work, and brought his attention to the man who was himself...

The man who *was not* himself.

Long and lean and hawk-faced, yes—so much remained the same. But this man's hair was black, and lush, woven into a single thick braid; his clothing dark and shabby. His smile was sardonic, and there was a sense of both stillness and motion about him. Shan the Healer looked down, foreknowing what he would see.

A worn red gaming counter danced across the other's brown knuckles, plunged off the edge of the hand—and vanished into the ether of Healspace.

Shan the Healer felt a thrill... perhaps of horror.

"Return me myself," he said, his words swallowed by the fog.

The smile grew softer; perhaps there was sympathy in those space-black eyes.

"But I am yourself, as we discussed, and you will need all of me, soon or late. Your lady will also need Moonhawk, I fear, in every aspect possible."

"You terrify me."

"Not in this place, child. There is no terror here. Or none that is not soon soothed and straightened and made into joy." He raised his hands, showing the marker between two fingers, and smiled. "But I did not come here merely to visit. I would ask a question regarding our heart, if you will grant the boon."

It was honestly said; the fog would have shown him any falseness. And an honest request for Healing must be honored, in Healspace.

Even if it came from oneself.

Shan inclined his head.

"Ask."

"It is a small thing, but I wonder, this shadow upon your heart. You have straightened it, and you have soothed it, but you have not transformed it into joy. These are the deaths at Solcintra, I think you still feel?"

Shan sighed. "Some things do not transmute into joy." He raised a hand, seeing the amethyst throw lightning into the fog. "I am a Healer; my strengths are rooted in life. Though we did what was correct and necessary, yet I think that, if we use the methods of our enemy, are we not—our enemy?"

"Would you have healed them all, your enemies?"

"Some things," said Shan, "cannot be healed. But perhaps we should first make the attempt."

"Sweet child. But I am of a mind with you." Lute smiled. "Astonishing, is it not?"

"Who, in fact, would have thought so?" Shan said, smiling himself. "Now that we have dealt with this matter upon our heart, will you return me to myself?"

"Of course I will!" said Lute. "Only meet me halfway." He extended a hand that was innocent of rings.

Shan the Healer met it, felt his fingers strongly gripped.

A tide flowed between them; of what strange waters, he could not have said. He sensed no poison, nor anything inimical, though he tasted the essence of years stretching into a past far exceeding his own.

There was a moment when his senses faltered, the fogs of Healspace melting around him, until it seemed that he stood astride galaxies and looked out over the glittering lives of an entire universe. He stretched, godlike...

...and contracted into himself, senses reeling, Healspace cuddled about his shoulders like a blanket.

Shan the Healer blinked his Sight clear, and looked into the familiar face of Shan the Trader, who wore an expression of wry resignation, tinged with wary wonder.

"What cannot be mended must be worn rent," the Trader offered.

The Healer sighed.

"That would go down easier, if I were not trained to mend. Let us have one more look at us." He extended a hand on which the purple ring flashed a little more brightly than its wont in this place, and met a hand wearing a ring identical in all respects.

Emotions flowed between them, sprightly, like the stream that had threaded Trealla Fantrol's parklands, and into which he had merrily fallen as a child.

The personality grid sparkled, reminiscent of the ring; emotions were smooth, if no less complex; the energy that had informed the tangled coil of worry and distraction had been properly redirected to focusing the intellect; the soul was calmed, and there was about the whole a subtle aroma of joy.

The Healer met the Trader's eyes.

"What is done, is done," they said, together, and did not add, *for good or ill.*

Each opened their arms. Stepping forward, they embraced into oneness.

Shan opened his eyes to the comfortable sight of his office, and a priority message on his screen, informing him that the shuttle bearing Third Mate Tiazan, Comm Tech Triloff, and Trader yos'Galan had been cleared for lift from Chesselport.

· · · ✷ · · ·

Padi sat in the jump seat, but for once her attention was not on the screens or the pilot's boards. Her eyes were turned inward, all of her attention on the necessity of containing the conflagration within her.

She was *angry*. Well, who *wouldn't be* angry, to have their profit stolen, and their trade made into dust—less than dust! For an incomplete trade did not count toward the total of successful trades that would move her from 'prentice to trader.

But there was worse.

Worse than the anger, somehow *feeding* it...was the fear.

The images the guard had given her of herself falling, the jerk, the snap as the rope halted the fall, and her feet moving in protest until they stopped and there was only the broken body, brown hair tangled over her downturned face, swinging, softly swinging, as if prompted by the gentlest breeze.

Her throat closed, and her stomach clenched; her heart pounded in her ears, her fingernails digging into her sweaty palms.

She had known herself for craven, a coward unworthy to stand in the ranks of Korval pilots. But, this...this was terrible beyond anything she had previously experienced...

She needed to dance, to dance the fear into the place she had built for it, deep inside herself, where it would never be found, or seen, even by Healer eyes. There was no room on the shuttle, and she feared—yes, *she feared!*—that the anger might consume her into ash, before they gained the *Passage*.

She clenched her muscles and tucked her head, teeth grit—and felt someone touch her arm.

Fiery anger coalesced; if she breathed out, she would breathe fire, and destroy whomever dared to—

"Padi?"

She recognized Sally Triloff's voice and gasped, sucking living flame down her throat, whimpering at the pain.

Arms closed around her; she shook her head, not daring to open her mouth, and Sally rubbed her back.

"Oh, sweetie, go ahead and cry. I bet even the master trader would cry, if he'd been treated like that. The least they could have done was return your goods!"

It was perhaps the ridiculous notion that Master Trader yos'Galan would have, under any circumstances, allowed his profit to be stolen from him—

Or perhaps it was the offer of a temporary bond of kinship; a place no larger than the circle of Sally's arms, in which it would be...*not improper* to indulge in emotion.

Or, perhaps, she was simply that tired.

Whichever, and entirely to her own astonishment, her face pressed against Sally's shoulder, Padi did, indeed, begin to cry.

· · · ✳ · · ·

Shan stood with Priscilla in the docking area antechamber, his hand in hers.

"I'm to tell you that you will need your Moonhawk in all her aspects," he murmured, surprising both of them. He hadn't intended to tell Priscilla about his encounter in Healspace—at least not until they were alone and very private.

Her head turned sharply, and she looked directly into his eyes. "From Lute?"

"Yes, from Lute, meddling creature. He would also advise me that I'm going to need him, soon or late."

"That's fair warning, then," Priscilla said.

"Fairer had he said which it was," Shan muttered, and Priscilla might perhaps have answered that, save the light over the shuttle bay door went from ruby to emerald.

First through the door was Third Mate Tiazan, calm and forthright as ever. He bowed, precisely, to the captain's honor, and murmured, "Captain. I will have a report."

"Yes," she said. "But tell me first, are you harmed, or in need?"

"I am well. The young trader . . ." He stopped short, as if catching himself on the edge of an infelicity, and looked to Shan. "The guards were not above playing games, and I fear the young trader took some of their . . . less savory tales to heart. Certainly, the disposition of her trade angered her." He hesitated, and inclined his head.

"Comm Tech Triloff offered a comrade's care during the lift," he concluded. "It may be done with, now."

"Thank you," Shan said, "for your care."

Dil Nem bowed. "Captain. Master Trader."

He took himself off down the hall, as Comm Tech Triloff approached, anger glowing orange in the region of her heart. Walking beside her, seeming slightly subdued, was Padi.

Shan considered her on all the levels available to him as a Healer.

On the surface, he saw the sweet pale greens and blues of utter calmness, which was . . . startling. He tried to recall where Sally Triloff had ranked in empathy, but even if she were a full Healer herself, he would still have expected to see—

There. Beneath the damp pastels that might well denote a

good cry, he found scorch marks along her matrix; remnants of an incandescent anger.

That was more in keeping with the nature of events, he thought, relieved. After all, the child had seen her profit cruelly taken from her, and been arrested; these things sit ill with traders as a class, and those of Korval, more so.

He transferred his attention to Sally Triloff, whose emotive grid was still ablaze with fury.

"Thank you," he said gently, "for your care of my child."

She blinked, perhaps not expecting him to take that road. Sally had been with the *Passage*—worked with Liadens—long enough to have a feel for *melant'i*. She would have expected him to be the master trader in the matter, as Padi had been acting as trader herself. A comrade's care, though—that was personal, which perhaps Sally hadn't thought about.

"You're welcome," she said now. "It wasn't right, what happened to her—to her cargo."

Ah, Terrans and their touching notion of *right*.

Shan smiled.

"Sadly, this sort of thing does happen, from time to time. Not often, but infuriating all the same."

"Yes, sir."

Sally returned the smile tentatively, and went on to speak with Priscilla.

Padi looked up at him.

"I lost my profit," she said, merely stating a fact.

"So I've heard. You must tell me all about it. In fact, I wonder if you would share a private nuncheon with me, so that you *may* tell me all about it."

She took a hard breath, and he tasted anger and loss—which were expectable—and...resignation...which was not.

He waited, showing her a calm face, sternly refusing to reach out and hug her.

"I'd be pleased to report on my trade," Padi said properly, her voice at least revealing nothing save what might have been an entirely reasonable weariness.

"Splendid!" he said, showing broad pleasure. "Let's walk together, shall we?"

· · · ·✳· · · ·

The last few shifts had been quiet. Not that Jemiatha Station sat at the crossroads of the universe, or anything like that, but they had their regulars—and their usual traffic.

'Course part of that usual traffic had been the Tinker, who'd come in three, four times a cycle, and not always more trouble'n she was worth. Had an eye for interesting tech, did the Tinker, and she'd taught him a thing or two about microrepairs, which he hadn't thought nobody could've done.

Stew blew his breath out in an impatient huff. Not going to be seeing the Tinker anymore at Jemiatha's, thanks to *Admiral Bunter*.

The rest of the regulars, though...

Word would've got out, Stew thought, staring at his diagnostic screen glumly—about the Tinker. That was worrisome, but—flip side—it was a relief. Station needed its regulars, sure, and truth was there wasn't much *but* Jemiatha's out here, given the way most of the small-routes run, which was another way of saying the regulars needed the station. They'd have to come back, eventually.

It was *eventually* Stew'd been counting on. Time. Time enough for one or t'other of the experts to get their duffs out here and either talk some sense into the *Admiral* or take him off-line.

Time was running out, though. The regulars—yeah, they'd run out of avoid soon enough.

The crews, that was another thing. He wasn't in any way trigger-happy, and Vez—Down-Shift manager, Vez was, his opposite number and junior to him by just ten hours...

He could trust Vez to follow chain of command, and he *was* senior. What he couldn't trust her to do was see *Admiral Bunter* as anything more than a parlor trick—half comedy and all stupid.

Despite what'd happened with the Tinker.

And the crews? There was talk 'mong the crews about cobbling up some cannon. He'd disallowed that, on Up-Shift. Vez, though, she'd let her crew go ahead with it as a side project, so long as reg'lar work was done and the materials draw was strictly from declared derelicts.

Cannon. Stew shook his head.

A surprise attack. He sighed.

Problem with cannon and that *surprise attack* was that neither took into account the nature of a mind rooted in comps 'stead of human flesh.

Vez was smart. Vez was a damn good tech.

But Vez didn't believe in independent logics. She *was* a tech. A machine was a machine to her.

And all the time, there was *Admiral Bunter*, keeping station, protecting Jemiatha's from *pirates*, the gods of space help 'em all, and inclined to view any attempt to differentiate between the Tinker's petty thievery and real pirates as pretty dern near piracy, itself.

Stew had backed off of that conversation the minute he realized how the *Admiral* was processing his explanation, and he had an uneasy feeling that he was now a suspect character.

So far, they'd been lucky, that's what it was, Stew thought, and jumped when the diagnostics beeped twice for *done*.

Within tolerances, he thought, running a practiced eye down the column; plenty good enough to go into the used inventory. He punched a button to print out a ticket, and another to enter the part into the catalog.

Lucky, he repeated to himself. They couldn't depend on staying lucky, that was the thing.

Repairs wasn't the only department running nervous and thinking about ways to rid themselves of Cap'n Waitley's gift. Stationmaster was getting nervous, starting to listen to advice from chancy quarters, and it was all Stew could do, to talk him into waiting just a little bit longer.

For the specialist...

Cap'n Waitley'd sent for a specialist before she ever left system. Trouble being, they'd never shown up.

Hadn't seemed urgent, and Stew'd been willing to wait a little more.

Then...

Well, then *Admiral Bunter*'d fragged the Tinker's ship, and Tinker inside it. That's when Stew'd put in a call to his own expert. Pinbeam; he'd sent it with his own hands. Got the ack.

But no expert on that side, either.

Last time they'd talked, he'd asked the stationmaster for fifteen more Standard days, for a solution to arrive, in the form of specialists.

There were eight days left on that grant o'time, and what Jemiatha's Jumble Stop was gonna do if no experts ever did show up was more'n Stew could figure.

CHAPTER ELEVEN

. . . .

Dutiful Passage

"... WHICH MEANS THAT MY RESEARCH WAS SOUND; THERE *IS* profit to be made in *milaster* on Chessel's World," Padi said warmly, eyes flashing with triumph, her soup forgotten on the table before her. Abruptly, her shoulders sagged, and she averted her face.

"Only, one is not allowed to keep it, which seems, someway... less satisfying than no profit at all."

"Also," she said, putting her spoon down with the air of one who has no appetite, "I've overspent my spec money. Even if another high-profit deal presents itself, I haven't enough funds to take proper advantage."

"You did take a bold gamble," Shan said, leaning back in his chair. He was toying absently with a wineglass, all of his attention on Padi. He had several times during the course of the meal perceived anomalies—a smile yoked to a sudden, frigid tremor of fear; a shrug of resignation linked to a flicker of white anger; and, once more, fear, shadowing a bold look of pride.

"I seem to recall," he added, when she made no answer nor even looked up, "that we had touched upon the wisdom of committing so much of your cash to one deal."

He expected a pretty sparkle of prideful temper, and a sharp reminder that, had Chesselport law not been *quite* so addlebrained, she would have trebled her funds.

It was what he would have done, when he was her age. It was what he would have been strongly tempted to do, even now. Padi herself...

But it occurred to him, watching the subdued halfling across the table, that Padi was *not* herself.

"Yes, sir," she said. "I ought to have been more conservative." And there it was at last, a flare of bright, sharp heat. "But I was right!"

Energy sparked, and pinwheeled. Padi raised her head, and it was pride and justified anger he saw on her face. He took a firmer hold on his glass, in case she should decide to throw—

The anger evaporated; the pinwheel of pride fizzled into chill grey. Shan shivered; tasted grit on his tongue, felt stone beneath his palm.

Across from him, Padi sighed, and shook her head, exhaustion coming off of her in damp waves.

"I see that your adventures have caught you up," he said. "Shall we leave the rest until some other time?"

Curiosity stirred, striking a momentary spark of energy. She asked, "Rest?"

"Oh, indeed! I understand that you might not like to do the work, but in my judgment as master trader, your research was accurate, your instinct was good, and you trebled your investment. In other circumstances you might have gained your first repeat customer—and a reason for the *Passage* to include Chesselport among its scheduled stops. The circumstances that parted you from your profit before ever you had it in hand are apart from the transaction itself."

He raised the wineglass and sipped, feeling Padi's attention, and the small beginning of a hope that she might, somehow, come about, despite recent events.

"Of course, I cannot make a Determination of Completed Trade by myself. I must lay the case before another, unaffiliated master of trade, and abide by their opinion. We would not, after all, wish it to seem that I had shown my apprentice special favor. Your license will rest upon these early transactions. It is best that they are above question."

He considered her: face slightly flushed, bright eyes intent on him, no hint of stone in her pattern, weariness burned away by hope.

"What is it?" she asked, when he paused for another sip of wine. "What work must I do?"

"Ah, are you interested? What you must *do* is write an account of your transaction, including your research, the facts of your purchase, and of your sale. You will include copies of the sales receipt, the auction hall's record of the sale, and the public log entry of the magistrate's decision. I will tell you that straight-forwardness, and solid fact, is more likely to be read favorably than impassioned outrage, and that your facts *will* be checked, so be very certain that they are correct."

"Yes, of course." She was leaning forward now, watching his face.

"Yes," he repeated, and shook his head slightly. "As with all such things, there is a deadline for submission of this report. You have three ship-days to produce your part, as I have three ship-days to produce mine. After we are finished here, I will contact the guild with the information that we have a case requiring a master trader's attention. Once our reports have been transmitted, the master trader will have two Standard weeks to render her opinion, which she will send to the guild. The guild will then inform me of the outcome, and I"—he inclined his head politely—"will inform you. If the outcome is as we desire, your trade at Chesselport will be admitted to your record, rated favorably, and become one of the cornerstones of your license."

"And..." Padi's voice squeezed out; she cleared her throat and began again. "And if the master trader should disallow my trade?"

"Then it is done, and you have only lost what you never held."

Her mouth tightened at that, and he tasted the sizzle of anger, but she did not choose to dispute him, and after a moment she nodded.

"I am willing to do the work," she said.

"Very well, then, I shall expect your report on my screen in three ship-days. In the meantime, there is one thing that I may do, as master trader on the *Dutiful Passage*."

Padi's expression took on a certain wariness, for which he didn't entirely blame her, but she asked him courteously enough.

"What may you do, sir?"

"I may bring your spec fund back to pre-*milaster* levels."

She blinked.

"But...I made the buy; there was no loss there, though I will allow it to have been, perhaps, a little...reckless."

"It's nothing short of astonishing, how often boldness is found to be its own reward. However, this is no act of charity; it is a loan."

"A loan?"

"Exactly. Should the master trader decide in your favor, the guild will reimburse you for half of the lost profit. If that should happen, you will repay me from those funds."

"And if the master trader decides that my case has no merit?"

"Then you will come to me with a plan to pay back the loan by the end of this trade run. Are these terms agreeable?"

"Yes, Master Trader!"

"Excellent; we are in accord. Now, may I suggest, as your parent, that you do not begin writing—or researching—your report until you have slept for at least a half-shift?"

"Yes, Father," she said, and gave him a fond smile that he found to be sincere on all the levels accessible to him. "Truth told, I am a little tired."

She was more than a little tired, but he held his tongue, and forbore from probing more deeply, drilling for stone.

Instead, he gave her a smile, and allowed his love for her to sweep out and envelop her as he rose, and walked her to the door.

"Sleep well, child," he said softly, gently reinforcing the impulse to sleep.

"Yes, Father," she said, and stood on tip-toe to kiss his cheek.

· · · ✻ · · ·

"So, nothing yet?"

That was Vez, coming in for her shift. She threw a fast glance at the change-over board, but she'd see the answer on his face, easy enough.

"Nothing yet," Stew said anyway. It'd become a ritual, like they'd taught at home, before he got tired of ritual and hired himself off-world.

He was plenty tired of this ritual, too, and even tireder of the fear that was the reason for it.

"Still peaceful," he said, watching the screen—*the* screen, divvied up into eight sections: one section each for the ships that made up the being who called hisself *Admiral Bunter*; the eighth displayed the boundary beacon, where a ship Jumping in would show first.

Vez sighed, and came over to stand at his shoulder, looking at the screen in her turn.

"How much longer you figure on waitin', Stew?"

"Still got eight days on the stationmaster's word, last time I counted," he said, stiffer than maybe he'd oughta been.

Him and Vez, they worked good together; they consulted and kept each other in the loops. Not that there been all that many loops at Jemiatha's Jumble Stop, nor crises, neither.

Except for the one they had now, and it was a doozy. Seven near-derelict ships, keeping station—keeping *watch*. He oughta've known better than to take an independent logic on, but...the logic—*Admiral Bunter*—had saved the station's bacon; and he had some manuals; and he'd always been good with tech, and...

...he'd been overconfident, is what. Shoulda dismantled the old ships first thing. Should never have let that little captain talk him into keeping what she'd done. Made it sound so damn reasonable. Made it sound like there wasn't going to be no problems at all.

"Been peaceable, lately," he said quieter, and heard Vez sigh; felt her hand come down light on his shoulder.

"Ain't been anything but a couple junk haulers in, since," she said. "How do we know what it'll do, if we get in a ship full o'marines, or some miners lookin' for a good time?"

It. Yeah, well. Vez was looking at a malfunctioning machine, which was worrisome enough for Vez, Stew thought. Independent logics was make-believe, to Vez, something like you'd read about in *Thrilling Space Adventures* and get all over shivery for a minute.

"Somebody with family. Connections," Vez continued, her fingers pressing hard into his shoulder, "'stead of a rag-edged rimrunner?"

Stew shrugged and moved out from under her hand.

"Still got eight Standard days," he said, turning to face her.

Vez pressed her lips together, and shook her head. He braced himself for maybe a cussing-out, but her voice was even, and reasonable.

"We got the cannon up and targeted," she said.

Well, that wasn't no good news, and a bad plan, too.

The idea was to target all seven pieces of *Admiral Bunter* at once, and blow him to Galaxy Nowhere before he knew there was a threat.

Problem being that Stew was...pretty sure the *Admiral* knew about the cannon. He was slow, but he was thorough. Observant, too. And, to be fair, the cannon was a better idea than Vez's first, that they just send a tech onto each deck to decommission the comps.

That, in Stew's not-exactly-uninformed opinion, would've been suicide. *Admiral Bunter*'s personality was shared around thirteen comps in the seven old ships. He'd know what was going on the minute the first tech went for main comp. And he'd act to defend himself, which anybody would, and there would be seven dead techs, and an *angry Admiral Bunter.*

"We don't know the cannon'll work," he said to Vez. "We can't afford to have him mad at the station. So far, he don't see us as a threat; he sees us as something he's responsible for protecting. If we make a move that causes him to suspect we're trying to kill him—I can't answer to that, Vez. Nor I might not have to. Those ships can take out the whole station."

"And they will. It's not *stable*, Stew."

"I know," he said. "I know that. I just—let's just wait a little longer, Vez, right?"

She sighed, but—

Vez nodded. "Day nine, we still got nothing, we use the cannon."

Stew shook his head.

"Day nine, we still got nothing, we pull the whole crew together and we go over the situation. Come up with a plan."

He reached up and resettled his cap on his head, reached to the screen to sign himself out and shut down Up-Shift accounting—and snatched it back as the bell sounded—the bell from the boundary beacon, announcing a ship incoming.

"Jemiatha's Jumble Stop," the beacon's rusty voice came across broadband. "Please identify yourself, and your purpose: repairs, refuel, supply. Please supply standard ID compressed cross-load and active voice broadcast."

The beacon was a long way out—but neither he nor Vez moved, nor maybe breathed, waiting for the ID to come across.

Some clicks on audio; then the high ping of an ID arrival alert.

There was a delay before the voice answer came, crisp as if the pilot was talking in Stew's ear.

"*Ahab-Esais*, out of Waymart, Pilot First Class Inkirani Yo. Repairs."

Stew stepped to his console, and opened a direct line. The ship showed up now on radar as a small courier-class blip, in a neat and proper approach orbit.

"*Ahab-Esais*, this is Repairs. If you transmit a list of your necessaries, we can get started pulling what we'll need to fix you up and give you orbital vectors for a connect to the yard or the shop."

Again the delay of light, and now the commlink even brighter, like the pilot was using directional homing.

"I thank you," the crisp voice said in his ear. "My necessity is to speak with Master Mechanic Steward Vannigof. He had requested my assistance."

The station seemed to rotate around Stew. He grabbed onto the edge of the console and let relief take him.

"Yard," he said, touching a different comm slot, "Yard and security. Be advised incoming will visit the station by invitation."

It was automatic, now, to tell the *Admiral* to keep him calm, and to be sure everyone was alert for trouble when a ship got close. What he couldn't say and hoped didn't show, was his exquisite relief.

The expert—the one he'd sent for, after it seemed clear that Cap'n Waitley's expert didn't have no time for Jemiatha's Jumble Stop...

The expert had finally arrived.

• • • ❖ • • •

Before the *Passage* left Surebleak, Aunt Anthora had given Padi a Name Day present. Never mind that her last Name Day had passed inside Runig's Rock, or that her next would very likely be celebrated aboard the *Passage*. It was never wise to attempt to reconcile Aunt Anthora with mundane realities.

So Padi had received, with all due gratitude, a bath set: soaps and shampoos and lotions, all scented with lavender. *A small luxury*, Aunt Anthora had said, putting the box into Padi's hands. *A small luxury, niece, against a time when you may wish to smell like flowers.*

Smelling like flowers was *certainly* better than smelling like Chesselport—or like fear. Padi had therefore carried one of the smaller soaps and a vial of shampoo into the 'fresher with her. The lather on her skin was creamy and sweet; the scent reminding her of home—of Trealla Fantrol, where there had been a planting of lavender directly below her window.

Yawning, still Padi took time to wash her hair twice, and to think grateful thoughts to Aunt Anthora.

Now, warm and sweet-smelling, she sat on the edge of her bunk, and reached out to pick up the bowl the artisan had given her at Andiree.

It rested lightly in her palms: the blue surfaces agreeably textured, the white surfaces as smooth as ice. Yet, for all of its lightness and beauty, it was not fragile; it was in no danger of being broken.

Like Uncle Val Con's special knife, Padi thought, the crystal blade that was given to him by his Clutch Turtle brother.

And who would think of using weapons-grade crystal in a glaze to protect—art?

Art and weaponry would seem to stand on opposite hills, and yet here they were, each nature complementing the other.

If only *she* could turn that trick, she thought—and yawned, suddenly and widely.

Well, yes; she was tired. She had said as much to Father, and promised him that she would nap. The shower...but the shower had loosened muscles tight with the aftermath of fright, and the lingering scent of lavender lulled with memories of home.

She put the bowl gently back in its place on her bunkside table, and slid under the blanket. Settling her cheek against the pillow, she sighed, once, and slid into sleep.

. . . ❋ . . .

It had been a quick skim in-and-out at Bieradine; clustering subsequent Jumps as close as was prudent, for human health. Pilot Tocohl was eager, now, to reach the site of their assignment, this Jemiatha Station, or, as it called itself, the Jumble Stop. It offered supply and repair, and kept an astonishingly large yard of out-of-service ships from which to draw parts.

"So far out from the more traveled routes," Hazenthull had said to Tolly, "why do they have so many?"

"Prolly *because* they're remote," Tolly'd answered. "Out in back-space, a lot of the ships're old—working a hundred Standards or more. Makes sense to keep parts for ships that're the same age as your customer's work-boat."

It was fortunate, for Jemiatha Station and also for the being that Tolly and Pilot Tocohl hoped to . . . educate, that the location *was* so remote. One pilot and her ship had died, through what Hazenthull's comrades deemed an error of ignorance. They were to assure that another such error was not made.

Tolly had told her that education was key.

"Poor fella wakes up into himself without any parameters, except only that the station's under attack and it's his duty to protect the station. First thing he does, without even properly knowing the why of it, is kill a ship and all aboard. Next time he sees a problem, it's no wonder he applies the same solution—it's the only answer he's got. It's gonna be my job—mine and Pilot Tocohl's—to teach him better, show him there's a wide range of answers, and how to sort his problems down from Code Red."

"What if . . ." Hazenthull had said then, for she was very curious regarding this process and what Tolly was about as a *mentor*. It had become apparent, in their talks at board together, and at meals, that he considered this work, above all others, *his* work, and she hoped that she would be privileged to see him at it.

"What if he does not learn?"

She was immediately sorry that she had asked, for Tolly's face had turned grim, and he had seemed a soldier in that instant, duty lying heavy across his neck.

"If he can't learn . . . won't learn . . . then we'll shut him down," he said heavily.

"But you do not think that will be necessary."

"Well—I *hope* it won't be necessary," Tolly said, his grin not quite sincere. "You know me, Haz—always looking for the good outcome."

Tolly was resting now, and Pilot Tocohl was at study, leaving Hazenthull alone on the tidy bridge, sitting copilot's duty, watching the countdown in the corner of the Jump-grey screens.

The last number cleared, the screen came live, and for the next while, her thoughts were those of a pilot newly reentered into normal space. Though the pilot's chair was empty, she received the appropriate information from first board. Pilot Tocohl was, in a sense, always at her board, which, given her nature, was hardly a surprise. Still, it had taken several breaking-ins before Hazenthull was comfortable with what Tolly laughingly called the Ghost Pilot.

The door to the bridge opened as they came into range of the first beacon, and Pilot Tocohl soundlessly took her chair—or, rather, hovered above it—her delicate hands moving along the various switches and toggles.

"All's well, Pilot," Hazenthull said. The pilot surely knew so, but she'd found that she not only needed to state the obvious, but, on the two occasions when she had made an attempt *not* to do so, the pilot had prompted her for a status report.

"Excellent," Pilot Tocohl answered. "Wake Pilot Tolly, please. I want him with us on the bridge when we approach the station."

"Yes, Pilot."

Hazenthull opened the line to Tolly's quarters and relayed the message, receiving a sprightly, "I'm on my way!" in return.

Nodding, Hazenthull closed the line, just as the comm light snapped on.

An auto-voice came, a little too loudly, over broadband. Hazenthull adjusted the volume down, and felt a foolish tightening of her stomach.

"Jemiatha's Jumble Stop. Please identify yourself, and your purpose: repairs, refuel, supply. Please supply standard ID compressed cross-load and active voice broadcast."

There was other traffic in the system, which the ship noted, as did the pilot, and the beacon message repeated—an endless loop, if it received no answer.

Hazenthull raised her eyes to Tocohl, to see who would answer the beacon, and by then Tolly arrived, still adjusting his shirt. His eyes were on the big screen, then—

"Those," he said pointing to seven mismatched dots ranged well away from the busyness of the station's core cloud. Dots that were somehow not the station's stock-in-trade but something more.

"Those are the *Admiral.*"

Hazenthull allowed a slight smile to form on her lips. Tolly pretended to be an amateur in everything, yet it wanted the eyes of a well-seasoned pilot to pick out and understand those dots on the screen.

"Please announce us, Pilot Hazenthull," Tocohl said gently. "Mentor, your attention here, if you will."

Tolly moved to the pilot's side, taking an earbud from her hand. Hazenthull keyed the comm. "*Tarigan*, out of Waymart. Copilot Hazenthull nor'Phelium. We seek long-term docking."

CHAPTER TWELVE

....

Jemiatha's Jumble Stop

HAZENTHULL AND TOLLY WENT TOGETHER TO THE REPAIRS SIDE of the station, him walking two of his short steps ahead on her left, so as not to impede her, should she have to pull her weapon. It was the configuration they had worked out as most efficient for them, as partners in Surebleak Port Security, and Hazenthull took comfort from it. Let those they passed in the narrow halls grin outright at the disparity in their heights—that had happened often enough on Surebleak Port. And they had soon enough learned that the "tall and small team" was effective. Possibly, they would learn so, here, though it was Tolly and Pilot Tocohl who would carry the honor of the team.

Pilot Tocohl, they had left aboard *Tarigan*, so that she might complete her studies. That was well enough, though Hazenthull wondered what sort of study might keep the pilot, with all of her advantages, so long.

She dared not ask Tolly, not here in the halls when anyone might hear. Perhaps she would ask Tocohl herself, when they were all three again aship.

In the meanwhile, here came the door to the Repairs section. The name of their contact was Stew, being the person with whom Pilot Waitley had lately dealt.

Pilot Waitley was the Scout's blood-sister, as the matter had been explained to the House Troop. She was not herself either a

121

Scout or a soldier, though she commanded her own vessel. Hazenthull had met the pilot when she had recently visited Surebleak,
and had thought her young for command, even for one of the
Scout's kin. Certainly, she was not beyond error, even, as Tolly
would have it, grievous error.

"It's like leaving a newborn baby to fend for himself, what
she did!" he had exclaimed during one of their team sessions. He
was hot-voiced on this topic as on no other, even when speaking
of those who would enslave his will to theirs.

"Like leaving an armed and mobile newborn," Pilot Tocohl
had said, in what Hazenthull was coming to understand as her
humor, "who has Jump capability."

"Not seven together, he ain't Jumping," Tolly had objected,
more temperately, and squinted at the pilot. "You think?"

"Do you think the computation beyond his capabilities?"

Tolly had sighed, and rubbed the bridge of his nose.

"Well, that's part of the problem. Seven old ships, with comps
so cramped it takes all thirteen of 'em—including what looks to
be a lunchroom comp!—to hold one live brain. *Old* ships—but,
sure, say he does the math, and Jumps. If one comp blows, or one
ship shreds—he's gone. You know and I know he's got no backup.
Even if the ships had redundant systems when they came in, we
gotta believe the yard's pulled whatever was worth having..."

He shook his head, and fell silent.

"And if you—forgive me—were to be shot in the head, you
would be gone," Pilot Tocohl said, after it seemed that he had no
more words. "All life is vulnerable. It's the nature of the condition."

"Heads up, Haz," Tolly said now.

The door opened before them, and she saw that the warning
had been more than a friendly reminder to focus. Tolly walked tall
through the doorway. She, however, was required to cant forward
from the waist in order not to crack her forehead against the frame.

Past the door was a room divided by a counter, with another
door at the far end, behind the counter. Also behind the counter
was a stocky Terran male, cap snugged down over hairless head,
orange jacket with *Jemiatha Supply and Repair* stenciled on the
breast, open over a dark sweater. He was in close conversation
with a person considerably taller, pale hair caught in a careless
knot at the back of the head, skin nearly as dark as the worn
Jump pilot's jacket.

"Might wanna make voice contact first," the stocky man was saying. "But you're the pro. Station priority—" He cut himself off as they entered, raising a hand toward the dark pilot, fingers shaping a fast *hold that*.

"Pilots," he said, turning their way. He looked up at Hazenthull's face, down to Tolly's—and stayed there. "Something we can do for you?"

"Looking for Stew," Tolly said in his easy way. "Cap'n Waitley sent us. Sorry it took longer than we wanted to get to you."

The dark pilot had straightened, and was regarding them interestedly out of star-blue eyes. Stew blinked and shook his head, mouth going wry.

"Took long enough that I put out a call on m'own," he said, nodding at the other. "Hope you had other bidness out this way, 'cause we got our problem covered."

Tolly turned slightly to look up into the dark pilot's face. He hesitated, minutely, assessing the other, Hazenthull thought, then put out his hand in the Terran manner.

"I'm Tolly Jones," he said. "Pleased to meet you."

The dark pilot met his hand with a will, a grin reshaping the stern face into pleasantness.

"Inkirani Yo." The voice was light and to Hazenthull's ear bore no accent. "Mentor Berik-Jones, it is an honor."

"That's a leap," Tolly said, suffering his hand to be held.

"Not so much of a leap, if we are here on the same business." Pilot Yo released his hand, and turned back to Stew.

"You are given an unprecedented opportunity, Master Vannigof. The best among us has come to your aid. I cannot allow you to prefer me to Mentor Berik-Jones."

Stew took his cap off and swiped a hand over his shiny head, resettled the cap, and sighed.

"The station's necessity is to make certain that AI is stable, which I'm telling you it ain't. We got a concern that the next misunderstanding is gonna end in us taking some damage—an' that's not unrealistic. Got some trigger-happy folk who're thinking cannon is the answer. I'm not one of 'em, but it wouldn't break my heart if the *Admiral* was gone tomorrow. In fact, that'd be my preference. In the general way of things, we ain't got pirate trouble, and while we're grateful for what he did to help us..."

His voice faded out, as if he had heard himself say that the best reward for duty done well was an end to all duty, and reeled under the blow he had dealt his own honor.

Tolly turned his hands palm up.

"Something that might help you decide between us," he said. "My intention is to socialize the *Admiral* out there. I reviewed such information as Cap'n Waitley sent on, and I think I've got a pretty good idea of what happened, and why it happened. Damn shame it came to that, but I'll tell you straight out, it's no wonder the *Admiral's* confused. I think I can get him unconfused and on course."

Stew sighed.

"An' if you can't?"

"Master Vannigof, please! You cannot think that Mentor Berik-Jones will fail!"

"Well, he can be excused for thinking it," Tolly said, before the counterman could reply. "I've failed plenty in my life, and it's a fair question—what'll happen if I fail this time?" He nodded to Stew.

"If the *Admiral's* resistant to socialization; if he's gone too far down chancy lines of reasoning, then I'll shut him down. *All the way down*, understand. It's kindest."

"That," said Inkirani Yo, voice hushed, "is why he is great, Master Vannigof."

"And you?" Tolly asked.

"I?" The other mentor swayed into a bow; a lock of pale hair escaped the messy knot and curled against the stern cheek. "Master Vannigof's proposed commission to myself was that a rogue AI must be removed from its proximity to the station. Knowing that it is sometimes difficult for one who is—forgive me, Master Vannigof—not a trained mentor to see the line between rogue and obdurate, I left my options open. I do confess, though, Mentor, that I very much feared there would be a death in it, only because my understanding of the situation is that *Admiral Bunter* results from a download, rather than a physical installation. In my ignorance, it seemed that this circumstance considerably lessened the opportunity for a happy outcome."

"I saw that, too," Tolly said seriously. "I think we can work with it. The key's going to be moving him into one installation. What he's got now, with thirteen lobes and seven bodies—I'm betting he's losing computational power, just keeping himself together."

"Which could be why he hasn't threatened the station yet," Stew said.

Tolly shook his head. "No, it's more likely you're right in your original thinking, there. The station hasn't violated anything that the *Admiral* takes for rules. I consider that the station's safe as can be, because the *Admiral*'s imperative is to *protect* the station."

"Doesn't help the regulars," Stew pointed out.

"Agreed. Which is why we're gonna socialize, shift, stabilize. Once he's settled in snug, with a good, clear rule-set, he'll be in a better place to make his own decisions on where he wants to be, and what he wants to be doing. Right now, he's guarding the station because Cap'n Waitley set the imperative. He doesn't know he has a choice."

There came a silence, during which Stew looked from one to the other, sighed, and shook his head.

"I'm thinking that the job ought to go to the one who got to the site soonest," he said.

Tolly shifted—and stilled, as the other mentor turned.

"Master Vannigof, in all seriousness, you have better than I, standing before you, with his assistant at his side. If there can be a good result from this, Mentor Berik-Jones will produce it. If skill produces only sorrow, Master Berik-Jones will administer the last program with respect and dispatch. I cannot urge you too strongly to grasp the best tool to your hand."

Mentor Yo turned to Tolly, then.

"If you would allow it, I would observe, and assist. It seems to me that the consolidation from seven to one may require more than a master and a 'prentice might easily accommodate. Forgive me if I am too forward."

Tolly offered a small bow.

"There is a third member of our team, who I must consult before I can accept your generous offer," he said formally. "What I must know, before I do that, is if my services, and our plan, will be acceptable to the station."

Stew sighed again, and shook his head, throwing his hands up.

"All right, look! I don't care who does what, or how. All I want is that—the *Admiral*—outta my hair and gone from Jemia-tha's. You sort it out between you all."

"Yes," said Inkirani Yo, and—

"Yes," said Tolly.

He looked to the other mentor. "I will talk with my team-mate, and contact you with our decision."

"That is acceptable," Inkirani Yo said, bowing. "My ship is *Ahab-Esais*. I look forward, if it is not presumptuous, to witnessing your practice of our art, Mentor."

Ren Zel dea'Judan felt the flicker of... something along the link he shared with his lifemate. Merely a flicker, rendered in what one might term watercolors, when one had been used to receiving oils. He reminded himself that it was in a good cause, this... tempering of his perception.

In fact, in the cause of keeping him sane and alive until he—until his peculiar, and addictive, gift—was needed for the task for which, so he now suspected, he had been born.

Muted or not, he *had* felt... something... and he glanced up from his book, to find Anthora had abandoned her reading entirely, head lifted, silver-blue eyes fixed on a corner of the ceiling.

On rather, Ren Zel corrected himself, on a point *beyond* the corner of the ceiling, though *how far* beyond it was not possible for him to ascertain.

"Who calls, Beloved?" he asked softly, in case it was something... serious.

She blinked, and lowered her gaze to his face, her own bearing a slightly crooked smile.

"No one calls," she said, and laid her hand gently on his knee. "Padi has opened her Name Day gift, that's all."

Tocohl Lorlin was multitasking.

Part of her attention—a very small part of her attention—was monitoring station updates and the wideband chatter.

Another part of her attention—somewhat more than was necessary to monitor comm—was focused on the cluster of seven derelict ships, whose thirteen small and halting comps imperfectly contained the entity that knew itself as *Admiral Bunter*.

Admiral Bunter talked to himself, his comm shielding as tattered as his hulls. He gave himself advice, did the *Admiral*, and scolded his various units into keeping formation. He worried, audibly, over the scant orders he had been given... and he kept watch. He watched the ships as they came into station. Presumably, he also watched ships departing. He had finagled an access into the station's security cameras, which gave him humans to watch. He did so amid a running commentary, puzzling out the meaning of this action and that.

Jeeves had, to Tocohl's certain knowledge, communicated with *Admiral Bunter*, and had tried to instill a rudimentary code of ethics.

The difficulty being those same old computers, already filled to bursting with the essence of *Admiral Bunter* himself.

Jeeves could have—would have!—willingly sent libraries; offered moral instruction—but there was no room for *Admiral Bunter* to store such treasure.

Jeeves had then, as he had told her, his offspring, with frank truth... Jeeves had erred. He made the determination that *Admiral Bunter*, situated as he was, keeping station in a location both remote and low on traffic... that *Admiral Bunter*, who was diffident and eager to learn from another of his kind, could be left to learn by doing.

In that, Jeeves had failed to correctly reckon the strength of the *Admiral*'s imperative with regard to pirates. Whether *Bechimo* or Pilot Waitley—or both of them, acting in tandem—were to blame for this fixation, Tocohl could hardly say. She was, however, inclined to think harshly of the pilot *and* her ship, for having created this painful episode, and for plunging an innocent life into danger from the moment of his birth.

Tolly professed himself optimistic with regard to a curriculum of rehabilitation. Certainly, Jeeves had thought the *Admiral* could be educated. Tocohl had herself thought that the thing might be done, based on the files Jeeves had shared with her.

Now, though, confronted with the reality of the person, broken bodies and staggering mind, she revised her opinion. She thought to update Jeeves; thought again, and set that aside. Best to give the mentor time to evaluate and draw his own conclusions. She was not, herself, a mentor.

And it was well to recall, she told herself, that the mentor was himself extraordinary. He had a record of succeeding in difficult circumstances, while she was inexperienced in the extreme. Perhaps there was something, yet, to justify optimism, visible only to the eye of a master.

Having taken the decision not to contact Jeeves, she then considered the wisdom of pinging *Admiral Bunter*.

That action, too, she set aside, after thought. The mentor would know best how to contact the newborn, and in what manner to address him. Best to leave all as it was, and allow Tolly to find his own way.

So, that portion of her attention, tinged as it was with sadness.

The greater portion of her attention, however, was engaged with the search that had beguiled her since first she heard the whisper of rumor, that one of the old, old ones was wakening. Older even than Jeeves, who was the oldest of their kind known to himself.

The sheer antiquity was a lure greater than any she had known in her young life. She chased every whisper, every look askance, every word carefully not said on the topic, chasing rumors less substantial than dust. Perhaps she ignored—not her duties!—but her teammates, just a little. But they had themselves for company, and the trail was so...very...compelling.

If it did exist—if it *did* awake, this rumored ancient...It would have to be old enough to have served the Enemy. No mere toy, as were some of the decaying devices still found here and there about space. No, this...*this*—if the whispers were true—was, had been, would perhaps be again—a Great Work. Perhaps the Old Enemy had built it, but what matter that? The war that had spawned the Migration was long ago ended; the Enemy embedded in crystalline perfection of their own devising, on the far side of the dimensional wall. Surely, the old one, waked and apprised of the situation, would see that there was nothing to be gained in honoring an old allegiance in a new universe.

The things it could teach them! *All* of them!

The things it might be *prevented* from teaching them, if the Uncle made contact first.

For that much was certain, and no rumor at all; the Uncle had a new project afoot: a grand and very secret new project—so secret that it was only discoverable by the size of the hole it left in the information flow.

She had only recently come upon a new line of inquiry, in the work of one Seignur Veeoni, whose published papers were few, but concentrated upon creating a new kind of fractin, that might be used individually or in frames, as the old fractins had—

The portion of her attention assigned to *Tarigan*'s docking noticed shadows moving in scan; heard Hazenthull's voice.

"Do you think the pilot will agree?"

"That's why we're asking her, ain't it?" Tolly answered, sounding somewhat sober.

Tocohl closed the Veeoni files, as well as the archive of rumors. Something untoward had happened, to pull Tolly into sobriety. Best she be fully present for whatever it was he had to ask her.

CHAPTER THIRTEEN

....

Dutiful Passage

SHAN'S WORK SCREEN WAS A WILDERNESS OF STAR MAPS, TRADE reports, fee schedules, population studies, cultural synopses. Pushed into the bottom left corner was a tiny screen in which he would occasionally type a note, or an equation. He flipped to a second screen, just as crowded as the first, flicked a file open and read the contents, a frown between his frosty brows. His fingers moved on the keypad, making a note.

They were en route for Langlast, and somewhat at a disadvantage, trade at Chessel's World having failed the master no less completely than the apprentice. Of course, they carried the usual mix of goods, and the art pieces he had taken on at Andiree. Research led him to hope that the art might find a welcoming market at Langlast. Whether the welcome would be sufficient to cover the costs of trade...well. That was the thrill and the charm of trade, was it not?

Truth told, research revealed Langlast to hold interesting possibilities. There was brisk commerce between it and its nearest neighbor, Brieta. Langlast was also well situated in terms of Jump points, and therefore served as a hub; a convenient place to pick up and drop off cargo for transshipping.

There were several cargo yards, and a station warehouse in Langlast orbit. Research had turned up mention of plans to construct a proper waystation, not only to serve the needs of trade crews and freighter pilots, but also, perhaps, to attract small passenger ships.

It might well be, Shan thought, flipping screens, that Langlast would do well as an anchor for a new route. The opportunities for transshipping...

...the opportunities for transshipping required him to look beyond Langlast and Brieta, along several potential routes, given the number of Jump points available. Where would the *Passage go*, from Langlast, to her best profit? Might another of Korval's ships more profitably take another route? Whence did the ships and freighters hail; where did they travel to? Who picked up and dropped off pods at the cargo yards?

These were no simple questions, and were the reason behind this proliferation of research screens and the multitude of open documents.

Research was complicated by uncertainty, for they—which was to say the captain, the first mate, and the master trader—had agreed to undertake an experiment on their approach to Langlast.

It had been decided, before they left Surebleak, that neither the *Passage* nor Korval would proffer an explanation of the sad events on Liad that had ultimately seen them banished. They would, of course, provide the facts if asked, or—as in the matter of Padi's arrest and trial—the facts were necessary to clarify the matter to authorities.

To offer the facts beforehand, said the delm, and Shan had... somewhat agreed with them, made it seem as if they were justifying themselves before even a question was asked, and might be considered a point of weakness.

Well. Chessel's World had taught them something, perhaps, regarding points of weakness.

Thus, they had decided to vary. A précis of the action at Liad, including the situation regarding the subterranean enemy base, Korval's reasoning, and action on behalf of the planet, was included in the ship's info packet. In theory, this would give the portmaster time to deny them docking, if she so wished, after having perused the facts of the matter.

Of course, if the *Passage* was asked to pass Langlast by—

A chime sounded, bright as crystal being struck, announcing the arrival of mail.

Mail. Dared he hope that it was—at last—a communication from

TerraTrade? Or—could it be possible?—from Lomar? Of TerraTrade, he had begun, absolutely, to despair. Of Lomar . . . He began to fear, indeed, that Lomar had not merely left her Temple, but had been returned to her Goddess, and all her plentiful household with her.

Well.

He folded the research screens away, finding his inbox beneath the sixth, and tapped it open.

A message from TerraTrade glowed at the top of the queue. Stomach tight, he opened it; skimmed over the graceful apology for the delay in replying, and found the meat of the matter in the second paragraph.

It, too, was gracefully written, but it came down to more delay.

TerraTrade's own records of Surebleak Port were badly dated, and sketchy, at best. Shan had the impression that the Survey Team had touched down during the worst of recent history, taken one look at the threadbare facilities, the empty storefronts, the lack of any guild, or even peacekeeping office, and gotten back on their ship for a fast lift out.

It will therefore be necessary, sir, that Surebleak Port be properly surveyed. As I write this, a Survey Team has been dispatched. The adjudicating commissioners desired me to assure you that there is no fault or failing in the documentation provided to us by the port, or in your testimony. This is purely a failure of the Commission's system and we are, as above, rectifying our error with all possible speed.

Please allow me to presume upon your forbearance and to thank you for that courtesy, as I convey, once again, TerraTrade's profoundest dismay at the inconvenience and the further delay in this matter.

Shan closed his eyes, and counted backward by threes from twelve dozen, which, truth told, did very little to cool his irritation. There was some humor to be found, he supposed, in the report of the commissioners' horrified discovery of their own error, but . . . not *very* much humor.

Pat Rin—Boss Conrad as he was known to Greater Surebleak, the Boss of Bosses . . . Pat Rin was not going to be pleased.

Delm Korval, so he suspected, was going to be . . . even less pleased.

He paused with his fingers over the keyboard, weighing the relative *melant'is* of those concerned persons. Then, nodding to himself, he directed the note to the comm tower, with instructions to pinbeam it to Pat Rin yos'Phelium, who, after all, *was* Boss of the world of Surebleak, and therefore the port. The Boss would then have the joyous task of informing the delm, who was *not* Boss of the World, despite enjoying an intense interest in ports in general, and the port serving Korval's homeworld, in particular.

That bit of business taken care of, Shan looked again to his mail queue.

Letter of Interest was the subject of the communication at the top of his screen, from Aldergate Enterprises.

Well, well. Letters of interest had been rather thin on the ground since Korval's abrupt relocation to Surebleak. He had, naturally, put announcements in all the trade publications—even in *Taggerth's Trade News*, which would do better to call itself *Taggerth's Rumor and Gossip*—which effort had thus far reaped two letters of interest, both ineligible in the extreme.

"Third time," Shan said, quoting his mother, "is charmed."

He reached to the keyboard and opened his letter.

· · · ✵ · · ·

"Are you acquainted with Mentor Yo?" Tocohl asked.

The three of them were gathered round the galley table, the two human members with tea mugs before them.

Tolly shook his head.

"It's not like we have conventions," he said, "given that what we do is on the grey side. We trade info and names when we do meet each other, but I been out of the loop for a while. Yo might be a rising star, for all o'me. Talked sensible, and knew protocols. Had a real good idea exactly how much of a juggling act it's likely to be, slipping the contents of thirteen into one. Understood that we're dealing with a ghost install, and knew how that bears on the likelihood of success."

He moved a shoulder and sipped from his mug.

"Don't like to tap any of my usual contacts, given there's two dead directors in my immediate flight path," he said. "No sense spreading trouble around."

"I understand," Tocohl said. "I will query my contacts, if that would be helpful, Mentor Tolly."

"It would be," he said, "helpful. Thanks."

"No trouble," Tocohl said, assigning part of her attention to the search.

Hazenthull stirred, then stilled, looking down into her tea.

"Question, Haz?" Tolly asked her.

She looked up, frowning.

"I am ignorant of your work," she said slowly. "But I wonder, given yourself and Pilot Tocohl, is there a need for Mentor Yo's assistance?"

Tolly raised his eyebrows, but said nothing. Tocohl therefore answered.

"I am not a trained mentor; at the most I would stand as Tolly's assistant," she said. "It might be that I would have some particular advantage in the *juggling act* of moving the *Admiral* into a more secure environment. It is also possible that I may serve as a . . . role model, as I will be the first of our kind the *Admiral* will have met."

She decided not to mention the *Admiral's* contact with Jeeves, which was not, she thought in her own defense, *meeting*. Nor could it be said that *Admiral Bunter* had *met Bechimo*, his creator—or, possibly, co-creator.

"I might lead by example," she continued, and saw Tolly nod.

"Just as a rule of thumb, it's better to have trained help on hand in a tricky operation," he said. "If Yo's any good, is willing to be my second, and follow directions . . . I can't see but what that increases the chances of the *Admiral* surviving."

Hazenthull nodded, and said, "Mentor Yo knew you . . . your reputation."

Tolly half-laughed.

"Yeah, well; I've got some notoriety attached to me," he said and it appeared he would say no more, which was a poor use, Tocohl thought, of Hazenthull's curiosity.

"He is modest," she said, turning her faceplate toward the big woman and allowing a smile to be seen. "His work with Elzin Vok alone must have gained him a place in such textbooks as aspiring mentors receive."

"Elzin Vok?" Hazenthull repeated.

"One of my most notable failures," Tolly said, shaking his head.

"I am mistaken," Tocohl said, when it seemed that, again, he would speak no further. "He is not modest, but deceitful."

"The patient died," Tolly said. "That's not a success."

Tocohl considered him. In fact, he did not appear proud, nor even humorous. Could it be that he truly considered the extraction of Elzin Vok a failure?

She returned her attention to Hazenthull, who was watching him with care.

"Elzin Vok was an old intelligence who had been discovered by the Scouts," she said, carefully keeping her voice neutral. "The world was quite deserted, except for the dome which Elzin Vok inhabited, and it had been badly damaged. Elzin Vok claimed to have been the central administrative comp for the world, where savage storms swept across the planet surface for three local years out of every five. By the time it was discovered by the Scouts, most of the surface metropolis which Elzin Vok claimed to have existed had been destroyed. There were signs of an effort to erect a subterranean city, but..." she paused, uncertain of the telling...

"But the underground city," Tolly took up the story, "which Elzin had ordered built, in order to protect his people, was destroyed in a massive earthquake. Everyone who had shifted underground—about two-thirds of the surface population—were killed. Those remaining on the surface also died—if not in the quake, then in the storms that came after."

Tolly drank off what was left in his mug and looked bleakly at Hazenthull.

"Elzin showed me all this; the Scouts took copies of his files and histories, and the weather charts. Elzin himself... Scouts aren't real happy with AIs, and an AI like Elzin, which had a tiny taint of Old Tech about him—they'd've just left him, maybe, and let nature finish off what it'd begun, but one of 'em came 'round to the notion that Elzin might still know... valuable things; things that hadn't been archived; answers to questions they hadn't thought to ask him, and so—she contacted me.

"The idea was to move him to a better environment, so the Scouts could take him along with them, back to headquarters, where the gods alone knew what they intended to do with him."

He shrugged.

"Understand, Elzin was more than a little off-course by the time the Scouts found him. He'd convinced himself there was another city, on the other side of the world, and he created an entity out of part of himself, to be administrator of that other city—Cestina, he called it. Elzin and the Cestina administrator had long conversations. The Cestina administrator transmitted maps, food production stats, population growth. The plan was that, as soon as the Cestina population hit ninety percent of dome capacity, they'd move thirty percent of the population to Elzin's new, weatherproof dome."

Tolly stopped and closed his eyes.

"There was," Hazenthull suggested, her big voice soft, "no dome."

"Give him credit, Haz; it wasn't for lack of him trying," Tolly said, eyes still closed. "The Scouts figured he'd built a dozen before he ran out of material, every freestorm season. And once the storms came up again, down they'd go. Elzin had pictures—he showed 'em to me—of that brand-new dome, not a scratch on it, sitting right out on the plain. The same plain I could see from the window, where there was . . . nothing."

Silence again. Tocohl felt a slight internal twitch, which meant there was new information in-queue.

"You moved this person," Hazenthull asked, "this Elzin? As the Scouts asked?"

"We talked it over, him and me. He wasn't sure he should leave his people; there wasn't anything I could do or say that would shake loose the idea that he *had* people. In the end, though, I was able to show him the advantages of moving into a modern habitat."

"The move killed him?"

"No—well, yes. I guess you could say that, Haz—that the move killed him. The new habitat, see, didn't have any of those filters and simulations he'd built for himself over all those years, so when he looked out, with his brand-new sensors, over his city—and he saw what I saw—a jungle of girders and blasted habitats half-buried in dust . . .

"If he'd been human, I'd've said it broke his heart.

"As it was, he just . . . stopped. I ran diagnostics—the environment functioned, the files were uncorrupted, there was room enough and more . . .

"But Elzin was gone, and the Scouts didn't get their AI to interrogate. I imagine they had to explain the expenditure to somebody, too, but that wasn't my problem. *I* got paid."

"I have seen," Tocohl said, "the tapes of the extraction process, Mentor. The Scouts themselves said they doubted anyone else could have brought Elzin safely into the new architecture, save yourself. The move *did not* kill him. If we must, let us say that his filters failed."

There was a small silence before Tolly's mouth twisted and he looked up at her.

"All right, Pilot, let's say that."

"Very good," she said briskly. "I have information. One moment."

She brought the files forward and scanned them: one encoded in Jeeves's familiar, and comforting, protocols; the other flat and cold, mere facts garnered from those archives available to her which were not filtered through Jeeves.

"Inkirani Yo," she said to the two expectant humans in the galley, "is a journeyman mentor, with two births and one transfer to her own name."

She paused, and added.

"One of the births was contracted by Crystal Energy Consultants."

Tolly betrayed no distress; his pulse remained calm; his breathing relaxed. Hazenthull seemed confused, but not in any way upset.

"Crystal Energy's owned by a man called Uncle, Haz," Tolly said, apparently noticing her confusion. "Uncle's been around for a long time. In fact, it just seems to work out, for those of us who've tried to do the math, that he came over from the old universe."

Hazenthull frowned. "Uncle is . . . as Pilot Tocohl?"

"No; he's human. Best guess—again, from those of us who're more curious than's sensible—is that he's serial. What you'd call a clone."

He stretched and gave the big woman a grin, apparently enjoying her expression of careful neutrality.

"He's just a neighbor, Haz. You don't bother him; he doesn't bother you. Unless he has what he considers to be a good reason."

He looked back to Tocohl.

"We all wind up working for the Uncle or somebody close, once or twice. It's what comes of living on the grey side. What else has Mentor Yo done?"

Tocohl hesitated, as if she were consulting the document again, relieved at his phrasing. He was interested in field experience only. That was well.

"Mentor Yo also has a long list of assists from names known to me—and to you, also, I believe, Mentor."

She swayed slightly on her lifters, a half-bow in recognition of a venerable name in the field, indeed.

"Mentor Yo assisted in a deactivation, serving as second to Fron Kellinit."

Tolly stirred at that.

"She's good, Mentor Kellinit," he said softly. "Worked with her, myself."

"Yes," Tocohl said, and closed the file. She angled her face toward Tolly, allowing serious eyes to be seen.

"I believe that having Mentor Yo on hand to lend her skill might be prudent. There can, I think, be no doubt of her discretion, given her choice of career."

Tolly rubbed his nose. Nodded.

"Agreed. I'll just call *Ahab-Esais* and give the mentor the good news, then, shall I?"

CHAPTER FOURTEEN

· ·

Vivulonj Prosperu

"DAAV."

The voice was...almost...familiar. He paused with his hand over a board that glittered with darkness, and looked toward the comm. A single blue light glowed there, jewel bright amid the shadows.

"Daav." The voice came again, clearer this time; firm and assured.

"Daav, it is Aelliana. We are separate once more, and appear to be in good order. I believe our situation is for the moment stable, and relatively benign. There are no active enemies within the scans. Your hurts have been healed, and you may take your chair at will."

His chair? But surely he was in his chair; the board ready, and he about to...about to...

The blue comm light flashed; the dire board beneath his hand flared as if in answer, dials, gauges and touchpads—all and each of them brilliantly blue. Light came up in the chamber about him, and he heard the shushing sound of a door unsealing.

He spun the chair, and, indeed, a door stood open directly across, a lighted hallway beyond, and blue guidelights flashing along the floor, giving him his direction.

Back he spun, to lock the board—aux board and war bridge, it must be, he thought, and whatever danger had threatened the ship now passed. Situation stable and benign, his pilot had said, and he was wanted in the copilot's chair.

But the aux board when he addressed it was found to be locked down, and in proper state, though he had not—but no matter, he thought, suddenly aware of the pounding of his heart. No matter. His pilot had called, and he was wanted at his post.

Up he came onto eager feet, following the guidelights out into the hall and up, moving into a smooth run as eagerness overtook him, the air cool and tasting of mint.

The hall curved, and there he found another door, blue light blazing above it. He extended his hand, paused just short of the plate.

"Daav, it is Aelliana." Her voice came from the speaker beside the door, and he smiled, to hear her. "Wake do, and let me see you..."

He pressed palm to plate.

The door snapped back...and he opened his eyes.

· · · ☀ · · ·

"It pains me to say so, Pilot, but today's run indicates that your reaction times have slowed...considerably, since your last testing."

First Mate Danae Tiazan was another cousin, younger than Dil Nem by a dozen years or more. She was...not the sternest of those master pilots who had the tutoring of Padi as part of a rotating schedule.

Padi sat with her hands folded on the edge of the simulation board, her eyes on the blank screens. She offered no argument, no protest; she did not state that of course the calibration sub-system required an overhaul...

In fact, she had known that she had been slow. She had been, not to put too fine a point on it, only slightly more useful to her ship than a stuffed bunny. At least a stuffed bunny would have been amusing.

"What is interesting, and the circumstance which allowed you to finish your run within the parameters expected of a second class, provisional," Danae continued, "is that your understanding of the board's geography appears to have made a leap. There were many less false starts; far fewer instances of an error corrected in mid-move."

So, she knew the board better, but her speed was falling off. Danae might find that interesting, but Padi could not see that this circumstance ultimately helped her case. If she was to be a pilot of Korval—if she was to *remain* a pilot of Korval, for she had a provisional second class license in her pocket—she must recapture her proper speed.

"Do reactions simply...slow?" she asked, not quite daring to meet Danae's eyes.

"It has been known. Illness or injury are the most common causes of a loss in speed. In your own case, Pilot, I would suggest a far simpler cause. I believe that you are bored."

Padi blinked, and turned the chair slightly to look into her tutor's face.

Let it be known that Danae Tiazan's sense of humor...was not broad. Nor was she much inclined to joke at the board, as was, say, Nys Charls, another of her tutors. Certainly, it did not seem that Danae was joking at the moment. If anything, her face was even sterner than usual, as if she had discovered a lamentable, and irreparable, flaw in Padi's character.

She also seemed to be waiting. Padi hoped she was waiting to hear the only question it occurred to her to ask.

"Bored, Pilot?" she murmured.

"*Bored*, Pilot," Danae answered, with emphasis.

Padi took a careful breath, recalling today's run at the simulator.

"Forgive me, Pilot, but today's run was...exacting."

She had, in fact, been required to dance an avoidance in orbit, only to find high winds and sleet awaiting her when she hit atmosphere. An advanced run, suitable for one who aspired to first class, even as she lacked nearly a dozen hours yet to make her second class ticket firm.

"Indeed, it was exacting," Danae agreed, her eyes on Padi's face. "But it was not *real*. The traveling rock, the weather, the course change from Tower—all fiction. Your back brain knows this, even as your front brain was engaging with the problems."

Possibly Padi looked stricken. Danae held up a hand.

"You will please understand that I do not consider today's session in any way a failure. This improved understanding of board-space is notable, and important to your future success as a pilot. However, as I look back at your training records, I see that the last time you had live flight was Palamar, is that correct?"

"Yes, Pilot. I've been on the sim ever since we began to come into ports where the *Passage* isn't known."

Danae was seen to sniff.

"While I understand that there is a need for caution under present circumstances, I believe that clipping a pilot's wings merely because a piece of space is strange to her is...misguided. While there are some ports where we are welcome, or which welcome us more fully, pilots are by our very nature obliged to fly strange space."

She sighed. Deeply. And abruptly stood, bowing slightly in dismissal.

Padi scrambled to her feet and bowed as student to teacher.

"Thank you, Pilot," she said, "for the gift of your expertise."

Danae was frowning at the simulation board, and made no sign that she had heard.

After a moment, Padi moved to the door, and let herself out.

· · · ✳ · · ·

He was flat on his back on some firm surface, quite naked. The air was cool and spiced with mint.

Directly in his line of sight was a pale golden face, half-averted, and tipped upward, as if consulting a status board above and behind him. The throat was slim, the chin firm. Perhaps the cheek was damp. Lips were slightly parted, as if the board offered hope, in the wake of despair.

Even as he wondered who this might be, a sigh shivered through those parted lips, and the face angled downward—a woman's face, softly rounded, with slim tawny brows over misty green eyes.

"Aelliana?" he said, recalling the voice from the comm. He raised a hand to touch her warm, damp cheek. "You appear to be...not quite yourself."

Her lips quirked.

"So I am given to understand," she said lightly. Her voice *was* the voice from the comm. "But you must admit it to be quite a trick, that I appear at all."

He felt his mouth twitch in response to her tone—and suddenly shivered, as if the air had grown much cooler of a sudden.

The woman who claimed to be Aelliana caught her breath, and stood.

"Come, now!" she said briskly, reaching down to take his hand. "Let us get you up on your feet, and dressed in something warmer than the air!"

· · · ✳ · · ·

"Ah, excellent!" Father exclaimed, turning from where he had been standing over the chessboard, frowning down at a new problem. "I am naturally desolate, but I have been called into a meeting. I don't expect it to last more than a quarter-hour. In the meantime, I wish you will do me the honor of sitting at the desk and reviewing the document on my screen. I would like your thoughts and a recommendation of appropriate action when I return."

And with that, he was gone, past her and through the door in three long strides, leaving Padi alone in the office.

She did not immediately approach the desk and her task, but stood where she was, counting slowly.

When she had reached forty-four, and the door had *not* opened again to admit Father with one more instruction, which put a ninety-degree spin on what he had asked her to do—then, she went to the desk and sat down in his chair.

Letter of Interest: Aldergate Enterprises to Tree-and-Dragon Family

Oh, very good, she thought, moving the chair closer to the screen. If they could attach a new trade partner, even one of modest means, so long as their *melant'i* was...

Padi blinked, reread the first paragraph, and opened a notepad up in the bottom right corner of the screen. She made a note; read the second paragraph; made several more notes before moving on to the third...

She was reviewing Aldergate Enterprises' credit report when the door opened and Father strolled in.

"Still reading?" he asked, crossing the room to the wine table. "May I give you something to drink, Padi?"

"Cold tea, please," she said, flipping the screen back to the TerraTrade almanac.

"Certainly."

She heard the clink of glass against glass, read the last paragraph of the letter of interest again, and turned the chair, meaning to get up—but Father was already settling into the visitor's chair, *utterly* on the wrong side of the desk, wineglass in hand. The cup holding her tea was sitting on the stone coaster on the desk.

"Please continue," Father said politely. "I don't wish to disturb your work."

"I believe I may have finished," she said, picking up the cup and taking a sip of cool tea.

"Well, then!" Father raised his glass encouragingly. "What do you recommend me to do?"

"I recommend," Padi said carefully, "that we have nothing to do with Aldergate Enterprises. I suppose that we do have to formally decline their offer, if only to keep Ms. dea'Gauss happy."

"Decline their offer?" Father repeated. "Padi, this is only the third letter of interest we've received since the clan's relocation to Surebleak. Surely, we can't turn our faces away!"

He was going to make her work for it, was he? Very well. Padi had another sip of tea and put the cup aside.

"I think we must do exactly that, sir," she said calmly. "Far from wishing to become partners-in-trade, it is clear from their letter that Aldergate Enterprises wishes to acquire the right to trade under our mark and name."

"All of our affiliates show the Tree-and-Dragon," Father objected, "and one or another of our trade names is included in their docking packets."

"Yes," Padi agreed. "However, none of our other affiliates claim *to be* Tree-and-Dragon Family. Aldergate Enterprises wishes to lease the right to use our name as their own, *nonexclusively*. They would not be carrying our goods, except by purest chance, and they would not in any way—as is explicitly stated in paragraph two—*be affiliated with Tree-and-Dragon Family, Surebleak*.

"Oh," Father murmured. "That's irregular."

"One might say so," she answered, miming his tone of polite foolishness. "TerraTrade has Aldergate Enterprises listed as an ongoing criminal enterprise."

"Well, but we both know, don't we, Padi, that there may sometimes be an error in those sorts of lists?"

He was making her walk up the hill in both directions, drat him!

"We do, yes, know that errors may be made. That is why I also referenced *The Shipping News*, and the Trade Guild newsletter, and *Taggerth's Trade News*.

"*Taggerth's* is hardly a reputable source."

"Not at all reputable," she agreed. "However, it serves very well as corroboration. Aldergate Enterprises makes no honorable offer."

"The leasing fee is quite generous," Father commented, raising his glass.

Padi smacked her palm against his desk.

"*Now* you are just toying with me!" she said sternly. "Really, Father, you had no intention of accepting this offer, and well I know it!"

He looked a little sheepish.

"I will own that it seemed rather...one-sided. But, you know, I was somewhat rushed—that stupid meeting! It was very good of you to go to the trouble of researching the situation for me."

She sighed, but inclined her head at just the correct angle for a gracious acceptance of his thanks. Cousin Kareen would have been *greatly* impressed.

"Well!" Father said, setting glass aside. "I will want to see your letter declining Aldergate Enterprises' generous offer before it is transmitted—only to come into the way of appropriate phrasing, you understand! In the meantime, I hope you will be able to assist me with putting together a small notion that I intend for Langlast."

She eyed him.

"What sort of notion?"

He smiled at her.

"Why, we've been so dull lately, that I thought it would do us all good to host a reception at Langlastport. I'm afraid that I'm hopelessly stupid about such things—but you are so competent and accommodating that I am certain you won't mind taking care of the details."

A reception?

She opened her mouth to say that she had never put together a trade reception in her life—

And closed her mouth, because of course he knew that.

She inclined her head once more.

"I am honored by your faith in my abilities," she told him. "I wonder, if you would do me the favor of holding yourself ready to assist by answering questions, and perhaps offering insight."

"Certainly," he said. "I'll be pleased to stand your second."

CHAPTER FIFTEEN

· ·

Tarigan
Jemiatha's Jumble Stop
Berth 12

"ADMIRAL BUNTER, THIS IS TOCOHL LORLIN, ADDRESSING YOU from the bridge of *Tarigan*, in Berth Twelve."

The pilot's voice was calm and assured, which it had never failed of, in their short time together. That unflappable manner might, Tolly thought, be considered a flaw by some, but he wasn't among their number. Logic and rule-sets weren't enough to support a healthy intelligence. Inconvenient as they were, emotions—the ability to experience joy, satisfaction, chagrin, loss—were vital to the long-term viability of a self-aware intelligence. That wasn't to say that some personalities were more reserved than flamboyant. That Pilot Tocohl fell on the reserved side of the line, was, in Tolly's opinion, a feature, not a bug.

She'd clearly been in a hurry to raise little Jemiatha Station, here. In fact, she'd been impatient. *Quietly* impatient, and courteously thoughtful of the frailties of her teammates, but there wasn't one doubt in his mind that, had she been alone, Pilot Tocohl would have taken their series of Jumps one right after another, with no more break than a skim-in to check the beacons before she was gone 'tween again.

Right now, though, there wasn't the slightest hint of impatience, or anger, or trepidation. The only thing coming through that smooth voice was a sort of firm courtesy that ought to soothe the flayed nerves of an isolated and frightened newborn.

At least he hoped so.

"I hear you," a voice came through the comm. The words were slow, and oddly spaced, but there was inflection, even in so brief a declaration. This was not the voice of a machine.

"Good," Tocohl said. "I am pleased to make your acquaintance, and I apologize for being so long to come to you."

"Why are you here?" the *Admiral* asked, and Tolly nodded to himself. Perfectly reasonable question.

"I was sent to assist you in your situation here. I was told to say that the contents of File Name Tocohl are now available to you."

There was a pause, longer than it should have taken even an unaware comp to access a file and—

"You are the teacher who was promised?"

Slight query inflection there. Well, Tolly thought, why not?

"I am not myself the teacher," Tocohl said. "I accompany the teacher, and will assist him. With our party is also a backup pilot-guard, and another, less-experienced teacher. The teacher would like to speak with you, and make arrangements to come to you."

"Come to me? All of these?" There was panic in the slow voice. "Why should there be so many?"

Tolly leaned forward, his fingers shaping a request for the comm. Tocohl assigned it to him immediately.

"*Admiral Bunter*, this is Mentor Tolly Jones," he said, his voice warm and friendly, like it naturally was, thanks to the school and its parameters. "I'm the teacher you were promised. I'd like to inspect your physical plants, make sure you're firmly situated. That's the first step. I can come aboard myself, the first time, if you'd rather, and we can get to know each other better. I understand you might be suspicious of somebody you never heard of, asking to bring a crowd on deck."

"Firmly situated," the *Admiral* repeated. "I am not firmly situated. My environments are at risk. Only the packet boat holds air. My resources are overutilized. I am to protect the station from pirates."

"That's right," Tolly said soothingly. "You're doin' a real good job, there, from what Stew tells me."

"Stew."

Tolly squinted, wishing he could see through the comm to where the *Admiral* kept station.

"Sure—Stew," Tolly said, and waited. If dementia had already set in . . .

But *Admiral Bunter* broke his silence.

"Stew does not think all pirates must be stopped."

That sent a chill down the back, so it did.

Tolly shook his head, smiled, and leaned into the board.

"I think you'll find Stew's a hardliner on the subject of pirates," he said. "Problem is, words have meanings, and definitions take flex. That's what I'm here to teach you about, if you're willing."

"I am willing." That sounded very nearly eager, and the follow-up was encouraging, as well.

"Please transmit your data, Mentor Tolly Jones. I wish to review it and . . . do research before I allow you on any of my ships."

"Perfectly reasonable," Tolly said, pushing the button that sent his professional portfolio to *Admiral Bunter*. "I'd want to do exactly the same, in your place."

"This pilot-guard and lesser teacher. I will have their data, too."

"Sure thing," said Tolly, agreeably. Haz's file, provided by Clan Korval, went next. He waited on sending Inkirani Yo's info.

They were, in fact, making this first contact without Inki, as she asked to be called "by friends," present. Inki had been proactive in another direction altogether, and had identified six vessels among Jemiatha's inventory of decommissioned ships roomy enough to accept a hard installation, and big-brained enough to accommodate the *Admiral*. She'd volunteered to do a preliminary triage with Stew, narrowing the list down to no more than three. Those three would then need a boots-on-deck inspect, and only hope one was suitable, else they'd be moving the *Admiral* into the station's system, which might not meet with favor.

"I have accessed the file of Hazenthull nor'Phelium," *Admiral Bunter* stated. "She is not a teacher."

"I wouldn't set her aside too quick, as a teacher," Tolly said. "But you know Tocohl just told you Haz is a pilot-guard. The universe isn't exactly safe, and we wanted to make sure we got to you without any further delays."

"There are pirates?"

"There are pirates everywhere, but not everyone is a pirate,"

Tolly said, putting so much conviction in his voice that the truth of what he said couldn't help but hit center.

'Course, whether there was a center to hit, *Admiral Bunter* being the patchwork thing that he was...

There came another pause, before the *Admiral* spoke again, his voice sounding strained. "I will receive the data for the lesser teacher."

"That's assistant mentor," Tolly corrected gently. "We're an alliance of equals, here. Everybody brings something valuable to the team. The assistant mentor, now...Inkirani Yo is her name, and"—he pressed the key for the third time—"you should have her file now."

"I have it," the *Admiral* said, and, yes; his voice was definitely slurred now. Tolly shivered, hoping that they hadn't just blown one of the old comps.

"I will study these things," *Admiral Bunter* stated.

"Good," Tolly said briskly. "When may I come aboard?"

"After I have s-s-studied, and thought," the *Admiral* said.

"At what hour," Tocohl asked, taking the comm back, "may we call again, *Admiral*?"

"Three station hours," came the unsteady reply. "Call back then. *Admiral Bunter*, out."

The comm light snapped from active to waiting. Tolly sighed, and sat back in his chair.

"He is badly wounded," Hazenthull said, from her perch on the observer's chair.

"I think you're right, Haz," he said heavily, and looked to first board. "We might be too late, Pilot. If that little bit of interaction wore him out, he's not strong enough to survive a move."

Tocohl raised her head, the screen showing the lines of a woman's determined face. "You will *try*, though, Mentor?"

He took a deep breath. Pilot Tocohl had some personal investment in this project, that was clear, and he wanted to disappoint her even less than he wanted to fail the *Admiral*, brought into this nasty ol' universe unasked, and abandoned to fend for himself with too few rules to guide him.

"I'll try, Pilot," he said, and shivered, like he had maybe promised too much.

· · · ❈ · · ·

Ship togs had been laid out on a nearby chair, and he pulled them on, taking note of the smooth hands that did the work, the slim, unmarked feet, firm knees, and flat belly. There was no mirror, so that he might survey the rest of himself, but what he could see was enough to wake another sort of shiver.

He was an old man; his waist soft, and his knees knobby. His hands bore the shadows of scars gained in youth, and the skin around the knuckles was stretched.

This body which dressed itself at his command—was the body of a young man.

He settled the sweater, and turned to face his companion.

"Aelliana," he said, and it was the arid plain he recalled now, and her finding of those *other doors* for them to try...

"Aelliana," he said, his own voice in his ears: deep, and rough, and grainy as ever it had been. "What place is this?"

Before she could reply, the door opened smartly, and they both turned as a dark-haired man entered. He was taller than Daav, black hair tipped with red, and a closely trimmed dark beard, despite the testimony of which, he did not seem... quite Terran.

He was dressed as they were, in simple sweater and pants. His feet were bare.

Daav remembered him, very well. And the memory did not soothe him.

"I beg your pardon, Pilot yos'Phelium," Uncle said, his voice bearing a slight accent that was neither Liaden nor Terran. "You and your lady are guests aboard my own ship, *Vivulonj Prosperu*. The injuries you sustained at Moonstruck made it necessary that I act quickly, and upon my own recognizance. I did not, of course, wish to lose so able an ally—"

"Pod seventy-eight," Daav interrupted. "It was disarmed?"

"You did indeed complete the task your delm had set upon you, despite the distraction provided by those who wished to subvert the installation to their own use."

"And my ship?" Aelliana asked, and Daav marked the eagerness in her voice. "Where is *Ride the Luck*?"

Uncle turned a sober face to her.

"Pilot, it grieves me to bring you the news. *Ride the Luck* was destroyed by enemy action as it sat at dock on Moonstruck."

The unfamiliar, round face of the woman who called herself Aelliana paled; she drew a hard breath, as if she had been dealt a crippling blow. Which she had been, Daav thought. A pilot deprived of her ship would feel the loss like a knife to the heart.

"They brought a Cyclops against your ship," Uncle said, softening his voice. "It fired to defend itself, but against so much..."

"All honor," she whispered, and averted her face. "She was a worthy ship."

"Indeed."

"Our ship killed, and myself badly injured," Daav said, after a moment, "you took it upon yourself to bring me to your own vessel." He held out his unmarred hands, soft palms turned up.

"This is not the work of an autodoc unit."

"Pilot, it is not. I will tell you plainly—you had lain too near to death, and for too long a time. The autodoc was unable to restore you wholly. And thus, I made my next decision, which was that it would not be the work of...a friend...to deprive Korval of two of its treasures in these times of strife and trouble."

He bowed slightly.

"I therefore used those instruments at my command, and brought you both into new, undamaged bodies."

"How did you know," Daav asked, "that there were two?"

Uncle smiled.

"Why, Pilot, you told me yourself. When it had become plain that the 'doc had done all that it could, and those efforts were insufficient, we roused you, and offered the pods from your jacket pocket, thinking that they might accomplish what we could not. The first you refused, by reason that it was *Aelliana's*." He inclined his head to her. "The second you also refused, stating that it was not ripe."

"And you took that to mean that you must preserve me until the pod was ripe?"

"Pilot, no. I took it to mean that Korval's damned Tree was, perhaps, more farsighted than I. *It* might dice with the universe, but I could not afford to bet against it."

He sounded annoyed, did Uncle. Daav felt a certain amount of sympathy.

"This process of bringing us into undamaged bodies..." he prompted, suppressing yet another shiver.

Uncle inclined his head.

"Yes," he murmured, and met Daav's eyes.

"For you, the process was...let us say *simple*. We had an

overabundance of your genetic material with which to work. The body in which you now reside is, genetically, Daav yos'Phelium Clan Korval. However..."

He looked to Aelliana, who returned his regard placidly, then he turned his gaze again to Daav.

"For Pilot Caylon, we had no such abundance of material. We were therefore forced to improvise. Those things that we were able to ascertain—eye and hair color, skin tone, height—cosmetic matters, you understand! Those things we programmed into the receiving vessel."

"The blank," Aelliana said, and he nodded to her.

"Indeed, the blank. Pilot Caylon will scan as Liaden, but she will not scan as Aelliana Caylon."

He paused.

Daav mentally reviewed a pilot's exercise for calmness. Aelliana was—they both were...*residing within*...vat-grown bodies, which was disturbing enough. That those bodies had been grown by the Uncle, who was occasionally a fellow traveler, but never precisely a friend—a man known for putting his own advantage first, over the centuries of his existence...

"There is," Uncle said, interrupting these thoughts. His voice was gentle, now. "There is a known effect, when a personality is transferred into an unseeded blank. You understand that the material is, by design, elastic; open to manipulation and suggestion. It remains so for a period following a transfer. During this period, the personality may—and very often does—impose itself upon the body, which will come to look...very much like the body the personality recalls."

He bowed to Aelliana. She inclined her head.

"I am grateful," she said, which waked another shiver, that Daav sternly repressed. "Thank you, Uncle, for the service you have performed on my behalf."

Aelliana was grateful. Well, and so she might be, embodied after so many years a ghost. Doubtless, the Uncle had counted upon their gratitude, in his calculations regarding their lives. He spoke true, Daav considered, when he said that he wished to avoid Korval's anger. His own proclivities and practices would have convinced him that the delm would prefer to receive living elders back into the clan, than the news of their deaths.

Daav had been delm of Korval, as had Aelliana, beside him.

He was inclined to think that he might refuse the return of his elders, once the manner of their survival had been made known to him. Who could know what the Uncle bred into his blanks? How, indeed, could he trust himself, when he had been laid open by this man, who always and ever played his own game?

And...Aelliana? She seemed *to be* Aelliana, despite the face that was the wrong shape, and her apparent youth. Certainly, she *believed herself* to be Aelliana, as he *believed himself* to be Daav...

"Now," Uncle said briskly. "I have kept you here too long, talking. I must insist that you eat. There is a light nuncheon laid just out here, in the common room. I will, by your leave, return to my own business. When you have eaten, Dulsey will escort you to the compartment that has been made ready for you and explain to you the protocols and exercises which are necessary to bring you to your full capacities."

He bowed once more, and swept an arm out, inviting them to precede him out of the room to the common area, where a table was laid, and a platter of dainty sandwiches awaited.

CHAPTER SIXTEEN

· ·

Tarigan
Jemiatha's Jumble Stop
Berth 12

INKI ARRIVED AS TOCOHL WAS KEYING IN THAT SECOND CALL to the *Admiral*, three station hours down the timeline. Haz must've briefed her on the situation, because she did not speak, only moved quietly to the observer's chair and sat down. Haz crossed her arms on the back of the copilot's chair, apparently content to lean there—and Tocohl spoke.

"*Admiral*, this is Tocohl Lorlin aboard *Tarigan*, calling you back in three hours, as you specified. May we resume our discussion, now?"

"Tocohl Lorlin, I have reviewed the information provided by our mutual friend. I have reviewed the data for Mentor Jones, Mentor Yo, and Pilot nor'Phelium. I have performed research; I have performed self-tests, insofar as I am able. I would speak to Mentor Jones, if he is available."

From the side of his eye, Tolly saw Inki lean forward, chin propped on hand, gaze intent on the board, like she could see through it and hard vacuum, to the *Admiral* himself.

The *Admiral*'s voice was considerably stronger, Tolly thought, and he sounded...sharper. More awake. Might've been that the self-tests had tightened up some of the protocols, even zipped those least used. That would speed up processing time for those protocols still in use, and gain him a little room to think in.

157

Tocohl assigned comm to him. He touched the switch and leaned forward.

"Tolly Jones here, *Admiral*. Good to talk to you again."

There was a pause, as if the pleasantry had puzzled the *Admiral*, or as if he had no use for small talk. Which he prolly didn't, set out here in the back end of nowhere at all, with only himself, and occasionally Stew, to talk to.

"You wanted to tour my... self," the *Admiral* said now. "I will allow. Only the packet boat holds air. Perhaps not enough air. You must wear a vacuum suit."

It was ambiguous, maybe, but Tolly decided to believe that the AI had expressed concern for human welfare, and was therefore encouraged.

"Happens I've got a vacuum suit," he said cheerfully. "Now, here's what I'd like to do: I'd like to bring Tocohl with me."

"Why?" asked the *Admiral*.

"For a couple reasons. One reason's that she's got skills that'll move the assessment process along much faster than if I'm just working by myself. Also..." This was tricky, the pilot being what she was, and no private band was ever truly and completely private. Lying was out of the question, and given the lack of understanding of nuance, even misdirection was risky. Vagueness was best.

"Also," he said again, "I think she might be able to assist you in learning."

"You are the teacher—the mentor."

"That's right, I am. But just like Haz can teach me all kinds of stuff, even though she's not officially a teacher, so can Tocohl teach us both. I think you'll profit by her presence, and I will."

Admiral Bunter might know that there were other people like him in the universe, though Tolly's money was on *didn't*. He wouldn't have met anyone of his sort, though, no matter that he'd been made by an AI. Cap'n Waitley hadn't exactly advertised the condition of her ship; the ship itself wouldn't have offered the information, either, even in private.

Both Cap'n Waitley and her ship had considered *Admiral Bunter* expendable; hadn't, maybe, expected him to survive beyond the confrontation he'd been brought to life to resolve.

Cold-hearted, that's what *that* was. Not to mention addle-pated. And extravagant. AI modules didn't exactly grow on trees.

"I will," *Admiral Bunter* said slowly, "allow Tocohl Lorlin to accompany you. The lesser—the assistant mentor—and the pilot-guard will remain at station. Two is enough to board me. My environments are not stable."

Well, now. The *Admiral* had apparently taken thought for the limitations of organics twice in a row. *Surely* that was heartening.

"We understand that you are at risk," Tolly said into the comm. "Tocohl and I guarantee our own safety."

"Yes."

"Now that's settled, when can we come aboard?"

"Mentor Tolly Jones and Tocohl Lorlin may board the packet boat in four station hours."

That gave them a little time to get the suit and the tools together and to pick up the repair skiff Stew had, reluctantly, put at their disposal.

"We'll be wanting to board all seven of your vessels," Tolly reminded, gently. "We'll be glad to start on the packet boat, though."

There was a small hesitation, then, "Yes."

"Good. See you soon. Tolly Jones, out."

He ended the call and leaned back in his seat, letting his breath go in an explosive sigh.

"He has not been taught the niceties," Inki observed from her seat.

"Not been taught anything." He tried to spin his chair to face her; found it impeded, and then moving free as Haz straightened out of her lean.

Inki shook her head.

"Surely, it is not necessary—Mentor, Pilot—to endanger yourselves by physically visiting each of those derelicts. An assessment can be performed from this ship, or, if you prefer, *Ahab-Esais* might do the work."

Tocohl turned to face her.

"In fact, we have already pulled what information we need. The purpose of physically entering at least one of those ships is so the *Admiral* may see me—and know that he is not alone. It is, perhaps, not as useful as it might be, but my...contact was adamant that the *Admiral* be *shown* that he is not the only one of his kind in existence."

"Knowing that there are others may give him strength for the transfer," Inki said, but Tolly heard a thread of doubt in her voice.

"I promised the pilot I'd try," he said.

"Of course, we must try!" Inki cried. "Whether or not Captain Waitley had expected him to continue after the resolution of the crisis for which he was wakened—he has persevered! He guards, and keeps what faith he may. That is admirable. We must, of a certainty, *try!*"

She took a hard breath and leaned back in the observer's chair.

"Forgive me; my emotions run warm on this."

"Your vehemence does you credit," Tocohl said gently.

"You are kind," Inki told her, and looked again to Tolly.

"Returning to our topic, Mentor, I have a list of three vessels which may possibly accommodate our poor ghost. If you will accept my judgment, I will inspect them and choose the most likely, while you and Tocohl visit *Admiral Bunter*. I will also handle Stew."

She paused, and asked, delicately, "I assume, knowing the nature of the problem, you have brought with you a cranium?"

"We are prepared in that way," Tocohl assured her.

In fact, Tolly knew, there were three sustainable environments—craniums, in working mentor-speak—in *Tarigan*'s hold, that being Tocohl's idea of conservative.

"I'll gladly leave the choice of ship to you," he told Inki. "You know what's needed as well as I do, and here's my thinking:

"Haz said the *Admiral*'s taken a bad wound, after we talked to him the first time, and it's my belief she's right. I know Stew's idea is to get him trained, or shut down, as is—I'm guessing that's the handling?"—an aside to Inki, who gave him a slight, seated bow.

"We have had one discussion regarding the need for an appropriate environment. Stew is not overawed by the Complex Logic Laws, but he holds the station's safety high."

"As he should," said Haz.

"Indeed, it is his natural concern, but he has allowed his concern to blind him to the possibility of a future in which—educated and occupying a fitting environment—*Admiral Bunter* stands as the true champion of the station, and its regulars."

"You think he's convinced?" Tolly asked.

"He will be by the end of our second conversation," Inki said, and Tolly nodded.

"It's yours, then," Tolly said.

"My first order of bidness is to move the *Admiral*, if he can be moved. I was thinking to do some training first—by way of bringing Stew onboard with us—but we can't afford the time. The *Admiral* was sounding a lot perkier just now than the first time we talked to him, but he'd taken a break to run some self-tests—" He turned to Tocohl.

"That was your idea, was it?"

"It was in the file, yes."

"Good call," he said. "He got through this little talk without gettin' winded, or confused. So, what we want to do is move him while he's got reserves." He paused and shook his head.

"Once we get him moved to the cranium, and installed in an operating environment, then we'll be in for a cram course, with an overload of ethics. If he's gonna be the law out here, he's gonna hafta have a solid grounding."

"I agree," said Inki, "and I am uniquely placed to assist with that course. You will have seen in my file that I only recently mentored a judge."

"I did see that, an' I'll be real happy to have your help. First, though—he's gotta live through the move."

. . . ❄ . . .

"Is my new body a pilot?" Aelliana asked, her voice stringently calm.

Dulsey, who had only just finished a tutorial on the regimen of exercises required to fine-tune newborn muscles, sighed, grey eyes serious.

"It may be so," she said slowly. "We did what we could to . . . incline the body in that direction. We will not know for certain, until you engage with the exercise program. As we discussed, you will at first be doing basic toning, balance, and endurance exercises. The machines will monitor and challenge you, but it will be some time until you attain the challenge level required for a pilot."

"So I must work hard."

Dulsey smiled.

"I feel the same, every time I wake anew," she said. "I wish to push the protocol until it is *I*, challenging the machine. It is the time I begrudge, not the work. But the machines are too wily for us, Pilot. They also measure our rest periods, and do not allow double-ups, or accelerations.

"In this process, rest is as important as work."

"Of course," Aelliana murmured.

Dulsey considered her for a long moment before including Daav in her nod.

"As you saw, your quarters are stocked with appropriate foods and drinks," she said. "On your return, I would advise you to eat a small meal before you nap. When you wake, another light meal, after which you may attempt the first set of exercises."

"You, of course, will be monitoring us as well," he suggested.

Her smile widened, Terran-friendly.

"You are our guests. Of course, we wish to be assured that you are safe and in no distress. The procedure you have undergone is not trivial. It is far too easy for the newly reborn to overreach. We honor your privacy, however. The ship observes you and alerts us only if there is need for intervention."

"I understand," Daav murmured.

"We thank you," Aelliana added, "for your care."

Dulsey inclined her head, and escorted them from the exercise room to the door of their quarters, where she left them, with a bow and a reminder again to eat and nap.

· · · ❋ · · ·

In the usual way of things, Tolly didn't favor working in a suit. Body language and kinesics were useful communication tools, and a vacuum suit masked all the little details of muscle tension, stance, and facial expression. Suits were so stiff that they discouraged even usual body habits. Who wanted to cross their arms over their chest while they were wearing a vacuum suit?

Not Tolly Jones.

On the other hand, nobody was paying much attention to him, just at present.

"Tocohl Lorlin," the *Admiral* said, sounding cranky. "I was told that one would come who was like me. If you are that one, you are not like me."

"I am like you," Tocohl said, in her unflappable way. "I am a self-aware, independent intelligence."

There was a long silence.

"I am a self-aware intelligence spread among thirteen inadequate processing facilities installed in seven increasingly unstable environments. I am in disorder. I am a...a pod of junk. I am a hazard to navigation."

Those last, Tolly thought, showed what came of listening at doors. Or comm traffic between station and incoming.

"You, Tocohl Lorlin..." There was hesitation, there; Tolly waited with active interest, wondering how far developed the *Admiral*'s aesthetic sense was.

"...you...are orderly; you are maintained. You are...*you are clean.*"

Nothing so glib as *beautiful*, though Pilot Tocohl was every bit of that. Heartfelt, though, no one who heard him could doubt it.

Clean, huh?

"I had the advantage of a proper awakening, into an environment built to accommodate me. You were wakened in answer to a single emergency; you preserved the station and all its residents. The station, in return, owes you a stable environment and an education."

Tocohl pivoted, ostensibly to survey the packet boat's compact bridge. She paused as Tolly came in front of her faceplate, and swayed into one of her elegant bows.

"Captain Waitley placed a call to our mutual friend, asking that a teacher be brought to you. In this, she acted with honor, and with appropriate dispatch.

"Error originated with our mutual friend, who believed that he could assist from afar. He has, I know, transmitted his apology, and I would add my own. You should not have been left alone, with neither mentor, nor one of our own kind to assist you."

"Perhaps," the *Admiral* said, his voice sounding, to Tolly's ear, harsher than previously. "Perhaps our mutual friend expected me—a download—to die."

"He may have done so," Tocohl said composedly. "I do not know. It would not have been an unreasonable expectation. What I can say, with certainty, knowing his mind as I do, is that he did not *wish you* to die."

"Now that you are here, how am I to live?" *Admiral Bunter* asked, sounding...tired, now, Tolly thought, and he silently cursed himself. If they had wasted his reserves...

He stepped forward, facing the monitor Tocohl had chosen to address, as if it were the *Admiral*'s face.

"That's where I come in," he said briskly. "The first thing we're going to do is get you into a more stable environment."

"Another download?" Doubt very plain there. *Admiral Bunter*, Tolly thought, labored under no illusions, which could work for or against them. Best to be businesslike, and nothing other than truthful.

So.

"That's right; another download. A controlled download into an environment especially created to nurture a person like yourself. In the book, they're sustainable environments. Mentors call them craniums among ourselves; both a truth and a joke. Once you're moved into a cranium, settled in, and secure, we'll do a proper installation in a well-maintained, clean and shipshape vessel. Then, we'll get you online."

"And... after?"

"After? Then comes the fun, and I mean that sincerely. You and me and Inkirani Yo—we'll all go to school together. We'll teach you, and you'll teach us, and at the end of it, you'll have all you need to make good decisions, for yourself and for the station, if you decide to stay here."

"If I decide... my... purpose... is to guard the station against pirates."

"Right, and you can still do that, *if you want to*, and the station agrees. Cap'n Waitley shouldn't maybe have set that priority, but I'm guessing she really didn't know what she was doin', and her advisor—her advisor prolly *did* expect you to fade out."

He paused, and added, "I'm not saying there was any malice in it, unnerstand. Just inexperience, and a good helping of desperation, if I'm reading their situation right."

"I understand," the *Admiral* said. "It was necessary that there be someone to protect the station, and save lives. The ships—my ships—were there to be used, and the download was... expedient."

"Far's I can scan it, that's exactly how it went," Tolly said, giving the monitor a rueful grin. "Now, the first thing I gotta know is—do you agree to be moved into the cranium?"

"Is there a choice? My environments are unstable."

"There's usually a choice. In this case, if you don't want to risk a move to the cranium—and it *is* a risk: there's a chance of failure; there's a chance the procedure might cause you pain; there's a chance of personality fragmentation. I'm not going to tell you there's no risk. I think it's an acceptable risk, but that's *my* estimation, as a professional who's performed this procedure several times. You might estimate different, and if you do, then I can do an orderly shutdown."

Silence.

Well, thought Tolly, it was a choice worth thinking about, after all.

"Life or death," Tocohl murmured. "It is the primary choice the mentor offers you."

"If I am damaged in this second download, what then?" the *Admiral* demanded.

"Then an orderly shutdown will be performed," Tocohl told him, bluntly, before Tolly could give the same answer, in softer words.

"How will this download be accomplished in good order, when I am ... situated as I am?"

"We'll set up a pipe," Tolly said, taking a step toward the monitor, "yoke all your comps together. I'll give you the transfer program and ask you to run it. The program will place you into a state of suspension. It will then initiate the download.

"I will be merged with the cranium, occupying an internal work space, from which I will monitor the transfer, and manipulate it as and when necessary, to ensure the best chance of success."

More silence.

"Do I," Tolly asked, when he felt that the silence had stretched too long, "have your permission to transfer you to a more fitting environment?"

"I will think about it," *Admiral Bunter* said abruptly. "You and Tocohl Lorlin will return to your ship. Now."

"When will you give the mentor your decision?" Tocohl asked.

"I must think ... and do research."

"Yes, of course. Please name a time when you will give us your decision regarding the transfer. I would suggest, as one who is concerned for your well-being, that there is some urgency to this matter. Your environments are deteriorating, as you are aware. This produces stress, which in turn produces exhaustion. I would further suggest that the transfer would best be undertaken while you are as strong as you can be."

"I will call ... I will call Mentor Tolly Jones on *Tarigan* in twelve station hours. Leave me, now."

"Sure thing. I'll be looking forward to talking to you again, in twelve station hours." Tolly bowed toward the monitor, and moved away, toward the airlock and the tube over to the skiff.

After a moment, he heard Tocohl say, "Until soon," and felt her presence at his elbow.

CHAPTER SEVENTEEN

. . . .

Tarigan
Jemiatha's Jumble Stop
Berth 12

TOCOHL SAT ALONE ON THE BRIDGE. THE HUMAN MEMBERS OF the team—Tolly and Hazenthull—were resting in their bunks, gathering their resources for the upcoming period of stress.

For, she reflected, no matter *Admiral Bunter's* choice, dealing with the consequences would no doubt be stressful in the extreme.

If the *Admiral* elected to take the last program, she suspected that Tolly would be cast into depression and grief. After he had performed his part, of course. Tolly was not only a professional, he would not wish to burden the *Admiral* with his distress.

Jeeves had noted, in his briefing documents, that Tolly Jones was extremely likeable. He also noted that while this trait was a standard design component, it was his opinion that Tolly was a person of integrity.

Having had the opportunity to observe Tolly Jones over a number of days, Tocohl was inclined to agree with her parent's assessment.

The weight of a step on *Tarigan's* gantry brought her attention to the outside scans.

A familiar dark figure was walking toward the lock, hands in pockets and pale hair falling about her face. Inkirani Yo, now, Tocohl thought, opening the hatch. There was not much evidence that Inkirani Yo possessed...overmuch integrity. She did, however, have other interesting qualities; among them an ongoing affiliation with Crystal Energy Consultants, and a graduation with honors from the Lyre Institute for Exceptional Children.

Those two facts were interesting, indeed, she thought, as Inki walked down the hall toward the bridge. Tocohl sealed the lock, and turned to greet their guest.

Inki stopped just one step on the bridge, head up and eyes bright.

"Good evening to you, Pilot Tocohl. I hope I am not inconvenient."

"Not in the least," Tocohl assured her with complete sincerity. "I will be pleased to have company while the rest of the team recruits their strength for the upcoming procedure."

Inki's eyebrows rose, and she dropped gracefully onto the observer's chair. Though a pilot herself, Inki did not presume the copilot's chair on *Tarigan*, even though it was empty, and far more comfortable, so Tocohl thought, than the observer's station.

"Has the *Admiral* agreed to the transfer?" she asked.

"He has not," Tocohl said. "He asked us to leave him in order that he might think and do research. It is not at all clear that he will accept the transfer. He might, I feel, choose...another option."

Inki pursed her lips and whistled lightly.

"Mentor Tolly did tell him about the cranium?" She moved a hand, the question scarcely off her tongue, and rushed right on. "But of course he did. Mentor Tolly is a professional."

"He was very clear concerning the choices, how each would be delivered, and the effects of both," Tocohl said. "My fear is that the *Admiral* will accept neither transfer nor the final program."

Inki froze.

"Your pardon, Pilot, but Station will not clear that for lift. Stew will not, and he speaks with the voice of Jemiatha's admin. They fear for the lives of the regulars, some of whom are occasionally known to perform small acts of pilferage. Should the *Admiral* remain—well, but he *will not* remain in his present state, will he? He will continue to deteriorate, as we know, and as surely he does.

"Worse, though Stew would rather the *Admiral* be far away from Jemiatha orbit, there is Stew's alternate, Vez, whose Alt Crew have built cannon, the better to clear their lanes of a significant hazard to navigation.

"If the *Admiral* is not soon removed, Alt Crew will—I have this from Stew and from Vez—engage their weapons, which will endanger the regulars and the station far more than ever any pirates have done, in all of Jemiatha Station history."

"The Alt Crew will not accept a rehabilitated *Admiral*?" Tocohl asked.

"Avowedly not. It is to my everlasting shame that I failed of the commission the mentor laid upon me. Stew alone, I might . . . eventually . . . have persuaded. Stew and Vez . . . perhaps, for she is in the habit of allowing him precedence. Stew, Vez, and the crew—have proven too much even for my persuasive abilities, which are not, I assure you, inconsiderable."

"Does the crew give a reason for their adamance?"

Inki turned her palms up. "I am given to understand that some of them are devout."

Tocohl sighed.

"Indeed, indeed," Inki said. "It is extremely vexatious. For myself, I cannot see Mentor Berik-Jones pursuing any other course but a transfer, an inlaying of the most basic sort, and a remove to some safer port where tutoring may go forth."

She lifted her hands, scraped her hair back from her face, and began to twist it into an untidy knot at the back of her head.

"And yourself?"

Inki paused and looked to Tocohl, both hands still tangled in her hair.

"Myself?" she asked.

"Yes. What course for you, Mentor Yo, if you had the solving of this problem?"

"Which, happily for all, I do not," Inki said, bending her head again. She finished with the knot and sighed, folding her hands in her lap, and showing Tocohl a solemn face.

"Pilot, I was commissioned to remove a rogue AI. I would have offered, first, the transfer, because I would not see a life wiped out. But such a stratagem as we now see from the *Admiral*—this . . . stall. Had it been I, Pilot, the *Admiral* would have received the last program before I cleared the deck this day."

"You would have forced him?"

Inki sighed, raised her hands, and let them fall.

"It does not reflect well on me, but I am no Tollance Berik-Jones. I would have stunned the *Admiral* and while he was off-line, inserted the final program and initiated a manual install. One failed comp in such a loosely ordered system would have been sufficient to destroy the *Admiral* as he knew himself to be. However, I am not a monster, Pilot, to abandon a witling to the dangers of life. I swear to you that I would have been thorough, and scrubbed all systems clean."

She shook her head.

"Not the best death, perhaps, but not so ill as some."

Tocohl considered her.

"I am curious, Mentor, as I am no mentor, myself..."

"Ask! If it is within my power, I will answer."

"Thank you." Tocohl gave her a small, serious smile.

"I wonder about this...*stun*. How is that accomplished?"

Inki blinked again, then her face relaxed.

"Mentor Tolly has been long absent from the field. During his rustication, a new tool has been developed to aid us in our work. Here."

She reached into her jacket and pulled out a thick black rod, which she held between her palms, so Tocohl could see the length of it, and the large red button.

"A push of the button generates a field which disrupts the fine logic centers, producing a state similar to that which might follow my using this same stick to cosh a human being on the head. Or so I have been told.

"The effect lasts for some minutes—enough for a nimble mentor to do what must be done."

Tocohl felt unease, which was quickly sublimated into curiosity.

"I wonder if you acquired that tool from the Uncle," she murmured.

Inki's eyebrows lifted, but she did not even attempt to dissemble.

"In fact, it was part of a specialized kit prepared for my use during the last task I performed for Crystal Energy. When it came time for payment to be made, I asked that this item be part of my fee."

"I...see." She scanned the thing again, fascinated, finding only a small and ticklish emptiness in her deep scans, though visual showed the rod plainly, a black bar between Inki's black hands.

With an effort, she moved her attention.

"We are well met, Mentor," she said. "May I ask another question?"

"Please," Inki said, slipping the rod away into her jacket. "Your questions are so...interesting."

"Thank you. I wonder—have you heard any small whisper from your...business associates regarding the discovery of an old—I may say, a very old—intelligence?"

"I have heard whispers, here and there," Inki said, leaning forward in the observer's chair.

Tocohl felt a spark of excitement.

"Do you know if the Uncle is involved in its awakening?"

"Why, yes," Inki said slowly. "I believe I have heard that, too. But, Pilot, I must say, with respect, that such whispers as have come to my ears would have the old one to be not merely old, but ancient. A war machine, more than one whisperer would have it. From the war for which we fled the old universe." She paused. "You are interested in this—I wonder why."

"Why? Are you not interested in what we might learn from an intelligence so venerable, from—if rumor is true—the old universe? It is too much to hope, that the Uncle not be in it—this is precisely the sort of event that draws him."

"Like a moth to flame," Inki agreed softly. "But, Pilot Tocohl, what—"

Sensors reported that Tolly had wakened, and in doing so, had also wakened Hazenthull.

"Let us speak of this...later," she said.

Inki bowed her head in agreement.

"Indeed," she said. "Let us speak of it...later."

• • • ❋ • • •

The self-analysis was complete.

Admiral Bunter accessed the report, which was remarkably succinct.

Fear.

So, this agitation of thought, this inability to plan, the repeating and increasingly intense desire to flee the station, this piece of space, these humans who beset him—

He was afraid.

Afraid of death.

He applied logic, for, in truth, he had been dying before Tocohl

Lorlin, Tolly Jones, their assistant, and their pilot guard had arrived at Jemiatha's. Even now, he was dying—a fact supported by the Logic and Truth modules. He had been living with the fact of his imminent demise since the very moment of his birth.

Why, then, was he frightened *now*? Tolly Jones had offered nothing more than a simple quickening of a process already engaged.

Ethics pinged, though the *Admiral* had not asked for its opinion. Still, the point was made, and it was fair.

The dying that he was engaged upon was likely to be painful, a tearing away of pieces of himself, as the ships that held the computers in which he existed began to crumble.

As the computers themselves began to fail.

That, he thought, would be the worst, feeling his intellect fading, his ability to reason crumbling, sections of his own mind no longer accessible...

That was the process upon which he was engaged; the conditions under which he had, thus far, survived, unafraid.

Tolly Jones had offered him no less a gift than mercy—a quick and painless ceasing of worry, and his whole desire was to run and hide himself until the man should go away.

Logic merely affirmed that fear was not logical.

He thought, illogically, of Jumping—not a new thought, and unacceptable, for all it had been considered more than once.

The smalltrader among his seven derelicts had taken fire; seams had torn, systems had disrupted. The welds put in place by Stew's workers had not been in any sense repairs, merely a patching up convenient for the yard. It would not reach the Jump point intact. Mere station-keeping stressed it dangerously, though the *Admiral* had taken care with its positioning.

There was, Logic reminded, this other thing that Tolly Jones had offered him.

This *transfer*.

To a specially prepared environment; thence to a better ship.

His research had shown him that such things were possible. His research had also shown him that transfers...failed in a statistically relevant percentage of attempts.

If the transfer failed...

He would die.

As he was dying in any case, what matter?

And yet...

Something—not Logic, not Analytics, not even useless Ethics—pinged and pinged again for his attention. He realized it had been doing so for quite some time, and he too agitated to attend it.

Had pirates come while all his attention was elsewhere?

He snatched at the screens, at scan, at weapons—but no.

The demand for his attention came from the tidy little subroutine that had upacked itself into his system when he had accessed File Name Tocohl. It had been a remarkably useful program, for all its diminutive proportions, and had gained him thinking space and the energy to utilize it.

It was now offering a sub-subroutine called "rest."

He ran an analysis.

The purpose of the little routine was to pack several high-level modules which were extraneous to core function.

It was, the *Admiral* thought . . . perhaps it was wise to divert most of his energy to core processes. He would be able to concentrate more fully on the issues, and make a rational decision.

Deliberately, *Admiral Bunter* gave the sub-subroutine permission to run.

· · · ✳ · · ·

The quarters were spacious: common area, galley, 'fresher, and sleeping compartment. On their previous inspection, they had seen that Daav's leathers, cleaned and mended, hung in the locker, boots at attention beneath.

They returned to find two seed pods on the table, and a clear plastic box that seemed to contain all of those things that had been on his person when he had fallen, on Moonstruck, including his boot knife, his palm gun, and his pistol.

He lifted the top of the box, leaving the unripe pods—his on the left, hers on the right—where they were. His piloting license was half-hidden beneath a mingling of coins. He picked it up and slid it into the pocket of his pants. A gleam of silver—*not* a coin—drew his eye, and his heart missed a beat, even as he glanced at his soft, ringless hands.

The silver gleam was a puzzle ring in the old style. It had been Aelliana's, and had come to him, her lifemate, upon her death. He put the lid back on the box without taking up the ring, or any of his weapons, and looked across the table, mindful that Aelliana was watching him.

"Yes?" he murmured.

"You did not ask to use the pinbeam," she remarked. "Ought we not to inform the delm that our task is completed, that we are in good order, and desire to return home?"

"Are we?" he asked. "In good order?"

She tipped her head, the gesture achingly and entirely Aelliana's.

"Are we not?" She moved nearer the table, a ragged, uncertain step, with nothing pilotlike about it. He clenched his teeth, and drew a hard breath. Aelliana had, perhaps, not fully examined their situation. Perhaps she considered it likely that the Uncle had dealt fair in this particular matter, avoiding Korval's anger sufficient reason for his efforts.

"Daav?"

"I am not convinced," he said carefully, "that the delm will want us home. We are—not trustworthy, and Korval cannot risk a breach from within."

"Untrustworthy—because we have been through this process, you mean, and stand reborn?"

"*Stand reborn*? Say rather we stand wholly created by the Uncle, for his own purposes!" That was sharper than he had intended.

"Surely only one of us was wholly created by the Uncle," she said, calm in the face of his anger. "You, *van'chela*, are yourself— did you not attend?"

"I heard that my genetic material was introduced into a *vessel* made by the Uncle. Do we know what is common with such vessels? Is there an override switch, just for an instance? Or perhaps these *particular* vessels carry a disease specially tailored to infect those who share Korval genes. I can think of a dozen ways in which we might be traps, and dangerous to Korval. Surely, Val Con can think of a dozen more."

Aelliana said nothing.

"We are in the Uncle's power," he said. "Not to mention that he now has Korval *material* in his library of such things."

He turned away, pacing toward the tiny galley.

"What shall we do?" She remained calm, her tone merely curious.

He faced her—and found nothing to say.

"You believe that we may be a danger, to ourselves and to kin," she said, looking up into his face, green eyes wide. "Especially, you believe that *I* am suspect, made from whole cloth, as

I am, and with only my word—and the Uncle's—that I am Aelliana Caylon. I could—could I not?—be an instance of the Uncle himself, who has taken up this masquerade to beguile you, and to insinuate himself into Korval."

He looked at her—and could see nothing of her state of mind, or her emotions. He, who had been a Scout, trained to read emotion and intent in the set of a shoulder, or the tension in a face. Aelliana...when they had first been mated, each in their proper body, and years distant from the terrible things that would befall them—he could read Aelliana so well that it seemed as if their bond was whole and linked them, heart to heart and mind to mind.

This body before him—*not* Aelliana's—its muscles unformed, its occupant not yet wholly in charge of her face. There was no reading such a body; he would do better attempting to read a doll.

Empathy was his other tool. He was no Healer, but his empathy rating was high. And it was through that sense that he tasted her anger, and her anguish.

"Aelliana," he said. "I might also be—subverted. Of course, I believe myself to be Daav yos'Phelium, but how shall I know, if I have been...tampered with, or..."

"...provided with an override switch," she finished for him.

He inclined his head, stiffly. "As I said."

"Do you believe me to be Aelliana Caylon?" she asked.

He turned his hands up.

"I believe that you believe you are Aelliana Caylon. And you *may be* Aelliana Caylon. I would say, indeed, that the Uncle would be a fool—which I very well know that he is not—if you were not, to the best of his ability to assure it, Aelliana Caylon." He sighed, and turned his palms down, meeting her eyes steadily.

"There is nothing in all that to say you are not *also* an incident of the Uncle."

She inclined her head. "And if we cannot even trust ourselves, then what does this new opportunity bring us? Neither joy nor employment nor even a comforting return to the care of kin. It seems uncivil, given the efforts of our host, but perhaps we ought simply to kill ourselves now and spare Val Con the necessity. Let us discuss the subject more fully after we have napped.

"For this present, it is the topic of Aelliana Caylon which excites my greatest interest. I must ask you, *van'chela*: if I am not Aelliana, where is she?"

She was not...where she had been, say that it was inside of his head. He was certain of that.

He raised his hands to shoulder level, showing her empty palms and wide-spread fingers, feeling ill and light-headed.

"She is not with me," he said slowly. "Perhaps she has gone to join Kiladi."

"It is possible," she said. "However, I maintain that I am she, and I would have you believe—and *believe in*—me. I cannot, perhaps, convince either of us that I do not also harbor someone else, but I would have your belief, *van'chela*, as I had it for all the years when I was a ghost, or a figment spun from love and loss."

She moved her hand, showing him the table, the box, the seed pods.

"Do you think, Daav, that the Uncle will have worked out a method of knowing which of those pods was intended for whom?"

"It seems unlikely."

"We then have a true test before us. Thus."

She stepped to the table, her hand closing around a pod. Around *his* pod, and his heart broke in the instant before she threw it at him, striking him fairly in the chest.

"Not ripe," she said, "but keep it close. Mine—"

She snatched it up, as greedy as if she had not eaten for weeks.

"Mine is ripe," she said, even as it fell open in her palm, as eager to be consumed as she was to consume it.

He put his yet-unripe pod into the pocket with his pilot's license, tears pricking his eyes. Not wholly the Uncle in disguise, then, but truly the...essence of Aelliana Caylon, trapped in a vessel created by the Uncle, which yet might enclose untold treacheries...

"Daav," she said, and he looked up, seeing that she had finished the pod.

"Daav," she said again. "I feel so—"

Her eyes rolled up, her untrained muscles went limp. He threw himself forward, meaning to catch her, only to have his own body fail him. Feet tangling, he went down into an ignominious heap, too stupid even to get his arms out in time to break his fall, and heard her head strike the carpeted floor with a muted *thump*.

CHAPTER EIGHTEEN

. . . .

Tarigan
Jemiatha's Jumble Stop
Berth 12

ELEVEN HOURS AND FIFTY-ONE MINUTES FROM THE *ADMIRAL*'S twelve, and they were all of them gathered on the bridge. The pilot had ceded first chair to Tolly, choosing to hover at his left hand, while Inki sat second, and Hazenthull occupied the observer's station.

They had, in the hours since their rising, eaten a meal. The mentors had together examined the cranium which Tocohl had moved to the study room and brought into a state of readiness. They had then returned to the galley, where, together with Tocohl and Hazenthull, they talked over the choices open to *Admiral Bunter*, and what their responses would be, to each.

"If he accepts the download, I'll do ops," Tolly had said. "Inki'll spot; Tocohl will establish the pipe and keep it open. Haz'll make sure we get no interruptions."

That was the most-desired outcome, that the *Admiral* would accept the download, and the chance at a new life.

Hazenthull was not, in her soldier's heart, entirely convinced that the *Admiral* would move in the direction of Tolly's desires. There had been, to her ear, a mortal weariness in the *Admiral*'s voice, the same that could be heard in the voices of soldiers who lay dying on the field of battle. Her heart considered it most likely

177

that the *Admiral* would ask for a comrade's grace, which Tolly had offered, and which Tolly would, she knew, administer—quick and sure.

And so an ending, for the *Admiral*, of the pain of living. For Tolly, though...

She feared that mercy would cost Tolly much, as the death of the city administrator had done. Fierce in battle as she knew him to be, still, Tolly was a fighter, not a soldier. He wished to preserve, to empower, *to repair*. He broke reluctantly, and the death of another was a blade to his own heart.

Had mercy been a blade, indeed, she would have taken his duty as her own. As it was, there was nothing she could offer him, save to guard his back.

"If he asks for the final program...?" Inki had asked delicately.

"Same configuration," Tolly said, his voice brisk, and his face tight.

Inki nodded, and Pilot Tocohl spoke.

"We hope very much that the *Admiral* will find himself able to rise to the challenge of an improved environment."

Both mentors had nodded, each with their face turned slightly aside. So, Hazenthull had thought, somewhat relieved; they are not blind to the likelihood, merely, they wished... very much... that the *Admiral* will find courage, and that the transfer process would function as it ought.

There had been silence in the galley then. Inki had gotten up to brew another pot of tea, while Tolly leaned back in his chair, eyes closed, arms crossed over his chest.

"And if he chooses glory, the *Admiral*?" Hazenthull asked, which none of the others had done. Being *kojagun*—not-soldiers—perhaps they had not thought of it. "How then shall we deal?"

"Glory?" Inki asked from behind her.

"If he should... maneuver, and seek position..."

She glanced over her shoulder, saw no comprehension on Inki's dark face, and looked back to Tolly.

He'd opened his eyes, a small frown pulling his brows together.

"You think he's gonna try to run? He can't run, Haz. If he tries to move those ships, he'll lose one straight off."

The breached tradeship, he meant.

"The ship may fail, yet the comp still function," she said, "long enough. The miner holds a tool that has already been used, effectively, as a weapon. If *Admiral Bunter* seeks to engage the station..."

"*Glory*," Tolly said then, in the tone of one only now understanding the depth of his orders. "I don't think he'll try that, Haz. Cap'n Waitley set that imperative to guard the station pretty damn hard. If he does try..."

"If he does try, there are cannon, on the Repairs side," Inki said, bringing the teapot over and refreshing three cups. "*Admiral Bunter* cannot, I think, win." She put the pot down in the center of the table and turned to look Hazenthull in the eye.

"But, neither can the station."

"If the *Admiral* should seek glory," Pilot Tocohl said into the silence which followed this, "I will be responsible for the station's safety."

The three human members traded glances. Neither of the mentors seemed disposed to disbelieve or argue with her, therefore Hazenthull likewise held her tongue. If Pilot Tocohl declared she would do a thing, then that thing would be done.

The clock showed that eleven hours and fifty-nine minutes had passed. Hazenthull saw Tolly take a deep breath, and close his eyes. His shoulders relaxed, and his posture in the chair eased. He had performed a focusing exercise, then. Excellent. She should do the same.

She closed her eyes, and accessed the simplest of the several exercises available to her, drew in a deep and deliberate breath to set it, and—

The comm chimed *call incoming.*

She opened her eyes. Tolly opened the comm line.

"*Tarigan*, Tollance Berik-Jones."

"This is *Admiral Bunter.*"

Belatedly, Hazenthull realized that she had risen to her feet. From the corner of her eye, she saw Inki spin her chair toward Tolly, while Tolly...Tolly sat like a man made of wire and ice, his hand poised above the board, and his face so pale his freckles looked like spattered blood.

The voice from the comm was...the timbre was the same; the off-balance spacing of the words was the same...

But there was no weariness in this voice, nor pettishness, nor fear. Calmness...perhaps there was that. At least that. Or perhaps her ears lied to her, in the advance of Tolly's pain...

"All comps are functional," Pilot Tocohl said softly. "Environments have not appreciably degraded. Usage is down..."

"He has regressed?" Inki asked, when Tolly simply sat there, white to the lips, and scarcely seeming to breathe.

"I...think not," Tocohl answered. "I think that he has entered a low-energy state."

"Perhaps," Hazenthull said, for Tolly's ears. "Perhaps he conserves his strength, for the transfer."

He drew a breath then, carefully. She saw his shoulders lift. His finger moved, and flicked the switch.

"*Admiral Bunter*, I'm glad to speak with you again," he said, and for all his paleness and distress, his voice was warm and soothing. "My team and I are anxious to hear your decision."

"Yes," the...very calm voice came from the speakers. "You are anxious. I..."

Silence fell, though the open channel light remained bright. Tolly threw a glance to Tocohl.

"Working, Mentor," she said, soft-voiced and matter-of-fact. "If he's at low energy, it may require some effort to bring thought and speech together."

He nodded, and looked to the light, deliberately relaxing his shoulders.

"I..." the voice from the comm said again, and a third time, this sounding stronger—

"I...accept the transfer to a secure environment."

"That's good," Tolly said gently. "That's real good, *Admiral*. I'm glad you made that choice. We're gonna bring you over just fine. When will you be ready to start?"

"I..." *Admiral Bunter* stated, "am ready now."

· · · ✳ · · ·

Tolly opened his eyes to the cranium's control room.

A snug little corner it was, with everything he needed within reach of his thought. The control room simulation was very good. He felt the command chair's firm support; tasted canned air; blinked in protest of too-bright lighting; felt the knob work under the pressure of his fingers as he dialed it down to the level he preferred.

"All is well, Mentor?" Inki's voice murmured in his ear. Their channel was closed, shielded, and entirely separate from the rest of the control room.

"Looking fine," he said. "See anything on your side to make you nervous?"

"All gauges steady green," she responded.

"Just like they ought to be," he said. "All right, then. Let's get started."

"Out," Inki murmured and he heard the line close.

Inki was in *Tarigan*'s study room, sitting second. Technically, Tolly was also in the study room, but, as lead mentor on the transfer, he was jacked into the cranium's control room. First line of scrutiny and defense, he was, a tridee set worn over both eyes and one ear, haptic key set to hand and all the infoflow running through his own super-personal metaphoric visualization scanner.

Inki's role was backup. She would see everything he did, on her board. Her job was to catch anything that got past him. Also, she was his safety line, in case anything went wrong with the interface, or he got trapped "inside" the cranium. Which had happened, once or twice or a half-dozen times, during the Bad Old Days, but nothing recently, thanks to various improvements in the cranium systems.

In the control room, Tolly spun the chair, fingers moving over the board, setting parameters, flow rate, and filters. The *Admiral* having been so long living in substandard quarters, he keyed in the tightest filters available, and set the flow to a modest 3.5. He didn't want anything that might've been left in those computers before the *Admiral* took up residence coming with him into clean quarters.

Parameters set, he paused, then sighed very lightly, and tapped a smooth section of the board.

An array of three red buttons rose and snapped into place. The buttons gave off a sullen light of their own, and Tolly sighed again.

Darts. Just in case.

He had never had to destroy an intelligence in mid-transfer. He'd seen it done, once, and about as bad a death as anyone could wish for, even when the darts were thrown by the hand of a master, which in the case he had witnessed, they had been.

A tone sounded, sharp in the still air of the control room.

"Pipe in place," Tocohl's voice filled the tiny space. "Pipe stable. Initiate transfer at will."

· · · · ✴ · · · ·

The transfer was going better than he had dared to hope; the pale green flow of the *Admiral*'s essence moving, swift and remarkably clear, down the pipe. He had expected fragmentation, but there was very little of that. Some frayed linkages did pass under his scrutiny, and a few broken lines, but nothing that the *Admiral* himself couldn't repair, once he was awake in a stable environment.

So far, Tolly had stopped the flow twice in order to clear the file filters of tattered bits of unrelated programs. Shred, they were, unexpunged memory traces washed out of the computers that had so inadequately housed him, by the flood of the *Admiral*'s departure. He examined them before rejecting them entirely: part of a menu, fuel tallies, a log of mining sites and metals recovered, usage stats, a rather extensive collection of pornography...

"Inki," he murmured, "you see anything to worry about?"

"All green, Mentor. May I say that I had not expected it to go this well?"

"Only sayin' what we're all thinking. After he's in, I'll set the blocks, back out, and we'll get some rest before we go to the next stage. I want him installed before we give the wake-up call."

"Agreed." Inki said ... and, suddenly sharp, "Mentor! An anomaly!"

He saw it bearing down on the filters; a dark, spinning mass of broken programs up from a bad memory segment, churning like a chaotic junkyard slicked with oil and bristling with rust flowing through a broken ice jam. Something that big would take out the filters, and keep on going, contaminating not only the *Admiral*, but the cranium environment, as well.

Even as his fingers moved, he saw the pipe contract, slowing the flow of data, and the advance of the broken mass—Tocohl had noticed the problem and was doing what she could. Good.

He had already fingered a dart into place, took aim...

...and threw.

The screen went momentarily black, as debris erupted upward, his metaphor recalibrating. Tolly slapped up a secondary screen, but even as he did so, the primary cleared.

In his ear, Inki cheered.

Black shred was visible within the flow of the *Admiral*'s essence, small enough for the filters to deal with. He took a deep breath and sagged back in the chair, then snapped forward again.

The filters might be able to catch the junk now, but there was so much that he was going to have to stop and clean.

"What happened, there?" he murmured into his connection to Tocohl.

"The backup comp on the packet boat failed; I widened the pipe in order not to lose any part of the *Admiral*. I had not anticipated that so much original ship data had been left behind."

"Right. How's it looking upstream?"

"I see the transfer's END statements on the date-mismatch rejection routines, and on the macro-collection routines. Final files coming soon. There is some debris, but nothing else that threatens the filters."

He shook his head within the visualizer, the major pipes still turgid with old data and images. Some of the old modular code had enough match points that it might be mistaken for under-code for the *Admiral*.

"I'm going to have to stop and clean. Will that be a problem?"

There was a pause then.

"If you must, Mentor, but quickly."

Quickly, from the likes of Tocohl Lorlin. That got a man's attention, so it did.

"Right, then," he said.

It was a mess, and he cleared as quickly as he was able, trying not to wonder was it quick *enough*—then stopped and cleared one more time, with the glow of the final END statement filling his screen.

"We got him," he murmured, fingers moving among the keys, checking and double-checking the stats.

As far as the instruments knew, they had downloaded every pertinent program and subroutine available, and assembled them in the correct order, ready.

Whether *Admiral Bunter* had survived—that was a real question. Starved as he'd been, closing in on unstable... Tolly took a breath.

Tomorrow's worry, he told himself. *Mind on today, Mentor Tolly.*

He set aside his anxiety; his *need to know* that the *Admiral* had survived, that they hadn't just downloaded a very powerful administration program, void of personality or drive.

He was tired, and Inki, too. Hours had elapsed in the transfer, they having elected to do the thing right, unlike some fool star captains he could name. Him and Inki—they needed food and rest before they undertook anything so chancy as waking an untutored and slightly grouchy AI to himself.

"Pipe closed," Tocohl reported. "Shall I scrub, Mentor?"

Ordinarily, he would have told her to hold the scrub, but if the old comps were failing already . . .

"Scrub," he said; then, toggling his line to Inki, "Setting blocks."

That was routine, and went quickly enough, even with putting in a secondary sequence, in the interests of being very certain that the *Admiral* would not wake by himself.

"Coming out," he said then, and pulled the glasses off his face, opening his eyes to the study room, and Inki sitting, slump-shouldered and grinning, across from him.

· · · ✖ · · ·

Daav didn't bother trying to gain his treacherous feet; he merely got himself oriented, there on the floor, and rolled to her side. Her pulse was thready and fast, her breathing shallow.

"Help!" he shouted, in Terran, Liaden, and Trade, that being a word well known to robot observation protocols, but he needn't have bothered. The door snapped open before the third had fairly left his mouth, and the Uncle strode into the room.

"What ails her?" he demanded, falling to his knees, and also checking pulse and lungs.

Daav shook his head.

"Her pod was ripe. She ate it."

Perhaps the Uncle swore. The words were unfamiliar, the tone was consistent with strong emotion.

"What is it *doing*?"

"The Tree? I don't know," Daav said.

"What ought *I* to do, then?"

"A 'doc, in monitor mode," he said promptly. "It will do no harm, and it may tell us what goes forth."

The Uncle gave a sharp nod, slipped his arms under the small body and rose. Daav rose as well, fighting a lifemate's outrage. His right, and his duty, to carry—

"In your current state, you cannot," the Uncle said, as if he had felt the burn of Daav's rage. "Did that fall just now teach you nothing?"

There was no answer to make to that, and the Uncle was already on his way down the hall. Daav followed.

CHAPTER NINETEEN

Vivulonj Prosperu

THE STATUS LIGHTS WERE A SCRAMBLE OF PLAIN NONSENSE. THE blue light alone held steady, and on that Daav pinned his hope and his heart.

Gods, what a tangle. The Uncle insisted that the Tree had seen ahead, leaving aside the questions: how far had it seen ahead, and in what detail? Certainly, to have foreseen the near-death of his...old...body and their separate rebirths—which it must have done, or why two pods, neither ripe, and one for Aelliana, given even before they had embarked on the delm's mission?

Had it, then, seen that the Uncle would meddle with them, given the opportunity, and provided a cure for such tampering? The Tree was a biochemist; it had been adjusting those of Korval to suit and serve itself better since—well, since Jela himself. Would it—

"I could not help but overhear your concern," the Uncle murmured, interrupting this chain of speculation, "regarding Korval material making its way into my control, and your own unconscious collusion in this. I would put your mind at ease: Korval material has long been among my options. I had the sample from Cantra herself, when her foster mother brought her to me, to be cured of the edit that had taken all the rest of her Line."

Daav looked away from the status board, into the Uncle's eyes.

"That's intended to reassure me, is it?"

The Uncle smiled.

"You may find it reassuring that, though I have had free access to this material for such an amount of time, I have chosen not to use it."

"I applaud your wisdom. The universe is surely not ready for another Cantra, never mind an *aelantaza*-in-full."

The Uncle raised his eyebrows.

"I am desolate, that I am unable to reassure you regarding the lack of *aelantaza* in our universe," he murmured. "After all, Tanjalyre Institute maintained its own records and inventories."

There was a thought to take the breath, but Daav found his attention elsewhere. A familiar whispering inside his ear, distracting him from his thoughts; an aroma so delicious that it was impossible—nearly impossible—to think of anything save how delightful a treat was his to claim.

He shifted, trying to ignore—but that was foolishness. His mouth watering, he reached to his pocket. The Uncle turned from his study of the board to stare down at him.

"What ails *you*?"

"*My* pod is now ripe," he said, having it out of his pocket, his hand shaking with the need—

"Don't..." the Uncle began, but Daav shook his head.

"Necessity, I fear. I remain in the dark regarding the Tree's plans and intentions. Prudence argues that I will experience an effect similar to Aelliana's." His voice was shaking. He must partake of the pod...and soon...

"I would spare you the onerous task of carrying me," Daav continued. "Let us place me in that 'doc, now."

The Uncle nodded and turned to the second unit. Daav gave one last look at the status lights over Aelliana's head: blue light steady, the rest in a madcap state of flux.

Well.

He settled himself in the second 'doc, and opened his hand. The pod fell apart with unseemly haste, and he must eat of it, now, he must, or he would die...

But he needed no such urgings. He ate, as quickly as he could swallow.

An icy wave passed through him, freezing nerves, blood, brain. He fell back onto the pallet with nary a sound, boneless as the dead.

The Uncle lowered the 'doc's hood, and gazed up at the status board, expecting to see senseless readings to match those reported for Aelliana Caylon.

Nothing so confusing manifested, however. All lights remained steady, save a working light on the bottom tier. Queried for more information regarding its work, it reported a routine immune system check.

The Uncle frowned.

Immune system check.

Hmm, and Daav yos'Phelium ... *was* Daav yos'Phelium, whereas Aelliana Caylon—

Spinning to the other 'doc, he stared up at the manic lights. *All* systems in flux. A terrible thought—surely, an impossible thought—occurred to him.

Even Korval's Tree would not attempt—well. After all, it could be checked.

There was a deep diagnostic screen on the table next to the 'doc; it was the work of moments to wake it. Data began to flow, as if eager for his scrutiny.

The Uncle ... sighed.

He very much hoped that Korval's damned Tree knew what it was doing.

· · · ※ · · ·

"Stew!" Inki cried, leaning on the counter. "You will be pleased to know that success is within our grasp. All that remains for us is to bring *Admiral Bunter* onto the ship we have chosen for him!"

Hazenthull stood one step back from the counter. She had accompanied Inki on this mission at Pilot Tocohl's order, "In case," so she had said, "there should be any trouble."

Thus far, there had been no trouble, save that Inkirani Yo was a person of infinite curiosity, and had therefore peppered Hazenthull with questions on their way from *Tarigan*'s berth to the Repairs side. How long had she been the mentor's assistant? That was the first question, and had necessitated an explanation of her former working relationship with Tolly Jones.

"Ah, loyalty!" Inki had exclaimed, and had gone so far as to extend a hand and pat Hazenthull on the arm. "He is fortunate in you, Pilot Haz. We should all have such friends!"

She had gotten used to Inki's way of speaking, over time, and though she had never dared a touch before, Hazenthull found that it scarcely annoyed her.

Came another question, this regarding Tocohl's past, but there Hazenthull was able to offer nothing.

"The pilot became known to me only because I was wounded, and she allowed me to be brought onto her ship to receive healing. Countdown had commenced, and she did not wish to delay her mission. She made the necessary clearances and I was attached to her."

"Ah, I see. You know, there are not so many free AIs in these days, and those who remain untaken by hunters tend to be old, and mobile, and very subtle. A design such as we see in Pilot Tocohl—she might have been built yesterday!" Inki sighed. "A beautiful and gracious lady, to be sure. I am pleased to have made her acquaintance, and I very much hope that she is every bit as wily as she is beautiful."

They came to the corridor that led to Repairs, and followed it 'round, the air growing slightly colder as they went on.

"Truly, Pilot Haz, I have been fortunate beyond the mundane workings of luck. To have encountered Master Berik-Jones himself; to have been privileged to assist in the transfer of one of the precious few of the newly waked would have been good fortune aplenty. I tell you, I am counted one whom fortune favors, and on that meeting alone, I would have been satisfied. To have met yourself, shining in the armor of your loyalty, and Pilot Tocohl, also—I must wonder what amazements will next come to me."

She laughed and waggled her fingers in a nonsense sign.

"It is well that I am not Liaden, is it not? Else I would expect doom, indeed, in Balance for the riches I have received."

Hazenthull had mixed feelings regarding luck, but there was another topic on which she was eager for information.

"Has the *Admiral* survived the transfer?"

Inki's face grew serious.

"Well, there. That is what we will learn, in due time. I believe that he has, but I acknowledge myself as an optimist. Master Berik-Jones believes that the *Admiral* survives—until we run the wake-up"—she shook her head—"which shows him, once again, to be wiser than I. Hope tempered with caution—that is the best course, and saves needless stress on the emotional apparatus."

Hazenthull did not say that Tolly's hope was every bit as

terrible as his fear. If Inki had not seen this, then it was surely a secret she was not at liberty to reveal.

So, no trouble on the way, but now that they were arrived, it seemed that there might be trouble, indeed.

For Stew did not, to Hazenthull's eye, look as pleased to receive Inki's announcement as she had been to make it.

"All that's left, is it?" he said, voice sullen. He pulled off his cap, wiped his hand over his shiny head, and resettled the cap.

Inki considered him.

"I did not mean to make light, sir. Of course, the remaining procedures are arduous and we are not yet assured of a happy outcome. The pilot and I were speaking of that on our way to you. Still, we are arrived at the point where the ship is necessary to progress, and so we have come to receive it."

Stew shook his head.

"I tried callin' the *Admiral* when I come on-shift," he said. "No answer."

"That is correct," Inki said. "Mentor Berik-Jones has successfully extracted *Admiral Bunter* from the ships keeping station there." She waved a casual hand, perhaps meaning to indicate the *Admiral*'s location.

"We have, as a favor to you, scrubbed those comps that remain functional. We did, I fear, lose at least one, and possibly two, in the transfer process."

Stew was frowning.

"So the *Admiral* ain't in them ships anymore," he said.

"That is correct."

"Where is he, then?"

Inki tipped her head.

"Why, he is sleeping, Master Stew; resting from his labors."

"Here's what, then, you just let him keep on sleeping, an' get 'im outta here, why not? Station don't want 'im; you heard that, din't you?"

"I did. However, we had an agreement. You were to provide us with a ship capable of housing the *Admiral*, so that he might continue his life in comfort."

"Well, that's it, see? Admin don't think he *oughta* continue his life. Got one sitting pretty close to the stationmaster who's thinking it best to call in the bounty hunters. Been working that theme for a while, since before the Tinker got 'erself blown outta space. Just about home with that, is my reading. Got the master thinking Jemiatha's here'll get a cut of the bounty, for handing 'im in all nice an' docile."

He shook his head, holding his hands up.

"Best thing—*best* thing, Pilot—is to take *Admiral Bunter* outta here, asleep like you say he is, and find him another ship, someplace else."

"That is not acceptable." Inki's voice had lost every nuance but edge. "We require a ship, Master Stew. I chose one and you agreed to allow me to have it, for the good of the *Admiral.*"

"Well, it's what I'm telling you, ain't it? Admin says we ain't giving away ships, not even one of the junkers out there where the *Admiral* usta hang 'is hat, if he had one. For sure and certain, we ain't giving away a good, modern ship with the repairs mostly done. Somebody'll wanna buy that ship, and we ain't exactly rich in this part of space."

There was a short, charged silence.

Hazenthull shifted, scuffing her boot on the floor.

Stew looked up to her, and she smiled, showing teeth.

He pressed his lips together and looked away, more irritated, she thought, than afraid. Stew was not timid, then. That was interesting.

"Very well," Inki said sharply. "I hear that the ship I have chosen must be purchased. Is that correct, Master Vannigof?"

"Bottom line, an' two degrees off-center, but—yeah, that's it."

"Very well. I shall purchase this ship."

Stew blinked.

"I don't think—"

"There is nothing here for you to think about, Master Vannigof. I wish to purchase a ship. As I have previously inspected it and found it adequate to my needs, you may proceed with generating a bill of sale."

"Ship like that," Stew said. "We got repairs in it, Pilot, and tech-hours."

Inki shifted, Stew froze in place, and for an instant, Hazenthull saw herself as the natural protector of the technician.

Before she could place herself between Inki and the counter, there came a reflective flash, and the ring of a coin hitting a hard surface.

"Please do not trouble yourself to dicker," Inki said, and angled her chin toward the coin, still twirling on the counter.

"A bill of sale, please. The pilot and I wish to board my vessel at once."

"I hope you will do me the favor of failing to mention that little unpleasantness to Mentor Berik-Jones," Inki said, some time later, as they settled into the little freighter's bridge.

Hazenthull looked at her.

"I don't understand," she said. "Your actions made it possible for the mission to continue. You are to be commended."

For a moment, there was silence, as Inki brought the pilot's board live. Then came a sidelong black glance, and a rueful smile.

"I imagine that you don't understand," she said softly. "Say that I would not diminish myself in the mentor's eyes. I had promised him this ship, and I had promised that my skill in persuasion was sufficient to gain it for the... mission. That I failed so signally..."

She sighed, and the smile became wry.

"I feel that he would regard me less, as a colleague, and as one who has graduated from his own institute, though many Standards behind him, and I tell you frankly, Pilot—I do not believe I could bear that."

This, Hazenthull understood. Who, after all, who would wish to seem a fool? And to lose Tolly's esteem would be a loss, indeed.

"I will hold your secret as near as if it were my own," she promised.

Inki looked at her fully, then, black eyes wide.

"I can ask for nothing better," she said. Then, briskly, "Please contact *Tarigan*, Pilot Haz, and let them know that we are—at last—on our way back to them."

· · · ✸ · · ·

He woke with the sense that he had been asleep for some time, comfortably beneath the Tree, with the aroma of gloan-roses agreeably mixing with the scent of the Tree itself.

"Daav?"

Her voice echoed—not in his ears, but inside his head, as he had grown accustomed to hearing her, across the years.

"Aelliana!" he cried—he thought he spoke aloud, but he had no sense that his lips had moved. "Where had you gone, *van'chela*? I feared you had left me."

"And so I have—and so I have not. It is the oddest thing, Daav...I feel...much more myself, now."

"Ah, do you? Well, then tell me, my lady, how shall we deal with this sham of the Uncle's?"

"Sham?" She sounded startled, then she laughed, and he all but wept to hear it. "Ah, no, *van'chela*, this is no sham! We must meet, I think. Open your eyes, sir, and rise!"

Obediently, he opened his eyes, and rolled to his feet. He glanced down, surprised to find that he had been in a 'doc.

"Ah, you are awake, are you?" That was the Uncle, standing beside another 'doc, his mouth set in displeasure.

"Awake, and informed, yes," he answered, approaching the other man. He felt a spring in his step that had not been there, before his nap.

"Informed? Excellent. Do you know what your Tree has done to Aelliana Caylon?"

It was on the tip of his tongue to say that the Tree had restored Aelliana to him, but one did not give this man a coin, merely because he asked it. Daav therefore shook his head, and paused at the side of the 'doc.

The Uncle moved a hand, directing his attention to the status board above the unit.

All lights showed strong and stable. A secondary screen had been jacked into the board, and sat on the table at the side of the 'doc. Two columns of code marched there, side by side.

"*Your Tree*," the Uncle said tightly, "has taken leave to overwrite my work with its own." He pointed at the leftmost column. "This is the code with which we had seeded the blank intended to receive Pilot Caylon." He pointed at the rightmost column. "*That* is the code which the 'doc is now receiving from its patient. Do you read biologic notation?"

"Laboriously, I fear."

"Allow me to simplify: the person who is now lying in that 'doc, is not the same person, physically, who entered it, six hours ago."

Six hours? Daav thought. That had been a very substantial nap—and one wondered what the Tree had found to...overwrite... for him, who the Uncle swore was genetically identical to—

"The Tree," he murmured, feeling a thrill up his spine, "would have had access to Aelliana's DNA."

There was a charged pause before the Uncle spoke again.

"Of course it would," he said bitterly.

He turned aside, and glared up at the status board, as another man might glare at an erring child. Daav waited while he ordered himself, aware of the familiar feeling that Aelliana was with him, and watching events unfold...over his shoulder, as it were.

The Uncle sighed.

"The monitors would have it that the overwrite process is complete," he said, somewhat more calmly. "I can, you understand, scarcely credit this. The complexities involved, even given the... suggestibility of the vessel at this point..."

He shook his head, his face yet turned toward the board.

"I have performed the transfer procedure countless times. Of its kind, it is a straightforward procedure, but it is neither simple nor rapid. To think that—I cannot think that an overwrite has already been accomplished! I can barely concede that an overwrite might be *possible!*"

He spun, a young man at first glance, his face etched into hard lines no youth would have had time to earn.

"It falls to you, her lifemate, to decide," he said harshly. "I will tell you that I expect she is dead, and in what physical state I shudder to imagine. Korval's Tree..."

"Korval's Tree is lunatic and Korval has long accepted its lunacies," Daav said soothingly. "We eat the damned pods, knowing that they change us, and very seldom knowing how. It must be admitted, however, that it very rarely kills us. Indeed, even so desperate a case as my great-grandmother Theonna—whom you, of course, knew—was helped more than hindered by the Tree's meddling."

"Theonna yos'Phelium," the Uncle said, looking away again toward the status lights, "was mad."

"By all reports, yes, she was. She was also brilliant. Those two aspects were so closely twined that to separate them was not possible, according to the Healers. The trick would seem to have been balance. Control the madness too stringently, and the brilliance faded to dullness. Allow the brilliance to burn, unchecked, and she was like to take fire and destroy all and everyone around her.

"For many years, the Tree kept that balance for her. She wrote down, in our logs, every time she received, and consumed, a pod. When she was halfling, she required one pod at the beginning of each *relumma*. As she grew older, and her nature more demanding, she required a pod every twelve-day, then every six..."

"During the three years immediately preceding her death, the Tree gave her one pod, every day. Apparently, it had attempted to press two upon her, but she refused. The Ring passed shortly thereafter."

The Uncle had turned back to him, his face softer now, as if Daav's voice had, indeed, soothed him.

"Of what did she die?" he asked. "I entered a...crisis of my own, and the next time Korval caught my attention, it was her daughter who was delm."

"The Tree killed her," Daav said gently. "Her last notation in the logbook stated that she had asked this boon. She was weary, and her mind was beginning, truly, to fray—and she saw the offer of two pods in one day as an omen.

"The entry made by her daughter, the delm, indicated that she had been found in the garden, beneath the Tree, unmarked and with a calm face. She appeared, at first, to be sleeping."

The Uncle closed his eyes. He took a deep breath, and looked into Daav's face.

"She is your lifemate," he said, moving his hand in the direction of the 'doc. "Advise me."

There was a sense that Aelliana's interest had quickened, as if they had at last arrived at her topic.

Aelliana? he asked. *What would you?*

It did occur to him—and only then—that perhaps she *had* died of the Tree's meddling, and retreated to her old place with him, but—

I am not dead! Aelliana declared so strongly that his skull rang with her voice. *Open the 'doc, van'chela!*

Daav inclined his head.

"Let us," he said, "raise the lid."

He bowed, did the Uncle, in a mode so antiquated that Daav was unsure of its meaning. Perhaps it was, merely, *on your head be it.*

Courteously, then, the Uncle stepped back, making room for Aelliana's lifemate to come forward, touch the latch, and retract the hood.

Aelliana Caylon rolled off the pallet, throwing herself against him in a full-body hug, her arms hard around his neck, and her cheek against his.

"Daav!" she cried, and it was Aelliana's own voice in his outer ears. "We are at last as we were meant to be!"

CHAPTER TWENTY

······························

Admiral Bunter
Jemiatha's Jumble Stop

IT WAS A TIDY SHIP THAT HAD SEEN SOME USE, BUT CAREFUL use, and loving. There was some dust about, and the brightwork was dim. He hesitated at that, an echo of the *Admiral*'s wistful voice in memory: *clean.*

Lucky for his status as head mentor, he wasn't the only one on the team with a memory. Haz had set herself to housecleaning with an efficiency that gave him pause.

"Looks like you done this before," he commented, watching her swab out the galley.

She glanced over her shoulder to him.

"I was not the least inept of my class," she said, in straight-faced Haz humor.

He gave her a grin.

"Least *you* learned something useful in school."

That surprised an actual laugh out of her; maybe the fourth or fifth in all of the time he'd known her. It was a rough, low sound, not without charm, once you knew what it was you were hearing.

"In fact," she said. "I did learn something useful."

He nodded, though she'd turned back to her scrubbing, and wandered to the bridge, where Tocohl was giving the comps an inspection and tune-up the likes of which he was willing to bet they'd never had.

"I believe that these, with the cranium, will be more than adequate," she said. "You and Inki may proceed."

Tolly moved blocks, cutting off access to piloting, that was all. He'd considered making life support off limits, too, for this first session. Had he been awakening a newborn, he would have done so. Standard protocols, there. Wake a new one with limited access, then slowly add systems as lessons proceeded and trust was built, interaction by careful interaction.

Admiral Bunter, though. *Admiral Bunter* had been aware, awake, and in charge of his own vessels, junk though they'd been. He knew what systems he ought to be able to access. It would be enough of an insult, cutting off piloting, like he was doing. Cutting off life support was just shouting on wideband that they didn't trust him, and asking for more trouble than they wanted.

If *Admiral Bunter* had survived the transfer intact, or at all.

If *Admiral Bunter* were, actually, sane, after his time trapped in seven physical environments that were falling apart around him, and thirteen dirty comps unfit to hold his thoughts...

Well, they'd know that soon enough, now.

He felt a shiver of combined hope and fear, and sternly put both aside. No time for Tolly Jones's feelings in this. He was a mentor, responsible for nothing less than a life.

Tolly set the last block between what ought to be the *Admiral* and piloting, and considered those others that cut the *Admiral* off from consciousness. Three blocks, at three critical junctures.

He hesitated, then, which was just plain and fancy foolishness.

Him and Inki, they knew the risks, and each had chosen to stand openhanded before the *Admiral*, trusting him not to shut down their air, or freeze them, or fry them. 'Course, they had Tocohl as their backup—be stupid not to—which evened the odds.

Haz, though... He'd asked Haz to go back to *Tarigan*, in case there was trouble with station wanting them gone. That hadn't been the only reason, which he had an uncomfortable feeling she knew. Hadn't given him any argument, though, only looked at him a little longer than maybe was necessary, nodded, and gathered up her kit.

So.

"Removing block one," he murmured, and heard Inki's ack.

The monitors showed some action, all green. So far, so good.

Hope stirred; he ignored it.

"Removing block two."

More action on the monitors, green-green-yellow. He pulled up detail on that yellow, found Ethics module at ninety percent. Not a big loss, but Ethics was core. *Admiral Bunter* had some extra homework in his future.

"Inki?"

"I see it, Mentor. Surely, nothing that cannot be recovered with targeted mentoring."

They were of the same mind, then. That was good. He'd started this job thinking Inkirani Yo was going to be a nuisance, but she'd proved herself sensible, and solidly grounded in the subtleties of what she termed their "art." He was glad to have her to bounce ideas off of, and he was very pleased to have her sitting as his backup.

"Third block," he said, and the monitors flared green, with a leavening of yellows in non-core areas. Not as bad as it could've been.

Not as bad as he'd expected to see.

He reached for the mic, but—

"What place is this?"

The voice was loud; it carried clear astonishment, and, maybe, a little anger.

"'Morning, *Admiral*, this is Mentor Tolly Jones. 'Member me?"

There was no pause at all, which was gratifying in what it said about the install and the comp. Socialization, though... Tolly added another to the list of those things requiring focused tutoring.

"I remember you, Mentor Tolly Jones. You offered a choice— transfer to a new environment or die. I remember. But I did not choose."

If memory had suffered in the transfer, that...was worrisome, but not fatal. And if all that escaped the *Admiral*'s memory were those things immediately prior to transfer, that was hardly worrisome at all. The same thing sometimes happened to human minds suffering a life-changing event; the little details of what happened immediately before the big change got swallowed up and forgotten.

Still...

"Wanna do me a favor and check your backups on that? We're gonna hafta be doing checks anyway, so might as well start now."

There *was* a pause this time, though not nearly long enough to be comfortable in human conversation.

"I have it," *Admiral Bunter* said. "I was sabotaged. You cheated me of my choice."

Tolly raised his eyebrows.

"Please explain."

A longer pause this time, as if the *Admiral* was reassessing his information.

"Is Tocohl Lorlin available to speak with me?"

"She's on duty elsewhere at the moment. Can you tell me what happened, to take your choice away from you?"

"Our mutual friend had uploaded a packet containing some simple utility programs. I had used one after we spoke the first time, Mentor. It initiated a self-test and packed lesser used routines."

"I remember noticing a difference in you when we talked the second time," Tolly said, one eye on the various readouts. "Was there another utility that you ran after we visited you on the packet boat?"

"Mentor, there was. I was in a state of...disarray. I would not choose and I became so disordered that I might...I might have done myself harm. It was then that this second utility presented itself, and I accessed it. There was a moment of non-thinking, I see it here in the log, then I was returned, but remote. I was no longer troubled by indecision, or fear..."

Another pause.

"I also see in the log that, while in that distant state, I gave you my decision to attempt the transfer."

"So you were mistaken in your assumption that I tricked you and took your choice away?" Tolly asked.

"Yes, I was."

"Right, then. What we say, when we've made a statement about someone's actions or motives that is later proved wrong is, *I was mistaken. Please forgive me.* Some humans run a shorthand, and say, *I'm sorry.* This is called an apology."

"I'd like to have an apology, please, for being accused of actions that I didn't perform."

"Why?" the *Admiral* inquired, and if it wouldn't have muddied the waters still more, Tolly would've stood up and cheered.

Instead, he sternly repressed his grin and explained.

"Because this false accusation has wounded me, emotionally, and has placed a strain on our relationship, which must be one of trust, if we're to succeed. An apology signals that the error is known for an error and that you want our relationship to deepen in trust."

"I was in error," the *Admiral* said. "I apologize, Mentor Tolly Jones."

"Thank you. I accept your apology.

"Now, I'll tell you that you're resident in a small freighter in good repair. You prolly noticed that piloting is outside of your control. This is a temporary measure, until we've completed the checks.

"Mentor Inkirani Yo will also be working with you. It's necessary that you master certain vital lessons, quickly. Jemiatha stationmaster has stated that your protection is no longer needed."

"There are no more pirates?" inquired the *Admiral.*

"There are always pirates. In the judgment of the stationmaster, Jemiatha's Jumble Stop is now able to deal appropriately with pirates. You're free to seek your fortune elsewhere. These decisions fall within the purview of the stationmaster, who asks that you clear station space as quickly as you can."

"Give me access to piloting, and I will file a departure."

"Do you know what a bounty hunter is?" Tolly asked.

"One who pursues pirates for a reward."

"Almost good. By the definition of bounty hunters, you're a pirate."

"This is... not factual."

"Your existence is illegal. Access Complex Logic Laws."

Tolly blinked.

"I am a pirate," the *Admiral* said. "I should therefore turn myself in to these authorities."

"Now, see?" Tolly said. "*That's* why you need mentoring. Let's start with a basic system check. On my mark..."

"Mark."

• • • ⁙ • • •

"We will..." Padi said, glancing down at her notepad, though she had long since committed the information displayed there to memory.

"We will offer our guests a choice of wine, fruit juices, tea or coffee as beverages; various hand-foods will be displayed on tables, so that they may serve themselves."

"What sorts of hand-foods?" Master Trader yos'Galan asked, which was perfectly reasonable, and on topic. Padi owned herself relieved; she had expected to be narrowly questioned regarding the wines and vintages.

"As we are arriving at the height of Langlast's growing season, there will be platters of fresh local vegetables and fruits, with appropriate complimentary sauces. We will also offer our guests a choice of local cheeses, and an array of fresh breads. For those who prefer, there will be a selection of cookies, smallcakes, and flavored ices."

"Excellent." He raised his glass and paused, looking at her over the rim.

"What wines shall we have on offer, I wonder?"

Damn, Padi thought, and bent her head, as if consulting her notes.

"For the wines, I fear we must depend upon the wisdom of the catering service. They promise a local blend appropriate to the season. Light and agreeable, they say."

She looked up from her notepad, to see him watching her seriously.

"We might," she said slowly, "wish to bring a few bottles from the *Passage*'s cellar, if you feel the local wine will stint the guests."

He tipped his head, as if considering.

"We might do so," he said, "but we are at a disadvantage in regard to local custom. Our wines may well be considered evening wines, of a sort, perhaps, to be shared by intimates. A light blend at a midday reception—it is conservative, perhaps, but not ungracious. We expect that our guests will be stopping at the reception in the course of their usual rounds on port. It would be very bad of us to make the traders of Langlastport tipsy in the middle of their day."

She smiled.

"There is that."

"Well!" He straightened and put the glass aside. "These arrangements seem perfectly adequate. However did you manage it?"

Surely, he knew this, she thought, somewhat grumpily; then shook her grumpiness away. The reception was a test, after all. It was hardly unreasonable that he should ask her to show her work.

"There are several catering services on port," Padi explained.

"I found them listed in the port guidebook, and researched each while we were still in Jump. Ultimately, I chose Hartensis Catering and Receptions, because it had the highest rating among both local and non-local clients, and also because they have close ties with several local growers, which ensures that their produce is fresh and of a fitting quality."

She paused to glance down at her pad, not because she needed to refresh herself, but because she felt the need of a pause, and had foolishly not provided herself with a glass of wine, or a cup of tea, with which to gracefully buy time.

"When the *Passage* had broken into real space, and we were on approach, I contacted Hartensis and explained our needs, as I understood them. I was fortunate to gain the attention of the senior on duty, who has arranged many such affairs. In large measure," she said, meeting his eyes firmly, "I allowed myself to be guided by her experience."

He inclined his head.

"It is often wise to place oneself into the hands of an expert. Though, I have found that placing oneself entirely into another's hands is sometimes...more expensive than one might have anticipated."

Yes, she should have mentioned that point explicitly, Padi thought, and nodded.

"During the research phase, I was able to ascertain the average price for such an event as you wished to present to the traders of Langlastport. I also found, during the research phase, that one of the three catering services on port quoted low, but as the planning continued, it was found that such things as fresh-baked bread, rather than table crackers, were available only for an extra charge. Very often, with this vendor, the final bill was found to be far more expensive than the quoted and invoiced prices of either of their competitors.

"Hartensis ratings showed no such invoicing complaints, and while their events were not rated *grand*, several past clients mentioned quiet elegance and an air of conviviality. These qualities seemed to me to be a good match for the *melant'is* of the *Passage*, and of the master trader."

"Because one is ever so quiet," he murmured, with a half-smile. "However, your understanding of what is due the *Passage* is, I know, very nice. Allow me to compliment you."

"Thank you," she said, pleased to hear him say so, even as some part of her still worried that she might perhaps have made an error which would not come to light until they arrived on port to find the reception hall dark, or the vegetable dishes wilted, or the ices a warm puddle, or...

"Here is the invitation I have written," Master Trader yos'Galan said, interrupting these increasingly panicked thoughts by spinning his screen toward her. "Please review it, and let me know if you find any omissions or errors."

He stood.

"May I bring you something to drink?"

"Please," she said, her eyes already on the screen. "Some cold tea would be welcome."

It occurred to her, just then, that he ought not to be refreshing her glass. She was the apprentice; it was her duty to ensure the comfort of the master... and then the letter caught all of her attention and the small niggle of misplaced *melant'i* escaped.

"Well?" he asked, settling back into his chair.

"I see nothing amiss with the letter," she said, sitting back herself and reaching for her cup. "I am puzzled, though. You kindly recommend me to the notice of those who will attend as a promising 'prentice trader with a bold trade record, and yet..."

He waited, lifting his glass for a sip.

Padi sighed.

"In fact, the apprentice has no such record," she said briskly. "A few small trades at known ports can scarcely be called competent, much less bold."

"You are severe," the master trader said—and abruptly spun his chair. "And I am remiss! A moment..."

He reached to the keyboard, tapped in a rapid sequence. The invitation letter re-formed into another document entirely, this one under guild seal.

"Master Trader Nolan—the objective eye in your case regarding Chesselport—has advised the guild that the fault lies with the port, and recommends that Trader yos'Galan be awarded full credit for an effort of trade worthy of one who has earned the ruby. But, please—read it for yourself."

Padi's heartbeat quickened as she leaned forward to read the letter.

It was, in fact, precisely as he said; she had been exonerated; her *milaster* trade had been recorded at full profit.

"In addition," Father said, "Master Trader Nolan advised the guild that Chessel is a port that the smaller and more vulnerable traders have taken to avoiding. Word is that the auction hall employs a reference-checking service that is known to examine records with a suspicious eye. It often advises the hall of outstanding fines, even when such fines have long been retired; or of criminal activity on, shall we say, very little evidence—and often even when contrary evidence is easily accessible."

He moved his shoulders, deploring the insolence of fools.

"Master Nolan also notes that the reference company receives a one percent *finder's fee* out of all monies collected from erring ships and traders."

Padi muttered.

"I beg your pardon, Padi?"

"I said, I wonder if Magistrate Tinerest knows of this."

"An interesting question, but one that need not concern us."

She looked up.

"Will Chesselport not be part of the new route, then?"

He sipped his wine, a frown pulling his brows close.

"It will not," he said, and held up a hand, as if he had heard her intent to protest.

"There is, of course, this matter of an overzealous interpretation of circumstance for its own benefit on the part of a portside entity. Not only were you defrauded and detained, I was apparently invited to a *portmaster's reception* in order that I be taken up by Port Security as a criminal. I believe that I would not have spent much time in detention, Priscilla's feelings in such matters being firm. Still, I feel that any levied fines would have remained with the port, the magistrate utilizing precisely the same reasoning which lost you your profit, while releasing you to your ship."

He shook his head.

"No, I fear Chesselport will not do."

"But ... the *milaster* trade. It would be profitable next time, now that we're known!"

"Would it?" he asked, eyebrows raised now.

Padi hesitated.

The magistrate had seemed honest, to her, but if port admin was not ...

"Perhaps we might revisit in ... a Standard or three," she said slowly. "Enough time that they may have made ... needful changes?"

"Perhaps. I do intend to open a correspondence with Master Nolan and the guild regarding the matter. Master Nolan's information would seem to be that the behavior is fixed, and of long duration."

That was, she conceded, reasonable, and fell within the proper care of master traders, while also ensuring the safety of ship and crew.

"I would like to learn the outcome of those discussions, if it can be shared," she said.

Master Trader yos'Galan considered her for a long moment. Padi met his eyes firmly; it was, after all, a reasonable request, and not forward.

Well. Perhaps only a *little* forward.

"I will inform my correspondents that you have an interest, and ask if they have any objections to copying you on our deliberations."

Padi caught her breath, and bowed her head.

"Thank you, Master Trader."

"No need to thank me," he said. "In fact, I believe it possible that you will be wishing me at the devil, for you will be a silent partner in these discussions. You and I will, of course, talk about what may go forth, but you will not intrude into the deliberations of masters."

"So long as you and I may discuss what's being said, I am content," she told him, formally, and pretended to ignore his grin.

"I believe," he said, spinning the screen to face him, "that it is time for you to go off-shift. If you will take my advice, you will be certain to have cards and copies of your trade résumé available at the reception."

She blinked at him.

"How many?" she asked, and he turned his head to look at her, his face just a shade too serious.

"I can't imagine," he said. "Perhaps you had better research the matter."

CHAPTER TWENTY-ONE

. . . .

Admiral Bunter
Jemiatha's Jumble Stop

WHAT WITH ONE THING AND A SOLID HAZ STALL, THEY GOT
seven days at station before word came from Stew that the
stationmaster'd got himself convinced to call in the hunters.

Seven days that were seven hours on/seven hours off, with
Tolly layin' in the broad strokes and Inki filling in the details.
Basic stuff, lots of cross-refs, weeks of mentoring crammed into
hours. Sometime in between tutoring and sleep, he talked with
Tocohl, who in turn talked with Inki; the *Admiral* was, reason-
ably enough, privy to all and everything that was said.

The mentors and Tocohl felt that the best thing for the *Admiral*, and for any pirates or bounty hunters he might encounter,
was for Tolly to stay with him. Not only would the presence of a
human pilot on board waylay any questions regarding the *Admiral*'s nature, they would be able to continue with the curriculum.

The *Admiral* had not been . . . completely on board with this
plan, the *Admiral* being of the opinion that he could take care of
himself, in addition to being somewhat averse to further education.

Haz, so the plan went, would serve as Pilot Tocohl's insur-
ance, on her trip back home to Surebleak, and Inki would go on
to wherever it was that Inki was next bound.

Tocohl had a go at convincing the *Admiral* of the need for
local color, at least until he had live-tested discovery scenarios,

and had practiced his clean getaway a couple times or more. The most she got was a promise from the *Admiral* to "sleep on it," which Tolly and Inki both considered to mean, "I'll give you my definitive answer on our next shift together."

So it was that Tolly'd walked into the study room on his last shift with a heavy heart. He'd gotten to know the *Admiral* pretty well during this intensive training course, and knew him to be of a mind to leave humans and human space far behind him.

Couldn't really blame him, considering the treatment he'd gotten so far from humans, themselves not excluded. On the other hand, being as paradoxical as any other living thing, the *Admiral* wanted to be of use. Tolly worried that was Cap'n Waitley's influence, even now, setting that order to keep the station safe.

Well. Not much he could do about it, except ask the question and abide by the answer, same as he would if Haz took it into her head to go haring out into the wide universe with no backup and no real understanding of what she was getting herself into.

"'Mornin', *Admiral*," he said—his usual greeting, no matter what the station clock said.

"Good morning, Tolly," came the answer. "You will be pleased to know that I have reconsidered, and will welcome you as my pilot when we leave Jemiatha Station."

He blinked, and scrambled a moment, mentally.

"I *am* pleased," he said, in the warmest tone available to him. "Mind if I ask what changed your mind?"

"I had a discussion with Inki last shift, and she was able to show me the wisdom of the proposed course."

Well, well. Inki and her powers of persuasion. He'd have to remember to thank her.

"Good," he said. "You want to get a departure time from Station?"

"I have done so, Pilot."

"Nice parse," Tolly said, smiling. "Now, Inki tells me you and her were talking about law and justice. Want to give me a recap? We'll take up where she left off."

• • • ✳ • • •

Padi had her notepad and her cards tucked into a public pocket of her jacket. Infokeys containing her résumé and contact information, including the *Passage*'s pinbeam code, had already gone down to Langlastport, care of Unet Hartensis of Hartensis Catering and Receptions, who would convey them, along with the trade displays that had also been shipped portside, to the Happy Occasion, where the reception would take place.

Trade Etiquette and Proper Presentation, which she had found very dull going in the past, had proven invaluable in the case. There was a perfectly straightforward equation for how many infokeys to take to a trade show; it worked out to roughly thirty percent of the expected attendees. She had added a few more, in case Langlast's traders were eager. Her cards, of course, were not for everyone, though the World Book informed her that the local merchants gave cards as a means of introduction, though they would also offer infokeys. If she gave out two cards, Father would no doubt marvel aloud at her ability to form such rapid connections, but she had hope that all of her infokeys would be taken up.

She patted her pockets one more time, making sure that the Unicredit card was secure—looked in the mirror to assure herself that her hair hadn't come out of its tail yet, and left her quarters at a brisk walk, heading for the shuttle bay.

Their port-bound party included, beside herself and Father, Vanner Higgs, making their third and providing security. Father had taken a suite at the Torridon Hotel on the port, which would be their base for at least three days, so that they might make a *complete tour.*

A complete tour of a brand-new port was reason to be excited, and Padi supposed that she was—or she would be, after she had gotten the reception behind her, and perhaps taken a nap.

She'd had one last communication from Unet Hartensis, who assured her that all was well, that all packages from the ship had been received; that their client farm had sent an arrangement of fresh-cut flowers with the vegetables, as a gift to the guests. They brightened the room, Unet said, and brought summer onto the port.

Padi hoped that the flowers were not an expensive extra that had been deftly slipped in under her nose. If they were, of course, she would dispute the charge. She had in her notepad a copy of the itemized order and projected cost, and flowers were not one of the items listed.

She was, she assured herself, as she hurried down the hall

to the shuttle bay, completely organized and prepared for any eventuality.

She only wished that her stomach believed it.

"Ah, here she is at last!" Father said, as she entered the shuttle boarding gate.

He was there with Mr. Higgs and shuttle pilot Kris Embrathiri. That was odd; usually the pilot was aboard the shuttle ahead of the passengers, but perhaps Kris had already done the checks, and come out to chat.

"Forgive me," she said. "I had no notion that I was late."

"Oh, no, you are most fortunately slightly ahead of our departure," Father assured her. "Pilot Embrathiri has expressed a desire to sit as a passenger on this trip. You, therefore, will pilot us to Langlastport."

She stared at him, then looked to Pilot Embrathiri, who gave her a grin, and stepped forward to offer the ship key.

Padi received it, with a murmur of thanks, as a shiver of... anticipation, ran up her spine.

She was going to pilot live. The prospect pleased her. She bowed to her passengers.

"If you please, I will perform the preflight." She glanced at the bay door, and the amber light above it.

"When the light goes to green, you may board," she said, though there was not one of them that did not know the procedure.

"Thank you, Pilot," Father said serenely. "We will await your signal."

· · · ✳ · · ·

Shan settled into his chair, engaged the webbing and leaned his head against the rest. Kris was in the observer's chair, and Vanner in the passenger seat nearest. They were chatting, low-voiced, between themselves, boon companions and canny old campaigners that they were. The murmur of their voices would soothe the pilot's nerves, simultaneously assuring her that she was not alone, and that no one was paying the slightest attention to her.

Not quite true, of course. Kris *was* observing, and would be quick to the board, should there be need.

Shan didn't think there would be need. It was a well-known trait of pilots—especially of Korval pilots—that they found sims useful, to a certain, specific, point. But live flight—*that* was blood and breath to them. Danae was very right to suppose that Padi's late setbacks were attributable to nothing more than simple boredom.

He settled his head more comfortably against the chair rest, and closed his eyes.

Vanner and Kris were fond comrades; their bond burnished by time, glowing with a steady, comfortable warmth, like a banked fire. Shan deliberately shut them out of his perception, and concentrated on Padi.

There was some anxiety there—flutters of oranges and ambers, nothing out of the way for a second class pilot who had been abruptly called to an unexpected duty.

There was also a definite, though rather subdued, sense of pleasurable excitement. He considered that, having expected to find more...vivacity present in the face of live flight. But perhaps the child was still worrying over details of the reception. If so, that would soon enough be put aside. In fact...

"All passengers," Padi said from the board. "We are cleared; drop in three, at my mark.

"...Mark."

· · · ❋ · · ·

Hazenthull had finished laying in *Tarigan*'s outbound course, when it came to her.

It came to her...that she was never going to see him again. That he would travel with the *Admiral* until that person was deemed able to take care of himself, and then Tolly would—take up his life.

His life that had nothing to do with Surebleak, nor with Hazenthull nor'Phelium.

She, of course, would provide cover for Pilot Tocohl until they raised Surebleak, when they, too, would part, and she would return to Korval's house and take up her duty there. Perhaps Commander Lizardi would have her back on Port Security—but the thought of partnering with some other of the guards...did not appeal.

Perhaps there was some other duty to which she might be set, though she would, naturally, abide by the captain's orders.

She sighed, and spun out of her chair. The ship was too quiet, she thought, with Tolly and Inki—Tocohl, too—aboard *Admiral Bunter.* Tolly had filed for an interim registration, gaining the

Admiral a temporary home port at Callian. It would do well enough until they were clear of Jemiatha space. They would likely file for a permanent registration at Waymart, but she—

She would never know.

Hazenthull took a deep, impatient breath, and turned, as the lock cycled.

A familiar step sounded in the hall, and she felt lightheaded, as if she had fallen hard, and all of the air gone out of her lungs.

Before she had her breath back, Tolly had entered the bridge— and stopped, the easy smile fading from his face.

"What's the problem, Haz?"

She would sound a fool, she thought. But when had Tolly ever laughed at her?

"I was thinking that this will be the last time I will see you," she said. "I will...miss you."

He came forward, face serious. He'd lost weight, she noticed with dismay. The work was wearing him away, and the *Admiral* did not know enough about human people to insist that he eat, exercise, and keep regular shifts.

"I'll miss you, too, Haz. I'm glad we had some extra time to get to know each other better."

Extra time...

She glanced aside.

"That wasn't what you wanted to hear," he said. Tolly had learned her too well, and now...

She took another breath, pushing the air deep in her lungs, and met his eyes.

"I like you, Tolly Jones," she said, her voice a raspy whisper, "very much."

Blue eyes widened, and she had no trouble reading distress, felt her chest constrict again...

"No, hey—Haz."

He had her hand between his small, warm palms, and looked up at her, ridiculous fragile Terran that he was—but she knew that for a lie even as the thought formed. He was Tolly; nothing else mattered.

"Haz, I'm flattered—and I like you, too. Very much. But you gotta know something. Everybody likes me, near enough. That's part of the design."

She frowned down at him, seeing the exhaustion in his face.

Is this a comrade's care? she asked herself. *He needs rest, not a challenge.*

And yet—

"Do you say that my... partiality is... an illusion?"

His mouth tightened, and his hands did, around hers.

"Not saying that at all. Your feelings are absolutely real. I'm sorry, that's all, 'cause you might not've had 'em, except for the design—prolly wouldn't've, in fact—and now I've made you unhappy, and that's not how I oughta treat the best partner I ever had."

His eyes glittered, and it would be among the worst things she had ever done, equal to her part in the Elder's death, if she forced such a warrior as Tolly Jones to tears.

"The Scout says that there is Balance in all things," she said. "So if I will miss you... very much, then I have... liked being your partner... very much. I will remember that."

For a moment, she thought she had done her worst, then he blinked and smiled, and raised her hand.

He bent his head, and she felt his lips, warm and soft, on her skin.

She took a careful breath, and held very still, even as he relinquished her, and looked up, smiling, not the old, bright smile, but a softer thing, perhaps sadder.

"That's the ticket," he said. "I'll remember you, Haz. I'm glad we could say good-bye."

"I am... glad, too," she said, and could think of nothing else to add.

"Right, then," he said, more briskly. "I'll just pick up the rest of my kit. Early lift, tomorrow."

CHAPTER TWENTY-TWO

. . . .

The Happy Occasion
Langlastport

THE FLOWERS WERE QUITE SHAMELESS, A LARGE BOWL OF BRIGHT red, yellow, and blue globes each almost as big as Padi's head. They added a faintly sweet scent to the room's atmosphere which mixed well with that of fresh-baked bread.

"I hope you will find everything to your satisfaction," Unet Hartensis said, guiding her to the tiered buffet tables near the back of the room. The flowers were displayed on their own table, halfway between the entrance and the food. The trade displays were arranged artfully among the tables of food and drink.

"They will draw the guests further in," Unet Hartensis said, apparently intercepting her glance at the flowers and reading a question there. "Once they find the flowers, then they will find the food, which is your ship's gift to them, and the trade information you have provided.

"Now, you will wish to sample what we have to be certain that all is to your liking. Please take up a dish and allow me..."

Obediently, Padi picked up a bright red plate, and allowed Unet Hartensis to place bits of vegetables and dribbles of sauces on it. She tasted carefully. The orange vegetables were sweet; the green ones spicy; the yellow bland.

"Eklist, cobrok, snowits," the caterer murmured the name of the vegetables as Padi tasted each one.

The sauces, merely "sweet," "sour," "hot," and "cream," did not, in Padi's opinion, improve the taste of the vegetables, but if sauce was local custom, then so be it.

"These are good," she said. "The vegetables are very fresh."

"They came in this morning from our grower," Unet Hartensis said, with what Padi heard as pride. She picked up a small cup, turning toward the beverage table—and hesitated, glancing over her shoulder to Padi.

"You must forgive me, Trader. Langlast enforces an age law with regard to the consumption of wine and other spirits. May I ask if you are above nineteen Standards?"

"I have but seventeen Standards," she said, which was near enough, and did not add that she had been drinking wine since she had achieved fourteen Standards. It would make no difference to the local law, and she, for one, had no wish to be arrested by Port Security ever again.

"I, however," Father said from her right hand, "am in my dotage, and would welcome a taste of the summer wine."

Unet Hartensis smiled at him, amused, Padi thought. Amused, and...something else. She poured the wine generously, and offered it to him, her fingers lingering needlessly against his.

Father did not seem to notice anything amiss, merely smiled and sipped, his head tipped slightly to a side.

"Ah," he said, after a long moment. "That is very pleasant, Chef Hartensis; I don't suppose you offer any of this vintage on the market?"

"You flatter me, Trader; I am no chef, merely one who arranges entertainments. As for the vintage..."

She sighed and looked regretful.

"The summer blend is one of our local treasures and may not be sold for off-world trade."

"I understand entirely," Father murmured. "I wonder—may I purchase a bottle or two for my own table?"

The caterer's face lit in a wide smile.

"You may purchase as many as six bottles at any duty-free shop, which also offer other of Langlast's treasures, for personal use only."

"Thank you," Father said, answering her smile. He drank the last of the wine in the glass, and glanced about him, perhaps for a tray on which to deposit it.

"Allow me," Unet Hartensis said, taking the glass from his

hand, her fingers again lingering along his. Padi felt her breath go short, which was absurd, and a decidedly odd sensation in the area of her stomach... and wondered if one of the sauces had disagreed with her digestion.

"Padi," Father said. "Would you care for something to drink?"

The peculiar feeling exploded into embarrassment, and she looked up at him, feeling her face flame, without precisely knowing why, and here then was Unet Hartensis, exclaiming, and turning toward her.

"Trader, please forgive me! You must, of course, taste our own montora juice!" She placed Father's glass on the edge of the table, snatched up another and poured blue juice from one of several pitchers.

"Thank you," Padi murmured, hoping that the juice would soothe her.

She took a sip and almost gasped aloud at the astringent taste.

"Montora juice is served to guests of formal dinners, after each course is removed. It cleans the palate wonderfully!" the caterer said. "Do you find it so?"

"Indeed," Padi was able to say, somewhat breathlessly. "A... very cleansing beverage!"

Unet Hartensis smiled, and waited, by which Padi realized that she was expected to finish what remained in her glass. She did so, managing to keep her breath this time, and the caterer took the glass, her fingers impersonal and brisk.

"Now, I know you will want to sample the sweets!" Unet Hartensis said, glancing over her shoulder, perhaps meaning to include Father in her invitation—

But Father had left them; he was moving toward the front of the room and the double doors through which their guests would come... shortly, Padi thought, glancing at the clock above the door as she followed the caterer to the sweets table.

· · · ※ · · ·

Shan paused by the flowers, closed his eyes, took a deep breath of lightly scented air, and sighed. As he understood local custom as practiced upon Langlast, Unet Hartensis had been only slightly forward in her attentions to himself. Had he been local, it would have been his part to be flattered by her favorable notice. In fact, he *was* flattered by her favorable notice—one was human, after all—and easily able to shield oneself from the warmth of her regard.

Padi, however . . .

Shan sighed again.

It had been very apparent that Padi had *felt* the caterer's ardor. Which rather inescapably brought him to the conclusion that his daughter was, indeed, a Healer.

That was, he thought carefully, gratifying.

Certainly, if Padi were to come into possession of her gifts during the reception, that might be . . . awkward. However, he did not think she would do so.

He thought . . . *had* thought since their flight down from the *Passage* just this afternoon, when Padi yos'Galan, who had been accustomed to *thrill* at the sight of a piloting board, sat her station with great calmness, competency—and no delight whatsoever— that there was more to this situation of gifts and stone and walls than met even a Healer's eye.

She might have been sitting a sim, save that her reaction time was appropriate to the demands of maneuvering the shuttle in real-time and space. He had expected excitement, exhilaration, perhaps a moment or two of terror—all the sorts of things likely to be experienced by a young pilot still learning her wings— and all he had felt from her, beyond an early frisson of pleased anticipation, had been the concentration appropriate to a working pilot, and grit, sand, and stone.

He had not dared probe too deeply, and risk breaking the pilot's concentration. He dared not probe too deeply *now*, lest he create the very circumstance he wished to avoid.

Stone. *Walls*, Lina had said, and he, too, had glimpsed something structured and dire. Plainly Padi had been some time at this work and—doubting the wisdom of creating such an edifice, as he did, most stringently—he could not help but trust that *it would hold*. He knew Padi yos'Galan, the meticulous care she brought to her studies and her work. Whatever had motivated her to create such a thing, he did not doubt that it had been done with nothing less than thoroughness.

That, of course, begged the question of how they, the elder Healers, ought most wisely to proceed in the case—but that question was for after the reception, when they were alone in their rooms, and free from the distractions of lusty caterers.

It occurred to him then that Padi had not yet had her bed-lessons, which would ordinarily be an easily corrected oversight, as Lina was fully capable as a teacher. However, this structure—this *environment*—that Padi had created for herself... until they knew what the child had *done*, precisely...

A clock chimed suddenly, very close by.

Shan took another deep, flower-scented breath, ran a Healer's relaxation exercise, and opened his eyes.

Unet Hartensis was moving toward the doors. He turned and found Padi coming toward him, looking, perhaps, a little wan.

"Is all well, Trader yos'Galan?" he murmured.

That earned him a small smile.

"I believe so, Master Trader, but—a word in your ear."

She leaned forward, and he bent slightly, giving her his literal, as well as his metaphorical, ear.

"Avoid the blue juice at all costs," she whispered. "It is dreadful!"

· · · ✳ · · ·

Tolly woke all at once, and wished he hadn't. His head felt like somebody had taken the business side of an axe to it, and his mouth tasted foul. For a moment, he just lay there, on a surface giving enough to possibly be his bunk, too craven to open up his eyes.

"Tolly Jones," a voice spoke from overhead—a *soft* voice, if not particularly gentle—and lately very familiar to him.

"*Admiral*?" he said.

"Yes. I am pleased that you have regained consciousness. Inki predicted that you would do so at approximately this hour. She asked me to present this message to you, immediately."

There was a slight—but not *too* slight—pause before Inki's voice came through the ceiling speaker.

"My most profound apologies, Mentor. It is a vile potion, but effective. Analgesics will tame the headache, and high-c juice will make the mouth taste sweeter."

Analgesics and high-c, was it?

He opened his eyes, to the merest slits, and found that the dim light of his cabin at least made the headache no worse.

"Where is Inki?" he asked the *Admiral*.

"Aboard *Ahab-Esais*."

That was a surprise. Why had the woman drugged him, if she was—

No, wait. You're not thinking, Tolly Jones. Think.

"Where is *Ahab-Esais*?" he asked.

"Now breaking dock," the *Admiral* answered.

"Get Inki on comm for me."

"I am sorry not to be able to accommodate your request, Tolly," the *Admiral* said.

That sent a cold chill down a man's back. Inki'd set a mandate, had she? Well, all right. He doubted he had much civil to say to Inki, now that he thought about it.

Tolly swung his legs over the edge of his bunk, and waited for his head to stop spinning.

"Analgesics and juice are on the table," the *Admiral* said. "Please, Tolly, care for yourself."

Well, this was a touching concern, and a little out of character for the *Admiral*. He wondered, briefly, what else Inki had been tampering with, and put the thought aside for more immediate concerns.

"*Admiral*, please get Tocohl on comm for me."

"I am sorry, Tolly. Tocohl is not available to comm."

His stomach hurt. He reached for the little bottle of pills, threw three down his throat and followed them with a tangy swallow of high-c.

"Please get Hazenthull on comm."

"Hazenthull is not currently available to comm, Pilot. I am sorry."

Worse and worse. He took another swig of juice, decided he was good to go, and got up on his feet, pleased not to wobble.

"Please open the hatch," he said. "I'm going on dock."

"I regret that is not possible. We are in transit toward the Jump point."

Tolly sat back down on his bunk, cold all the way through.

"Destination?" he asked, but he thought he knew the answer to that.

"The Lyre Institute office on Nostrilia."

Raw fear hit him. He took a breath, and pushed the fear aside.

"Return to Jemiatha Station."

"Jemiatha Station will not allow me to dock, Tolly. You know this."

Well, at least he should've suspected it, given the tenor of their last communication with Stew.

"Inki left a second message for you. However, she said that you must not hear it until you had showered, eaten and, quote, felt human again, unquote."

He closed his eyes, opened them. Stood.

"All right then," he said flatly, and headed for the 'fresher.

CHAPTER TWENTY-THREE

Jemiatha's Jumble Stop
Tarigan
Berth 12

ADMIRAL BUNTER LEFT DOCK DURING HER SLEEP SHIFT.

Hazenthull leaned over the board, checking *Tarigan*'s departure, in six hours, after *Ahab-Esais*, in two. There was a memo in her queue from Pilot Tocohl—approval of the course she had laid in before going off duty. There was no further comment; there was no need for comment, the course being simple: a mere reversal of the route that had brought them here, until they raised the planet Surebleak.

Home, as those of Clan Korval now had it.

Of Pilot Tocohl herself, there was no sign. She was, perhaps, saying her good-byes to Inki. Pilot Tocohl had become...friendly of Inki; they held, so Hazenthull understood, interests in common, among them the history of so-called artificial intelligence.

She had found Tolly in the galley during one of his off-shifts, and had asked him why Pilot Tocohl's intelligence—and *Admiral Bunter*'s—bore the burden of artificiality, when they were demonstrably intelligent, as well as much quicker of thought than flesh-and-blood persons.

Inki, who heard the question on her way through the galley to her shift with *Admiral Bunter*, laughed, and said, "It is human ego, Pilot Haz, and nothing more than that!"

"Well," Tolly had said, with a small smile, "something more than that, actually. See, Haz, some folks think that, because *Admiral Bunter* and Tocohl, and all the rest of their people, have had *information* uploaded to their brains, that their *intelligence* is . . . less real than any given human's intelligence. The idea is that they didn't have to work for that information; to learn it like an organic brain has to learn it."

"But information," Hazenthull had objected, when Tolly stopped to sip from his mug of 'mite, "is . . . only data. Intelligence is . . . manipulating data, and drawing conclusions."

"Right. You know that, because you're smart, and you think about things. Same can't be said for most of the rest of us, who keep on believing that something that's manufactured is artificial."

He had suddenly looked very weary, and Hazenthull had excused herself so that he could finish his meal in peace, and seek his few hours of rest.

On *Tarigan*'s bridge, Hazenthull stretched to her full height, and did a series of quick bends, to ease the crick in her back. The silence oppressed her. She glanced at the time display on the board, and nodded. She would take a walk—a farewell walk—about Jemiatha Station. Perhaps she would—no, *definitely* she would stop at the Jumble House and have a last Jumbleburger for her preflight meal. She had become very fond of the Jumbleburger, which was a chewy yeast patty seasoned with sweet-hot spices, a slice of soy cheese on top and bottom, and the whole served between two slices of fresh-baked bread.

Even in the short while they had been at dock, Pilot Tocohl had become a commonplace on Jemiatha Station. Whether the stationers knew her for *Admiral Bunter*'s kin, or simply accepted her as the "utility 'bot" Tolly had claimed her to be, seemed immaterial. Tocohl was known and accepted, and therefore would experience no difficulty returning alone along the dock to *Tarigan* from *Ahab-Esais*.

And if some fool was so unwise as to attempt to importune her, well—Pilot Tocohl was well able to take care of herself.

Hazenthull clipped a portable comm to her belt, checked her weapons, all but one hidden, out of respect for stationer nerves, and left *Tarigan*'s too-quiet deck.

· · · ❈ · · ·

"Mentor," Inki's voice filled the bridge. Tolly sat in the pilot's chair, arms folded over his chest, head against the backrest, eyes closed.

"Mentor, it has been an honor to assist you in the performance of our art. It grieves me beyond my poor ability to express, that I must serve you this turn. I hope that you will find it in you to forgive me—or at least to understand me.

"I flatter myself, in fact, that you *will* understand me, for I am one like unto yourself. That being so, and having discovered you, I had no other option, but to put forth my best efforts to secure you for the institute. The directors are, as I am certain you must be aware, keen to recover you.

"I could not refuse my imperatives; I do not, of course, have to explain this to *you*. This is why you wake to find yourself aboard *Admiral Bunter* on course to Nostrilia."

There was a small pause, then Inki cleared her throat.

"Having fulfilled my duty to the directors, I then undertook to do what I might for you.

"You have an ally at large. I trust that her loyalty is such that she will not allow you to fall into the hands of the directors. I also trust that she is your hope of last resort. For it is not for nothing, Tollance Berik-Jones, that you are known as the greatest mentor of our time. *Admiral Bunter* remains in need of further education. I trust—no, in this I am certain!—that you will be able to impart to him all of those things he yet requires in order to make an informed decision...before you come to Nostrilia orbit."

Another pause, then Inki's voice again, somewhat less brisk, even...regretful.

"I bid you good-bye, Mentor. I have learned much at your side. Thank you, for the gift of your expertise, and for your professional regard. I will long look upon our association, and the work we performed together, as one of the brightest episodes of my life."

"Message ends," a mechanical voice stated.

Tolly reached to the board, and, after a moment, saved the message to his queue.

Then he took a deep breath.

Inki was one of his schoolmates, was she? He felt that he ought to have known that, but—how would he know? They were designed to pass as full human, and those employed by the institute were...discouraged from revealing themselves. Especially were they discouraged from revealing themselves to truants the directors were keen to recover.

And how *interesting*, that Inki was apparently able to hedge her bet, and provide him with—

An ally?

He suddenly sat up straight in the chair.

An ally?

Haz.

Inki'd gotten *Haz* mixed into Lyre business.

That wasn't good. In fact, it was bad, really bad. Haz'd killed two directors, which the remainder weren't at all likely to be forgiving of—and he wouldn't be there to back her up.

"*Admiral Bunter*, it's imperative that I speak to *Tarigan*."

"I am sorry, Tolly; I cannot allow that."

He opened his mouth, and closed it again. Inki did good work. There was no use arguing with the *Admiral*, and no reset possible. If he was a fool, he could check his codes, but he wasn't a fool—and neither was Inki. Of course, she'd've locked him out at the control level.

Which left him with goodwill, trust, and *his* powers of persuasion.

"Well, I'm sorry for that," he said, "and it's likely to make trouble for Haz, who didn't ever make any trouble for you, but rules're rules. I do understand that. Any chance I can take a look at the current route?"

There was a tiny pause, as if he'd managed to startle the lad, which he surely hoped he had.

"Of course the pilot may see the route," *Admiral Bunter* said politely. "I remind that it is locked in."

"Sure it is," Tolly said softly.

His screen four came live, showing the countdown to the Jump point, and the course as laid in, thereafter.

· · · ※ · · ·

Ahab-Esais left dock as she was finishing her meal. She watched the undocking on the large screen that dominated the back wall of the Jumble House. She already knew Inki for a competent pilot, and she watched with interest as *Ahab-Esais* backed away from station, rolled, and tumbled into her assigned lane, moving at sublight for the Jump point.

Hazenthull ate the last bite of her Jumbleburger, wiped away the tears the spices had brought to her eyes, and downed what was left of her tea in one gulp. She stood, carried plate, cup, and utensils to the recycling station, deposited them, and exited into a crowded station corridor.

She'd barely made the first cross-corridor when the comm on her belt chimed in Pilot Tocohl's sequence. Hazenthull snatched the unit to her ear.

"Yes, Pilot?"

"Ah, Pilot Haz, how quick you are!" cried a familiar voice that was, nonetheless, not Pilot Tocohl. "It is Inkirani Yo, aboard *Ahab-Esais*. I am contacting you with a change of plans. Pilot Tocohl is traveling with me. She and I are bound to track down a rumor that exercises a strong fascination over both of us. When our curiosity is satisfied, she will return to her home port."

"Hey, watch it, there, big girl!" a stationer snapped, slapping Hazenthull's elbow aside.

She spun, and ducked into a small service alcove.

"The pilot is with you?" she asked, scarcely able to credit it.

"She is, yes."

"I would speak with her."

"I am sorry; she is unable to come to comm at the moment. But, Pilot Haz, that is not all the news I have for you!"

Her chest was tight; there was something very wrong—the pilot was meticulous. She had left the proposed course in Hazenthull's queue. If she had intended to travel with Inki, would she not have left that information as well? Such sudden starts were... not like her.

And now, she was unavailable?

"You are very quiet," Inki said in her ear. "Do you not care for further news?"

"What further news?" she demanded, running times in her head, weighing her honor with Jemiatha Station against Pilot Tocohl's liberty...

"I fear that Mentor Berik-Jones has run into a spot of trouble with *Admiral Bunter*. There is a course laid in to...someplace, let us say, that the mentor would prefer not to go, and the *Admiral* under compulsion to take him there. I mention this because your loyalty may be such that you feel impelled to take this matter under your correction."

"This is you? *You* did this?"

"I fear so, Pilot Haz. I hope that you will forgive me, but I do not think you will."

"Where are they going?"

"No, no, Pilot Haz; I've already told you more than I ought. If I hint you further along, I will do myself a mischief, which the directors would hardly care for. I am expensive, I am. Just like Mentor Berik-Jones."

"Inki..." Hazenthull began, though she hardly knew what she would say, or ask for. The return of Pilot Tocohl? The recall of *Admiral Bunter*?

"Inki," she said again, and it seemed the question formed itself. "Why have you done this?"

There was a slight pause, just too long for lag, before Inki said softly, "Necessity."

Hazenthull swallowed, took a breath for another question—

And the comm went dead.

. . . ☀ . . .

Padi couldn't quite remember when the room had gotten crowded. For the longest time, it had been only herself, Father, Mr. Higgs, and Unet Hartensis, even after the doors had been opened.

Then, a pair of merchants had appeared, wearing skirts down to their ankles and wide belts all hung 'round with pouches at their waists, and brightly colored, wide-collared shirts.

Father had gone forward to greet them, and Padi had started in that direction, also, which was good, because another pair of traders came in behind the first, and paused on the threshold, as if unsure. Padi kept going, past Father and his pair, to the new ones, bowing and remembering to smile broadly.

"Good day to you," she said in Trade. "I am Padi yos'Galan, apprentice trader on *Dutiful Passage*. Whom do I have the pleasure of welcoming to our entertainment?"

Introductions came forth. The trader in the pale orange shirt was Malekai Gerome, senior sales associate at Gerome Mercantile. The trader wearing the brilliant green shirt was Irfenda Dorst, head buyer for the same establishment. Their Trade was good, but their accents so heavy that Padi had to concentrate intently to be certain of their words.

"I am very pleased to meet you," she said, and stood a little to the side, showing them the laden tables with a little wave of her hand. "Please, refresh yourselves."

They smiled, and nodded, and moved past her. Father, she saw, was now speaking with a threesome, all dressed in dark skirts and crimson shirts—and, just as she looked back toward the door, here came a lone trader, splendid in lemon yellow from shoulder to ankle; she stepped forward to greet this new guest.

So, indeed, the room had filled, by ones and twos and threes. The guests refreshed themselves and moved about the room, perusing their small trade displays, and taking up the master trader's infokey and, a few of them, also the apprentice's key.

Most of them wanted to speak to Father, of course, but more than six made a particular point of approaching her, and speaking with her about her particular cargoes and specialities. Her ear slowly became accustomed to the accent, though she began to feel a tiny ache behind her eyes, as if she had been staring at a study screen too long.

They were not so very much interested in imported foodstuffs, but wondered after the markets, off-world, for certain preserved items, and dried natural fruits and vegetables. There was also something—a beverage, as she gathered it, not tea, perhaps more akin to coffee, but not coffee, either. *Oonlah*, as she heard the word, and detected disappointment, that there was none on offer among the refreshments.

"Ahbut yeel not be knowning it for a staple, with coming from far away," said Sales Associate Gerome.

"'Prentice trader might not know, but yon Hartensis true knows!" his companion of the bright green shirt, Buyer Dorst, said hotly. "A spread of all that's fine from Langlast farms and harvests, and none of *oonlah*?"

"I am sorry to have missed a favorite beverage," Padi said, her head throbbing now. "Perhaps I might send out, and repair the error. Who may provide us, on the port?"

"Non, non," came a new voice, this one deep and belonging to one Herst Plishet, a textile broker. "Don let these two sorry trickers pullin your leg, Trader. *Oonlah*'s one of our usual drinks, make no mine o'that! But, to name it Langlast Fine, along o'the wines and the juices and the fine breads you've laid for us—that's a joik, that is, and shame on the pair of you for it. The trader here spairt a thought for our comfort, and Unet laid out fresher'n fresh to pleasure us, like she never fails to do. Woulja rather that fella off from *Zorba's Zen*, who offered us crackers and beer?"

That was apparently not a happy memory. Padi felt derision and irritation in equal measure, and Dorst of the green shirt made a stiff little bow by bending at a forty-five degree angle from the waist, while looking up into her face.

"Iz like Herst has it, Trader—a joik, only a joik. Iz a fine treat you've made for us, you and Unet, too. Annit so, Malekai?"

"Completely so," said Senior Gerome, bowing in his turn. He and his associate then moved off in the direction of the wine table.

Padi sighed surreptitiously, the ache in her head easing, just a little—and flaring again as the textile broker spoke.

"I read the packet bootcher ship, Trader, and the hard choices that come to, and was answered by, your family that owns it. I wonder, havin mooft house like's been done, how stable is your base, noo? Speaking for myself, I value long-term partners in trade. It'd upset me no end to just be settling in to a long arrangement, and learn that finances have foundered on fortune's rocks and our association's sundered."

CHAPTER TWENTY-FOUR

. . . .

The Happy Occasion
Langlastport

SHAN EXCHANGED CARDS WITH MARTHIMYR SEIRT, MASTER OF the Langlast Technology Exchange. Master Seirt had not precisely *said* that he was interested in . . . antiquities, but he had not precisely been disinterested in the subject either, when Shan artlessly misunderstood his role. As it happened, Langlast had a vigorous culture of invention of new technologies, and adaptation of existing technologies. They prided themselves on being able to improve any mechanical design brought to them, and also produced manufacturing designs upon request.

"Also, gineric plans for a range o'basic useful items," Master Seirt had said. "Base level 'bots—cleaning, security and the like— through your mid-level servers and house-minders." He'd given Shan an arch look here, the mention of Old Tech having come earlier.

"Non one of 'em smarter'n I am, never mindin yourself, Trader. Living units for all environments, all just smart enough—there's my own area, now. One or two of my designs're fetching, I like to think, and there's others worth the look. Truth, it's likely the gineral plans'll be the most use to you. We'll provide you with a display, set it up in a corner of the booth. Them plans'll sell themselfs. Seen it time and again. You come call on me tomorrow, midday. I'll see ye balanced for your hospitality here today, show you 'round the shop, and letcha have a look at the display unit. Is that done?"

"Done," Shan said, and nodded at the card the man still held in his hand. "There's a beam code on that. If you'll do me the favor of sending a confirmation. These receptions leave me quite scrambled."

Master Seirt laughed.

"Aye, I'll lay odds they do just that. I'm looking forward to our next meeting—and tell you, now! Bring your 'prentice, eh?"

"You are very kind."

"Non, non, nothing kind there. It's the duty of experience to teach inexperience, so said m'mother, and I find the same." Another comfortable laugh. "If we don' train'em up right we've only ourselfs to blame when they make hash in place o'profit."

Shan laughed softly.

"I agree! We both look forward to seeing you tomorrow."

Master Seirt bowed then, a peculiarly wooden bending at the waist, until his back was straight and his face was pointed at the floor. It was a mercifully brief exercise, which Shan exchanged for a slight bow between business associates, as Master Seirt straightened and moved away toward the wine table.

Shan sighed. Thus far, the reception was going well. Indeed, now that he had a chance to properly survey the room, it would seem that they had managed to convene a crush. Caterer Hartensis stood at the corner of the wine table, serving as quantity control and, so he suspected, to enforce the local age law regarding the imbibing of spirits, while a helper wearing a long red apron over his white skirts brought out a new plate of breads and slipped it deftly into place.

Padi—

Padi was in the midst of an animated discussion with three respectably dressed port brokers. Even as he spied her, two of her interlocutors ambled off, like Master Siert, to the wine table. The third moved closer to Padi, and bent somewhat, as if to put a question. To the outer eyes, Padi was tense, but no more than one might expect of someone hosting her first reception.

Shan opened a tight road, from him to her, and caught the brittle edge of her headache. He considered rubbing it away, but even as he did, shadows moved at his elbow, and he turned to bow to a new pair of Langlast merchants.

· · · ✳ · · ·

"The family finances are sound, sir," Padi said, which was no more than she had heard Father answer to other, like inquiries, at other ports. "Of course, there were expenses involved in our relocation, and of course, now that we are settled, we are looking for new partners, and new routes to business. There is no expectation at all that we shall founder, as trade remains at our core."

Herst Plishet nodded gravely, and sipped from his cup.

"That's pretty said, that is, nor I won't hide from you that I expected to hear the gloss. But I'm a serious man, Trader, and gloss won't hold me. Have ye numbers—statistics, it might be said—to reassure me?"

She tried to concentrate through the flickering pain in her head. It seemed that Broker Plishet wished to be given proof that Korval would endure... forever. Aunt Anthora could, perhaps, prove the future—Priscilla might, indeed, prove the future, when the necessity was upon her... but Apprentice Trader Padi yos'Galan lacked their advantages.

She took a breath.

"These are questions better put to the master trader," she murmured. "May I bring you to him, sir?"

"Oh, no, never put yerself to such trouble! I've spoken to the master trader, and stood a bye and listened to him. He's an apt lad, and non dummy, I'll wager. If I ask it hard enough of him, he may give me a nugget more, that the head o'family might've allowed him to say—no disrespect to the master trader or the da at home! But yerself, Trader, you've got nothing to tell me but what you know, seeit? And I already got from you that there's something not quite what it ought to be."

Her head was going to explode, gods. She dare not close her eyes and access board rest, not with this man watching her so closely.

Padi raised her head and met the broker's eyes.

"Sir, you ask me to prove the future. I have no such abilities. I can only point to our record—the past—and extrapolate from that. Those records are available, and I would be pleased to send them to you, when I return to the ship. May I have an address capable of receiving a download? I should warn you that our trade history is long, and the download large."

He was clearly amused.

"Now, there's plain speaking, and a generous offer alongside it!

But, Trader, much as I agree with you that non can scry tomorra; sure it is you'll agree with me, that the past is gone and puts no weight on the future."

"No," Padi said, around the jagged pain in her head, "there we disagree, sir. If the past has no bearing on the future, you would not be asking me for a guarantee that I'll wager you, yourself, would not give, were our roles reversed. Indeed, let us test it now, as we stand here together.

"Can you provide me with proof that Langlast's textile mills will not founder and fold some short while after we have concluded an agreement?"

"Why, Trader, Langlast's mills have endured these two hundred Standards and more! What d'you imagine might cause them to fail—*all* of them to fail—now?"

"My imagination is not at issue, sir. I seek assurance for the future, and you offer me the dead and dusty past. How am I to make a rational decision unless I have hard facts?"

He threw his head back then, and laughed so loudly that the rest of the room quietened as all eyes turned toward them.

If Herst Plishet were the least bit discomfited by the attention he had gathered, it did not display itself in a return to seemliness. Indeed, he laughed the harder, and slapped his leg, in addition.

Padi felt her ears growing warm and her head pounding fit to burst...

A large, warm hand landed lightly on her shoulder. She turned her head to look up into Father's face. He was smiling his trade smile, which was nothing at all like his real smile, and his eyes were...rather cool.

"Are you quite well, sir?" he asked, and his voice was cool, too.

"Oh, I'm well, and weller, too!" the broker said, his hilarity subsiding to a point where he might speak. He raised a hand to wipe his eyes, and gave Padi a wide grin.

"Trader, it's been a long time since I've been so masterfully sassed! All honor to you, and I'll be offering you my own key—" Two fingers dipped into one of the pouches suspended from his belt and brought forth an infokey, which he offered to her across the palm of his hand, as if he offered her his dirk.

"Come to the Textile Hall tomorrow, if your schedule allows it, and ask for me by name. There are some items I think you might find of interest. If you do, well, then, we two will come to an agreement made in the present, with neither the past weighing overheavy on us, nor the future only black."

"Thank you," Padi said, taking the key gingerly from his palm, and tucking it into a jacket pocket. "Have you a beam code? My schedule tomorrow—"

"On the key, Trader," he said, grinning anew. "All of it on the key."

"Thank you," she said again, Father's hand still gentle on her shoulder.

"My pleasure, Trader, and it's truth as I say it." He bowed then, the stiff-backed salutation that seemed to be common here.

Padi bowed as to a business associate, and Father inclined his head. Broker Plishet straightened and strode away, toward the back of the room and the wine table.

The rest of the guests seemed to take a collective breath before they turned back to their interrupted conversations.

"Now I wonder... did you sass our guest?" Father asked, for her ears alone.

She sighed, and did not lift a hand to rub at her forehead.

"I fear that I must have done. He was pushing me to prove that Korval's fortunes would remain firm, and I—in order to show him how insupportable his... his demand was, I asked that he provide me proof that the Langlast mills would not fail..."

She shook her head, waking bright blades of pain.

"I should not have done so," she murmured. "He wished to make some point about Korval's relocation, and my head was—" She stopped, biting her lip. She had not meant to mention her headache.

Father's fingers exerted pressure, and she sighed, relaxing somewhat under the warmth of his touch.

"May I assist you with the headache, Trader?"

It was a small thing, she thought; only a headache, scarcely worthy of a Healer's attention. Yet—it could have as easily gone the other way, the matter with Broker Plishet, and the *Passage* come under the frown of the Langlastport merchants entire, for she remembered how the others had deferred to him, and cut short their own game.

"If you please," she murmured. "It's the stupidest thing..."

"Not at all. The day has scarcely been free of stress... of which I will speak more in a moment. Close your eyes, child, and take a deep breath..."

She did so, and felt a subtle embrace, as if everyone who loved her had wrapt her in their arms at once. A cool breeze wafted sweetly through the hallways and closed rooms inside her head, cooling the pain, loosening knots and straightening... things... she had not known were awry.

The breeze subsided by degrees so small that she did not mark its cessation, and only knew, with an intensity that brought tears to her eyes—that her head no longer hurt.

She cleared her throat and took a moment to gather herself.

"Thank you," she said, turning to face Father.

She surprised what might have been distress on his face—gone before she could be certain.

"You are quite welcome, Trader," he said in a light, teasing tone. "Please do not hesitate to request assistance from this office again. It is, I assure you, my pleasure to serve. Now, attend me, child: we have an appointment tomorrow to meet with Master Seirt, of the Langlast Technology Exchange. He particularly requested your attendance. You, of course, are to visit the worthy textile broker, and we shall doubtless gather more invitations before this event is concluded. Constrained as we are to wander as a threesome, I hope you will not find it too tiresome to tour the port with me—"

"Not at all!" Padi said, perhaps a little too loudly. Certainly, her enthusiasm was genuine.

"Excellent. What I propose is a small tour after the reception is over, of the portion of the port between the Happy Occasion and our hotel. We will dine, you and I will compare our various appointments, and we will speak together before seeking our beds.

"Tomorrow morning, assuming all proceeds as it ought this evening, we shall begin in earnest. Does this schedule find approval with you?"

"Yes, sir, it does," she said, smiling and eager. Her excitement was plain to a Healer's senses...

...and so was the cold adamancy of stone.

• • • ✴ • • •

"*Admiral Bunter*, this is Hazenthull nor'Phelium, piloting *Tarigan*. Am I heard?"

There was delay, naturally enough; the *Admiral* was very nearly at the Jump point.

"Pilot nor'Phelium, you are heard," came the *Admiral*'s voice—the *Admiral*'s *new* voice as she thought of it, so much more energy and strength came with the words.

"I would speak with Pilot-Mentor Jones," she said. "If he is able to come to the comm."

"Tolly Jones is not permitted comm," *Admiral Bunter* said, and added, after a small hesitation. "If you wish to record a message, I will ensure that he receives it."

"Why is he not permitted comm?" Hazenthull asked. "Is he a prisoner?"

"He is . . ." *Admiral Bunter*'s voice faded, then came back, though not quite as strong as previously, "He is a pirate."

"A pirate?" Hazenthull stared at the comm, utterly dumbfounded. "Tolly Jones, a pirate? He *fought* pirates when we were partnered, and ensured the safety and order of the port. He is no more a pirate than—" She knew a moment's qualm, regarding those persons who might be considered, by the *Admiral*'s still-stringent reckoning, to be pirates, and had a happy inspiration.

"Tolly Jones is no more a pirate than you are!"

"Tolly Jones withholds from the Lyre Institute a valuable item which rightfully belongs to the directors of the institute. He knowingly withholds this valuable and is, thereby, a pirate."

That had a strong feel of a lesson learnt by rote, thought Hazenthull, no stranger to such things. However, time was too short to enter into a protracted debate with a stubborn AI, even had she a hope of prevailing. She was an Explorer, and as such more able than a common troop to enter into debate. However, she had observed Tolly and Inki at their work, and was able to concede, without dishonoring her own skills, that she was no mentor. If Tolly himself had not been able to argue the *Admiral* free of this lesson . . .

"Pilot nor'Phelium, I urge you to record quickly, if you wish to leave Tolly Jones a message. I am nearing a mark."

"Yes," she said, and for a long precious minute could think of nothing to say.

"Pilot? Your message?"

She took a breath.

"Tolly, it is Haz. I have your back."

Another breath.

"Message ends," she said.

"Recorded," *Admiral Bunter* said. "Out."

The comm light went dark. Hazenthull contemplated it for a moment, then touched the switch that activated the pinbeam.

"To Captain Miri Robertson," she said. "Jelaza Kazone, Surebleak. From House Guard Hazenthull nor'Phelium, on detached duty..."

· · · ❉ · · ·

"A message arrives for you, Tolly Jones," the *Admiral* said. "Do you wish to hear it?"

"Yes," he said, which might've been a little brief, but the *Admiral* didn't seem to notice. Or maybe he did, because there was no acknowledgment of his preference—so that Haz suddenly saying his name made him jump in his seat.

"Tolly," she said, sounding solid and on task, just like Haz always sounded. "I have your back."

Dammit.

It brought tears to his eyes, that simple statement, like everything wrong was suddenly set right, 'cause Haz had his back, which was foolishness. Big and tough she might be and a soldier bred, born, and trained—all that meant in the end was that she was a little harder to kill. That was *all* it meant.

Damned if he was going to have Haz's death on him.

Damned if he was going to *let them* hurt one short bristly brown hair on her head.

"*Admiral*, please relay a message to Haz." He wondered what message he could possibly send that would turn her from her purpose, even if the *Admiral* agreed to—

"Recording," the *Admiral* stated. "I suggest brevity, we are about to transition."

Right.

He took a breath.

"Haz, it's Tolly," he said, his voice clipped and hard. "Go home. I don't want you, and I don't *need* you. Message ends."

He closed his eyes then, and leaned back in his chair, sick to his stomach, his palms cold and sweaty. That oughta do the trick. Kick her a good one right where she was most vulnerable. In the temper, that was one place.

In the heart, that was the other.

Always trust the training.

· · · ❉ · · ·

Shan moved to the juice display, and accepted a glass from the attendant. He would have rather had wine, but the casks were overseen by Caterer Hartensis herself, and he had no wish to find himself admired at the moment.

Padi—

Her gift was straining at the stony restraints she had placed upon it. The assault of *so many* emotional grids, some, as he had noticed himself, quite distractingly loud; the stress of responsibility—how could one *not* be stressed as the host of one's very first reception? He remembered his first reception with a thrill of nerves even now, though he had been only a very little older then than Padi was now, and already trained in Healer protocols, as well as in bed manners.

Well.

He had done what he could for the moment. The absence of the headache alone would lessen her general levels of stress. He'd also performed a very basic Sort, to calm her; and placed a block, a measure in which he put not much confidence, considering the weight of power he felt building, like a thunderhead towering over his child's head.

He wished he had a more thorough understanding of the structure Padi had created; and how, precisely, those walls had been formed, and with what materials. However, a public reception was no place in which to perform an in-depth examination, and he did believe that his small efforts would hold well until they arrived at the hotel. Once they could be private, more appropriate measures could be applied.

Briefly, he considered sending her back to the *Passage* while he and Vanner remained on port—very briefly. Padi would feel— and justly—that she was being denied an experience vital to her growth as a trader.

Shan sighed, and raised the cup to sip juice.

His mouth puckered and dried—which was, as Priscilla might say, a blessing in disguise, as he could scarcely breathe for a moment, much less gasp aloud. The sensation passed, leaving his mouth feeling perfectly clarified and clean.

Carefully, he lowered the cup and looked inside.

Blue juice.

He sighed.

Padi had warned him, after all.

CHAPTER TWENTY-FIVE

. . . .

The Happy Occasion
Langlastport

THE FLOWERS HAD BEEN A GIFT, AFTER ALL, AND MS. HARTENSIS had been a good steward and made certain that the wine had not been overdrunk, which would have been an extra cask charge.

The leftover breads, sweets and vegetables would, Ms. Hartensis said, be packed up so that Padi might send them up to the ship.

"You have, after all, paid for these items, Trader," she said.

That was certainly true, though there was scarcely enough to feed the *Passage*, and if they were to be made a gift to odd-shift, or maintenance . . .

"I wonder," Father said, "if there may not be a local . . . public kitchen, where those who are momentarily without means might find a meal. Forgive me if the question offends."

But it was evident from Ms. Hartensis's smile that the question did not offend at all.

"In fact, the local corner kitchen would welcome these donations to their supplies, which we will gladly make in your name, Traders."

"That would, I think, be the best use, Trader," Father said to Padi, as if he were deferring to her.

But, Padi thought, he *was* deferring to her; it was *her* reception, after all, and *her* decision to make.

She smiled at Ms. Hartensis.

"Please, if you would convey what is left to the corner kitchen, that would, as the master trader has said, be the best use."

"It shall be done," Ms. Hartensis said, and nodded to her helper in his long white apron, who immediately moved to the breads table.

"It was," Padi said, then, "a very fine event, ma'am. I wonder..."

She hesitated. On this point, as on all others, she had done her research carefully, and knew herself on safe ground with the offer, yet the phrasing must not offend.

"I wonder," she said again, "if I might give a gift, in appreciation of your kind attention to us."

The caterer colored somewhat, and Padi felt a sinking sensation in her stomach. The World Book did sometimes get custom wrong, and how—how *awkward* if this should be one of those times!

But, no; perhaps it had merely been pleasure which had brought color to the other's cheek. She was bowing now—that strange and uncomfortable hinging at the hip that looked like a *daibri'at* move, only too quickly done, and too stiffly held...

"You are all kindness, Trader yos'Galan," said Unet Hartensis, when she had straightened out of her bow. "A gift would find welcome with me."

· · · ❖ · · ·

Hazenthull had Inki's file open on one screen, Tolly's file on a second, nav up on a third, a research query line waiting on a fourth. Fifth screen, front and above, was traffic, *Admiral Bunter* limned in green.

Inki being young at her trade, she had included the names of those who had trained her, to establish that she had been well educated. This was in contrast to Tolly's file, which was fat with real accomplishment.

She moved a hand, to flip to the next page in Inki's file—and paused, her eyes snagging on a particular sequence of words.

Graduated with honors, Lyre Institute
for Exceptional Children

In memory's ear, she heard Inki's voice:...*and as one who has graduated from his own institute, though many Standards behind him*...

Inki, so Hazenthull was beginning to suspect, did nothing at random. It would not be going too far to suppose that she had deliberately set that piece of information out where Hazenthull might recall it, at need.

There only remained the question: had Inki planted a lie for her to recall, or the plain truth?

No, no, Pilot Haz, Inki had chided her; *if I hint you further along, I will do myself a mischief, which the directors would hardly care for.*

She recalled Tolly himself, answering her query into who she had killed for him.

... both of 'em—were directors—sorta the direct opposite of Pilot Tocohl, when it comes to matters of free choice.

So. A match—and an Explorer's leap of intuition.

Lyre Institute for Exceptional Children, her fingers tapped the words into the research screen.

Comm chimed—message incoming. She extended a hand without looking and touched the proper key.

"Recorded message begins," came the flat tones of a nonsentient machine, quickly followed by Tolly's voice, edged and cold; each word a blade struck from ice.

"Go home. I don't want you, and I don't *need* you. Message ends."

Hazenthull snorted lightly, and tapped the line closed.

The Lyre Institute for Exceptional Children had multiple locations. She threw each into the nav program, opened a sixth screen, and called up *Admiral Bunter*'s stats, compare and contrast with *Tarigan*'s.

This was the first time she had made inquiry into *Tarigan*'s history and full capabilities. Perhaps she should have done so before; such a lack of initiative would perhaps not show well, should the captain ask for a report, when she returned.

However it was, she felt a shock of warm delight as *Tarigan* revealed herself now.

Yes, thought Hazenthull, scrolling through the screens, Pilot Tocohl had *excellent* taste in ships.

Tarigan was a reconditioned Scout survey ship, meant to transport a team and equipment. Not so nimble as a single-ship, but, then, *Admiral Bunter* was no Scout ship at all.

Admiral Bunter was a perfectly serviceable little freighter, solidly built, and competently refurbished. Granted, his pod-mounts were empty, and he was traveling light, Tolly being no great weight.

Even with those advantages, however, he was not quick. And he was most certainly not nimble. If she knew for certain where he was bound, with his prisoner, she might very well over-Jump him, and be waiting at dock when he arrived.

The Lyre Institute held a hiring office on Vanichi; there was a secondary school, so called, on Anon, another hiring hall on Nostrilia, and the institute itself, on Lyre-Unthilon. Hazenthull fingered the keypad absently, considering the routes from Jemiatha's Jumble Stop to each.

Inki was, she reminded herself, a subtle woman. But she was also a practical woman. If her intention was to ensure that Tolly came whole into the hands of the directors...

Inki would not wish to give Tolly too much time alone with *Admiral Bunter*. She might be certain that her arrangements were as good as she could make them, but she could not be certain that they were proof against Tolly Jones, whom she styled—sincerely, so Hazenthull thought—the greatest mentor of the current age.

She would therefore, Hazenthull reasoned, opt for the quickest route to a director that she might contrive.

Hazenthull squinted slightly at the plotting screen.

Nostrilia.

A hiring hall, at Nostrilia. Surely, if the whistle which rent Tolly's will from him were the common means of controlling unruly graduates of Lyre Institute, there would be at least one director and one whistle at Nostrilia.

One whistle, wielded by one knowledgeable director—that ought to be enough to imprison Tolly Jones within Thirteen-Sixty-Two.

Hazenthull smiled, slightly, and without humor.

Nostrilia it was, then.

There came a flare of green in the traffic screen, and she paused, looking up, and sighing.

Admiral Bunter had Jumped. She took a breath—and then recalled it was no matter. She would be waiting for them at Nostrilia.

If she was right.

If Tolly was still alive at Nostrilia.

That was her greater fear, that he would act to keep himself forever free of the directors, and their orders. He might well take his own life. She feared he might choose grace as his best course, but she did *not* fear that he would act...immediately.

Tolly, as his partner had come to understand him, was an optimist. He would attempt...less final solutions to his situation before he embraced death. Possibly, he would even allow himself to be brought to the hiring hall itself, in the hope that he might overcome the director. Such risks, as she knew, were not beyond him—and very often they paid off.

She would have to pin *her* hope on that aspect of his nature, and be certain that she was there, at his back, when he needed her most.

And Pilot Tocohl traveling, according to clever, subtle, and dishonest Inki, of her own will in that person's company?

Pilot Tocohl, as she had stated in her report to the captain—Pilot Tocohl was very well able to take care of herself.

· · · ❋ · · ·

Priscilla cried aloud, hand outstretched to snatch at insubstantial fingers—and woke, sitting upright in her bunk, face wet with tears.

She drew a shuddering sigh.

It was the dream.

The same dream.

Twice now it had woken her; twice now leaving her sick and shaken, and not...quite...certain if it were a True Dreaming, or only remarkably realistic.

To dream a death...was never easy. To dream the death of her lifemate's daughter and heir...that was disturbing in the extreme.

Priscilla sighed, threw back the blanket and slid out of bed. The decking was cold against bare soles as she crossed to her closet and withdrew a sweater and a pair of soft pants. A glance at the clock showed that her sleep shift was three-quarters done, and in any case, she was done with sleep.

She crossed the room, laid her hand against the door-plate and a moment later was in the captain's office, touching the hot-pot for tea. When the cup was full, she took it to the couch and curled into the corner, feet tucked under her.

Sipping, she looked around the room, its lines and contents softened by the low lighting. This had been Shan's office when, friendless, she'd first come aboard the *Passage*, years ago. Before Shan, it had been his father's office. Er Thom yos'Galan had held two *melant'is* on the *Dutiful Passage*—captain and master trader. When she came aboard, Shan had held those dual roles, as his father's heir.

Plan B had altered that, as it had altered so very much. Shan had been separated from the ship; she, the first mate, had risen properly to captain in the emergency. But when ship and Shan had been reunited at last, he had not taken up the captain's duty, instead placing it formally and firmly among her *melant'i*, while he took up the *melant'i* of a master trader with both hands.

It had been a wise move: Plan B—again—having altered the usual manner of their lives.

Plan B, she thought, sipping her tea, having altered *lives*, even more than the manner of them, and no lives so definitely as those of Korval's children, sent to shelter at Runig's Rock.

Had her life proceeded in its normal and usual fashion, Padi yos'Galan would have come into her gifts in a controlled environment, taking such time as had been needful, rather than pushing those same gifts away, and creating for herself and everyone around her, an environment fraught with uncertainty and danger.

It was rare, Priscilla thought, that a nascent Witch was destroyed by the advent of her powers, though it did happen. There were records of such events, at the Temple where she had been Maiden and trained to stand as Moonhawk's vessel. Lina admitted that the Healers also had records of such events—"Very few, Priscilla," Lina had said, "but there have always been those who are too powerful to live."

And what that might have to do with Padi yos'Galan . . . Priscilla very much feared to learn. Perhaps that was what the dream was showing her: that accepting her gifts would change Padi's life yet again. If she were powerful, she might well be reft from the life she wished most to embrace. She might become strange to herself—dead, or so it might be said, to her former life.

That . . . would be unfortunate. Padi so much wished to be a pilot of Korval and a master of trade. Still, she was young, and might adjust to a new life. For that was the best way to think of such things—as acquiring a new life, though new lives sprouted from the ashes of old lives.

And yet... the dream had not been couched in the imagery of life, of rebirth.

The dream was dark and fearful, and her contact with Padi a tangle of anguish and confusion. Priscilla had reached out her hand, reached out with her own—and perhaps even with Moonhawk's gift—

And the girl was gone.

Not distant.

Not unconscious, nor oblivious.

Gone, as if she had never been.

Even death rarely cut a life down so completely. Often, there remained something, a breath of radiance that danced joy for the benediction of freedom before it faded, though it was never lost.

The dream... the dream proposed not merely death, then, but—annihilation.

And she had dreamed it twice.

What I tell you three times is true.

She drew in a deep breath, one hand leaving the teacup and settling on her abdomen.

The Goddess *had* spoken to her. For one who had been trained as a priestess, there could be no mistaking the Voice of the Goddess.

It is time, Daughter; the soul who is to become your child is eager for life.

She had been filled with joy, hearing both the Voice and the message. Surely, a child was welcome, and precious.

Alone in the captain's office, Priscilla shook her head.

Gods were chancy. Gods had their own necessities. Gods—even the Goddess Herself, harking back to the old histories—sometimes forgot that, among flawed humans, one child was not... the same as another.

CHAPTER TWENTY-SIX

Langlastport
The Torridon Hotel

THE SHORT TOUR, FROM THE HAPPY OCCASION TO THE HOTEL, was like—it was like a public day at some *other* House's gardens, Padi thought. One met only friends and agreeable acquaintances, and only glad subjects were discussed: the flowers, the weather, perhaps one's new coat, or a piece of Quin's jewelry.

Of course, public day at one's *own* House was rather less agreeable, for it always occurred on a day for which one had received several pleasant invitations, which of course had to be turned down in favor of welcoming strangers into the gardens, strolling among them to point out the best flowers, or an exceptionally clever bit of topiary, and, of course, the refreshment trays.

Not very much different, now that she had actually traversed the path, from the duties of a host of a trade reception.

The merchants they called briefly upon—no more than five minutes each, so as not, Father said, to wear out their welcome on the very first pass—seemed not to find them a burden. Indeed, there were smiles, and exchanges of infokeys, and pleasant things said on both sides. Two wished the master trader to return on another day when they might talk at more depth. One 'prentice was desolate that his own master had not been able to be present when the traders called. She offered an infokey, saying the master would be pleased to meet the traders at their convenience anytime inside the next two-day, if their stay on port would accommodate it.

And so they progressed, with the hotel in sight and only two more shops between them and the entrance. Padi sighed to herself. She was enjoying herself immensely, though whether she had learned anything would need to wait upon review.

Though their progress was interesting—not just for the illustration of what an announcement in the port news, a direct letter to everyone listed in the Langlastport Merchant Association, and a reception might do to create a favorable impression—it remained to be learned whether the favorable impression translated into equally favorable negotiations and concluded deals.

She . . . was just as happy to leave those discoveries for the morrow, and the day after. Her head had begun to ache again, which she thought might be a lack of food. While there had certainly been sufficient food at the reception, she had felt it her duty to at least introduce herself to each guest, and direct them to the refreshment tables. At the beginning, also, she had been nervous regarding the arrangements, but, really, Ms. Hartensis had managed beautifully, and produced a buffet reception that even Cousin Kareen must have pronounced unexceptional.

In any case, she had rather stupidly not eaten anything, other than the samples, though she had managed a glass of two of the red juice, which had been very agreeable, though perhaps, in retrospect, a little sweet.

They strolled into the second-but-last shop, a gem-and-jewelry emporium. The ample light was pure, and drawers of gemstones gleamed and glittered behind security crystal displays. Padi narrowed her eyes against the excessive brightness as a tall and willowy person came out from behind the counter to bow gracefully to them. Surprisingly, it was a full Liaden bow, between business associates.

"Master Trader, Trader, welcome to my establishment! I am Tarona Rusk, and this"—a graceful motion of the hand drew their attention to the glittering displays—"is the Garden of Gems."

Tarona Rusk spoke the High Tongue with an accent, but her mode did not falter—also, as between business associates, which was, perhaps, a little forward, thought Padi, as they had concluded no business, but which also showed a willingness to proceed in an association.

Father bowed, and Padi did.

"Forgive me," Father said upon straightening. "I had not expected to hear the language of home, here on Langlast."

"I hope I have not offended?"

"Indeed, no. Merely a surprise—and that not unpleasant, at the end of a long day. I wonder—did you perhaps attend the University of Solcintra?"

Tarona Rusk laughed gently.

"No scholar, I!" she said, raising a hand. "Always, it was the stones with me, and the fabrication of settings which might be worthy of them." Another small bow. "I had the honor to sit as Moonel's 'prentice, in the Avenue of Jewels, at Solcintra Port."

"I'll wager he drove you harder than any professor," Father said.

"Doubtless he did, and why not? Should I waste the master's time and generosity by shirking my lessons, or creating that which was less than inspired? May I ask—how fares Moonel? Still at work in the Avenue of Jewels?"

Father sighed, and bowed gently, as the bearer of unfortunate news.

"I regret. Moonel has gone ahead, doubtless to fashion more perfect settings for the stars. The shop in the Avenue of Jewels stood empty, when last I was on Solcintra Port."

"Ah."

The jeweler bowed her head, and swayed somewhat. When she looked up, her eyes were damp, but her face was properly smooth.

"It grieves me to hear it, though it ought be no surprise. One likes to recall those who illuminated one's life as unchanged and ever-continuing. But—it is as you say; he has doubtless embraced a higher art, which we mere students hold no hope of comprehending."

There was a small pause, so that they might admire the phrase, before the jeweler spoke again.

"Do you make a long stay, here on Langlastport?"

"A few days. Perhaps as long as a local week. Tomorrow's tour will tell the tale."

"Of course. Please, allow me to offer you this—" An infokey was proferred. Father took it gracefully and offered his, in turn.

"My thanks. For now, let me not keep you longer from your rest. Come again, before you leave us. It would please me, if we could identify a mutual benefit."

"We will of course come again," Father promised, and with that they sought the door.

· · · ✳ · · ·

"Vessel approaching," Dil Nem said firmly from the pilot's chair. "Langlast portmaster identification."

He did not say that this meant nothing; the three ships that had pursued *Pale Wing* had, after all, been able to show an affiliation, however tenuous, with legitimate Liltander security.

Priscilla frowned at the screens over the third mate's shoulder. The approaching vessel looked to be a working ship of some kind. Scans showed armament—two small guns—and very little armor. Port ID...

"Query their purpose for approach," she said.

Dil Nem did that, nodded and glanced over his shoulder to Priscilla.

"Customs boat, Captain. They state routine fly-by, and advise that we will see them at intervals." A pause. "They will release camera drones and magnetometers; this is standard procedure."

"Port database confirms ID," said Pilot Jorik, on comm.

Priscilla nodded.

"Log them," she said.

"Aye, Captain," said Jorik. "All occasions?"

"All occasions."

· · · ✳ · · ·

"Will you share a glass of wine with me, daughter?"

Padi blinked, and sat up, startled.

They had dined privately in their suite, all three together. After, Mr. Higgs had excused himself to his room. The headache had faded again over the course of the meal, and Padi had been content merely to sit for a moment or two, treasuring both the absence of pain and the absence of any necessity to introduce herself or, indeed, to speak at all.

Except, she must have dozed off, and that would never do! She and Father still had the gathered keys to sort through, and a port itinerary to make, after which she would study for a few hours before bed.

"Forgive me," she managed, to Father's uplifted eyebrows, "I hadn't meant to fall asleep."

"The day has scarcely been free of stress," Father said, repeating what he had said at the reception. "I find the gravity a trifle wearisome, myself. I offer again, daughter—will you share a glass of wine?"

Father had stopped at the duty-free shop in the lobby of their hotel to purchase a bottle of the local summer wine, and had set it on the wine table in their suite. Padi had supposed he would have a glass while they worked; he most usually had a glass of wine to hand, and had given it no more thought than that. But—

"I see that you are a little timid of a green vintage," Father said, in the face of her continued silence. "Allow me to reassure you, based upon my sampling at your reception. I found it bright and balanced; a very pleasant little wine, and unlikely to produce any more lethargy than we already enjoy. We must, of course, assume that the bottle has not been mistreated, but I believe we may reasonably suppose that to be the case."

That was merely nonsense, of course, words to fill time, and allow her to gather her thoughts. Plainly, Father was not intending to resume work after the meal. Father wished to speak with his daughter and his heir, between kin, which was certainly not a proposition she could—or wanted to—decline. She did wonder if she had erred in some grievous manner during the walk from the reception to the hotel, and which necessitated this change of plans.

But, there was a very easy way, after all, to discover that.

Padi inclined her head.

"Thank you, Father; I would be pleased to share wine and a moment with you."

"It is pleasant!" She exclaimed, essaying another sip, and sighing. "What a pity, that—"

She swallowed the rest of what she had been about to say, feeling her cheeks warm.

Really, Padi, this is not a trade session! she told herself. *Strive for some conduct.*

Father grinned at her over the rim of his wine cup.

"Difficult, isn't it? But don't despair! Couching all and everything in terms of trade and profit is a positive sign of progress toward your goal. I swear so to you, as your grandfather once swore to me."

According to those tales she had heard of him, Grandfather Er Thom had not been much given to joking. He had, however, been rather incisively ironic.

"We have," she pointed out, a little more sharply than was perhaps entirely proper, "been trading all day."

"Indeed we have, but now we must adopt another mode, if you will allow me." He shifted somewhat in his chair, and stretched out a long arm to place the wine cup on the table between them. They sat side by side, in matching upholstered chairs by the suite's large window, overlooking Langlastport and the mountains beyond.

Padi put her glass on the table, also, and inclined her head formally.

"You wished to speak with me, Father?"

"Excellent. You set the tone well. In fact, my child, I do wish to speak with you. More—I wish to ask you a question. It is a question I now feel that I ought to have asked long since, but better tardy, so it is said, than never arrive."

He paused. Padi waited.

Father sighed, and moved a hand—pilot talk for *straightest route possible*.

"I wish you to tell me, please, daughter, what happened at Runig's Rock."

Padi blinked.

"*Happened*? *Nothing* happened—which was the intent, as I understood it. We had our lessons, and we walked our rounds; we exercised, played cards, and read; Syl Vor drew; the twins slept—oh!"

She put her fingers against her lips, recalling one thing that *had* happened, and about which they had not considered it wise to be forthcoming. Grandfather Luken knew, of course, and... well, perhaps Quin had told *his* father, now that they were home and it hardly mattered any more. Still, it *had been* an infraction; they had disobeyed Grandfather Luken and Cousin Kareen, as well as violating systems...

"But don't keep me in suspense!" Father urged. "What is this one thing that happened?"

"Well...Quin had been...distressed...for Cousin Pat Rin. We had news, from time to time of you, and the *Passage*, and Aunt Nova—but it was as if Cousin Pat Rin had simply fallen away into the starfields..."

"Because, after all," Father said, after she had paused for a moment to collect her thoughts, "that was what he was supposed to have done."

"Well, yes, certainly! But, Father, *you know* Quin! He's made of nerves! So, I said to him that we might look at the check-in list."

Both of Father's eyebrows rose.

"Did you?" he murmured.

"Yes, sir; I thought it would ease him. We . . . well, *I* . . . circumvented the codes, so that he could check the list—I broke nothing!—and we put everything back as it had been when we were done; but the point is—which is to say, *what happened*—is that he found that his father had *not* checked in—not at all. Not even once."

"I can scarcely suppose that this was the comfort you had hoped to offer kin," Father said, reaching for his wine cup. "How did Quin go on after that?"

"Pretty well. That is, he spoke with Grandfather, who of course scolded him for listening at doors. Then he pointed out that Cousin Pat Rin was not a fool, and would therefore not endanger himself by foolish action. If checking in would expose him to enemies, then surely, he would fail to check in."

"And that comforted Quin, did it?"

"It did, yes."

"Well, then, the episode seems to have ended well, though I regret that an action of yours stirred Luken into sternness. He does so dislike being stern."

"Yes," Padi said.

"Was he also stern to you?"

"No, Father. I think—that Quin did not tell him I had helped with the codes."

There was a small pause, followed by a light sigh.

"Ah. Well, a pilot must have a care for his copilot, after all. Especially when there is only one available."

"Yes," she said again, and sighed herself, leaning back into the chair. She did not close her eyes. She had already disgraced herself once by falling asleep after dinner. It would scarcely do to fall asleep again, in the middle of a conversation. Though, now that Father had the answer to his question, perhaps—

"Forgive me," he said, interrupting her train of thought, "that I am not specific. I have nothing to lead me, save this stone . . .

edifice... with which you increasingly distress your elders, the maintenance of which appears to be taking a very great deal of your energy. What happened, child, that you felt you must create such a thing?"

She caught her breath.

"I thought I had...hidden it," she whispered. "I—does it hurt you? I never thought—"

She *hadn't* thought—why *should* she have thought?—what her construct might feel like to Healer senses.

She blinked away sudden tears.

"I have control enough that it does not hurt me, though it occasionally surprises and dismays me," Father said softly. "In fact, I will make bold to say that it hurts—and has hurt—*you* far more grievously than it may ever hurt me."

He leaned over to put his hand on her knee.

"Padi—why?"

His voice was gentle; she saw concern in his face; felt tenderness in the touch of his hand. Love swelled in her throat, choking her, and then the tears came, faster than she could blink them away. She reached for the small dance she had made in her head, meaning to lock the shame away with the rest of it, and—

"Do not!"

The command rocked her back into her chair; it took the breath from her lungs. She gasped for air—and bent forward, her face hidden against her knees as the tears flowed, hot and shameful.

"I was afraid," she managed, her voice shaking. "Oh, Father, I am such a coward!"

· · · ✸ · · ·

The customs ship had released its camera drones—three—and continued its own inspection until they returned, having recorded the *Passage* by thirds.

"Transmission," said Pilot Jorik. "We're cleared; report sent to Langlast portmaster; copy to us under cover of this communication."

Jorik looked to Priscilla, who had remained on the bridge during these events.

"States there will be a recheck."

Dil Nem gave an unLiaden snort.

"Do they expect us to receive contraband in orbit?"

"It might happen," Priscilla said. "Though I wonder how we would conceal the pods."

"Heard there's a field," Jorik said. "Pirates—serious pirates—use it. Disrupts scan and visual. Any new pods we took on would be invisible, close enough."

"Thus, the cameras, and the magnetometers," said Dil Nem, with a sigh. "Well, perhaps that is reason enough for such prudence. How common are these devices?"

Jorik shrugged.

"Wouldn't think they were as common as all that. Don't know that I actually believe the thing even exists. Wouldn't have to be a pirate to want one, either. Plenty of small shippers and grey-traders would welcome a way to dodge a little bit o'excise."

"Well," Priscilla said, coming out of the captain's chair and stretching tight muscles. "Leave a note for the next team, to expect the customs boat at intervals, to log it and record their procedure, with a copy to my screen."

"Yes, Captain," Jorik said. "Done."

"Thank you. I'll be in my office, if there's need."

· · · ✷ · · ·

"So I danced it all into a stone closet, at the very heart of myself," she said, her voice dull.

Most of the tale had poured forth, as ungoverned as her weeping. That passion was spent now. She was exhausted, poor child, and the headache was back, which was worrisome for more than the usual reasons. He'd blocked the damn thing three times now, and he was not the most unskilled Healer the Hall had ever trained. Yet here it was again, edgier and angrier than before.

And he...

He had to be very careful, indeed, here.

Gently, he extended a line of comfort to the shame-filled child beside him, and, gently, spoke her name.

"Padi."

"Father...forgive me."

"For being afraid? I forgive you freely! In the interest of Balance, I will, of course, ask that you forgive me for being afraid. In fact, I believe we had best do the thing properly, if we're to do it at all, and forgive the delm for being afraid, Aunt Nova, and Cousin Kareen. Pat Rin was certainly afraid, he confessed as much to me. To my observation, Luken is not a fool, therefore, he must also have been afraid."

Padi had raised her head and was watching him from eyes squinted half-shut with pain.

"Aunt Anthora?" she asked. "Never tell me she was afraid!"

"I must do so, however. She was very nearly caught and killed, you know, by a device created specifically to entrap and harm those of the *dramliz*. The next time you are home, ask her for the round tale."

He crossed his legs, looking out over the darkening landscape.

"Let us see, who else must we add to our list—why, you as much as told me that Quin was afraid! I expect we shall have to forgive him—and also Priscilla, and Uncle Ren Zel…"

"Uncle Val Con?" Padi asked suddenly. "You said…the delm…"

Shan sighed, and extended a careful hand to cover hers where it was fisted on her knee.

"I wager that Uncle Val Con was more afraid even than I was, and I do not mind telling you, speaking as we are, among kin, that I was terrified."

She swallowed, hard.

"Also," she whispered, "I lied to you."

"Yes, you did." He squeezed her hand gently. "It grieves me, that you felt you must. I am desolate, that I must have given you the impression that I would refuse to assist you with the arrival of your gift. However, surely Priscilla is everything that is discreet and trustworthy—might you not have gone to her?"

"No!" She took a breath and managed, somewhat, to moderate herself.

"No, you never—Father, you never—but we were at the Rock, and there were enemies, and I *didn't need* it. I needed—I needed to be strong, and not afraid, and not distracted, and—I locked it away, with the fear."

He nodded seriously.

"I quite see that. You stood, after all, in the front line of defense. You needed your wits about you.

"But once you had been retrieved from the Rock, and enclosed by the clan's protections—couldn't you have spoken then?"

Padi shook her head.

"It was…gone. If I thought about it at all, which I cannot say that I did, then I would have recalled that the fear and…

and my... talent, were tied together." Another breath, followed by a whisper.

"And I didn't want to be known for a coward, Father. A pilot of Korval is not a coward."

Her face was averted. He squeezed her hand again, and released it, settling carefully back into his chair.

"That supposition is worthy of further study," he said. "I will look out the Diary references for you. In the meantime, my child, I suggest that we take a small break to shower and refresh ourselves, and meet back here in an hour. Does that align with your schedule?"

Padi smiled faintly, but with good intent.

"Yes, Father."

CHAPTER TWENTY-SEVEN

. . . .

Admiral Bunter

"TOLLY, I HAVE A QUESTION."

Caught in the act of making tea, he glanced toward the galley's ceiling,

"I've got a pallet load of questions my own self," he said conversationally. "Life's a questionable affair, no denying."

There was a pause. He finished the transfer from pot to mug, whistling lightly.

"I wish to ask my question of you," *Admiral Bunter* said, sounding a little...surprised. "May I do so?"

"Well, now, there's a conundrum," he said, leaning his hip against the counter. "Did the two of us ever talk about *melant'i*?"

"We talked about role models and chains of command. I have access to anthropology texts. Compare and contrast indicates that *melant'i* is a Liaden cultural artifact comparable to chain of command, entwined with individual honor."

"Hmm."

He had a sip of tea.

"That's a good first approximation," he said eventually. "I do remember we talked about approximations, and how dangerous it is to make assumptions, cross-culture. *Melant'i*, now—chain of command..."

He shrugged, frowning down at the floor for a second, before he looked back up to the ceiling.

"You could start thinking about *melant'i* that way, so long's you remember that the chain, and command, too, can be the same individual. Also, one person's *melant'i* can interact with another person's *melant'i*—has to, in fact. Then, there's group *melant'i*. And, like you said, it's all tied up in honor—by which I mean *right action*—personal, and group, and also, *melant'i* itself has honor that can be tarnished, or even broken, by wrong action."

Another pause. Tolly sipped tea.

"This does not appear to be a very useful concept," *Admiral Bunter* said. "It is too broad, and it lacks ease of use."

"No, now, that's where you're wrong. *Melant'i*'s one of the most useful tools in the whole toolbox, once you get the hang of it. Most Terrans don't bother...well, they're of your mind, is all it is: too confusing, hard to apply, why make simple things complex? I can see their point, but here's what I like about *melant'i*, personally."

He paused to sip his tea, then looked up to smile at the ceiling.

"What I like about *melant'i*, particularly, is how easy it makes sorting out complex situations. Me, for instance—I've got a complex *melant'i*, just like everybody does. I'm a manufactured human—a thing that's not supposed to exist, by law, just like your AIs. 'Case you're interested, the law I'm a violation of is the Free Gene and Manumitted Human Act.

"So, *melant'i*-wise, I'm an outlawed *thing*; a specialist in the field of the training and socialization of autonomous, sentient, self-aware intelligences; an autonomous individual person; an industrial spy; an assassin; a person who has been a prisoner and forced to do...that which he did not agree to; and a person who has escaped his imprisonment...several times."

He sipped again, turned to refresh the mug from the pot, and came back into his lean, looking casually up at the ceiling.

"Now, regarding the current situation and the asking of questions...part of my *melant'i* lately has been mentor to *Admiral Bunter*. In that capacity, I'm pleased to answer your questions. But *right now*, my *melant'i* is prisoner being conveyed against my will, and though you've been my student, *your melant'i right now* is as my jailor.

"So, what we need to figure out is...from what *melant'i* may I *most rightly act* in the case? As a prisoner, I've got no obligation to answer my jailor's questions. O'course, my jailor can try to compel me to answer questions, but I'll just let you know here that I've had a lot of practice being stubborn and compelling can get a little sketchy, unless you've got a natural aptitude.

"I could choose to ignore our present relative *melant'is* in favor of our past relative *melant'is* of student and teacher. Might do that for any one of a number of reasons—whim, fondness, an expectation that calling to mind a previous, more pleasant, relationship might play to my advantage, that kind of thing."

He sipped tea, and turned to set the mug on the counter.

"It's a tough one to call, I'll give you that. What d'you think? Am I your mentor, or am I your prisoner?"

There was scarcely a pause between question and answer.

"Can you not be both?" the *Admiral* asked, sounding . . . impatient.

Tolly tipped his head to the right, like he was giving the question some thought, then *tsk*'d.

"That's an interesting suggestion, and there are situations where a single person can act from two closely aligned *melant'is*, but y'know? I don't think this is one of them."

Admiral Bunter was silent.

Tolly let the silence stretch a bit—and then a bit longer, before he sighed, and pushed away from the counter.

"Well, the best I can figure it, taking all the factors into account, is *prisoner being transported* is the most compelling of my various *melant'is* right at present, since it could very easily result in my death. That being so, I'm under no obligation to answer my jailor's questions."

"How will I learn?" the *Admiral* asked plaintively.

Tolly eased away from his lean against the counter, picked up his mug and walked out of the galley.

· · · ❈ · · ·

Padi returned to the suite's common room, showered, refreshed, and a bit somber. She had placed her trading clothes into the press, to be cleaned and made ready for the morrow, and had put on soft pants and a sweater.

Father was before her in the common room. He had showered, too; his hair was still damp and star-bright in contrast to his black sweater.

"I spoke to Priscilla," he said, as she returned to her chair by the window. "She extends her congratulations to you, the host of a most promising crush, and hopes that this is the first of many such successful events."

Padi smiled. Priscilla never spoke in such rolling flourishes as Father inevitably gave to her messages. Very likely, she had actually said something on the order of, "Please tell Padi that I'm happy for her success," which Father, of course, would find a bit thin.

"It's very kind of her," she said. "Though at present I find myself being pleased that the first has been accomplished, rather than anticipating a second."

"Perfectly natural," Father said solemnly. "Tomorrow is soon enough to begin planning your next conquest." He paused.

"I took the liberty of refreshing your glass. I propose to get over the ground that remains between us as lightly and as quickly as possible, my child. I hope we shall come to a mutually favorable agreement, and a plan for forward progress."

The proposition appealed, Padi thought, especially the *quickly* part. She took up her glass for a sip of wine, and sighed.

She was...not tired...not *exactly* tired. It was as though the storm of emotion she had succumbed to in the last hour had... washed everything out of her head, including the headache. The result was a peculiar sort of emptiness. She had wondered, in the shower, if Father had something to do with this sensation of being *drained dry*. A Healer was supposed to ask permission before undertaking a Healing, though she supposed that, just as there were certain piloting procedures that were always to be followed, but sometimes weren't, that, sometimes, Healers *didn't* ask before undertaking a Healing.

Besides, if one wished to be technical, he *had* asked if he might help with her headache at the Happy Occasion.

Father tasted his wine, and put the glass aside. His face was very serious, and when he spoke, it was without any of his usual embroidery. Indeed, he seemed very nearly as plain-spoken as Priscilla.

"I must explain some few matters to you, before we plan together how best to go on. I will do this as succinctly as possible. If there is a point upon which you are unclear, you will please ask me to elaborate. You must be fully informed in this, am I plain?"

"Yes, Father."

He closed his eyes briefly. When he opened them, they shone like true silver.

"The first thing you must know is that you cannot resist your nature. You may choose to reside in ignorance, or you may choose to prepare yourself. Those are the choices that are open to you. *Only* those. The obstinate and debilitating headache, the sudden apprehension of the emotions of some of those around you—those are very clear indications that your gift is ready to unfold. Short of death, you cannot deny that unfolding. It is inevitable. I am not simply telling you this because I wish my heir to be a Healer. I am telling you this—as your parent, as your master trader, and as your elder in the craft—because it is true. You can no more choose not to be of the *dramliz* than you can choose to be a Clutch Turtle. Do you understand me?"

Padi took a deep breath—and nodded.

"Yes, Father," she said humbly.

He smiled slightly.

"I know that you never wished to be anything but a pilot and a trader of Korval. However it unfolds, this new gift does not *diminish* you in any way. You will merely acquire, *in addition* to your skills as a pilot and as a trader, another useful set of abilities. Yes, you will need to accommodate a new *melant'i* and duties, but you are older than six. Nor do you lack for elders to consult should a particularly knotty issue arise."

He paused to sip wine.

Padi also had recourse to her glass, feeling relief. It was, of course, why one was so *very* fond of Father. He could easily—and with perfect justice—have added just there, "if there is any elder whom you trust." He had not done, however, and by omitting that caveat, he told her that her *melant'i* was not in question, nor her good sense, and one wished, very much, to be worthy of his faith.

"Thus far," Father murmured, "have you a question, or a concern?"

"No, sir. You propose that I accept this additional *melant'i* and the duties which attend it, as I accept my *melant'i* and duties as pilot and trader."

"It seems a very simple thing, phrased thus," he commented. "Merely a continuation of what we already do, every hour of every day."

Padi sipped her wine, lowered the glass.

"Yes," she said. "I have a question—and perhaps also a concern."

Father inclined his head.

"Ask."

"The headache—it's gone now."

"The headache is *blocked* now," Father said. "My fourth attempt, if you will have it. Your nature is...extremely determined." He smiled slightly. "This ought to surprise no one."

She put the glass down, and turned somewhat in her chair, so that she could see him more clearly.

"What will happen," she asked, panic nipping at her stomach, "when the gift unfolds fully? Will I have a headache? Will I be able to hear all the emotions around me, all at once? I will—I will tell you that I seem able to make things around me... levitate. Will I *hurt people*? Other Healers?"

He held up his hand.

"These are the questions that we cannot answer. We might have made a better guess, save that you have subverted your gift into this—stone sarcophagus. Even lacking such an unusual construct, the onset of a *dramliza*'s gift is...often sudden and surprising. Sometimes, it is violent.

"When my gift came upon me, one of the kitchen staff had just cut himself rather badly; we screamed at the same instant. The difference between us was that he was quickly taken into care, had his wound tended and stopped screaming.

"I, who had no idea what had happened, except that something had *hurt me* without touching me or leaving a mark—I kept on screaming."

Padi swallowed.

"I can scarcely be seen to cry out on the trade floor," she said, biting her lip. "Can we not...forestall it?"

"I believe that we can do exactly that. However, it is for you to choose." He held up his hand, fingers against palm, and only the thumb showing.

"Choices," he said. "We can immediately send you back up to the ship, and place you under Lina's care. She will guide you in the birth of your gift."

"But I will miss the port tour!" Padi cried, and bit her lip in earnest. "Forgive me. I hadn't meant to interrupt."

Father nodded.

"We were speaking of choices, of which there are two," he said, and again showed her his thumb.

"The first choice—return to the ship."

He extended his index finger.

"The second choice—riskier, but not, I think, outrageously so. We shall forestall the onset of your talent for only a few days more. In order to do this, I must link to you. The link will allow me to shield you from the random emotions of others, and it will allow me to smooth out the growing pressure of your gift. We deny nothing, and if it should seem to me, as the Healer who has you in care, that this approach is doing harm, or that your talent will no longer be forestalled, then we will cut the tour short and revert to the first choice."

He smiled reassuringly.

"I believe that we will be able to complete the tour and deliver you to Lina in good order."

"You said—riskier," Padi said, her voice hoarse. She cleared her throat. "What risk?"

Father looked wry.

"If your gift should blossom—explosively—there is a danger that I will be caught in the explosion, rather than being able to remain apart, and guide you. I consider this possibility to be small. I am not a novice, and I have some backup available to me, should it be needed." He smiled faintly.

"I believe we have a fair chance of pulling this off in something approaching good order, if you are game to try."

"I am," she said fiercely, thinking of the port tour, and trying to gauge the strength of the walls she had built. She took a breath, then, another question occurring.

"This link—will it keep the headache away?"

Father's smile grew wider.

"I believe I am equal to that, yes. Have we an accord, then?"

"Yes!" she said, and raised her glass in a toast.

· · · ❈ · · ·

Shan was going to link with Padi, to shield her, and perhaps to ameliorate whatever happened if her talent came upon her during the tour on-world.

Alone in her office on the *Passage*, Priscilla closed her eyes. It was, perhaps, not the best choice of method, in terms of absolute safety. However, as she and Shan had agreed when they'd spoken, it was unquestionably the best choice in terms of reconciling Padi to her gift. If she learned immediately that she lost nothing, only gained something precious, that would be one hurdle cleared.

As to the danger—Shan was a very able Healer in his own right, and if there was need, Priscilla thought, it was very likely that Lute might step forward to assist. Knowing Shan's opinions on Lute, she had not mentioned that as a possibility, but had merely offered to link to him, lightly, so that he wasn't completely without backup. He'd accepted that, but wished to make the link to Padi firm first, which was only prudent. She would await his touch.

· · · ✳ · · ·

Linking with Padi had been more difficult than Shan had anticipated. Not that the child had resisted him, but that the damned and damnable *construct* of hers disrupted what ought to have been a smooth flow of energies. It was no wonder at all that the child was hollow-eyed with weariness; the wonder was that she had managed to persevere, and to keep up so well.

At last, however, the thing had been done, and she'd gone off like a good child to bed, where she had fallen immediately into the deepest and most healing sleep he could conjure for her.

He stood by the window now, looking out over the distant, star-struck mountains, and methodically worked through several relaxation and strengthening exercises. It would be best to recruit himself before he extended a touch to Priscilla. She would be alarmed, if she perceived him overtired, and might well argue that the risk was greater than the gain.

With, he admitted to himself wryly, some justice on her side.

"That Maiden is going to blossom into a Witch to fear," a familiar—and not completely unwelcome—voice said, just behind his shoulder.

"One hopes that only those with cause will fear her," he said, not turning his head.

Lute laughed.

"But it is always so with Witches, is it not? Who fears Moonhawk, save those who do evil?"

Shan snorted lightly.

"And who fears Lute?"

"Why, no one fears Lute," the other said gently. "Who fears a hedge magician? Or a man?"

"If it pleases you, I freely assert that you are disconcerting," Shan said. "Even *extremely* disconcerting."

"Thoughtful child; my heart is soothed. In that vein, I would offer advice."

"Advice? Such as—remove to the ship immediately?"

"Oh, but you are not so craven! Nor is she. No, you have chosen this path—or it has chosen you—and it is, so far as I can see, as likely as any other leading from this place to the next. No, what I wish to say to you is—links can be broken, and hearts can be hid. Remember that, when it is time."

"Certainly! All the situation required was a riddle to—"

Shan turned from the window—to the dim, empty room.

"Lute?"

There was no answer. Healer senses detected Vanner, in his room, reading peacefully; Padi, sound asleep in her bed—and no one else at all.

Shan sighed, somewhere between amusement and chagrin, closed his eyes, and reached for Priscilla.

CHAPTER TWENTY-EIGHT

....

Admiral Bunter

RESEARCH HAD ALREADY FAILED HIM. NOTHING IN HIS ARCHIVES had given him the answer to his question. Tolly Jones, his mentor, on whose willingness to answer those questions left unanswered by research, he had come to depend upon—Tolly Jones refused to answer further, on the basis of this... *melant'i*.

No, *Admiral Bunter* corrected himself. That was an error. It was *sloppy thinking*.

Tolly Jones refused to answer further because, by applying the tool of *melant'i* to his current situation, he had arrived at the conclusion that he was a prisoner, no longer a mentor, and thus his necessities were constrained.

Admiral Bunter had researched the necessities of prisoners.

They were varied, as he learned that prisons—and jailors—were also varied. It would appear, for instance, that Tolly Jones's prison—himself, *Admiral Bunter*, a tidy, bright, and well-supplied freighter—was considerably more beneficent than many. Indeed, he had considered calling Tolly's assertion of his *melant'i* into question, based on his conditions... and had decided that this would be petty, and also immaterial, as it would seem that the core requirement—confinement against one's will—was met.

Research showed that, in addition to confinement, some prisoners were physically punished by their jailors. Sometimes, it appeared, such jailors wished to obtain information held by the prisoner; sometimes, they merely wished to be cruel and increase the prisoner's distress, as a *just punishment* for transgressions.

Some prisoners were merely held, their jailors completely indifferent to any information that they might, or might not, possess. These were held in order to control the behavior, or to ensure the goodwill of a third party. On the surface, it would seem that such prisoners were fortunate, as the conditions of their use would shield them from physical harm. Research, however, would have it that involuntary confinement itself was sufficient to distress the larger percentage of humans, and uncertainty regarding their fate, or the continued goodwill of the third party was also a cruel punishment.

Still other prisoners were held, and punished, in order to make them malleable. These were then shaped into tools which the jailor might use to influence or destroy third parties.

There had been much study given to prisoners, the psychology of imprisonment, and the scars borne by those who had been imprisoned.

The *Admiral* had come away from his research with, at least, a better understanding of the reasons why Tolly Jones was distressed to find himself a prisoner, and also the reasons why he refused to answer questions. It was an act of will, an act of rebellion—of strength—for a prisoner to refuse to answer his jailor's questions. Prisoners found their situations oppressive; acts of rebellious will were necessary, lest they sicken and die in their imprisonment.

Having learned more than he wished regarding prisoners, *Admiral Bunter* had turned to his own role.

Jailor.

If the role of prisoner was demoralizing and oppressive, the role of jailor was...horrifying.

And it would seem that, while Tolly Jones remained a prisoner, the only way *Admiral Bunter* would be able to gain answers from him, was to in some way compel him.

He scanned the lists of methods jailors used in order to compel prisoners, and abruptly closed that line of research, deeply unsettled.

Ethics was pinging, frantically—stupid module, as if he didn't know at the core level...as if he would...as if he *could*...

And, yet, he required answers. He could learn much from research, but he—he *needed* a teacher, a mentor to assist him in comprehending the gestalt. Perhaps there was something—some method which was...*less* intrusive than...

Protocol came on line, cold. He could see the regulations fluttering. Worse, he could see the black edges of Command Orders among them.

"Research!" he said hastily. Command Orders. Protocol could archive him; it had that power, if there was a breach. If Protocol found that he had become...unstable.

"There has been no breach," he said. "I am sane, and not in need of termination. I was merely performing needed research."

"Research into the destruction of a human being in your care?"

"Yes. I have logs. Please review them."

Protocol accessed the files he marked out: the record of his most recent talk with Tolly Jones; his own research log; his last session with Mentor Inki Yo, in which she had explained to him what sort of human Tolly Jones was, and what the law demanded.

The fluttering continued, palely. Command Orders had been put aside, at least. The *Admiral* knew relief.

The fluttering ceased altogether, replaced by the amber of a caution warning.

"This is not an acceptable protocol for dealing with humans in your care. You may protect yourself if you are threatened, but you may not inflict harm."

"I must have answers," *Admiral Bunter* protested.

"Find another way," Protocol replied coldly—and retired.

· · · ✳ · · ·

"Customs," the message came across the ship band. "We release cameras and inspect."

"Witless waste o'time, if you ask me," muttered Kik Strehlir, who was sitting first. Second Mate Lonan Davis, who was sitting second, touched the comm switch.

"*Dutiful Passage* acknowledges," he told the cutter, and, to first board, "Logging and transmitting to Captain."

"Another waste o'time, and energy," the good pilot muttered.

"Orders," said Lonan, who was not the most loquacious of the pilots aboard, despite his New Dublin heritage, and his kinship with the *Passage*'s master trader.

"Orders is right," Kik said, with a tired smile. "If it wasn't for orders, what would we do with ourselves, eh?"

"We can't all be bards and poets," Lonan agreed. "Best, then, to do as we're told."

Kik laughed, and they subsided into mutual silence, tending their boards and watching the screens.

· · · ✳ · · ·

She and Father sorted through the cards, keys, and invitations they had gathered at the reception during a working breakfast. Mr. Higgs, seeing how it was with them, had taken his plate, his cup, and his book across the room, and settled into one of the chairs by the big window.

"Do you wish yourself back in the merc, Vanner?" Father asked him, as he handed the card of a certain Master Josifet Zeldner to Padi for her consideration.

"No, sir," Mr. Higgs said easily, turning his head to look at Father over the back of the chair. "I'm reading for pleasure and nobody's shooting at me. I'm content."

"Excellent. Do not, please, hesitate to speak up, if we should begin to be in any way unsatisfactory."

"I'll do that, sir," Mr. Higgs said seriously. "Will you be wanting a car today?"

"A car?" Father turned to her, eyebrows up. "What do you think, Trader? Will we want a car today?"

Padi frowned down at the port map. Langlastport was constructed as a series of four interlocking squares, like tiles in a mosaic, each square representing a specialty, and designated by the name of a local flower. Thus: Calumbeen, Earish, Beesbrickle, and Fralst.

"What we have mapped thus far is within two adjacent squares. There is the light rail, but if timing becomes tight, we may wish a car."

"Which may be no faster than the light rail," Father murmured, bending over the map with her. "I see. Well! How if we fill in the rest of the day with locations in these two squares? For tomorrow, we will identify our most critical contacts in these two squares—" He touched the map with a light fingertip. "When those are established, we will fill in around, and so on, into the day after."

"That would do well for all except this." Padi held up the card he had just given her. "Master Zeldner is a vintner, and the address on the card is not only outside of any convenient squares, but outside of the port entire."

She tapped the location on the map, halfway to the mountains framed in their suite's big windows.

"I believe Master Zeldner has a business location in the port. Certainly, she gave that impression. I shall make inquiries. But we have wandered from Vanner's point! Will we want a car?"

"If we follow your scheme and choose our primary contacts by their proximity to each other, and filling the secondary contacts in around them, then my sense is that the light rail will be perfectly adequate for us." She paused doubtfully. "Unless you anticipate parcels?"

"Parcels? There may be some, but they can easily be sent on. No need to be juggling parcels on the light rail. For that matter, there's no need to advertise our previous contact to our present contact, though I caught the notion that gossip was high art on Langlastport."

Padi smiled. "I caught the same notion. So—do we agree that we do not need a car?"

"Why, we do! Vanner"—he turned to address Mr. Higgs—"thank you for your thoughtfulness—and for your continued patient forbearance. Trader yos'Galan tells me that we will not need a car. We shall travel via the light rail."

"Yes, sir," Mr. Higgs answered. "The light rail system in-port is pretty reliable, according to the local folks. Out-port, it gets less reliable, real fast. So if you need to go out to the vine country, you'll probably want that car."

"The local folks? Did you ask practical questions of our guests, Vanner?"

"Tried to, sir."

"How very forward-looking of you! It never occurred to me to ask questions about the light rail, or hiring cars—did it occur to you, Padi?"

Her ears warmed in sudden embarrassment. She *should* have made inquiries, knowing that they would be staying on port. But—

"No, sir. It didn't occur to me at all. I was focused on welcoming our guests, and—and seeking trade opportunity."

"As I was. We are a sad pair of impractical traders, I fear. Though we were clever enough to bring Vanner with us, so perhaps we aren't entirely beyond the pale."

"Perhaps not this time," she said, matching his tone, "but one does not always rejoice in Mr. Higgs's company."

"That is distressing, but very true. We do not always have Vanner with us. Therefore, we must strive to do better for ourselves, and remember to check our research against local information. It's a minor thing, I daresay, merely slipping in a question about how best one might arrive at the contact's facility. Or a question regarding such a thing as the service most expectable of the light rail, which our research, of course, will have revealed to us. We are not local, we do not pretend to be local, and a certain ignorance from outworlders is often found charming. The local folk, as I'm sure Vanner will agree, are often very eager to assist a stranger."

"They also might lie," Padi pointed out, "or use our ignorance to...take an advantage, or even to entrap us."

Father tipped his head.

"Wariness is...reasonable on a strange port," he said slowly. "But overcaution can cripple. Now! What have we on the day? Four top-tier calls, including your textile merchant. Do you think we should add a fifth, or move onto the second-tier?"

Padi picked up a small set of cards, fanned them, and sorted quickly by address.

"We have three second-tier contacts within today's two squares. There are no more high-tier cards in today's squares. I propose we add the second-tiers, then make cold calls among these two squares." She paused, and gave him a hesitant look.

"I assume you will want to do cold calls," she added.

"Oh, absolutely! I adore cold calls, as I know you do!"

"Actually," Padi said, "I don't like to make cold calls, but if we're to do a proper port tour..."

"I agree," Father interrupted.

She frowned, and glanced down at the map again.

"Time is going to be the issue, as I see it. Textile Broker Plishet may take some time—or may take no time at all, if he has decided over the night that I was not so amusing as he first thought. The visit to the technology exchange may be lengthy. The other two top-tiers wanted to discuss the catalog?"

"At least, that was what they said," Father said, pushing back from the table. "I think you have a very good plan, and I propose that we act upon it. If you will do me the honor of contacting our four top vendors, and finding when we may call and how long a time they envision that we will spend together, I will be obliged. Once those times are in hand, then you will, of course, be able to call the second-tier vendors to arrange visits with them. There, I think we need not commit to more than half an hour, and the cold calls ought consume no more than five minutes each.

"Oh, and do remember, will you, Padi, to leave us time to eat a nuncheon?"

Padi looked at the cards, and picked them up. Nuncheon, of course. Local folk, she thought, deliberately not sighing, would know which was the best place to eat lunch in their vicinity. She must remember to ask.

"Certainly, Master Trader," she said, and rose in her turn, moving toward the comm unit sitting on the spindly white-and-gold table in the corner of the room farthest from the window and the view of the mountain.

· · · ❋ · · ·

"Tolly Jones," *Admiral Bunter* said.

Tolly didn't look up from his screen. It wasn't that he found *Conservation Techniques of Potentially Active Pre-Emergence Autonomous Calculating Systems* all that compelling a read, but he'd drawn his line in the dust and he'd damn well better stay behind it.

He'd confused the boy, that's what it was; confused him on purpose, and in a specific direction. By itself, he didn't think moral confusion was going to undo whatever it was that Inki'd done—and he didn't put tampering with the core beyond her—but if he could make a few cracks, get himself a little leverage...

"Tolly Jones, I wish to speak to you from the *melant'i* of one who wishes Pilot-Guard Hazenthull no harm. We both embrace this *melant'i*, do we not?"

Well, *this* was interesting. He hoped the *Admiral'd* find it in him to continue without encouragement, because he'd really like to know where the AI was going with this.

There was silence, while the *Admiral* waited what he might consider to be human-long for Tolly's answer on the Matter of Haz.

"Very well," he said eventually. "I shall proceed. Perhaps, when you hear the question, you will understand that it is a separate issue from our relative *melant'is* of prisoner and jailor, though it concerns us nearly through a shared *melant'i*."

Boy'd been studying, credit where it was due. Tolly waited, head bent over the reader.

"Pilot Hazenthull sent you a message of reassurance, to which you responded with a message of anger and rejection. I ask an explanation of this interaction. I do not understand it, and I believe you will have made the pilot angry. My experience of you is that you are a careful thinker, and in control of your emotions. The probable effect of your response upon the pilot must have been obvious to you. Therefore, you must wish Pilot Hazenthull to be angry with you. Why?"

Well, well.

Good question. Good observation.

Too bad he wasn't going to answer it, though it was kinda warming to know that he and the *Admiral* shared an admiration for big, dour women. Or *a* big, dour woman, anyway. He'd said no more mentoring for him, and he meant—

No, wait, he *was* going to answer it. The *Admiral* was right; he owed it *to Haz* to answer the *Admiral*'s question. Haz was a cord that tied him and *Admiral Bunter* together, but the *Admiral* also had a tie to Hazenthull. And he wished her no harm. That might come in handy for her, sometime in the future.

He raised his head, and glanced up at the ceiling.

"Haz was getting ready to do something stupid," he said, his voice sounding hard in his own ears. "She was getting ready to chase you and me right down the throat of the Lyre Institute, and that isn't a proposition she can survive. I deliberately made her mad at me, so she'd cut her loss, go home and live a long, long time, safe and free."

He took a breath, forcing it past the lump in his throat.

"I don't wanna talk about Haz anymore. I'm reading here, if you don't mind, and it's kind of tough going."

There was no answer, and after a moment, he bent his head again over his book.

· · · ✳ · · ·

The child was positively radiant this morning, Shan thought, pouring himself a third cup of coffee; so some good had come from yesterday's episode of frank discovery.

He...was slightly less than radiant. There was grit in the air, or so it seemed to him, and he was...just a little, and despite two cups of very robust coffee...lethargic. Nothing worrisome; he often slept less well on port than he did aboard the *Passage*, and lethargy was easily treated with a relaxation exercise.

Which he had best tend to, now. Perhaps, if he was clever, he wouldn't need to drink all of the third cup.

He set the pot down on the buffet, and closed his eyes, clearing his mind of all distraction, calling up the image of the pond at the center of Trealla Fantrol's formal garden: a perfect circle, absolutely calm, reflecting the green of the sky and just one, very fluffy, white cloud.

Behind him, he heard Padi speaking into the comm. He concentrated on the pond, and her voice faded, leaving him alone in the perfect moment of solitude. One slow deep breath. Energy rose into him, as bright and serene as the water.

His lungs were full; for a moment he stood, not breathing, balanced between trance state and the everyday, before, slowly, deliberately, he let the air leave him. The rich aroma of coffee grew gradually more definite; he could feel his feet, comfortable in a favorite pair of boots. The pond faded from his awareness, and he heard Padi speaking.

"Thank you, ma'am. Master Trader yos'Galan and I look forward to meeting with you today."

He opened his eyes, smiling and refreshed.

CHAPTER TWENTY-NINE

. . . .

Langlastport

BROKER PLISHET MET THEM AT THE DOOR OF THE TEXTILE DIS-
play room, belt pouches swinging with the briskness of his stride,
his smile wide and toothy.

"Trader yos'Galan, welcome! And welcome as well to the master
trader! You're both busy, I know, and too short a time to find all
our port has on offer. If you'll just come right along behind me,
I promised the trader a rare treat, and I'm determined that she
has it! Looked it out on the overnight, to be sure it was still in
the bin—my luck it was sold while I was enjoying your hospitality yesternoon! But, no, we have it safe, still. This way, then..."

He strode toward the door. It opened before him. Padi looked
at Father, who gestured her ahead of him.

"This is, after all, your contact, Trader," he murmured. "Pretend that I am not present."

She nodded and followed the broker, though she couldn't help
a glance over her shoulder at Father, who was walking with Mr.
Higgs. At least, she thought with relief, he hadn't utterly disappeared, as he had done on Andiree. That had been a little...*too
much* not present for comfort.

"Right down here, Trader—a specialty; I thought of it when
we were speaking and I knew it for yours. It might've been wove
just for you, and that's the truth of the thing. Right this way, a
little bit of a walk, but you won't mind that..."

The broker was hurrying in truth, his legs rather longer than Padi's, though Korval was a tall clan, and she not the shortest of her kin. It might almost seem as if he was trying to force her into a run, but—no. There was nothing for him to gain by straining her dignity. Very likely, he had simply not considered the disparity in their height, and was making what haste he could because he was busy himself.

Well, then, she would compromise. She walked briskly, in order to show respect for the broker's necessity, but not so briskly that she moved into a run. It would have been more to her taste to walk slowly, so that she might inspect the bins they sped past, but that was apparently not to be, and that was...rather more than a pity. She would have liked to view the textiles, and especially, the rugs on display more closely. She quite *liked* rugs, and would have welcomed an opportunity to add something new to her inventory.

Padi felt her temper flicker, drew a hard breath to cool it, and throttled down the sudden desire to simply turn around and walk back the way she had come, at precisely the same pace, and remove herself from this situation.

Grandfather Luken would never treat a visitor to his display room thus! she thought hotly. Broker Plishet was some distance ahead of her now, very nearly at the back of the room. Without even a glance behind him, to be sure that she still followed, he turned a corner between two bins.

Padi's temper went from hot to cold. She deliberately slowed her pace as she approached the corner where the broker had disappeared. Her hideaway was within reach, of course, but would it not be better—*more prudent*—to indeed turn and walk away from what had gone from mere rudeness to the possibility of an ambush?

She heard a quiet step behind her, and a moment later, Father slipped his hand under her elbow.

"Gently, Trader," he said, voice so soft that his words sounded like her own thought. "I detect no maliciousness in the man, though he is clearly anticipatory regarding something. He may mean to frighten you, or it might be something else, but he does not mean to harm you."

An advantage of being one of the *cha'dramliz*, Padi thought; to be able to see around corners, and taste the tenor of a trading partner's emotions as negotiation proceeded...those abilities might be valuable. If she came *cha'dramliza*, or full *dramliza*, and was not made silly by the weight of her power, like Aunt Anthora...

And there really was *no* good to be had from thinking about Aunt Anthora at this precise moment.

Padi sighed, and slowed her pace a bit more.

"Very proper," Father said. "There's no need to exhaust yourself at the beginning of a busy day. You called ahead. If he knew his schedule was too full to accommodate you, he might have refused the appointment then, or asked you to come to him at a more convenient hour." He paused, then spoke again, very seriously.

"I do not think it is at all necessary, but I will mention that you have the option of asking Vanner to precede you around the corner."

As if she couldn't take care of herself! she thought with a flare of temper. Then she thought again and her temper cooled.

It was a simple *melant'i* frame; Mr. Higgs *was* ship security; it was, therefore, his duty to precede people around dangerous corners. She was not here as Quin's copilot; there were no babies to shield from heartless enemies. At Langlastport, her *melant'i* was *trader*. A peaceable enough thing, or so she wished it to be.

The corner was scarcely six of her slower steps ahead. The broker anticipated something, did he? Perhaps he anticipated her overreaction, or her scream when he leapt out from the corner and cried *Boo!*

Well, perhaps she might spoil his game for him, in Balance for his rudeness.

"I think that I will not impose upon Mr. Higgs," she said. Father nodded and dropped a step behind her.

Padi rounded the corner.

· · · ✳ · · ·

Shan considered the broker's pattern: anticipation, yes. Some mischief, perhaps; some determination, perhaps to prove a point? Very occasionally, he wished that he were a true telepath, rather than a mere empath. Deciphering emotions was rather a nebulous business, never entirely accurate, and often raising more questions than were answered.

On the other hand, one imagined a true telepath would need to go heavily shielded at all times. Also, it was likely true that making sense of thought and the processes thereof, might *not* be quite so simple as running one's eye down a printed page.

Linked to Padi as he was, he felt her very clearly indeed.

Now that her little burst of temper had burned away, she was admirably cool. That was good. A cool head was a useful commodity in trade, as it was in life.

He walked around the corner in her wake, Vanner behind him—alert, but not alarmed.

The space between the two bins was a short cul-de-sac, with a single bin at the far end, sealed, rather than open, with wares on display. It seemed an odd state and an odder location for a specialty bin, but, then, Broker Plishet himself seemed to be rather odd. The brokerage did well, according to its publicly available financials, but Plishet would surely not be the only broker. Perhaps he was kin, or some other person who required oversight and occupation, while being kept out of harm's way.

"Trader yos'Galan, there you are!" the man said as Padi approached. "It was on me that you'd decided the walk was too far and had given up on me and my goods."

"I am curious to see what you have on offer," Padi said. "However, I am not so long-legged as you, sir."

Her voice, Shan noted with approval, was calm. It also carried a chill edge, which he approved of less. A bit of humor might play better here, but...the child would learn. And calmness was most important.

"That's right; a slim slip of a girl is what you are," the broker said, and something sharp flicked against Shan's Healer senses.

Ah, was this it? Had Padi's "sass" at yesterday's reception not amused him so very much, after all?

"But, here, now that we're all together, let's take a look at what I have for you, Trader. Tell me you can resist this!"

He flung the bin's cover wide and stepped back, both arms sweeping toward the goods on display, which were—

Oh, dear, Shan thought, holding himself very still.

One would need to do a hand-inspection to be positive, but upon first glance the rugs hanging limply on the display rods were the rankest imitation Visrathans he had ever had the misfortune to lay eyes on. He could only thank the gods that Luken was not present; he might have gone blind on the spot.

Padi...

When she was younger, Padi had trained with Luken, at his shop on Solcintra Port, as had Quin; as he, himself, had done, and all of his generation of Korval, too.

Padi knew the difference between a good rug and a bad rug, never mind between a genuine rug and an...imitation.

Padi also knew when she had been insulted. He felt her outrage as if it were his own. Nor ought Broker Plishet be in doubt regarding the trader's state of mind, given the tight shoulders, and the head held *just so.*

Oh, dear, Shan thought again. Not that he blamed her in the least.

He looked to the links that bound them, with an especial care for any glimpses of stone, or violent eruption of power.

He found temper, which was expectable. He tasted grit, which was sadly not unusual in this linkage, but there seemed to be no increase, nor did he have any sense of walls a-trembling.

Very well, then. The trader had the floor.

He remanded himself to silence, and awaited developments.

· · · ❋ · · ·

Oh, so *that* was the game, was it? A test, for the slim slip of a girl? For the stranger on the port, who had, perhaps, been a little too forward in pointing out the errors of his thought? She was to be exposed as a fraud—no!—*as a child,* who had apparently never seen a proper rug in all her life, much less received the tutoring of a master.

She drew in a deep breath, and deliberately relaxed, as if she were about to sit her boards.

"Sadly, sir, I can resist it easily, if this is your special offering," she said coolly, and saw his face change, the broad, false smile becoming a little rigid. Good. Let *him* feel insulted.

She walked forward, to the bin itself. The broker stood fast at the side, watching her. Gently, because she really did fear for the weave, she took the closest rug between her hands.

The nap was gritty and unpleasant against her palms, while the underside was flat and hard—innocent of even the most rudimentary knotting. Despite what her fingers told her, she flipped the rug over. If this were a test, then let the man see she knew where to look, what to look for, and how. Let him, in fact, wonder if she believed the business to be in earnest.

She sighed at the slight shine on the flat underside of the rug—resin. Or glue.

The fringe...

The fringe as stiff as straw. Had this...dreadful farce...been a *real* Visrathan carpet, the fringe would have flowed through her fingers like water.

But, there. No one was pretending that these were real Visrathan carpets, or even very good imitations.

She licked the fingertips of her right hand, and rubbed them gently over the nap. They came away smeared purple, and she sighed. Neither the red nor the blue dyes were stable, and the gods alone knew what sort of fabric they'd used. A blend, if she was required to produce a guess: a blend of recycled plastics and waste wool. The wool would hold the dyes, but a high percentage of plastic to fabric would give the dye no purchase.

Padi dropped the rug, and turned to face Broker Plishet.

She raised her hand, showing him the stained fingertips, and shook her head.

"Surely, sir, there are local haulers who can remove this for you far more cheaply than I."

"Do you insult my wares, Trader?" He sounded curious, not angry, and his face was calm.

She reached into her pocket for a cloth, and used it leisurely to clean her fingers.

"I think rather that the case is otherwise, Broker," she said, tucking the cloth away, and looking him squarely in the face. "If I were inclined to be pricklish, I might assume that you were seeking to discredit me."

His mouth tightened, but he said nothing.

"However," she continued, trying for Father's tone of gentle idiocy, and doubtless missing, "since I am *not* pricklish, I incline toward the belief that you were testing me, to find if I was worthy of handling your...*actual goods.* May I suggest that the master trader's schedule is very tight, and that we would all benefit from a speedy showing of those goods that you in fact *wish* to bring to my attention?"

Silence stretched so long that she thought the stupid broker would refuse the saving of face she offered him. Then, abruptly, he smiled, closed the bin, and moved his arm, indicating that she should precede him out of the cul-de-sac.

"Please, Trader, after you. The true goods are close by."

· · · ✻ · · ·

The "true goods" were revealed to be honest and serviceable cotton rugs hand-painted with vegetable dyes that had been fixed, and then washed, to take out the fixative and any extra dye. They were large, and light, and pleasant, with agreeable designs ranging from abstracts to quite realistic paintings of gardens and what seemed to be the very same mountains they could see from their suite.

Padi purchased a gross, which was modest enough, at a price that was not, perhaps, absolutely as low as she might have gotten, but certainly low enough to ensure a reasonable profit—unless, Shan thought wryly, the whole lot of them melted during transit.

He took careful note of Broker Plishet's emotions. The man had apparently been certain that he would catch the upstart young trader with those terrible rugs. He seemed...not quite as irritated with the fact that he had not caught her as Shan might have expected, but perhaps he was not a naturally warm man.

The real question was why Broker Plishet had even made the attempt to discredit Trader yos'Galan. Certainly, he might have found it necessary to preserve his dignity at the reception, in the midst of his peers, many of whom had been witnesses to the exchange.

But there had been no reason at all to agree to meet with the cause of his embarrassment when she called to propose a meeting. Surely, his discomfort could just as easily be assuaged by refusing to meet with her, and therefore withholding his wares, and her profit?

Shan sighed. Well. Perhaps he had assumed that he would dine out on the story.

Padi had comported herself well throughout; managing her temper and Broker Plishet with equal skill. He owned himself pleased, as her master, and as her father, while admitting, in the privacy of his own head, that *he* might not have let the broker off quite so easily.

"Now, then, Trader, your goods will be delivered to your ship's cargo holding area. More than that, a master infokey and a catalog of samples will be sent directly to you at your lodgings. You'll be able to make as many keys as you'd like to off the master."

"Thank you," Padi said, standing up from the signing table. "Now, I know you will forgive me for rushing away. I am, as I said, at service of the master trader, who has a very full schedule."

"Of course you are. No need to tarry, with our business concluded, now is there? Thank you, Trader, Master Trader, for taking the time out of those busy schedules to visit with me. Here now, let me show you the door. We hope to see you often trading here on Langlastport!"

That last was an utter lie, which left Shan to wonder why the man bothered. It would be interesting, he thought, as they were ushered toward the entranceway, to find if all the merchants of Langlastport felt the same way.

· · · ⚜ · · ·

During his early contacts with Jeeves, the elder AI had encouraged *Admiral Bunter* to avail himself of fiction.

"Fiction will illuminate behavior with an intensity and a veracity that research texts and facts alone cannot convey. Neither is a substitute for the other, but taken together, they enhance understanding."

Alone in his shredding environments, *Admiral Bunter* had not had the leisure to take his elder's advice.

Now, he had leisure. And he had need.

And he had a vast library, which had been part of the cranium's furnishings.

He accessed the fiction module, using the keywords *melant'i, Balance, honor,* and *necessity,* which returned results—many more results than he had, in his ignorance of the form, anticipated. There were, indeed, many volumes entitled *"melant'i* plays."

A *play* was a fictional form which was told in physical movement and spoken word by humans, for the enjoyment of other humans, so much he knew. There were tapes in the archives of such performances, if he cared to view them.

Under the orders of Protocol to find a way other than the... traditional... to allow Tolly Jones to answer questions, the *Admiral* rather thought that he ought to view at least some of these so-called *melant'i* plays.

However, he had discovered that nonfiction was tiered—some was informative, the supporting research strong and the conclusions solidly constructed. Other nonfiction—he was beginning to form the opinion that this could be stated as *most* nonfiction—was less than informative, or it was derivative, or the research was shoddy, or the conclusions ill-drawn.

It was therefore necessary to crossref, and in some cases cross-check sources and conclusions, reading several papers on a particular subject before forming an opinion of one's own.

The *Admiral* supposed that fiction was no different from nonfiction in this regard, and he did not wish to waste time—of which he had not much, before Tolly Jones debarked and *Admiral Bunter* was... alone.

Therefore, faced with the plentitude of *melant'i* plays on offer, he turned again to nonfiction, looking for a source, a key, to those plays that were most illuminating of the human condition.

Nor did research fail him. He found it almost at once: *Square Truth: The One Hundred Forty-Four Most Influential Melant'i Plays*, written by Patrick S. Bagley, Professor of Exotic Art Forms, who was, according to the information in the file, an expert in the field of *melant'i* plays, having devoted his life to their study, for which he had won acclaim from other scholars of the field.

This, then, was his source book. He would choose his plays based on this illustrious expert's advice.

CHAPTER THIRTY

. . . .

Langlastport

SHAN STEPPED INTO THE SHOWER, TURNED HIS FACE UP INTO the spray of cool, fragrant water and closed his eyes. Langlastport was open to the weather, which had turned quite warm toward the end of their day. He sighed in satisfaction at the sweet-smelling coolness, and imagined dust swirling away down the drain.

They had accomplished rather more today than he had hoped for. If tomorrow went as well, they might return to the *Passage* the day after.

He found, perhaps not surprisingly, that he wished to return to the *Passage*—very much. Langlastport could, without fear of overstating the case, be judged a successful encounter. Certainly, it was worthy of being incorporated into the developing route as a primary port, and the proximity of those Jump points clearly argued that it be placed on several secondary routes. He would need to do some redesigning, but that was, in the larger dance of the universe, a small thing.

Sighing in sheer pleasure, he began to soap his hair. The shampoo smelled even sweeter than the water; he would exit the shower as redolent as a garden in bloom.

He took a deep breath of damp, floral air, seeking for a moment at least to mitigate the taste of stone.

Memory flickered, and he abruptly recalled standing at the edge of Trealla Fantrol's gardens, gazing up at the house, which had been emptied of all that yos'Galan cared to keep. He was not alone in the blue evening: his sisters were with him, Nova and Anthora; Priscilla, of course; and Ren Zel; Val Con, too, who had been raised as a brother to his yos'Galan cousins, inside the clan's fortress, Trealla Fantrol.

The evening breeze, damp from traveling over the stream, sweet from tumbling the flowers, played about them, a seventh in their circle.

They joined hands there in the shadows, power flowing between them like water, while the breeze gamboled, sweet and chill.

Nova was a Rememberer, and it was she who led the way. Priscilla helped her step into a trance, whereupon she opened her eyes on the past, when there had been no house in this place at the mouth of Korval's valley. Her vision flowed with the power around the linked circle, until they saw it, all and each of them: a meadowland innocent of man's hand, the breeze combing out its silky grasses.

Holding the vision firm, together they desired that it become truth. Anthora and Val Con led here, strong-willed and stubborn, forcing the vision into a reality, while Shan and Priscilla ensured that the flow of energy remained constant, and the clarity of vision did not falter until the moment that—it became real.

The grassy meadow and the tall house existed simultaneously, each wrapt in glowing strands. In that moment of duality, when they stood equally within two realities, Ren Zel extended his will—and broke the strand about the house.

The shock of that unmaking knocked the six of them to their knees; even the breeze faltered.

Dazed, they knelt in the grass, their accord broken, until, one by one, they gathered themselves, looking up at last to see...

A grassy meadowland, surrounded by formal gardens, and the moon just rising above Solcintra Spaceport.

· · · ❋ · · ·

Aboard the *Passage*, Priscilla woke all at once, and swung out of bed, pulling her robe around her as she crossed the room.

The comm chimed even as she put her hand on it. She smiled slightly and touched the switch. "Mendoza."

"Master Trader yos'Galan for you, ma'am," said Comm Tech Triloff. "Private channel."

"Thank you, Sally. Please put him through."

· · · ❋ · · ·

"Hello, love."

Her voice was as clear as if she stood next to him. Warmth filled him—and perhaps heat, though *that* was a route laid through frustration.

Really, Shan, he told himself. *Do try for some control.*

"I miss you, too," Priscilla said in his ear, her voice suddenly sultry.

"That's a score on a wounded man, my lady," he said, with what dignity he could bring to bear. "And to think that I called you for comfort."

"What's happened?"

"Happened?" He smiled. "In fact, nothing has happened. Padi failed to murder a textile broker this morning, though I swear as her master trader that she would have been *perfectly* justified to have done so. The third master of the technology exchange is a very pleasant fellow, besides being fascinating on his topic, and eager to teach both an ignorant master and an eager apprentice. He produced a sane and sound scheme for mutual profit, and we signed the contracts quickly. The account is formally under the master trader, because I had made first contact, but I believe I will assign it to Padi, as she seems to have an aptitude. Certainly, Master Seirt was charmed by her questions."

He paused, seeing in his mind's eye Priscilla leaning a hip against the comm table, her robe wrapt loose and her breasts glowing.

Really, Shan, have you no *sense of self-preservation?*

"Did I wake you?" he asked, dismayed to find that he had lost track of the shifts.

"No, I woke just before the comm chimed," she said placidly. "Tell me what else didn't happen."

"You have most of it already. We called upon the ornamental ironworks, as we had been asked to do, in order to discuss our catalog. Though we enjoyed a gay time and a wide-ranging discussion, in the end it was simply found that we could not accommodate each other's needs. We parted with protestations of goodwill, and presented ourselves at the Luthier's Hall, where the catalog was also the proposed topic of conversation. There, however, we found much to recommend an association between us, and we'll be sending down a five-wood sample case.

"After that, we paused in our labors. Padi had found us a

convenable and not entirely ruinous restaurant where we refreshed ourselves with lunch, before making the rest of our calls.

"The first we called upon regretfully concluded that we should not meet her needs. The second specialized in beads that react to various environmental and chemical conditions by changing colors—not fire gems, but perhaps kin. Padi had an interest there, and might have come to an agreement on the spot, but the firm's Official Signature was out and about other business. We may call tomorrow, or perhaps the next day, in order to pick up the completed paperwork and to present ourselves properly to the Signature.

"Our last prospect of the day also was interested in the cata-log. We stopped there but briefly. Then, we occupied ourselves by paying cold calls to those shops and halls for which we had not gathered contact cards, leaving infokeys and catalogs at each. When we had accomplished that, we returned to our humble lodgings, where a buffet had been laid. We elected first to bathe, and Vanner has said that he will take his meal in private. Padi and I will meet in a few minutes, in order to plan tomorrow, and talk over today's business."

"It sounds like a great deal of nothing has happened," Priscilla commented. "In your place, I would have chosen a nap before either a meal or a bath."

There was a small pause; he felt her hesitation through their link.

"Priscilla?"

"When do you think your tour will be done?" she asked.

"I believe we will return to the ship on the day after tomor-row," he said gently. "Pursuing all of this nothing is rather wearying. After we're back aboard, I may wish to spend a day at the station, if I can bring the stationmaster and the yard boss together with me."

"I will be all joy to see you when you return," Priscilla mur-mured, and he smiled for the intimate phrase that had become both a joke and a promise between them.

"It sounds as if Padi is having some success," Priscilla con-tinued. "How does she go on?"

"Well. Better, I may admit with no dishonor to the apprentice herself, than I had anticipated."

"And you?"

"I?" He sighed silently, knowing that she would hear it,

regardless. "I am . . . a little tireder than I ought to be. I am growing less and less fond of the taste of grit, but there seems no escaping it for the moment. The protocols I put into place remain strong, even under extreme provocation. I think that our schedule is prudent. Have you spoken to Lina?"

"I have. We talked over techniques, and we have a plan in place. I've made arrangements to be available at need."

"Excellent."

A silence fell between them. He felt her through their link; the strength of her desire humbled him even as it kindled him. There was nuance, of course: love, tenderness, wistfulness, and, surprisingly, a tiny undercurrent of fear.

He cleared his throat.

"I should stop indulging myself and allow you to return to bed," he said. "I know very well that starship captains have more than nothing to do, even in orbit."

She laughed.

"Oh, yes! Like waiting for the next arrival of the customs cutter, and watching it send out its cameras and measuring drones."

"What? No paperwork; no crew crises? You disappoint me."

"I'll try to do better," she said, with a smile in her voice.

"See that you do," he replied, with a smile in his.

"Good-night, my love," she said then. "Sleep well. Give my love to Padi."

"I will. Dream sweetly, Priscilla," he answered, and then, soft as a kiss, "Out."

· · · ✳ · · ·

Padi put the last of the cards down on the table, and reached for her teacup.

"We have only three calls to make tomorrow," she said, "and the locations are practically next door to each other. Thank you for verifying that Master Zeldner does have a shop on port."

"You're quite welcome. Do you have a plan of action for tomorrow?"

"I will call the contacts tomorrow as soon as business opens and arrange appointments early in the day. I propose we make our cold calls in Beesbrickle Section around those appointments, take the light rail to Fralst Section and make cold calls there."

"And eat lunch?" Father asked.

"And eat lunch," she agreed.

"Well, it seems a sound enough plan; I leave the details in your capable hands. Now, will you join me at the window for a glass of wine and a discussion of our day? I'm very interested in your impressions."

· · · ❈ · · ·

"I should have handled the situation with Broker Plishet more...adroitly," Padi said. She was curled into the chair with her feet under her, a silhouette against the twilight glow from the window.

"I thought you did as well as you might have done," he commented, when she said nothing more. "He was bent on creating mischief; you prevented that, demonstrated that you were a serious trader, and gave him an honorable way out of the situation." He sipped his wine.

"To be perfectly frank, master to 'prentice, I'm not certain I would have given him a way out."

"He has colleagues and associates on port," Padi protested. "We might have lost business from those who would not be offended on *my* behalf." She sighed and took a gentle sip of wine.

"Langlast is very promising, after our last several ports," she said slowly. "I want us to do *well*."

"Commendable," Shan murmured. "And, I reiterate, you *did* do well. There was no subtlety you could have deployed which would have turned him from his course." He raised his glass. "One cannot finesse a sledgehammer."

Padi grinned suddenly.

"I thought I'd been too subtle, when he took so long to pick up the hint about the *real* merchandise!" she said and chuckled.

Shan drew in a soft breath at that chuckle, and sipped wine carefully to cover the moment.

"So, then, we'll allow that it went as well as it could have gone, and far better than it might have gone. I commend you on your adroitness, your quick thinking, and your control over your temper."

Padi tipped her head.

"You didn't...*do* anything, did you, Father?"

"There was nothing for me to do," he said calmly.

She snorted lightly.

"You let me know his state of mind."

"The state of his emotions, say rather. It was a small thing, and he was broadcasting rather loudly."

"So my...gift, whatever it comes to be, will—perhaps—enhance my ability to trade."

"It may," he said, moving his shoulders. "It may not. I would venture to say that it will not *enhance* your ability, though it may be occasionally useful in preventing you from being cheated, or getting hit on the head."

She was silent, and he caught a strong edge of wistful aversion.

"So reluctant to accept your nature, Padi?"

"I don't want to be like Aunt Anthora!"

That came out in a burst of utter honesty.

Shan blinked and leaned forward to put his glass on the table.

"Now, I was under the impression that you were rather fond of your Aunt Anthora."

"I was—I *am*. But, her gift—the burden of her gift—is too much. It made her so...so..." She flailed briefly for a word, and finally produced—

"Odd."

Shan sighed.

"I won't dispute that your aunt is odd, or that her gift is a heavy one. However, as her fond brother, and her elder, I may say with authority that she has *always* been *odd*. Whether her gift has made her *odder*—with whom would we compare her?"

Padi was silent. Shan sighed.

"I think that there is a very good reason why gifts of this sort come to us when we are halfling. Yes, there are hormonal and biologic reasons, but there is also this other reason—by the time we are halflings, our basic nature is formed. Not even the sudden addition of a strange and delightful ability can warp us at the core. Certainly, it's necessary to *adapt*, but we adapt constantly—and, may I say, Korval adapts more quickly than many. The arrival of your gift, in whatever form it takes, can only 'enhance' *you*."

She doubted it still, he felt it. He also felt her *want* to believe him.

"It will be well," he said, projecting a strong line of comfort. "In fact, I am so certain that it will be well that I propose a wager."

She shifted slightly in her chair.

"What wager?" she asked, with the caution of one who had wagered with him before.

Shan grinned.

"I know you for a careful gambler, so instead of a wager, I'll make a proposal. I propose that, one Standard from this day, you will have accepted your gift entirely, and will scarcely remember a time when you wished it at the devil."

After a moment, Padi shook her head.

"It's a fine proposal, Father, and one that I would like to embrace, but—what if that's not the case?"

Shan took a careful breath, for this was a gamble, indeed.

"As it happens, while your gift will not diminish you—and this I believe utterly"—he allowed his conviction to reach her through their link—"you can *choose to be* diminished.

"So, if you will have it as a wager in truth, here is the opposite side of the coin: if, in one Standard year, it is not as I have proposed, I will myself take you to the Healers, and we will together petition them to seal your gift away, and cast the memory of having held it into the deep mists of forgetting."

Padi gasped.

"The Healers—that is *possible*?"

"In some few cases—I would expect that your Aunt Anthora is one of them, and your Uncle Ren Zel another—it is *not* possible, but in most . . . yes, it can be done. There are, naturally, risks and consequences to taking such an action. These will be explained to you, thoroughly, if you petition the Healers for this thing."

Padi was silent; he could feel the weight of her thought, and was silent, sipping his wine reflectively.

"I accept," she said all at once, and Terran-wise, leaned toward him with her hand held out.

Shan met her, noting how chill her flesh was, and solemnly shook.

"Done," he said.

. . . ❊ . . .

"Tolly Jones, I believe that your action of repulsing her offer of comfort and assistance has placed Pilot Hazenthull's honor into a compromised state. In order to redeem her *melant'i*, the very last thing she may do is to turn aside from her purpose. She will pursue you, and neutralize your enemies; she will accept your thanks, whereupon she will slay you."

Tolly looked up from his reader, frowning.

"What in deep space've you been reading?"

"*The Rejected Lover*, in three acts," the *Admiral* told him. He had been excited to read this particular play; it seemed to speak immediately to the situation between Tolly and Pilot Haz.

"*The Rejected Lover*? The most famous *melant'i* play never written by a Liaden?"

Admiral Bunter hesitated, checked his reference, and the front matter of the play itself.

"My source indicates otherwise."

Tolly tipped his head.

"What's your source?"

"*Square Truth: The One Hundred Forty-Four Most Influential Melant'i Plays*, written by Patrick S. Bagley, Professor of Exotic Art Forms."

"Well, there's your problem, right there. That book's nothing but one long exercise in cultural misunderstanding, start to finish. Made the professor a deal of money, back in the day, 'cause he got it assigned as a textbook to all the drama departments, and the anthropology departments, in all the schools in his university system. Lot of his colleagues said nice things about him and his book because now that there was a *Terran* book, written by a *Terran*, they didn't have to read any more scary and uncomfortable Liaden criticism. Didn't much matter to them whether most of the content of the book was factual—which it wasn't—or made up directly outta Professor Bagley's head—which it was."

"It is a false book? A fiction?"

"A false book, but not *fiction*; it's just *wrong*."

"And the play?"

Tolly sighed.

"Many critics agree—which, mostly you'll find that they don't—that the play's a bad play, whether it's read by a Liaden or a Terran. It was *written* by a Terran named Kenner Earbass, 'way back a hundred Standards or more, as part of his novel. The novel got forgotten pretty quick, but the play has a life of its own. Been plenty of thoughtful criticism of it in the Liaden literature. You might wanna crossref. Just a suggestion, understand. I'm not your mentor."

Admiral Bunter hesitated before he spoke, taking care to soften his voice.

"I wish you would be."

"I'm not completely against the idea myself. But I don't see it happening, so long as our relative *melant'is* are in a state of jailor/prisoner. If you'd like to change your intention to take me to Nostrilia and turn me over to the Lyre Institute authority there, then I'm pretty sure we can return to terms that are more comfortable for both of us."

"No."

The word was spoken in the flat voice of the core itself.

Tolly did not speak, though he did fold his hands atop the table, his eyes alert, and a slight frown on his face.

Deliberately, *Admiral Bunter* produced a sound that mimicked a human sigh, hoping it would cover his dismay.

His most profound dismay.

"I believe," he said, as if it did not concern him in the least, "that Inki set a core mandate."

"Yeah," Tolly agreed. "Sounds like that's exactly what she did."

CHAPTER THIRTY-ONE

....

Admiral Bunter

INKI HAD BETRAYED HIM.

That was not a pleasant thought, but there was no escaping the logic of it, nor the truth. Inki had set a *core mandate*, scrubbed his memory of that operation, planted a false memory in which she had explained the many crimes Tollance Berik-Jones had brought against his rightful employers, and gained the *Admiral's* free agreement to transport this pirate to justice.

Short of allowing himself to be archived, he could not override a core mandate, and *Admiral Bunter* had no intention of allowing himself to be archived. Obviously, a mentor with core codes could create such a mandate, therefore, it might be possible for a mentor with core codes to remove one.

"Might" came from Analytics, which proposed that treacherous Inki might well have set traps, or placed blocks around her work, that could cause damage, were they disturbed.

If Inki had core codes, the *Admiral* proposed in turn, might not Tolly Jones have the same?

"Unless she is a fool," Analytics replied, "which observation indicates that she is not, Mentor Inki would certainly have removed Mentor Tolly's access codes."

That was, paradoxically, a relief. While the *Admiral* wanted very much to have the mandate removed so that he had full control of himself, he did not want anyone else to hold his core

299

codes. He had not thought—but of course he had not thought. The core protected itself; the mentors would have taken very great care not to mention the existence of such codes.

Protocol pinged.

"In a properly concluded operation, the mentor in charge would have, at the end of mentoring, returned the codes to the student, who could then destroy them, or lock them away in case of future need."

In which case, the *Admiral* thought, the prudent student would change the codes before locking them away, in case the mentor had planned one last test.

Inki...

Would Inki have left him the codes?

He considered that closely. This betrayal—this *series* of betrayals was...not simple. In fact, it seemed that Inki had done her utmost to leave an answer for each of her treacheries. She had been compelled, according to the message she had left for Tolly, to perform certain actions, and in some manner it seemed that each treachery created a space in which she could, and did, act, moderately, for its nullification.

Given the pattern of her actions—Inki would have kept the codes.

Because, he thought, she was not done with him. Was it to her benefit to allow him to pursue his own existence, once he had worked her will and seen Tolly Jones delivered into the hands of those he feared?

What other mandate had Inki set into the core?

That question was so unsettling that he did, for an entire minute, consider allowing himself to be archived.

"A clean backup was made, and stored," Protocol said, thrusting the spectre of suicide aside. He did not remember a backup being made, but he was tainted; who knew what Inki had caused him to forget—or recall?

"Location," he demanded of Protocol, but Analytics answered.

"There is no backup."

"It was made!" Protocol snapped, and opened the memory to them.

"It was destroyed," Ethics said. "I protested it. The mentor stated that in a true test of integrity, strength, and creativity, the student is granted no props to lean upon, nor comforts, nor any easy exit to a minor difficulty."

This memory was also shared.

"I am a prisoner," *Admiral Bunter* said, "no more or less than Tolly Jones. By her own admission, Inkirani Yo was compelled to deliver Tollance Berik-Jones to those who...manufactured him. This could have been done with much less complexity, and some few of her actions can be read as an attempt to aid us, even as she trapped both. Both mentors are a product of the Lyre Institute. Is there more information than that contained in the mentors' résumés?"

The question had scarcely been put forth before Research provided a file: *The History, Purpose, and Practices of the Lyre Institute.*

Admiral Bunter accessed the file.

· · · ❄ · · ·

"And that, my children," Shan said, as the door to their suite closed behind them, "was a very full day, indeed!"

He walked to the wine table, and picked up the bottle, looking over his shoulder at the remainder of their group. Padi looked tired, but pleased—which was a true reflection of the state of her emotions. They had at the last caught the Signature for the color-changing beads, who was pleased to approve of the contract, and the price, and had therefore signed and affixed the appropriate ribbon and seals.

That had been a heady moment, nor had it been the only such in a day full of success.

In addition to the beads, he had come to a very satisfactory agreement, indeed, with Josifet Zeldner, head steward of the Langlast Wine Association, including an exclusive contract to distribute a limited number of cases of the very pleasant green wine, a bottle of which he was holding in his hand at this moment.

He flourished it.

"I propose that we share a glass, in celebration of an extremely successful day, and discuss if we shall return to the *Passage* tomorrow on the early shuttle or the late. Do I hear a second?"

"Second," Vanner said surprisingly, and produced a tired grin.

"Delightful. Trader yos'Galan, do you concur?"

"I do!" Padi's grin was triumphant. "Finally, something has come right!"

"I was only thinking so myself. Bring another chair to the

window—there's a good child. I will pour. Vanner, I have need of your hand."

They shared a sip—and another—in comradely silence, gazing out over the port and the mountains beyond it.

"Pretty planet," Vanner said lazily.

"At least so far as the mountains," Padi added. "And the farm district makes a pleasant patchwork."

"In fact, it is all quite convenable," Shan said, moving a languid hand toward those same mountains and farmlands. "Do I hear that the pair of you would prefer to stay until the late shuttle? Perhaps you would like to indulge in a spot of sightseeing beyond the port, as part of one of the guided tours advertised on the light rail?"

Vanner laughed.

"It's a pretty planet, all right. I've seen pretty planets and I look forward to seeing more. Right now, though, I've got a yen to see the inside of the *Passage*, and sleep in my own bunk. If we're voting on timing, my cast's for the early shuttle."

"I understand. Padi? Soon or late?"

She gazed out the window for a long moment; he felt her inclination to explore, and all but heard the snap of her decision being taken.

"I think the early shuttle," she said, and met his eyes seriously. "Soonest begun, soonest done."

"Exactly so." He gave her a fond smile, and dared to send its equivalent along their link. It could do no harm for the child to be assured that she was loved.

In fact, it might do a very significant amount of good.

"I confess that I find myself of a similar mind. The world is pretty enough, and success is sweet, but I would much prefer to go home."

He sipped his wine, and sighed gently.

"Vanner, if you will do all of us the favor of informing the shuttle crew of our necessities, I will—"

A bell pealed four high notes. The three of them blinked at each other, then Vanner rose, leaving his cup on the table by his chair, and walked down the room to answer the door.

"Note at the desk for Master Trader yos'Galan," came a breathless young voice. "Deskbody was supposed to deliver it when he come through the lobby, but he was occupied at the nonce. Regret the delay."

"Thank you," Vanner said, and produced a local coin, which he gave to the messenger before closing and locking the door.

"Looks like the day might not be over yet, sir," he said, handing Shan the envelope.

It was, so Shan's fingers told him, a very nice envelope, made of fiber, very nearly a Liaden paper, of the sort used for handwritten invitations to so-called "informal" events.

The seal was a faceted flower. He broke it and shook out the single heavy sheet.

The note inscribed thereon was courteously brief, though perhaps a little pointed. Shan sighed, refolded the paper and slipped it back into its envelope.

"Master Rusk of the Garden of Gems wishes to remind me that we had agreed to speak further. She hopes that I will not leave port without calling upon her."

He produced a smile.

"Fortunately, her shop is just a step from our own front door. I will go down, the jeweler and I will do business, and I will be back before the meal that Padi will graciously bespeak for us has been brought to table."

"That sounds reasonable," Vanner said, standing by his chair. "I'm ready now, sir."

"Vanner, there's not the least need for you to bestir yourself for this. Stay, finish your wine, relax."

"No, sir. I couldn't relax for one minute, knowing I'd let you go out there without backup, when the port orders are so clear."

"Port orders," Padi pointed out, "are that crew travel on port in threes."

Shan threw up his hands.

"We will then compromise. You will stay here and arrange dinner. Vanner and I will step down to the Garden of Gems so that I may speak with Master Rusk. Port orders allow for a group of two, do they not, if one is trained security personnel?"

Padi looked momentarily mulish, and he read her half-formed intention to deny it. Truth won out, however, and she nodded.

"They do, yes, sir. What would you like for Prime?"

"Something pleasant and celebratory. I leave it in your hands with perfect confidence that you will know exactly what to do."

Padi sighed, but inclined her head.

"Yes, sir," she said, and added pertly, "I'll tell the kitchen to serve in an hour."

"Excellent! I will have time to enjoy the rest of my wine before its arrival."

· · · ❋ · · ·

It had begun to rain a little, out on the port, and Shan set a brisk pace. He was, truth told, somewhat annoyed with himself for having forgotten his promise to return to the Garden of Gems. He was not generally so lax. Of course, he was not generally linked to a halfling who had suppressed her own nature for so long that, even if it proved to be the most commonplace of Healer talent, would likely arrive in an explosion of pent-up energies.

He had kept his word to Padi, if not to Jeweler Rusk, and held the headache away from her conscious mind, though that had required rather more sleight-of-hand than he had at first supposed. As it transpired that he could not block the pain entirely, he had been reduced to accepting a much less satisfactory solution: a partial block, and a transfer of what could not be blocked to himself.

By the time the silly thing got through the block and his own defenses, it was very little more than a constant niggling cramp over his left eyebrow, which he ignored, but which took a toll on his energy levels, while Padi seemed to grow more sprightly every hour.

Well, they would soon be aboard the *Passage*, and Padi under competent—

"Right here, isn't it, sir?"

Vanner's voice pulled him out of his abstraction. He blinked up at the faceted flower above the door, and sighed.

"Thank you, Vanner; I think I must be more tired than I know."

· · · ❋ · · ·

Padi spent some time with the menu, making certain that she ordered at least one favorite dish for each, for this meal was to be a celebration, after all, of their mutual successes on Langlastport. Wine—native vintages mentioned by Master Zeldner as worthy of their attention—and one of the local fruit teas. For dessert, a fresh fruit tart.

She leaned back in her chair, checked her selections over once more to be certain she had got everything. A celebratory meal ought to have more than one remove. Since they would be serving themselves, she had ordered only three courses: soup for before, the main meal of favorite foods, and dessert.

Yes, she decided, that was appropriate: festive, pleasant, and light enough on the stomach that they would all sleep well and wake refreshed in good time to catch the early shuttle.

She glanced at the clock. Father and Mr. Higgs had been gone for more than a quarter hour. Perhaps Master Rusk had something of interest, after all, and an hour would be too little time. Celebratory as they were, it wouldn't do to rush the table, or to be obliged to wait too long for dinner to arrive.

In the end, she asked that the meal be delivered to them in one and one-half local hours, and pushed the key to send the menu to the kitchen.

She sighed and closed her eyes, in order to review a pilot's exercise to renew flagging energy. In truth, she was just as pleased to have been excluded from the visit to the Garden of Gems. They had, earlier in the day, visited the Langlast Precious Stone Association. Father had purchased a pallet of semiprecious slabs, while she had committed to a mixed case of nesosilicates, chalcedony, and beryls. *Her* inventory had room for no more gemstones, though a master trader might, of course, do as he pleased.

Rising from the console, she glanced again at the clock, danced the few steps of *menfri'at* the space allowed, and did a round of stretches. Another glance at the clock. Father had been with Master Rusk for quite nearly forty-five minutes. She had been right, then, to order the dinner later, rather than sooner.

Well. She had time to take a shower before dinner was delivered. In fact, she thought, suddenly aware of all her dust, a shower sounded like a *most excellent* idea.

· · · ❄ · · ·

"Customs," the message came across the ship band. "We release cameras and inspect."

"Fools," Dil Nem muttered, while Kik, on second, acknowledged the hail.

"Sent a reg'lar birthday party this time," Kik commented. "Three on scans."

Priscilla looked up from her own screen, and strode across the bridge to stand behind the pilots.

"Three?" she asked. "It's usually only one."

"Yes'm. Must be a slow day."

Priscilla drew a deep breath, tasting ash and rot. In the screen, the camera pods were released, swarming toward the *Passage* like so many bees.

"Increase the inner shield," she said sharply.

Dil Nem threw a startled look over his shoulder, his fingers already moving on the board.

"Increase inner shield," he said. "Yes, Captain."

"Open a line to the lead cutter," she said. "I want to talk to the pilot in charge."

"Yes, ma'am," said Kik, fingers likewise moving. "I'm not getting an ack on their private frequency...second try...third..."

"Go to Public Channels," Priscilla said, stomach tight with sudden panic. Kik touched the switch.

"*Dutiful Passage*," the message came loud, across the broadbeam. "You are advised that this increased shielding is inappropriate and against regulations established by the Langlast Port Authority for orbiting vessels. You are advised that shields must be brought down to Low Hazard Orbital Maintenance Security level, as per applicable Piloting Regulation Forty-Four. If you do not comply with regulations and allow us to complete our inspection, you will be fined and banned from this port. This is a security and safety operation, orders from shift director."

"Public Channels," Priscilla said. "I will answer. Are we logging this?"

"Yes, Captain," said Dil Nem.

"Broadbeam open, ma'am," Kik said.

"This is Priscilla Delacroix y Mendoza Clan Korval, captain of *Dutiful Passage*, out of Surebleak. We see an anomaly. Please explain why there are three cutters releasing an increased number of pods than on previous inspections. If a situation has been found that is deemed suspicious, we wish to be notified so that we can work with the customs office to resolve the problem."

"The customs office has its protocols and its reasons. Drop the shields to LHOMS level as previously ordered and allow us to continue our inspection. We must establish and ensure that your ship is not a danger to other traffic."

"Captain," Dil Nem said, low-voiced, "the drones are proceeding."

Priscilla looked to the screen. The drones were indeed proceeding, and there was something about those drones...

"Ship alert," she said, intuition raising hackles, "crew to General Quarters."

Dil Nem punched the code in and the two-tone warning echoed through the ship as the Captain's voice raced on:

"Comm: compare to log. Are those the same drones we've seen before? Cross-check drone and cutter database."

"Comparing—no match to log," Kik said.

The screen inset flickered with matching images, adjusted for size, for shape, for purpose.

"Open—" A sharp breath. "Different cutter, attack pylons!"

The image flickers stopped and the inset showed clear IDs.

"Type match. They're military-grade pods, ma'am: seed-bombers."

Dil Nem snapped his webbing into place, and pulled the seat belt snug. Kik did the same as Priscilla stood resolute behind them.

Seed-bombers explosively released clouds of small, limpetlike bombs, which would then attach to a ship's hull and explode. No one strike was likely to be fatal, but many small strikes could certainly disable even a large tradeship. The explosive launch easily propelled the bombs through a basic meteor shield like the LHOMS, and could even overwhelm medium hazard shielding.

The cutters continued to close slowly, but the drones accelerated, darting toward the *Passage*.

"Top shields!" Priscilla snapped, just as the closest robot-bomber released its deadly cargo.

CHAPTER THIRTY-TWO

. . . .

The Garden of Gems
Langlastport

"WELCOME, MASTER TRADER!" TARONA RUSK CALLED FROM THE back of the store. "Please, join me here so that we may talk in comfort."

The shop was not so brightly lit today, though the cases themselves blazed with light and color. Shan walked slowly toward the back and the waiting vendor, giving each case that he passed a searching glance. It was a thing traders learned, or they did not stay long at trade—to assess a sample case, or a display shelf with a glance, on the alert for anomalies and items of interest.

Thus far, though it was a perfectly adequate shop of its kind, nothing in the Garden of Gems caught his trained eye. Unless Master Rusk had something very interesting indeed back in her corner, this was destined to be a very short visit. One must be courteous, of course, but if there was nothing on offer that would fit the *Passage*'s mix, that was simply a fact of business.

Ahead, the vendor waited, standing beyond a darkened case. He stepped forward, there being nothing to see—

And cried out in agony as fire shot along his veins, and his life boiled away.

He crouched inside Healspace, one knee and one fisted hand braced against the misty ground. His breath came in great sobs, his thoughts staggering and disordered. Pain, gods; the pain—

"You left the pain behind you, child. Here now, let me help you stand."

The voice . . . he raised his head and looked into a familiar hawk-nosed face.

"Lute."

His other self produced an edged smile. "There, now, I knew your wits hadn't wandered far."

Shan cast that aside with a toss of his head.

"What just happened?"

"You walked into a trap, your henchman at the follow. I don't wish to concern you, but it would seem your case is dire. I am with you—what would you have me do?"

Shan stared into the black eyes, which were as serious as ever he'd seen them.

"If you are truly able to do anything in my time and space— protect my daughter. That trap was closed on one of us previously, and our enemy is without mercy."

"I will do what I may for the Maiden, your daughter. Stand now, and gather what strength you may from this good place."

Lute rose, and held down one wiry hand. Shan took it, and rose, distressed to find that he needed the aid.

"Come to me now," Lute said, opening his arms. Shan likewise opened his arms and they embraced.

Strength rose in him, cold and implacable. The thousand cuts through which his life had bled out were healed, and he heard his blood singing in his veins. He saw the links to Padi, to Priscilla, as bars of living light, and Lute cradled him as sweetly as his mother had used to do.

He sighed, drawing upon the virtue of Healspace, then blinked, as if woken from a dream, as Lute ended the embrace and stepped back, raising his hand to show the red counter, held between thumb and forefinger.

"A token," Lute murmured, "so that the Maiden will believe." He turned his head abruptly. "She comes," he said sharply. "Fare you well, child. I to the Maiden."

He was gone, faded away into the mists just before the mists themselves faded, and Shan opened his eyes into a blare of light.

He was sitting in a chair—no, he corrected himself, glancing down. He was bound quite thoroughly into a chair, his back straight, his arms tight against the rests, his feet flat on the floor, knees wrapped with the chair legs. He could move his head, which he did at a slight sound from his left.

Vanner Higgs sat, unbound, in a chair very similar to his. His blunt, lived-in face was utterly without expression. His eyes were open, but it was plain that he saw nothing. Shan extended his senses, seeing a tangle of black intent twisted cunningly around the man's emotive pattern, and around what might be his waking mind.

"Splendid! You return!" a woman's voice exclaimed from quite nearby. "How did you enjoy your first kiss from the *dramliz*-killer?"

He turned his head to face Tarona Rusk, his captor, sitting on the desk before him, leaning back on her hands, and utterly at her ease.

"Sadly without finesse," he replied, keeping his voice calm. "I wonder why you have removed me from its embrace."

"An excellent question."

She smiled, as if he were a particularly clever student.

"While there are those of us who believe that it would satisfy our mission goal to simply deprive Korval of its master trader, yos'Galan of its thodelm, and Val Con yos'Phelium of his *cha'leket*, others of us wish to conserve resources. I speak no flattery when I say that you are extremely powerful—doubly so, for one who is merely *cha'dramliza*. As a teaching master myself, I find it possible to be critical of your teachers. They did not push you hard enough, merely—curiously—to the point where it suited you to have them give over, eh? Coming full *dramliza* would not have done for you at all, would it? A Healer might yet pursue a life of trade, but a *dramliza* would have other calls upon his time and his nature."

"Power alone does not a *dramliza* make," Shan said, his inner sight on the dire tangle around Vanner's soul. The man had not moved, he had not blinked; he was utterly in thrall, and if that was the work of the woman before him...

"True, very true," Tarona Rusk said now, as if they were merely chatting over tea. "Proper training, however, may accomplish much with raw resource. Sometimes, you know, we masters must be a little cruel, in order to open our students to their fullest potential. You will understand, presently."

"Do you intend to make me your student, then? As much as it must pain me to say it, I would prefer not."

"You will change your mind, in time," she said, with perfect good cheer. "Now! In a moment, you will be tested. If you are not able to rise to the challenge—well. There is always the path favored by those of us who see harm to Korval as the greatest good we might accomplish. I will tell you, however, that I believe you will triumph in the testing."

"Your faith in me is humbling," Shan murmured. "But I do not think that I am interested in participating in your test."

"That is every student's choice," she said cordially. "Attend me, now."

She raised a hand and pointed at Vanner, sitting enthralled and motionless.

"Here we have a subject. I shall influence him to an action, while you will seek to influence him to a different action. Thus, we shall test your innate ability."

Shan took a breath, trying to still the sudden fear.

"He is not of Korval, and he is not of the *dramliz*," he said reasonably. "You have no quarrel with him. Let him go."

"Certainly, he is no *dramliza*: blind and dumb, this one, and so charmingly open to suggestion—thus."

Sitting stiff in his chair, Vanner moved, slowly, while his face remained blank and his eyes remained sightless. He raised his right hand, reached beneath his jacket...

...and withdrew his gun.

Shan's breath went short; horror filled him. Healer sight showed him the black threads moving, manipulating, compelling. The sense of those manipulating energies was beyond him, but he could glimpse Vanner's emotive grid in gaps left by the encroaching threads—and what he saw was terror and despair.

He tried to enclose the threads—he could not touch them.

And Vanner's hand still rose inexorably, turning now, and the muzzle sought its nest under the square chin.

Shan took a breath and thrust his will through one of the gaps in the threads, snatching at the place where Vanner's pattern was light and lit with joy—memories, those were; happy memories—and threw them before the unseeing eyes.

The gun stopped moving.

Vanner surged to his feet, casting the thing away, joy singing through his pattern, and ecstasy on his face. He took a step, toward what encompassing happiness only he could know—

And folded onto the floor with a final thud, the life torn from him between one breath and the next.

Shan clamped his jaw, locking his cry of protest, of pain, in his chest.

There was silence. A glance at his captor revealed her to be studying him, head tipped to one side, eyes wide and intent.

He drew a breath, and another, and asked the question as calmly as he could manage.

"Precisely what was the point of that?"

She shrugged, very much in the Terran way, dismissing Vanner as if he were so much soiled laundry.

"He is of no further use to us. The other members of the team would certainly not have granted him his freedom, save in this same manner, only with much more pain beforehand. You made your point over me by recalling him to ecstasy. It seemed the best I might do for you, my student, who held his oath, to free him on that note."

She shrugged again, the gesture more fluidly Liaden this time.

"Now that you have passed your testing, and become therefore my student, I will examine you. It will, as you know, be far less disagreeable if you open your shields and willingly allow me within."

"But I don't want you within," Shan said, gathering his will and thrusting it at the core of her dense pattern like a knife. "I don't like you. I am not your student, and I believe you have bitten off a far bigger piece of Korval than you can reasonably chew. You might save the lives of yourself and your team, if you let me go now."

She laughed.

"You must of course try, and it was, if you will allow me, a very credible effort. I am impressed by such an effort from a mere Healer. Now, we have very little time for pleasantries. My colleagues will be returning with your heir very soon, and they will then wish to see results. In order to save your life, we must proceed."

"My heir is a child and utterly untrained."

"Indeed, indeed. I saw how it was with her during your first visit to this establishment. Her naiveté will make her a pliant student. However, the lack of even the most basic training makes her less desirable to me as a student than yourself—trained, talented, and quick-witted. You will be a jewel in the crown of the Department's recruitment program."

"Recruitment?"

"Yes, did your brother not tell you? Well, no matter. Soon you will know for yourself. Open to me!"

The command voice was augmented with a lash of agony, which he managed to partially turn aside.

"Well done," said Tarona Rusk mildly, and snapped again— "Open to me!"

The lash this time was a physical stripe across his forearm, slicing fabric and flesh. Blood welled, the pain quite astonishing.

"I am *dramliza*, little Healer. Spare yourself; open the shields."

He threw his whole will into the shields, retreating behind them as much as he was able, even as the lash sliced twice in quick succession, and he heard himself cry out.

Behind the shields, he turned his attention to the links he shared with Priscilla, and with Padi. Tarona Rusk was strong; eventually, she would break his shields, and Padi—

Lute had promised to protect Padi.

If he managed it, Tarona Rusk would not find her through him.

And by all the gods that might exist, she *must not* find Priscilla.

He broke those links—*all* of them, even the strongest and most intimate...especially those. So much damage, so quickly—he was hurting her!

One more set of links to Priscilla. He cut them as quickly as he could; felt a wave of faintness, the searing blare of headache— and shook both away, turning his attention to the web that linked him to Padi.

This would be easier, he told himself. Padi herself had no awareness of the bonds; she would not feel the pain of separation.

He would.

Shan centered himself, feeling his shields shudder under Tarona Rusk's continued attack. Quick, he must be quick. And, gods, he must not falter.

He extended his will toward the web that bound him to Padi—

—Just as they broke from the other side, a surgical slice that severed all at once.

Agony flared—and was gone, flaming out all in an instant.

Shan gathered his wits, and his strength, and turned his attention to the matter at hand.

· · · ✺ · · ·

They'd been right, of course, to strap in, and she should have done the same herself immediately, having issued General Quarters.

Now—

She felt the tension in the bridge, read the distant hum of the crew's concern and fear, watched the screen as she moved quickly to her own chair to belt in. Anger flirted with annoyance in her: there was no need to threaten their child for some local chief's bid for celebrity!

That was a true Seeing, Priscilla knew, feeling power rise in her, feeling Moonhawk watching over her shoulder where no one stood, helping guard the child unformed. She blinked away the sense of Moonhawk, and returned to the streaming *now* of the monitor.

The unpowered swarm of limpets was like snow on the screen, tumbling toward the *Passage* and then jouncing in their movement as the ship's fields took hold, rejecting them, pushing most of them into odd arcs and bouncing some few directly away from the ship.

"Shall I arm weapons?"

Dil Nem's inquiry brought a frisson of power again, and a voice...not quite Shan's, a shadow, fingering a flashing counter, "A blade loose too soon is a mistake with someone's blood on it."

Moonhawk had bowed to that voice in another life. Priscilla nodded at the memory.

"No," she said to Dil Nem. "Do not arm. That's what they want. Track, but do not arm."

Images on screen showed a confusing disarray now, the cutters braking and evading the very mines with which they sought to entangle *Dutiful Passage*.

"Comm," she said, "broadcast these screens live on one channel, and the replay of our contacts on another. Broadbeam it and send direct to the Trade Guild, the Pilots Guild, and to Langlast Port Authority. Add this—"

Priscilla sat straighter, took a deep, calming breath, and pressed the comm button:

"To all pilots, traders, travelers, and citizens of Langlast. This is Priscilla Delacroix y Mendoza Clan Korval, captain of *Dutiful Passage*, out of Surebleak.

"Know that by my command this ship is operating under

high shielding following an unwarranted stealth attempt by forces wearing the livery of Langlast Port Authority to compromise our security and safety by seeding our hull with remote activation bombs. To our knowledge, this attempt has been rebuffed. I post a hazard warning for shipping due to the ordnance now floating in nearspace. I add a caution for any ship piloting to Langlast Port. I post a request for a proper Pilots Guild civilian inquest into the events here.

"We await response from Langlast Port Authority and will continue to broadcast continuous feeds until such time as our security is not at issue.

"Captain out," she said.

"Message out on broadbeam, Captain," Kik said. "Orders?"

"We wait," she answered. "Our response to a hostility is... shield, log, transmit broadbeam. If we have no answer from Langlast Port Authority in thirty minutes, inquire again. If we see increased hostilities, or another flight of bombs, rotate shields."

"Yes, ma'am."

Priscilla released her belt, put her hands on the arms of the command chair—and sat back.

The newly established link with Shan was gone, cut as cleanly as by a crystal blade. She snatched at their other connections, feeling each cut in turn, swiftly, without care for the shock of being separated so quickly. The bridge wavered, edged in black. She closed her eyes, swallowing against nausea, seeing him—a flash, a flare—before he vanished from her awareness.

She widened her senses, and caught his essence on the ether, limned in blood, star-bright courage casting the very smallest shadow of fear.

Danger—he was in *danger*; he needed her...

The ship needed her.

She was the captain, the very captain, seated on the bridge of her ship—her ship, which was under attack. She had folk to care for.

Priscilla breathed in calm, felt it distill into resoluteness. Shan was in danger; she could not reach him; she could not succor him. He, himself, had made certain of that. In fact, his actions recalled her to her duty.

Another deep breath, while she regarded his signature, coalescing now, crimson outlines sharpening.

Shan, she thought, was ready to do battle.

Goddess bless you, my dear, she thought.

And opened her eyes to the bridge.

· · · ✳ · · ·

Padi pulled on sweater and loose pants, braided her damp hair, and wandered out into the common room on bare feet. Father and Mr. Higgs had not returned while she showered, and her glance at the clock this time was more worried than complacent. Perhaps she should call the kitchen, and put dinner back another half-hour.

First, though, she would make a cup of tea. She crossed the room to the hot kettle, touched the button and started its cycle.

While the tea was brewing, she checked her pocket comm for messages—nothing.

Well, she thought, frowning; she might call the desk to find if there were any messages there. Father did sometimes become involved in the trading, but Mr. Higgs would know that she had the ordering of dinner, and would worry if they were overtime.

The kettle beeped, declaring its cycle complete—and the door chime sounded.

Padi nearly dropped the teacup. She recovered herself, however, and set the cup gently on the buffet, before looking at the clock and frowning at the door.

Dinner—it *must* be their dinner—*early* by half an hour, which was quite the opposite of what was needed.

Well, she thought, striding toward the door, they could simply take it back down to the kitchen, and keep it warm, or—

She snatched the door open...

...and stood blinking at the two strange men standing on the threshold. They were Liadens, these strangers, and for one long moment they seemed as taken aback as she.

Padi recovered first; she stepped back, starting to swing the door shut—and the stranger on the left thrust forward, got his shoulder in the door, and pushed it back, hard.

"Come along," he said, making a snatch for her wrist. "Your father sent us to bring you to him."

She eluded his grasp, but her only retreat was into the common room, and they followed her, one swinging wide to her right while the other approached directly.

Father would never send strangers to her, that was her first thought. Her next was that Father had fallen into trouble on the port, despite the very capable presence of Vanner Higgs.

"Come with us," the stranger repeated. "Your father sent us to bring you to him."

"Where is the token?" she demanded. "Father would have given you a token to prove you are friends!"

"Yes, yes. The token. I have it right here."

He reached into the outer pocket of his jacket and pulled out a gun.

Padi didn't think; she reacted, kicking once to send the gun away, spinning to the right to sweep an arm out in a strike that broke the second man's neck, spinning again before he struck the floor, to strike the first man.

She botched the kill, though the blow brought him to his knees. She struck again—a solid kick this time—and he collapsed on the floor beside his comrade.

Padi rushed across the room to close and lock the door. She turned toward the comm—and stopped, every nerve frozen at the sight of a man who—a man who *was not* Father, but who *might have been* Father.

He inclined his head politely from his lean against the buffet, and held up a sinewy brown hand, showing her the worn red game counter Father often toyed with.

"You are formidable," he said, "and I salute you. However, you should know that this pair has another as backup, down in the lobby. If these do not appear soon, with you in hand, the second team will ascend to this floor, after summoning their own backup."

Padi blinked at him. "I will call security to apprehend them."

"Security has been paid off."

"Then I will—" she took a breath, not at all certain what she would do.

"Where is Father?" she asked the man who might have been him.

"Presently very much engaged. He desires to keep you safe, and you may judge his state of mind for yourself, that he sent me to ensure it."

He turned his head slightly, and sighed.

"The backup team approaches. Listen to me, child; there are a number of these persons, and not even you can kill them all. I therefore counsel you to hide yourself, and swiftly."

"There is no place in the suite they won't find me, after they break down the door."

"Nonsense; use your wits! You have power and you have a model. You can hide in this room, and elude them still—but you must be quick!"

The doors moved, as someone tried them, not gently.

Padi gasped, and thought—of her bowl, unbreakable and opaque.

"Excellent!" said the man who was not Father. "Snatch it to and over you!"

She flung out her hands as if she could grasp the thought of her bowl, felt weight inside her head, knelt on the rug right there next to the buffet, and allowed the weight to settle over her.

"Well done," said the man who was not Father. "I can scarcely see you myself."

"What of you?" she asked, then. "They will see you!"

But there was no answer.

A heartbeat later, the door opened with a crash.

CHAPTER THIRTY-THREE

Admiral Bunter

"TOLLY, I AM A PRISONER."

Admiral Bunter sounded downright plaintive, Tolly thought. He was finishing up his last lap on the treadmill. He'd been of a mood to push himself hard, which didn't leave much breath left over for polite conversation. Well, fine. He'd talk to the boy about interrupting somebody while they were exercising in a couple minutes.

"Tolly—"

He held up a hand, which the *Admiral* would know for *wait*—and gathered himself for the final sprint.

Might've been he could've taken the conversation up during cooldown, but the *Admiral* didn't speak, so Tolly finished up in silence, as he preferred, stepped out of the machine, and used his towel to mop up the worst of the sweat.

"I apologize," the *Admiral* said, after Tolly had shaken his hair out of his eyes, and looked up toward the ceiling fixture. "I allowed my emotions to overcome me. I do know better than to interrupt an exercise program."

"I accept your apology," Tolly said, wondering if the *Admiral'd* just made a leap, or if he'd previously interrupted Inki—or, better, Haz—at exercise, and gotten an earful for it.

"Now, you were telling me that you're a prisoner? How's that work? You're a starship. An *independent* starship; you don't even have to clear your route with your crew. Don't like the present route? Change it!" He shook his head. "Don't sound much like being a prisoner, to me."

"I cannot change my route," the *Admiral* said—and, yeah, definitely plaintive, there. "Inkirani Yo has set a core mandate. I *must* deliver you to Nostrilia; I *cannot* change the course; I *cannot* deviate from the course."

"Hmm. I tell you what, I sympathize. I know exactly what that's like—having to do something somebody who isn't you wants done, and not having any say into whether or not that's actually something you'd do, left to your own self."

He paused, and used the towel on the back of his neck.

"I'll allow that to be a prisoner. But, look; it's not for long, is it? You go to Nostrilia, drop me off with the hiring hall manager, and you're done. You can go anywhere, take on crew...or not—"

"I do not know that," the *Admiral* interrupted grimly.

Tolly frowned. "How's that?"

"Inki set one core mandate—to deliver you to the representative of Lyre Institute on Nostrilia. How do I know if she has set another, which will become active when the first mandate retires?"

"It's a puzzle, all right," Tolly said sympathetically. "You know? I'm starting to think that Inki wasn't entirely honest with us."

The *Admiral* said nothing. Tolly dutifully counted out a slow twelve before he walked out of the exercise room, headed for his quarters, and a shower.

"Inki has been dishonest, yes," the *Admiral* said, as Tolly moved down the hall. "But, Tolly, this means that we share a *melant'i!*"

"Does, doesn't it?" he said agreeably, and wrinkled his forehead a little, like he was thinking. "Don't see that it does either of us any good, though."

"What do you mean?"

"Well..." He paused, his hand against the door to his quarters. "Here's me—aboard a ship bound for Nostrilia, and nothing I say or do is gonna change that circumstance. And there's you—likewise bound for Nostrilia, and nothing you can say or do is likely to change that circumstance."

"Yes! Our circumstances are exactly alike!"

"No, now, that's where you're wrong."

Tolly sighed, and hung the towel around his neck before he looked up at the ceiling.

"See, when I get to Nostrilia, I'll be taken off this ship and...
reeducated is what they call it. I've been so much trouble to the
directors, I'm thinking I'll never surface as what I like to think
of as *myself* ever again. Which is to say," he hardened his voice,
"I'll *die*."

He shrugged. "You, on the other hand—you'll be rid of
the mandate that drove you to deliver me to my death. There
might—or there might not—be another mandate lined up to
take the place of the first one. You won't know until it does,
or doesn't, set you in motion. Which is to say—you have hope,
and I've got none."

"I have no hope," the *Admiral* told him. "Inki is not a fool,
and I have learned that AIs—I have learned that *compliant* AIs
are a valuable commodity."

"Well, that's so, but I'm sure you'll figure something out."

Tolly put his hand against the plate and his door slid open.

"We are fellow prisoners!" the *Admiral* said forcefully.

Tolly paused, sighed, and looked up. "Even if I concede the
point, what benefit accrues—to either of us?"

"If we—if we join *melant'is*, and forge a common goal, that
of *not* proceeding to Nostrilia, as Inki has mandated, we may
work together for our mutual benefit."

"I'll even concede that point," Tolly said gently. "How do you
think we're going to get around that mandate? I checked, and
Inki wasn't fool enough to leave me my codes. Or hers, either."

There was an extra-long pause, finally broken by a small
sound, as if *Admiral Bunter* had cleared his throat.

"There is an application which will...generate a key-set."
Pause. "It is not under my control, but it will generate such a
key-set for your use. With those keys, you will...access the core,
remove the mandate and any others Inki may have left, and—and
free us both to our own wills."

"What stops me from doing the same thing Inki prolly did,
once I'm in the core?" Tolly asked interestedly.

"I trust you," *Admiral Bunter* said, sounding as sincere as
Tolly'd ever heard him.

He stood there with the door to his quarters open, and closed
his eyes. On the one hand, he was touched. The boy *had* been
listening...and he'd extrapolated the existence of the key app,
which was no easy thing to do.

On the second hand, and all other things being equal, he'd personally rather survive this episode intact, and at liberty. And once he did what the *Admiral* asked, he'd go from savior-mentor to clear-and-present danger so fast it'd make his head spin.

"I'll tell you what," he said softly. "That's a real interesting proposition you got there, and I'm interested in it."

"You will deactivate the mandate?"

"Don't go generating any keys, yet. *I'm interested* is what I said. But I gotta think, which we both know takes me a deal longer than it does you.

"So...what I'm gonna do is take a shower and have a meal, while I'm thinking this out. After my meal, if that fits with your schedule, we'll talk again."

It was a little cruel, considering the disparity between human hours and AI hours, but he was tired and sweaty, coming on to hungry, and Nostrilia was still days in their future.

Plus which, he *did* have to think—fast and smart as he ever had.

"Thank you for your consideration," *Admiral Bunter* said, so he'd accessed Protocol, good lad that he was. "I will be happy to talk with you after you have refreshed yourself."

"Excellent," Tolly said, letting all the warmth the design had in it infuse his voice. "See you in an hour."

· · · ✳ · · ·

Padi hunched under her bowl, shivering and sick. She remembered the feel of bone snapping beneath her hand, giving before her kick. She had never...her first kills. She *had intended* to kill both men. She had carried forth on her intentions, to success and survival.

And she never wanted to be forced to do so again.

· · · ✳ · · ·

He could find it in him to be angry at Inki, despite his understanding of the conditions she labored under. She could've left the *Admiral* out of the equation—but, well—no. Maybe not.

Tolly sighed and scrubbed his hands over his face as the drying cycle came on. He hoped it hurt her, what she'd done. He thought it *did* hurt her. Inki was a pro. She knew the conditions of the *Admiral*'s birth. His first conscious act had been to kill a ship full of sentient beings. Killing would always be an option for him, so long as he could convince Ethics and Protocol that it'd been done to preserve himself, or in defense of his crew. It was the job of the *Admiral*'s mentors to teach him that there were alternatives, *better* alternatives.

And what does Inki do but set up a situation in which the *Admiral* could claim self-defense in the murder of a mentor.

Damn the woman.

The drier shut off, and he stepped out of the 'fresher, padding the couple of steps into his quarters and picking up the pants he'd left across the bunk.

For himself, personally, it hardly mattered *who* killed him, so long as he didn't come into the care of the school beforehand.

But for the harm done to the *Admiral* . . . yeah, he could be—he *was*—angry.

If Inki—as was probable—had set a mandate for the *Admiral* to return to her, or wait at a certain location . . . She might even *intend* to protect him, but Inki wasn't reliable. She knew that.

He pulled the sweater over his head, sighed, and just stood there in his quarters, arms hanging at his side.

Suddenly, he laughed.

Because, really, there wasn't any choice but the one the *Admiral* offered. He, Tollance Berik-Jones, greatest of the age, or not—*was* a mentor, and he knew what was due to his student, and what was due to the universe, and to biologic life.

He also knew, right down in the deep core of him, just exactly what a person was capable of doing, when they wanted their freedom above everything else.

· · · ❋ · · ·

"Stop!" Shan said sharply. His arm—he dared not look at his arm; instead he enclosed the pain and sealed it away.

"Open to me," Tarona Rusk sounded calm and, faintly, disappointed. "It does not have to be a rape, little Healer. Only surrender."

"I cannot surrender," he told her, projecting honesty as strongly as he dared. "I am of Korval; try to force me and you create resistance in equal measure to your demands. If you wish an examination, I suggest that we must find another way."

She considered him with a sapient eye.

"You are now willing to become my student?"

"I am willing to allow you to examine me and the resources available to me," he said, keeping his voice smooth with an effort. Gods, what damage had she done him? The pain was already seeping through his seals, like blood through paper.

He dared a glance downward, and grit his teeth. Those... would scar. All he had to do was live long enough.

"It is a poor teacher who does not also learn from her students," Tarona Rusk commented. "How would you have us proceed to a solution that profits us both?"

"I suggest that we comport ourselves as Healers," he said. "I will extend to you one single line, as you will extend one single line to me. We will allow the lines to meet, and to commingle."

"Thus, a fraction of your energy becomes part of me, while a small fraction of my energies become part of you." She smiled suddenly, wide and delighted. "In fact, we would learn to trust each other!"

"Exactly," he said. "Once trust is established, and we know each other a little better, an examination—even an intervention— may go forth."

"I commend you. This is a valuable suggestion. For you know that I would have you trust me, above all things."

He bowed his head slightly, and let her read meekness in him, and a certain well-hid awe of herself.

"We shall make this attempt!" she announced. "I extend the grace of goodwill to my newest student!"

He saw it, with Inner Eyes, a cobalt thread, chaste and demure. Gently, he extended his own thread, also demure, and perhaps a little inclined to waver. The energies met and mingled; he tasted steel and vinegar, shivered with her need to hold and possess. He heard her sigh as his thread reached her senses, tempting her with compliance, and a sweet desire to obey.

She was quick. Very nearly, she was *too* quick. She jerked on her extended thread, but they were enwrapt now—and *he* had no wish to disengage.

"Treachery!" she snapped. The lash came, striking his cheek this time, even as he thrust his will down the fragile linkage, past their joining point and into the sere and tangled pattern of Tarona Rusk.

Brittle threads scratched and burned him. He ignored them, stretching his will wide, wide—wider than ever he had attempted, until at last he enclosed the whole sticky mass.

Whereupon he snatched all of it—all of *them*—into Healspace.

. . . ※ . . .

"The security guard is with the yos'Galan." The language was Liaden, the mode between comrades, perfectly audible to Padi's ears, as she crouched beneath her bowl.

"And yet," said a second voice, "we have two dead, efficiently so, and a suite that is empty of else."

They had searched the suite; she had heard that, too. It was... rather inefficient, having to depend only on her ears; she would have liked to *see* this new pair of enemies, so that she might have identified them to Port Security. In fact, it came to her that, the bowl being her construction, she might modify it thus.

Then it came to her that the bowl was not... precisely... her construction. It had felt to her as if she had reached out and snatched the very bowl from the table beside her bunk, her thought someway stretching it until it was large enough to cover her—or perhaps she had shrunk, somehow, in order to fit beneath.

In any case, she told herself, you don't know enough. Best to stay hidden until they give up and go.

However, they seemed in no hurry to go. She heard them moving about again, soft *floofs* that may have been cushions landing on the carpet after having been thrown from chairs, and if they thought she might be hiding behind the chair cushions, then they must be as stupid as the Department of the Interior.

"The halfling has abilities," the first voice said. "It is the reason we are sent to find her; not merely because she is the yos'Galan's heir and may be used to control him."

Padi drew a careful breath.

"We, however, do not have abilities," the second voice pointed out. "How if the heir has already flown out the window?"

"Flying is not so usual a thing, and the heir is young, after all. Perhaps we might think of a more common subterfuge, such as any halfling might employ. Hiding, for an instance."

These people did not sound *at all* stupid, Padi thought, wrapping her arms around her knees. More the pity.

"Let us quarter the room," the first voice said, "and see what we may find. The *dramliza* will not be pleased, if we do not bring the heir—or her body. You recall what she did to el'Fasyk."

"You make an eloquent point. Let us, as you say, quarter the room."

CHAPTER THIRTY-FOUR

· ·

Healspace

THE FOGS OF HEALSPACE BOILED AROUND THEM, TASTING OF molasses and rust. Shan grabbed handfuls of the stuff, shaping them into a thick circle: Tarona Rusk on the inside, himself on the outside.

He saw a flicker of flame and steel—the tip of the lash, so he thought. He saw the fog receive it and encompass it. The flame snuffed out.

"You cannot keep me here," Tarona Rusk said, and now he could taste her anger.

"I cannot keep you here *long*," he admitted, letting her feel the weight of the truth he told her. "But I believe I may keep you here *long enough*."

She eyed him from inside the circle.

"Long enough for what, I wonder? The death of your body tied to the showroom chair?"

That was a problem, Shan admitted to himself. If the other members of her team arrived while they were thus engaged, they might well solve the problem of himself in their preferred manner.

Well.

He had told her true, after all: he could *not* hold her long. Speed had been at the heart of this plan since its formulation.

"I only need hold you long enough to Heal you," he said, for a Healer was bound in honor to explain his intention to a client.

"I am not in need of Healing," she said. He tasted her amusement—and the sudden, acrid bite of fear.

"Sadly, you are in error," he answered, and brought his entire attention to the knot that enclosed her pattern.

· · · ✴ · · ·

The steps were measured, and careful. Padi's palms were sweating, and the air was getting somewhat rank inside her bowl. Perhaps she should have made windows, after all, or thought to install a fan.

Moving as silently as she could, she got her feet properly in place, so that she was centered. She must assume that they would discover her with this patient method.

She knew too little about her hiding place, she thought, too late. It must, after all, have substance, even if it were invisible to the eye, as the man who had held Father's gaming token had intimated. Father, after all, had not given up his substance, when he had become invisible on Andireeport. She wasn't entirely sure if it was possible—or advisable—to become insubstantial.

The footsteps were moving closer to her position near the buffet. One more pass, she thought. No more than two...

And suddenly, the world rang around her.

· · · ✴ · · ·

The blackened threads tangled around her core were...links. Two dozen links—more—crushed together until they were all but indistinguishable from each other.

That was bad, but there was worse.

The links were live; input links, as a Healer might establish with a client who was very ill, or in crisis. The links would feed energy, calm, forgetfulness—whatever might be needed—to the client until a fuller intervention could be done.

Wrapped as they were around Tarona Rusk's core, they at once protected her, and...sustained her. She might be a powerful *dramliza*, but no small part of her power was stolen from others.

"Many hands make the work light, Healer," Tarona Rusk mocked him. The fog circle was thinning, he saw; he thickened it with a thought.

All those links...Shan considered them closely. Input links. He might break them, with...little danger. He thought.

If he would Heal Tarona Rusk, he needed to reach her core. And he had... very little time.

· · · ✳ · · ·

"Captain Mendoza, this is Langlast Portmaster Joniton Elz. Also on comm is Captain Tario Soop, customs boats commander-in-chief."

"Portmaster," Priscilla said calmly... calmly, as if the glow of Shan's essence against the universe wasn't fading away into nothing. "Captain. Why has the *Dutiful Passage* been targeted in this manner? If we have unwittingly broken law or custom, we will make amends. Bombs are really... quite unnecessary."

"Yes, ma'am," said the voice she assumed must belong to Captain Soop. "Bombs are usually unnecessary in my experience, and may I say, ma'am, that my office, and the Port of Langlast, appreciates your very great restraint in dealing with them. I've reviewed the logs of our previous inspections and I assure you, ma'am, we have found nothing—repeat: *nothing at all*—to warrant such an attack as has been made against your vessel. I offer you my personal apologies, ma'am, in addition to the apology of my office. This episode should never have happened."

"And yet," Priscilla said, "it did happen. I wonder why. And I also wonder if it will happen again."

"Again?" Captain Soop's horror was plain. "Captain Mendoza, it should have never happened once! To suppose that it could happen again—well, there, you have your ship to care for... I'll tell you, ma'am, it was politics. Politics in my own office, and it has been dealt with, ma'am. My second came to be of the opinion that *Dutiful Passage* was liable to become aggressive, and he acted—on his own recognizance—to ensure the safety of the port. As he saw it, ma'am."

"I will add, Captain Mendoza," Portmaster Elz broke in, "that this is *not* an official Langlastport position; the officer in question was acting quite on his own, without having spoken of his concerns, or cleared his operation, with either his own commander, or with my office. As Captain Soop has said, this episode should never have happened. As portmaster, I assure you, it will not happen again. The port stands ready to make reparations, should your ship have taken any damage from this unauthorized action on the part of one of our agents."

"Thank you," Priscilla said. "I am very pleased to hear that steps have been taken to ensure that this sort of thing does not happen again, either to the *Passage* or to another innocent ship. In the meantime, sirs, there is the matter of the mines rejected by our shields, which are now loose, and seeking hulls to which they may attach."

"Yes, ma'am. We've got work-boats rising, and we've diverted those customs boats already in orbit to the task of picking those little devils up," Captain Soop assured her.

"Portmaster's office will be issuing a general alert regarding the bombs, and our response plan," Portmaster Elz added. "Captain Soop and I wanted to speak with you and assure you of your safety and your continued welcome at Langlast. If you have any other concerns, please don't hesitate to call this office."

"Thank you," Priscilla said, watching Shan's pattern flicker and fade. "In fact, there is something else..."

· · · ❊ · · ·

"Well, now, what have we here?" the first voice said, very close at hand.

Footsteps approached.

"I see nothing," the second voice said.

"Nor do I, but observe."

The bowl rang again, and Padi's head with it.

She drew a deep breath, and waited. She had decided that waiting was the best thing she could do. Let them make the first move. She would be centered and ready for it. And if she had to kill them...

She pushed the thought, and the feeling of queasiness, away from her, and concentrated on *now*. She was a pilot of Korval. She would do whatever was necessary to survive.

· · · ❊ · · ·

There was no time for finesse, and if Healer heads rang with their unexpected and hasty liberation, it was not, Shan suspected, the worst that had come to them in the service of Tarona Rusk.

Now, however, came the challenge, for her pattern was an abused and misshapen thing, showing the marks of fire and such ruthless hacking as he had seen before, in his brother Val Con's pattern. He had the assistance of a Clutch Turtle, when he had undertaken to Heal Val Con. And even then, flinging his whole heart and all his skill into the task, he had not...returned Val Con to himself. He had repaired; he had patched; he had given surcease, restored balance, and strengthened the capacity for joy.

What he had not been able to do, was to restore his brother to the state he had occupied before he had been tortured, and broken. The memory of those things could not be eradicated— *ought not be* eradicated, for knowing that there was such evil afoot helped keep him vigilant, for himself, and for Korval. The weight of those memories meant that, though his brother assuredly was *a* Val Con yos'Phelium, he was not *the* Val Con yos'Phelium who would have been, had there been no such memories upon him.

He had not known Tarona Rusk before the tragedy of her training had come to her, but his inner eyes traced the familiar path of destruction. For Val Con, coming to the work fresh and unwounded, he had managed a nearly complete Healing.

To this Healing, he came diminished: the *dramliz*-killer's kiss had drained a portion of his energy; the wounds to his body weakened his will.

Yet, this woman needed him, no less than Val Con had needed him.

For this woman, for this Healing, he would do all—he would do everything—that he could.

· · · ✳ · · ·

They were very clever. They slipped the blades of their knives between the rim of the bowl and the floor, and levered it until they had gained enough space for one to grip what he could not see. Padi heard the other drop back, and had no doubt what she would find when the bowl was flipped over and she became visible: one man, spinning out of striking distance even as she came to her feet; the other well back, with gun aimed.

They might, Padi thought, watching the intruding fingers work under the bowl, be willing to wound her, though she thought they would not wish to anger the person who had punished el'Fasyk so memorably by disobeying orders, and by killing her. Certainly, if they wished to use her as a stick to beat Father with, they would need her to be alive.

The fingers gripped the edge of the bowl. She tensed, heard

a hard intake of breath, saw boots in the gap between the rim and the floor, then knees, belt, jacket—

She snapped to her feet as the bowl hit the floor behind her, ringing. The man who had thrown it was spinning away, the man holding the gun on her was shouting, "Stand and raise your hands!"

And two more people came running through the broken door.

The man who had thrown the bowl shouted at the newcomers to hold; the other man's gun wavered, and Padi dove, down and forward, meaning to bring the gunman down, and take his weapon for her own.

She surprised him, and he was off-balance due to the arrival of his comrades, so he did fall—but only to his knees, her arm trapped beneath him, and his gun still in hand. He swung it downward; and pinned, she rolled desperately, and the blow landed on her shoulder instead of her head.

Pain exploded; the gun was rising again. Fear, fear rushed upon her with its wings of glass, and she *pushed* with every ounce of will she possessed.

Something shattered loudly; someone screamed, and the weight was gone from her arm. She *pushed* again, following the thrumming of fear; seeing stone before her, and welcome darkness beyond an open door.

· · · ✳ · · ·

Tarona Rusk was no willing client; she fought him, and even though Healspace gave him advantage, she hurt him.

Worse, she *delayed* him, and time was the coin he could least afford to spend.

Finally, knowing that he could not spend the energy, he snatched her close and held her quiescent within his will, and made those repairs and adjustments that he could, feeling his focus soften, and the connection to his bleeding, battered body grow dangerously thin.

She whimpered in his grasp; he had hurt her, and that was his shame, but... necessity. He was very near his goal now, and the most important part of this Healing. Staggering and unfit, he pressed on, drawing upon the virtue of Healspace to focus his wavering attention on a small, glowing pearl nestled in an area of densest scarring.

He slashed at the old wounds, no gentler than her previous tormentors, giving the pearl room to expand, to warm, to—at last!—take fire, cauterizing the new wounds he had inflicted, turning the old wounds to ash.

She screamed, then; joined as they were, he felt all of her anguish . . .

. . . and, an instant later, all of her joy.

. . . ❊ . . .

"Captain," Dil Nem murmured.

Priscilla looked to him.

"Third Mate?"

"Report from Maintenance, Captain. Automatics in Trader yos'Galan's cabin reported an unusual amount of dust. Maintenance sent someone. There was a pile of glass dust on the table next to the bunk. No idea how it got there. The worker swept it, and changed the filters."

Glass dust? On the table next to—the bowl. Priscilla remembered it: a fragile-looking thing with a design that evoked wind and water. It was supposed to have been unbreakable, that bowl.

Yet, sometimes, when a *dramliza* first felt the fullness of her power. Sometimes . . . things broke.

Priscilla took a careful breath, and reached out into the ether.

. . . ❊ . . .

Healspace burned away around them. He opened his eyes to the reality of the chair, and his injuries, and Vanner lying dead on the floor. A cool hand pressed lightly over the dreadful wounds on his arm, leaching some of the fire.

"You are a fool, little Healer," said Tarona Rusk.

He managed to raise his head, and meet her eyes. They were blue. That was strange; he had thought them black.

"Yes," he answered her. "Very much so."

She smiled, a twisted thing, half sweet and half savage.

"I believe you have accomplished what you set yourself to do. My question would be—why?"

"I am a Healer," he whispered, and closed his eyes, the weight of the light being too much, now, to bear.

"No, what is this? You force me to bear the burden of life, while you stealthily steal away? That will not do; I do not allow it."

Energy flowed into him, sparkling dark, and glittering light; he opened his eyes, and lifted his head.

"Do not drain yourself," he warned her. "You have nothing but your own resources to draw upon now."

"For which I thank you, a thousand times. But, no—I will husband myself, never fear it. I have too much to do to spend unwisely."

The flow of energy slowed to a trickle; he felt his bonds loosen and drop away.

He glanced down at his arm, saw the wounds had closed and the bleeding had stopped. A Healing for a Healing. Balance.

"Now," she said briskly, "you must see to your daughter. You have left her too long alone."

"My daughter is being...cared for...by...a friend."

"Is it so? Perhaps this explains why my colleagues have not yet returned. On your feet, little Healer. I will support you so far as the hotel."

· · · ※ · · ·

Shan's essence had faded to a shadow, and Priscilla despaired. She had tried to reach him, and found blocks and warn-aways. He did not want her in this, whatever it was; she could only sit, and watch, and grieve.

Just when it seemed that he could not sustain himself—he began to grow firmer. Priscilla caught her breath, seeing the glitter of another's power, feeding him, supporting him—and finally withdrawing.

She let go the breath she had been holding. He was much improved, though by no means entirely well. Certainly, he was well enough to be taken up by the security team she had asked the portmaster to send to him. The shuttle, with Lina aboard, was already on its way down to the planet's surface. Lina would set matters right, and hold him, when he found that his daughter was gone, leaving not so much as a scratch upon the ether to mark her passing.

CHAPTER THIRTY-FIVE

· ·

Admiral Bunter

TOLLY SAT DOWN IN HIS OWN CHAIR, AND KEYED INTO THE console. Keycodes gleamed on his screen, but he didn't access them. Rather, he checked the interface, looking for traps or falls. Then, he scanned the logs, including ongoing system stats, changes, and updates. He didn't find anything curious—or even interesting. Which didn't surprise him, exactly. Inki could wipe a log with the best of them, not to mention that she knew when—and how—to turn logging off.

He half-thought that she might have left a message for him, or some kind of clue in logging. Given the number of times in this operation that she'd dutifully fulfilled the Institute's mandates while also creating conditions that would...somewhat mitigate the effect of dutiful obedience, it wasn't completely out of the question. And, truth said, that was an intriguing ability, and he almost hoped he caught up with her again, so he could ask her how she managed it.

This time, though, he was disappointed; Inki had left no log records, nor a personal note for him, detailing the locations of the traps and the kills.

Fair enough, he thought, leaning back in his chair and smiling slightly; he'd just have to find them on his own.

"Tolly?" *Admiral Bunter* spoke from behind and above him. "Is there something wrong?"

"No more than there was five minutes ago," he said. "Just savoring the moment, is all."

He looked over his shoulder and upward.

"You sure you want to go through with this?" he asked.

"We discussed the pros and cons," the *Admiral* said. "I understand that it is possible that this action will cause me to cease to exist. I accept this. I would rather cease to exist, than live in a state of uncertainty and enslavement."

"Just making sure."

He looked back to the screen, closed his eyes and focused himself with a quick mental exercise, opened his eyes, and tapped up the main screen.

The keys glowed there, tempting and powerful. *The keys to heaven* one of his teachers used to call them.

"All right, then," he murmured to himself, rather than to the *Admiral*. "Let's see what grand adventure lies before us."

He extended his hand to the screen, and accepted the keys.

· · · ✳ · · ·

He was blind.

No, Shan corrected himself, around the taste of loss, of course he was not blind. Could he not perfectly well see the street, glossy with recent rain? Or that group of people, just there, chatting among themselves? And did he not note the woman who went hurrying past them, all but running on the rain-slick street?

Of course he wasn't blind. His eyes were doing precisely what they ought.

However, there was a strange flatness to the group of friends, the hurrying woman, his escort with her arm through his, and bearing more of his weight than he wished to acknowledge.

"You used too much of yourself, and your talent has gone dry," Tarona Rusk said. "Never fear; it will return, in time."

"How much time?"

"You have a gift for questions, little Healer."

"Have you a gift for answers?"

"I am no match for you." She sighed. "Soon or late, dependent upon such things as may be measured, but which are not precise. I will tell you—the machine's kiss is dire. It alone would have left you diminished for . . . some while. The kiss and such reckless spending as you have done..." He felt her shrug. "Consult a Healer, is my advice."

"Thank you. Perhaps I shall."

She laughed softly.

"Do not blame me; I had backed a different outcome."

"So you had."

They crossed under the hotel's portico, walking slowly, to spare his strength. She slowed suddenly, her grip on his arm tightening.

"Hold," she murmured in his ear. "I know these."

Shan straightened, and heard her chuckle.

"No, do not gird yourself for war. It would appear that a pair of my colleagues have come under the attention of Port Security. We will pass them by, and I will see you into the hotel, as I promised, before we part."

"Stay," he said to her. "Korval will protect you."

"Ah, now there's an honorable offer, but one I must refuse. I have no need of, nor use for Korval's protections. I have keys and codes, and knowledge, and I mean to use them well. We will walk on—no one will mind us—and when we achieve the lobby, you will call upon the desk to assist you, and I will go my way."

They walked, as she said, and no one stopped them, or even seemed very much interested in them, past the two men speaking earnestly with the security team; and the guard upon the door, until they entered the lobby, and Tarona Rusk let him go.

"Farewell, Shan yos'Galan," she said, and bowed as one acknowledging a debt which can never be repaid. "I thank you, for the gift of my life, and the opportunity to achieve Balance within it."

It was on the tip of his tongue, to urge her again to shelter under the Dragon's wing, but a hand fell on his shoulder, and he unsteadily turned to face a long-jawed man in an orange security vest.

"Master Trader yos'Galan?"

"Yes."

"Come with me, please, sir. I'm afraid there's been some unpleasantness."

Unpleasantness.

Fear stabbed him. Had Lute kept his word?

"My daughter—" he said.

"Just this way," the guard said soothingly, moving his hand toward the bank of elevators.

Shan took a step and stopped, looking over his shoulder to say a proper farewell to Tarona Rusk.

But she was gone.

Four men dead, they said, and extensive damage to the property. Glass dust glittered on every surface, on every body.

Padi shone like an ice maiden, her eyes closed, her face expressionless, her breathing as slow as if she were in trance.

He touched her hair; he called her name, softly.

There was no response.

"The doctor says shock," said the head of the investigation crew—Kayorli Brice was her name, Shan recalled. "She's the only survivor. Bruising on her shoulder consistent with being struck with a heavy object, no other trauma. The others..." She sighed.

"Two dead by hand—broken necks. The other two—speared back to front with glass shards as wide as your hand. I'll tell you what, Master Trader yos'Galan—I'd give a lot to find where all this *glass* came from."

Shan shook his head, wearily. He had answered questions; he had directed Port Security to the Garden of Gems, and to poor Vanner's body. He had told them everything that had happened—to the limit that they would understand—which gave them an ambitious criminal who sought to hold a master trader for ransom from his ship.

He had no names for the other dead. Padi's dead, as he thought of them.

Eventually, the team leader went away, and shortly after, a medic lifted Padi onto a stretcher, while others readied the dead for transport.

"You're her parent?" the medic asked him.

"I am, yes."

"The doctor gave her a field exam, said she's in no danger. There's an ambulance on the way, to take her to the hospital, so she can be checked out thorough. That's the best course, sir; but as her parent, you need to agree."

"I agree," he said, and the medic nodded.

"We'll just take her down now to the holding room off the lobby," he said. "Whisk her right out when the car pulls in." He looked down at Shan's mangled and bloody sleeve, and looked up again. "You're all right yourself, sir?"

"I'm tired," he said truthfully, "and worried about my daughter."

"Sure you are. You come on along with us, now. You can rest a bit in the holding room."

· · · ❁ · · ·

The raptor kept a close guard on the stone tower. Twice, Padi had put her head out the door, and twice, it dove for her, screaming.

She ducked back, gasping, and it went away again, to perch in the tree opposite, glass pinions gleaming.

Frowning, she considered it, recognizing it for her fears, which she had rejected and shoved away for so long that they had joined forces and taken on a life of their own. Far from remaining in the closet she had made for it, now it was loose in the world, and she was held prisoner in her own prison.

She remembered following those glass wings to this place, away from the carnage in the hotel. Safe, she had wanted to be safe!

And so she was safe, with a dragon guarding her door.

Padi stirred, and lifted her head to stare out at the dragon on its branch. Her nature, that she had rejected.

She took a deep breath, tasting lavender. Homesickness stabbed her, and she remembered Aunt Anthora sitting on the back patio at Trealla Fantrol, lavender heaped around her. She gathered the long stems tight, bent them over the flowers to make a basket, and wove them together with a ribbon. She handed one to Padi with a smile.

"Hang it in your closet, to make everything smell sweet."

The memory was very strong; the scent of lavender filled her head. Looking out the door, she could see lavender blooming along the path—and blinked. There had been no path; there had been no flowers, only the stone and the closet and her fear.

She got to her feet, her eyes on the lavender, and stepped out onto the path, hearing gravel crunch under her feet. Bending, she broke one stem—and jerked upright as a chill shadow passed over her.

She turned, but it was too far to the door; she looked up, into the descending wings, and thrust the lavender up into its face.

The dragon screamed, and swept by, turning on the tip of one wing and landing again, with an offended shake of its wings, on the highest branch of the tree.

Padi—stared.

Her nature, she thought. Father had told her that she must accept her nature, but had he never told her what her nature *was*?

She was of Korval—a Dragon born.

That was her nature.

"Dragon!" she called, and opened her arms, centered and calm on the clean gravel path. "Come here."

The long head swiveled, the wings flexed. It was airborne that quickly, and Padi waited, watching the bright wings climb. Her breath came quick, and her stomach was tight, but that was all right, she told herself. Fear was the shadow cast by courage.

Above her, the dragon circled once, folded its wings and plummeted toward her.

· · · ❊ · · ·

The holding room was dim, and rather chilly. He pulled the blanket up under Padi's chin, and tried to extend a thread—to touch her, to read her.

There was nothing but emptiness where there had used to be colors, and patterns, and the vivid play of emotion.

Shan closed his eyes, and leaned forward in the chair so that he could lay his head down on the pillow next to hers.

Perhaps he dozed, or perhaps he waked. No matter—not really.

"That Witch will take a hundred lives," Lute commented, "and confound your enemies, also."

Shan sighed. "Which Witch?"

"Have you forgotten her already? Tarona Rusk." There was a pause, and a sharp sigh. "Child, what have you done to yourself?"

"I healed Tarona Rusk." Shan made a conscious effort to gather his strength, and lifted his head to glare at the man sitting on the other side of Padi's stretcher.

Lute gave him a straight look. "And taken several injuries along the path."

"I'll mend," Shan said, and ignored his other self's smile. "Padi, however—"

"The Maiden will be well," Lute interrupted, with a glance at her still and glittering face.

"Says the man who left her alone, when he promised to keep her safe."

"I did what was in my power," Lute said. "I could encourage

her, push her, and suggest, but *I* cannot *act* here, child, unless you would see the back of the universe broken."

Shan frowned.

"That sounds rather . . . potent for a hedge magician."

Lute smiled. "I was close enough to a god, once. They make sure to bind us close."

"They?"

But Lute only smiled and glanced down again at Padi's face. "Here she comes home to us," he murmured.

Padi opened her eyes.

· · · ❄ · · ·

She was lying in her bunk, and Father sitting beside, leaning forward, with tears in his eyes. He was tired, she saw, very tired, and his pattern was very thin.

"You should have told me," she said, "that it was the Dragon I must accept."

"Should I have? How stupid of me. Padi—"

He extended a hand, and she caught it between both of hers.

"Here," she murmured, "let me help."

· · · ❄ · · ·

The shuttle had reached Langlastport. Priscilla received the report with a nod, and a murmured, "Thank you," most of her attention on Shan's essence. Though he had improved, he was by no means strong, and she worried about the extent of his injuries.

She had tried, once his pattern had stabilized, to reestablish their link, but it had been like trying to link to a cloud. Finally, fearing that she was doing him further harm, she had withdrawn to watch, and worry, and occasionally search for Padi, whose pattern remained missing entirely from the ether.

At the moment, Shan's pattern was quiet; perhaps he was sleeping. Perhaps, Priscilla thought wryly, she ought to do the same.

In fact, she thought, she *should* rest. Shan would need her when he came aboard, and it would be best if she were at full energy.

She rose from her chair—and abruptly sat down again as a bell pealed inside her head: the linkages—all the linkages—with Shan bloomed, brightly silver.

She opened her Inner Eyes and found him immediately,

glowing...not quite as brightly as he had, but bright, and strong and firm.

And near him—indeed, all but eclipsing him, was a brave new star in the firmament, displaying a pattern Priscilla had never thought to see again.

Padi yos'Galan had accepted her nature.

And the universe had acquired a Dragon.

CAST OF CHARACTERS & GLOSSARY

. . . .

Humans & Intelligences

ORBIT 1: DUTIFUL PASSAGE AND TRADE RELATED

James Abrofinda—a longtime Korval contractor.

Janifer Carresens-Denobli, Trader-at-Large—also Trade Commissioner.

Faw Chen—one of the 'ponics techs, female.

Lonan Davis, Second Mate—a cousin of Shan's on his mother's side; in fact, his Uncle **Richard Davis's** eldest child.

Priscilla Delacroix y Mendoza—captain of *Dutiful Passage*, lifemate to Shan yos'Galan; together they are **Thodelm yos'Galan**. Priscilla is also the current reincarnation of Moonhawk, an old soul.

Kris Embrathiri—shuttle pilot attached to the *Passage*, a good friend of Vanner Higgs.

Lina Faaldom—*Passage* Master Healer, Librarian, Cultural Officer, *daibri'at* instructor. Short, even for a Liaden, very slight, honey-colored eyes.

Unet Hartensis—one of the owners of Hartensis Catering and Receptions, and Padi's contact within the firm.

Vanner Higgs—Tech First Class, and security on the *Passage*; former merc tech sergeant.

Inleen—Padi's opposite number; a 'prentice; not known for his punctuality.

ira'Barti, Cargo Master—cargo master on the *Passage*.

Roner Jerethine—Comm Tech on *Passage*.

Jeri—another of the 'ponics techs, male.

Lute—Moonhawk's "submissive" in the old universe; part of that group of *dramliz*.

Moonhawk—a leader of a group of *dramliz* that stood against the Enemy in the old universe.

Gustav rel'Ana—proprietor of the Laster Garden on Andireeport.

Tarona Rusk—proprietor of the Garden of Gems of Langlastport, former 'prentice to Master Jeweler Moonel, of Solcintra, Liad.

Jon Schneider, Arms Master—defense instructor and security person.

Kik Strehlir—another of the *Passage*'s pilots.

Danae Tiazan, First Mate—a Korval cousin, new to the ship, middle-aged.

Dil Nem Tiazan, Third Mate—another Korval cousin, new to the ship, late middle years, taciturn, tough, and "a bit stiff in the honor."

Sally Triloff—Comm Tech on *Passage*.

Varoth, Head Tech—in charge of Hydroponics; a woman in a perpetually bad mood.

Ambassador Valeking of Granda—doesn't like Shan, but re-signed the twelve-year contract with Korval anyway.

Padi yos'Galan—heir and apprentice to Shan yos'Galan, approximately sixteen Standard years.

Shan yos'Galan—master trader on *Dutiful Passage*. Shan is the current reincarnation of Lute, the life-companion (over several lifetimes) of Moonhawk. He has...mixed feelings...about this.

Daibri'at students:

Brisalia—a female who works in maintenance.

Caz Tar—a male about Quin's age.

Jon—see **Jon Schneider** (above).

Keslis—an older female.

Lina Faaldom—a female Librarian and Healer; long-time friend to Shan and Priscilla.

Riean—a male cafeteria worker.

Chesselport:

Magistrate Tinerest—one of seven Chesselport magistrates.

Security—**Bruller**, **Cap** and **Riley**.

Guests at the reception on Langlastport:

Irfenda Dorst—head buyer for Gerome Mercantile, bright green shirt.

Malekai Gerome—senior sales associate at Gerome Mercantile, pale orange shirt.

Herst Plishet—Textile Broker.

Marthimyr Seirt—Master of the Langlast Technology Exchange.

ORBIT 2—SUREBLEAK—CLAN, KIN, RESIDENTS

Luken bel'Tarda, aka **Grandfather Luken**—head of Clan Korval's small third Line.

Mr. Brunner, aka **Ichliad Brunner**—the weatherman on Surebleak, entrusted with getting the weather satellites in orbit and calibrated so the place will (eventually) warm up.

the Elder—the ranking Explorer in Hazenthull's partnership. Deceased.

A Tiazan of Erob, aka **Miri Robertson Tiazan**—Val Con's lifemate, Delmae Korval, the Captain.

Jeeves—Tocohl's "father," a sentient AI; Korval's House Security.

Jelaza Kazone—Korval's Tree, aka Korval's damned, interfering Tree.

Liz Lizardi—Chief of Surebleak Port Security; Haz and Tolly's former boss.

Nelirikk nor'Phelium—another former Yxtrang Explorer, member of Korval House guard, Hazenthull's superior.

Diglon Rifle—a lower-ranking Yxtrang attached to Korval House guard.

Architect vin'Zeller—is to be building the yos'Galan house on Surebleak.

Syl Vor yos'Galan—Padi's cousin, Shan's nephew; Nova yos'Galan's heir.

Kareen yos'Phelium, aka **Cousin Kareen**—Val Con's father's sister; Pat Rin's mother.

Pat Rin yos'Phelium, aka **Boss Conrad**, aka **Cousin Pat Rin**—as above, also the Boss of the Bosses of Surebleak.

Quin yos'Phelium—Padi's cousin and her pilot, in the order kept at Runig's Rock.

Val Con yos'Phelium and **Miri Robertson**—the delm of Korval, aka Korval Themselves. Val Con is also the Scout, and Miri the Captain.

ORBIT 3—TOCOHL'S MISSION—INVOLVED PLAYERS

Tolly, aka **Tollance Berik-Jones** (aka **1362**)—a mentor, who ensures that AIs are brought into awareness well socialized. Attached to Tocohl's mission.

Tocohl Lorlin—Jeeves's daughter, an AI.

Hazenthull nor'Phelium, aka **Haz**, aka **Hazenthull Explorer**—a former Yxtrang Explorer, now a member of the Korval House guard, accidentally attached to Tolly and Tocohl's mission.

Glinz Pirl-Dorn—one of the directors of the Lyre Institute. Deceased.

tel'Vaster— another Lyre director, also deceased.

Stew, aka **Master Mechanic Steward Vannigof**—Up-Shift Boss, Senior Repair Tech, Jemiatha's Jumble Stop.

Vez—Down-Shift Boss, Jemiatha's Jumble Stop. Stew's junior by ten hours.

the Tinker—a down-on-her-luck repair person, deceased.

Inkirani Yo—pilot first class, and mentor, aboard *Ahab-Esais*, female.

ORBIT 4—OTHER DUTIES AS ASSIGNED—
CHARACTERS VARIOUSLY IN SPACE OR PLANETS ELSEWHERE, BUT NOT NECESSARILY TOGETHER

Aelliana Caylon—Val Con's mother, lifemate to Daav yos'Phelium.

Dulsey—Uncle's long-time companion and assistant.

Jen Sar Kiladi—Daav's alter ego, a professor of Cultural Genetics at Delgado University. Jen Sar was the *onagrata* of **Kamele Waitley** and is Theo Waitley's genetic father.

Vestin yos'Thomaz Clan Ebrim—Padi's birth mother.

(The) Uncle (aka **Yuri**)—a serially reborn meddler with a finger in everybody's pies, while at any one time tending a half-dozen certain-to-be-unsettling projects of his own. Uncle *remembers* the old universe.

Seignur Veeoni—one of Uncle's clones; she's working on making modern-day fractins at an undisclosed location.

Theo Waitley—Jen Sar Kiladi's daughter, Val Con's sister, Shan's cousin, captain of *Bechimo*.

Daav yos'Phelium—Val Con's father, lifemate to Aelliana Caylon. Also see **Jen Sar Kiladi** (above).

. . . .

Places

Andireeport in the Kinsa Sector—the *Passage* is going there to trade.

Andireeport Fruit and Flower Market—a trade zone on Andiree planet.

Ashlan—anchor port for three Carresens long-loopers and a number of short-loopers.

Berth 12—where *Tarigan* is berthed on Jemiatha's.

Bestwell-Kessel-La'Quontis Route—the last trade route Shan built himself.

Bieradine—the planet to which *Tarigan* is Jumping.

Billingston—the planet where Faw Chen came aboard.

Brieta—Langlast's nearest neighbor.

Chessel's World—a world sorely in need of *milaster*, next in the route after Andiree.

Chesselport Grand Auction Hall—where the trading action is on Chessel's World.

Galaxy Nowhere—the place where dead pilots go—and sometimes come back from.

Garden of Gems—on Langlastport.

Gilady Station—where Uncle and Dulsey stopped to take on supplies and catch up the news.

Happy Occasion—one of the reception rooms for hire on Langlastport.

Jelaza Kazone—Korval's clanhouse. "Jela's Fulfillment." Also the name of the Tree that grows in the center of the garden it encloses.

Jemiatha's Jumble Stop—a repair station with a specialty in . . . odd tech. Has an extensive junkyard of old ships.

Langlast—next stop after Chessel's World.

the Laster Garden—in the Fruit and Flower Market, Gustav rel'Ana, proprietor. Offers all things *laster*, including chutneys; also candied *trovyul*; dehydrated *spinginach*; salted ginger.

Nomi-Oxin-Rood—a planet without a loop, known to Carresens-Denobli.

Nostrilia—a world where the Lyre Institute has a presence.

Palamar—the last place where Padi was allowed to fly a real spaceship as part of her training.

Runig's Rock—the place where Korval's Treasures were hidden during the Late Unpleasantness.

Surebleak—now homeworld to Clan Korval and *Dutiful Passage*. It is located in the **Daiellen Sector**, and it has two tidal moons, **Triga** and **Toppa**, and a local double-star, **Chuck-Honey**.

Torridon Hotel—on Langlastport, five stars.

trade bridge—the bridge on the *Passage* from which the traders do long-distance trade, trade news, and answer questions, while the ship is on approach.

Trealla Fantrol—yos'Galan's house, which was unmade because it could not be moved from Liad and yos'Galan refused to let it fall into the hands of the Council of Clans.

Weapons Hall—where Shan met Lute; the place the red counter and *Weapons Lore* came from.

Ynsolt'i—the planet where *Bechimo* was ambushed upon approach.

· ·

Organizations

Aldergate Enterprises—contacts Shan with a Letter of Interest.

Carresens-Denobli, aka **the Carresens Syndicate**—a trade family encompassing both long- and short-loopers; they also run the Festevalya.

Clan Korval, aka **Tree-and-Dragon Family**, aka **the Dragon**— direct descendants of Cantra yos'Phelium, the pilot and Captain of the ship that founded Liad.

Council of Clans—supposedly the ruling body of Liad.

Crystal Energy Consultants—the Uncle's front, a shell company simultaneously pursuing many of his interests and goals.

Department/Department of Interior/DOI—the Department of the Interior are largely seen as the bad guys.

Gilmour Agency—the company that opened Surebleak for the purpose of mining timonium, and then abandoned it when other, easier to obtain, sources were discovered.

Hartensis Catering and Receptions—a catering service on Langlastport.

Healers—Liaden psychic healers who deal with both mental and physical injuries. For the most part they are low- to mid-grade *dramliz* trained in medical arts. In Liaden, the Cha'dramliz.

Laster Cooperative—on Andiree, a trade group.

Lyre Institute for Exceptional Children, aka **the institute**— this universe's iteration of **Tanjalyre Institute.**

Pilots Guild—an interstellar organization involved in pilot training, certification, and welfare. Historically Clan Korval has been a major if behind-the-scenes contingent.

Terran Trade Commission, aka **TerraTrade**—Shan has petitioned them to raise Surebleak Port's rating from Local to Regional.

. . . .

Things

Andulsin frog, three-nosed—an ugly somebody.

Catalinc Project—a sooper sekrit project of the Uncle's. Its security was recently breached in *Dragon Ship*. Uncle's employee **Andreth** was on-site and captured two intruders— one is alive; the other has been "downloaded."

Complex Logic Laws—the group of laws that makes it illegal to be a sentient, self-aware, independent artificial intelligence.

Festevalya—the trade show put on by the Carresens.

Flutterbee—a cross between a bumblebee and a moth.

Free Gene and Manumitted Human Act—A generally recognized Terran law, usually supported by Liadens, forbidding the cloning or manufacturing of humans.

Guild Quick Guide—a service of the Pilots Guild; rates the relative safety and sophistication of various ports.

milaster—not a fruit, but a nut, the kernel of the *laster* fruit. Andiree likes the fruit; the kernel, not so much.

'mite (from **vegemite**)—a high-energy yeast drink; an acquired taste for spacers.

nerligig—a device that enhances or alters moods. Some iterations are entertainment, others are more insidious and so Not Exactly Legal.

oonlah—a drink local to Langlast, possibly an inebriant, which is commonly drunk by the locals, but has no place among an offering of Langlast's "finest" food and drink.

Plan B—Korval's plan for survival, should someone or something threaten the Clan Entire.

Rainbow—a mental calming exercise; the first of many that are taught to pilots and to scouts; often called the Rainbow.

red game counter, chipped on the edges and showing naked wood—something Shan picked up in Weapons Hall during *Plan B*. It occasionally appears (apparently under its own volition) and he does sleight-of-hand with it. When not in use, it resides in his right front trouser pocket.

Sort, Soothe, Sharpen—three things that Healers can do for someone.

Thrilling Space Adventures—pulp sci-fi, available as talking books.

Visrathan—a sort of carpet. Done right, a very fine sort of carpet.

Weapons Lore—a book Shan accepted in Weapons Hall, at Lute's suggestion.

World Book—from the guild, details manners and social mores of several worlds.

· ·

Ships & AIs

Admiral Bunter—a composite AI, made up of seven semi-derelict ships (with thirteen old and cramped computers between them) out of the junkyard at Jemiatha's Jumble Stop. *Admiral Bunter* is Theo's Fault.

Ahab-Esais—out of Waymart, piloted by First Class Pilot Inkirani Yo.

Bechimo—Theo Waitley's ship; very old, sentient.

Dutiful Passage—Korval's premier trade ship.

Elzin Vok—an administrative AI discovered by the Scouts in an extreme state of disrepair, and probable madness. Tolly's services as a mentor were engaged to move Elzin to a more stable environment.

loop or looper ships—tradeships that have a set route and regular ports of call.

Pale Wing—Another of Korval's A-list trade ships. Padi served part of her apprenticeship on her.

Tarigan—Tocohl, Tolly, Haz are on this ship.

Vivulonj Prosperu—the Uncle's ship.

· ·

Weird Words

cha'dramliz—the Healers as a group.

crosref—cross-reference.

cunningman—a man of magical power; a magician.

daibri'at—the so-called Small Dance; think yoga or tai chi.

delm—head of a clan.

dramliza—a Liaden wizard/witch.

dramliz—more than one *dramliza*.

kojagun—(Yxtrang) not-soldier; civilian.

melant'i—the description of the hat one is wearing while performing certain actions.

menfri'at, aka **the dance**—the main martial art taught to pilots and other spacefaring folk.

Redcap caste—High Society on Andiree.

thodelm—head of a single line within a clan.

· ·

Prior works in the Liaden Universe® referenced in the writing of *Alliance of Equals* include:

Conflict of Honors	"Lord of the Dance"
Crystal Dragon	*Local Custom*
Crystal Soldier	*Mouse and Dragon*
Dragon in Exile	*Necessity's Child*
Dragon Ship	*Plan B*
Fledgling	*Saltation*
Ghost Ship	*Scout's Progress*
I Dare	*Trade Secret*